MW01097326

THE RETURN

BRAD BONEY

Published by
Dreamspinner Press
5032 Capital Circle SW
Ste 2, PMB# 279
Tallahassee, FL 32305-7886
USA
http://www.dreamspinnerpress.com/

This is a work of fiction. Names, characters, places, and incidents either are the product of the author's imagination or are used fictitiously, and any resemblance to actual persons, living or dead, business establishments, events, or locales is entirely coincidental.

The Return
Copyright © 2013 by Brad Boney

Cover photograph by Tricia Dunlap
Model: James M. Brookes

Cover content is being used for illustrative purposes only
and any person depicted on the cover is a model.

All rights reserved. No part of this book may be reproduced or transmitted in any form or by any means, electronic or mechanical, including photocopying, recording, or by any information storage and retrieval system without the written permission of the Publisher, except where permitted by law. To request permission and all other inquiries, contact Dreamspinner Press, 5032 Capital Circle SW, Ste 2, PMB# 279, Tallahassee, FL 32305-7886, USA.
http://www.dreamspinnerpress.com/

ISBN: 978-1-62380-498-5
Digital ISBN: 978-1-62380-499-2

Printed in the United States of America
First Edition
July 2013

Sadness is but a wall between two gardens.

—Kahlil Gibran

PART 1:
TWO WEEKENDS

ROLL OF THE DICE

TOPHER MANNING replaced the oil cap, released the prop rod, and allowed the hood of the Chevy Malibu to close with a loud bang. He looked at the clock on the shop wall. He still had three more hours until quitting time. He wiped his hands with a towel from the bench and glanced through the glass window into the front office. Darrell, his boss and one of the co-owners of Groovy Automotive, was speaking to a customer. The woman had a distressed look on her face. Behind her, a man was talking on his phone and looking agitated.

Topher felt his phone vibrate in his pocket. He pulled it out and flipped it open. The tiny screen was blank. No call or text message.

"Hey, Travis," Topher yelled to the mechanic working beside him, "I'm going inside to help out Darrell. That guy waiting in line looks like he's about to blow a gasket."

Travis looked into the front office and smiled. "Damn. He's hot. Did you double-check the oil level on that job?"

"Yeah, don't worry. I double-checked it."

Topher put his phone back into his pocket. He crossed through the bays and stepped into the front office. Darrell looked at him and nodded to the waiting customer.

"Can I help you, sir?" Topher asked.

The man ended the conversation on his phone and said, "I sure as hell hope so."

"What seems to be the problem?"

"I'm visiting for South by Southwest and I stupidly borrowed someone's piece of shit...." Darrell and the woman he was helping stopped their conversation and turned to look at the man. "Sorry," he said. His strong baritone voice attacked the word like a cello player dropping his bow onto the

C string. "I'm driving someone else's car and it died across the street—in the parking lot of the grocery store."

"You mean the H-E-B?"

"If that's what you call it, yes. Look, I don't mean to be an assho—" He stopped himself. "I'm not trying to be difficult, but how long will it take to fix?"

"No way to know, sir," Topher said. "If it's just a dead battery, we could probably get you out of here by five or so."

"Shit," the man said to himself in a panic. He lit up his phone to check the time. "I only have ninety minutes to get downtown to the convention center so I can pick up my ticket to the Springsteen concert tonight."

"You're going to the Springsteen concert?" the woman asked.

"Not yet," the man said. "That's the problem. I don't have my ticket. And if I don't get downtown by five o'clock, they'll give it away."

"Why didn't you just call a cab?" Topher asked.

"I don't know. Because I'm not thinking straight. The owner of the car is hosting a panel downtown, so he can't help me. I have a dead car. I looked across the street and saw an auto shop. Am I an idiot to put those two things together?"

Topher grinned and said, "No, sir. You're not an idiot. Where are you from, though, if you don't mind me asking?"

"New York."

"New York City?" Topher asked. He could tell Darrell was looking at him and probably wishing he'd shut up.

"Yes," the man said.

"And you came all this way just to see Bruce Springsteen?"

"More or less, yes."

Topher shook his head and turned to Darrell. "Boss, can I run the man downtown so he can pick up his ticket? I'd hate to see someone miss Springsteen just because of a dead battery."

"You would do that?" the man asked.

"Drive the man downtown," Darrell said. "And take the rest of the day off. Sir, you're lucky this kid has such a big heart."

"Do I still get paid?" Topher asked.

"Yes, you still get paid."

"Sweet." Topher turned to the man. "My truck is parked outside. Give me one second to grab my stuff." Topher hurried into the breakroom, where he collected his backpack.

He was heading out through the bays when Travis called after him. "Where you going?"

Topher stopped. "I'm giving that guy a ride downtown so he can pick up his ticket to see the Boss tonight."

"Springsteen?"

"Yeah. It's my good deed for the year, but Darrell gave me the rest of the day off with pay."

"Good golly, boy. You got the damnedest luck sometimes. Git on out of here, then. I'll finish the paperwork on your last job and make sure everything's good to go."

"Thanks, man. I owe you one."

Topher looked into the front office and signaled to the man, who met him outside a few seconds later. Topher grinned and said, "My truck's out back if you're ready to take that long walk."

The man returned the smile. "That's cute, kid. You know your Springsteen, so we're going to get along just fine. Lead the way." Topher turned and headed toward his truck, which was parked behind the shop. The man followed him and said, "Thank you for doing this. I'll pay you."

"Stop it. I don't want your money. I'm a big Springsteen fan myself, and I would be pretty damned pissed if this were happening to me. I'm Topher, by the way."

"Stanton," the man said, shaking his hand. "Porter."

"Stanton Porter, the music critic?"

"One and the same."

"I've heard you on the radio. One of the mechanics likes to listen to NPR in the shop."

"Really? That's unexpected."

"You think mechanics only listen to classic rock and Glenn Beck?"

"I didn't mean to imply—"

"I know." Topher stopped and gave Stanton a once-over. It was hard not to notice how good-looking he was, so Topher's next question seemed like an obvious one to him. "With a face like yours, why aren't you on television? I mean, it's kind of going to waste on the radio, don't you think?"

Stanton turned a bright crimson, and Topher could tell he'd thrown the music critic off guard a bit. Still, Stanton smiled and seemed to appreciate the compliment. "Thank you. I think. But the radio keeps me anonymous. I like my privacy."

"Oh. Okay, I get it." Topher walked up to his truck. "I sure liked that piece you did on the Killers. They've been a huge influence on me."

"Thanks. So you're a musician?"

"Yep."

"A musician and a mechanic?"

"Guilty as charged. Of course, this week, it seems like everybody is. A musician, I mean."

"It does feel that way. So much music that will never be heard by more than twenty people."

Topher unlocked the passenger door and opened it, then walked around to the other side of his truck. "Smartass," he muttered under his breath. He got in and fastened his seat belt, then looked over and saw Stanton's knees butting up against the dashboard. "You can adjust that seat back if you need more room." Stanton struggled with the lever until it popped and sent the seat flying backward. Topher tried not to laugh, but he couldn't help himself. "Sorry about that. Travis sat there a couple of days ago, and he always pulls the seat up, since he's short like me. How tall are you, anyway?"

"Six one."

Topher suddenly felt small by comparison. "Yeah, you'd probably be more comfortable in an F-150, but Travis and I are partial to Rangers."

"Who's Travis?"

"One of the other mechanics. He works in the bay next to mine. You said the convention center? That's where we're going, I mean?"

"That's right."

Topher started the engine. He pulled out of the parking lot and headed toward Red River Street. "I figure we should avoid I-35."

"Is that what you call the big highway in the middle of the city?"

Topher tilted his head to check the rearview mirror. "Yeah, that's what we call it. This your first trip to Austin?"

"No, I visited once before, years ago."

"Your first SXSW, then?"

"Yes. I'm not a big fan of festivals, so I tend to avoid them, but when I saw that Springsteen was headlining… well, it was an offer I couldn't refuse."

"I take it you've seen him before? Bruce, I mean?"

"Yes. Just once, though. Back in 1981."

Topher glanced over at Stanton and asked, "How old are you?"

"Old enough. I don't need to hear the actual number come out of my mouth. You're what? Sixteen?"

"That's cute, mister. More like twenty-six."

"Well, I was younger than that when I first saw him. Hard to believe it was more than thirty years ago. I've always known he was an amazing artist, but after this afternoon, I'm even more impressed."

"What happened this afternoon?"

"He gave the keynote speech."

"Oh, that's right. How was it?"

"I'm embarrassed to say this, but I cried at the end. It was a history lesson in pop music held together by gratitude and sheer inspiration. The man is a poet, a musician, and now an orator."

"Why were you embarrassed?"

Stanton turned his head. "Excuse me?"

Topher kept his eyes on the road as he explained himself. "To cry? At the end? Why were you embarrassed to cry at the end of the speech?"

"Well, I didn't say I was embarrassed to cry. I said I was embarrassed to tell you I cried. There's a difference. I have a love/hate relationship with sentimentality, and I don't like to be thought of as soft."

Topher nodded and asked, "So you care what other people think?"

"Yes, don't you?"

"Not particularly. I wish I could have been there for the speech, but I can't afford to take off work—or the price of a festival pass."

"You can watch it for free online."

"Really?"

"Just Google 'Springsteen keynote'."

"I'll have to check that out."

They passed St. David's Medical Center and crossed Dean Keeton Street. Stanton stared out the window and said, "This is the university, right?"

"Yep. It goes all the way over to Guadalupe. They call it the Forty Acres."

"I remember eating at a place called Les Amis. It was right off the main street. What do you call it?"

"The Drag."

"Yes, the Drag."

"I've never heard of a place called Les Amis, so I think it's gone now."

"That's a shame. Did you go to school there?"

Topher shook his head. "No, I didn't have any interest in college."

"What instruments do you play?"

"Guitar, piano, some harmonica. I can find my way around a drum set too."

"Well, you've got that whole Adam Levine, tattoo thing going on there." Stanton referred to the ink that covered Topher's right arm and disappeared into the sleeve of his work shirt. "You've got that same wiry build too. Do you sing?"

"I think so." Topher looked over at Stanton and grinned. "A critic like you might have a different opinion on that, though."

"Who are your influences, other than Brandon Flowers?"

"Chester Bennington, Billie Joe Armstrong, Barry Manilow."

"Barry Manilow?"

"Sure, he was a great storyteller. Cee Lo Green, Steve Perry, Meat Loaf."

"You like big voices."

"Yeah."

"So do I."

"You ever heard of a band called Air Supply?" Topher glanced over and saw Stanton smiling.

"Yes, I've heard of them."

"I found one of their songs poking around YouTube the other day," Topher said. "Dude's got an amazing voice. You know who I'm talking about?"

"Russell Hitchcock."

"That's the guy."

"Are you in a band?"

"Yeah."

"What's the name?"

"Judecca Rising."

Topher could feel Stanton shift in his seat.

"Hmm," Stanton said, "you should rethink that, although it does take balls to name your band after the final circle of hell."

"Yeah, blame it on our drummer. It was his idea."

"You playing a gig this weekend?"

"Yeah, but nothing official. We were able to get one set at the Rooftop on 6th tomorrow night. They're pretty good about promoting local bands."

Stanton's iPhone lit up. "Excuse me," he said to Topher, and then he swiped the screen to answer the call. "Hey, buddy, what's up? ... Are you kidding me? ... Was it something you ate at lunch? ... Marvin, you can't miss this. ... Okay, okay... hold on a minute." Stanton put his phone down and asked Topher, "Do you want to go see Bruce Springsteen tonight?"

Topher slammed on his brakes. "Don't be pulling my leg like that."

Stanton put the phone back to his ear. "I have someone who can use your ticket. Have you picked it up, yet? ... Okay, I'll be there in a few minutes to get your badge." Stanton ended the call.

"What's going on?" Topher asked.

"That was Marvin, my best friend. He's throwing up and can't go to the concert tonight. Probably food poisoning, but it means there's a spare ticket. I wouldn't even be going if it weren't for you, so it seems only fair. We need to stop by the hotel so I can pick up his festival badge. We'll need that to get the ticket."

"Which hotel?"

"The W."

"I don't know where that is."

"Hold on, I have the address." Stanton turned on his phone and tapped the screen a few times. "Lavaca and Third Street."

"I'm on it," Topher said. He put the truck into gear and turned right on Sixth Street. He cut across town to Guadalupe, then headed south to Second and around the block to Lavaca. He pulled into the driveway of the hotel and Stanton jumped out.

"I'll be right back," he said.

Topher sat in his truck and tapped out a tune on the steering wheel. He thought about calling one of his bandmates, just to brag about going to see Bruce Springsteen, but he didn't want to be on the phone when Stanton got back. He waited impatiently for about five minutes, until finally the music critic reappeared.

Stanton jumped into the truck and said, "Go."

Topher didn't see any empty parking spaces downtown, so he drove north to Fifteenth Street and then back east to Red River. He turned to Stanton and said, "We're going to have to park and walk. We both need to be there to pick up the tickets, right?"

"Right."

"We're about fifteen blocks away, but it's as close as we're going to get. You up for a walk?"

"I'm up for it," Stanton said.

Topher parked across from the Erwin Center. He fed the meter with three quarters, which gave them forty-five minutes. As the two men started to walk south, Topher asked, "What were you doing driving someone else's car?"

"One of the local music critics offered. I think he works for the free weekly."

"*The Austin Chronicle?*"

"That's it. He was sucking up because he wants a job at NPR, so he offered me his car for the day. I thought it would be nice to drive around and see the city, but now he's on my shit list. I'm going to text him the address of that H-E-B thing and let him deal with it."

"Aw, come on—it wasn't his fault. Batteries die sometimes. That's what they do. I'm assuming that's what it was, at least."

"It's still his problem."

Topher decided to change the subject. "What do you think of Austin?"

"It's changed a lot, but it's a nice enough city. I'm originally from the Midwest, where every town looks the same. This doesn't seem too much different than, say, Columbus."

"The devil is in the details," Topher said. He took a few steps before he realized Stanton had stopped walking. Topher turned around and looked at him. "What's the matter?" he asked, but Stanton didn't respond. Topher's phone vibrated in his pocket. He took it out and flipped it open. The screen was blank again. "What the fuck?"

"What's wrong?" Stanton asked.

"Nothing. It's just this stupid crappy phone. It keeps going off in my pocket, but when I take it out, it's blank. No call, no text, nothing."

"It's called Phantom Vibration Syndrome."

"Are you kidding me? They've got a name for it?"

"Yes, I was just reading about it on the Daily Beast. People have reported being so connected to their phone that they feel it vibrating even when it's not."

"I'm not that connected to my phone."

"Maybe you just have a crappy phone, then."

"Why did you stop walking?"

"I... I don't remember. Really. I just spaced out for a moment, there. Sorry about that. It happens at my age."

"At your age? I'm pretty sure Bruce Springsteen is in his sixties, and I know you're not even close to being that old. So whatever chip you got on your shoulder, well—" Topher stopped himself. "Excuse me, my mouth is running, so I'm going to shut it now."

Stanton laughed. "No, it's okay. Let's keep going—we only have forty-five minutes." He walked away and Topher ran to catch up with him.

"And we're only ten minutes away," Topher yelled. "So calm down."

"You don't know what Springsteen means to me."

"Then tell me," Topher said as he fell into step with Stanton. "I'm sure you have some cool stories up your sleeve. I've never lived anywhere but here and Dime Box, Texas."

"Where is Dime Box, Texas?"

"It's about seventy miles east of here, between 290 and 79."

"Are you a small-town boy with big-city dreams?"

"Are you making fun of me?"

"No, I'm not. I was one too, once."

It suddenly dawned on Topher that Stanton had probably eaten lunch with Brandon Flowers, the front man of the Killers. In fact, he'd probably hung out with all of Topher's favorite musicians, doing those stories for NPR. "Have you met Bruce Springsteen?" Topher asked.

Stanton chuckled and shook his head. "No. He does very little press. That's one of the advantages of being a living legend."

"What about Billie Joe Armstrong?"

"Yes."

"Dave Grohl?"

"Definitely yes. I've done three features on Foo Fighters over the years."

"Did you ever meet—?"

"Kurt Cobain? Yes, in '93, the year before he died."

Topher paused. "What about Chester Bennington?"

"Next month. I'm spending two weeks in California with Linkin Park."

Topher sighed in resignation. "Okay, you're now officially the coolest person I've ever met."

"Please," Stanton said. "Hanging out with cool people so I can write stories about them doesn't make me cool. If anything, it makes me decidedly uncool."

"That's a stupid way of looking at it."

"Excuse me?"

"Sorry, that's just my mouth going off again. Can you give me some advice?"

"Advice? No, I don't think that's a good idea."

"Come on, now. Haven't you been around the music scene your whole life, practically?"

"Practically."

"Then what do I need to know? Getting started and all."

"I'm not a musician. Go home and listen to Springsteen's speech."

"I'm not asking him, I'm asking you."

Stanton kept walking. "Don't do it to make a living. I know that sounds harsh and jaded, but—"

"I don't mind jaded."

"The music industry is like a chocolate factory. There are a very limited number of golden tickets. Only one person can win *American Idol* every year, which means thousands of others have to lose."

"I'm not looking to win *American Idol*."

"Why not? David Cook. Adam Lambert. Kelly Clarkson. You should be so lucky."

"Adam Lambert didn't win."

"If you enjoy being a mechanic and making music on the side, then you're going to be a very happy man. Don't set your life up so you feel like a failure at the end of it."

"What does that mean?"

Stanton stopped and turned to Topher. "Many musicians have their lives destroyed by their dream. They feel like failures because they were never successful, whatever that means. They say there's only one thing worse than not getting what you want, and that's getting it. But from what I've seen, that's bullshit. Not getting it is way worse."

Topher didn't know quite what to say, except, "That's just about the saddest thing I've ever heard."

"I agree. Think of it as a cautionary tale."

Stanton started walking again. Topher followed him and asked, "Do you really believe those musicians would have been better off without the dream?"

"I think they would have been better off if they had weighed the dream a little more evenly with the rest of their lives. When following your bliss makes you miserable, but not following it makes you even more miserable, then what is a person supposed to do?"

"I suppose, but...."

Stanton stopped as they arrived at the convention center. "Unfortunately, we're going to have to table this discussion for the time being." He pulled a festival badge from his shoulder bag and handed it to Topher. "Here, take this. When we get inside, hand it to the person at the booth and say as little as possible. If they ask, you're Marvin Goldstein."

Topher took the badge and followed Stanton into the lobby. They walked to a booth with about fifteen other people in line. As they queued up, Topher asked, "Who's Marvin Goldstein? Other than your best friend, I mean. Is he a critic too?"

"Keep your voice down," Stanton whispered. "Yes, he's a critic. They used a lottery system to distribute the tickets for this concert, but certain members of the press were guaranteed spots."

"Like you?"

"Yes, like me. I asked someone on the inside to put Marvin and me together, but he couldn't promise anything."

"They're supposed to believe I'm Jewish?"

"Do they know the difference in Texas?"

"Aw, come on—don't be an East Coast dick about the Lone Star State."

Stanton shushed him.

Topher faced forward but then whispered, "Austin isn't like the rest of Texas, you know? We're a blue county surrounded by a sea of red. And just so we're clear, we do have Jews here."

"Don't say anything, then," Stanton whispered back. "Just hand them the badge and follow instructions."

After a few more minutes, they reached the front of the line and Stanton stepped up to the booth. He handed his badge to a blonde woman, who scanned it and smiled at him. "Hold out your wrist, please." Stanton held out his right hand and the young woman placed a band around his wrist. She handed him a ticket. "Enjoy the show."

Topher stepped forward and went through the same process. The woman did not ask him his name. Topher looked down as she snapped the wristband into place. It read, *Bruce Springsteen & The E Street Band.* Goosebumps ran up and down his arm. He turned to Stanton and grinned as the woman handed him a ticket. "Enjoy the show," she said. Topher looked down at the ticket and shook his head in disbelief.

"Come on," Stanton said. They walked toward the door and exited back onto the sidewalk.

"Where are you sitting?" Stanton asked.

"Mezzanine. Section 4. C5."

"I'm C6."

Topher grinned. "Looks like that insider knew not to mess with you. Since we're sitting together, do you want to meet out front first or something?"

"That sounds good. The W is right next to the theater. Here, give me your phone." Topher reached into his pocket and pulled out his phone. He handed it to Stanton, who looked at it like an alien piece of hardware. "A flip phone? Really?"

"Sorry."

"No, it's okay. I used to have one of these years ago. I can figure it out." Stanton opened the phone and punched in his contact information, then handed it back to Topher. "Call me so I have yours."

"Right now?"

"Yes, right now."

Topher scrolled through his contacts until he found Stanton Porter. He hit the enter key and put the phone to his ear.

Stanton pulled out his iPhone and waited for it to ring. When it did, he swiped his thumb across the screen and answered the call. Then he turned around and walked away.

Hey, Topher. How's it going?

"Not too bad. I sure am excited about tonight."

Me too. When you get to the theater, give me a call and I'll come down. We can get a drink beforehand.

Topher grinned as he watched the back of Stanton's head. "Sounds good. Thanks, again. This has just about made my year."

It's only March. Don't sell yourself short.

"Oh, you don't have to worry about that. Anyway, you know the way back to your hotel?"

Yes, I do. I'll see you tonight, Topher.

"Looking forward to it, Stanton Porter, the music critic."

Topher heard laughter, and then the call ended. He watched as Stanton stuffed his iPhone into his pocket and disappeared around the corner. Topher put his phone away and headed north. He hadn't gone two feet, though, when he felt his phone vibrate again. He reached into his pocket and pulled it out. Another blank screen. "Stupid piece of crap," he said out loud.

As he walked away, Topher made a mental note to Google Phantom Vibration Syndrome when he got home.

INTO THE FIRE

STANTON PORTER stepped onto the deck of the Blue Whale with his roommate and best friend Marvin by his side. He felt the thump of disco music coursing through the wooden floorboards beneath him. He raised his hand to block the stark afternoon sun and looked out across the sea of men. Some sat at patio tables talking, but most were on their feet dancing. Stanton had never seen gay men dance during the day—only in dark clubs well after midnight.

"So this is tea dance," he said to Marvin. Stanton glanced over and caught the attention of a blond, shaggy-haired bartender. The bartender smiled and Stanton turned away.

Marvin leaned in and said, "Everyone's staring."

"I keep telling you, Marvin, you're a stud."

"Very funny. They're not staring at me. Can't this be one of those movies where the ugly duckling switches bodies with the beautiful swan?"

"Ugly duckling? Please, you're like a young Dustin Hoffman."

"Don't patronize me. This is intimidating, for me at least."

"Trust me, buddy, you know perfectly well that you don't want to trade places with me. And besides, there's a niche for hot little Jewish boys. You just need to learn how to fill it."

"I suppose we can't all be universally attractive."

"I'm not universally attractive," Stanton said. "I've been shot down plenty of times. You know that."

"Our realities are not the same, my friend. The only reason we're even out here this weekend is because of the way you look."

"That's not true. It was blind luck."

"Blind luck, my tuches. Do you think Colby invites everyone to his house on Fire Island? And then lets you bring a friend? And then doesn't even ask you to sleep with him? That kind of thing only happens to beautiful people."

"Relax, buddy, and stop your whining. This is how the world works."

"This is how your world works, maybe."

"And you're a part of it. Think of this as a fresh start. It's a new decade. We're young, there's a movie star in the White House, and tomorrow, on the Fourth of July, John McEnroe is going to win Wimbledon. What more could a red-blooded American ask for?"

"Peace and quiet by the pool, preferably with some shade. And the most recent issue of the *Atlantic Monthly*."

"There will be plenty of time for that when we're old and fat. Years from now, we'll invite some cute boys out to lounge around our pool and drink our liquor, and maybe if we're lucky, they'll let us suck their dicks. How's that for a plan?"

"Let us suck their dicks? Why is it that you feel the need to bring every conversation we have down to the level of a locker room?"

"Because some of us actually played sports in high school."

Marvin rolled his eyes. "Just because it's authentic doesn't make it any less disturbing."

Stanton leaned over and tried to give Marvin a kiss on the cheek. "Come on, give me a smooch."

"Get away from me," Marvin said as he pushed Stanton back.

"Let's get a drink, then."

Stanton led them to one of the outdoor bars, where they waited for the blond, shaggy-haired bartender to finish up a large drink order for the two men in front of them. The bartender smiled as Stanton stepped forward and pulled out his wallet.

"Put that away," the blond said. "This one's on us."

"Who's us?" Marvin asked.

"The bartenders. Every day we vote for the cutest boy on deck, and today he won," he said, pointing to Stanton. "So, free drinks for both of you."

"Oy vey," Marvin said. "Will it never end?"

"Thanks. I'm Stanton, and this little troublemaker is Marvin Goldstein."

"I'm Hutch." He reached out to shake their hands. "What are you two drinking?"

"I'll take a Heineken, please, and Marvin will have a glass of red wine."

Hutch gave them a funny look, but then he said, "We can accommodate that, I suppose." He reached behind him into a cooler and pulled out the bottle of beer. He knocked the cap off and placed it on the bar in front of Stanton. He grabbed a wine glass, poured in a small amount of the house red, and then handed it to Marvin. "Would you like a taste, sir?"

Marvin blushed and smiled. He took the glass and tasted the wine. "That's lovely. Thank you." He handed the glass back to Hutch.

Hutch filled it, placed a napkin on the bar, and then the glass on the napkin. "You two are new on campus."

"This is our first time," Stanton said. "We're Fire Island virgins."

"Welcome, then. Do you need a tour guide?"

Marvin laughed and almost spit out a mouthful of wine.

"What's so funny?" Hutch asked.

"Tour guide? There's nothing out here except sand and wooden sidewalks."

"The devil is in the details."

"Well," Marvin said. "I suppose you could show us where Tommy Tune lives."

"Or Calvin Klein," Stanton added.

"Or Robin Byrd."

"Or David Geffen."

"Have we forgotten anyone?"

Hutch smiled. "Have you thought about taking this little act of yours on the road?"

"We've had offers," Stanton said. "Thanks for the drinks." He grinned and walked away. Stanton had reached the other side of the patio when he realized Marvin hadn't followed him. He turned around and saw Marvin still talking to Hutch. Stanton growled to himself, and a few moments later, Marvin rejoined him.

"What were you two talking about?" Stanton asked.

"The opera," Marvin said. He took a drink of the wine and grimaced at the taste.

"I'm serious."

"Do you think I'm not serious about the opera? Believe me, sister, I'm serious."

Stanton took a swig of his beer. "Don't do that."

"Don't do what?"

"You know I don't like to be called 'sister'."

"That is because you are an uptight homosexual who doesn't appreciate the subversive power of gender swapping."

"We don't need to have this conversation for the fiftieth time."

"Sorry, you're right."

"So what were you talking about?"

"I told you. He asked me if you like Italian or German opera."

"What did you tell him?"

"I told him the truth. If I'm supposed to lie about your lack of exposure to classical music, I did not get the memo."

Stanton took another swig of beer and grumbled. "You told him I don't know anything about opera?"

"No, I told him you have never been to the opera. There's a difference."

"Now he's going to think I'm some kind of hick."

"You *are* some kind of hick."

"Fuck you."

"Why do you care what he thinks? Didn't you just blow him off?"

"No, I smiled and walked away. There's a difference. Obviously, I care what he thinks."

Marvin shook his head. "It doesn't matter. Here we are, surrounded by gorgeous, successful men, and you want to shtup the bartender. Sometimes I don't know what to do with you."

"He's the hottest guy here."

"Mark my words. If you date him, people will call you Starsky."

Stanton paused and looked around. "So, what's the difference?"

Marvin stared at him with a blank look on his face. "Did you just change the subject?"

"I changed it back. What's the difference between Italian and German opera?"

"Oh, so now you're interested in the opera? I've been trying to get you to go for two years. You're impossible."

"Just give me enough so I can bullshit my way through it."

"That is not a discussion even you can bullshit your way through. Besides, don't worry—I took care of it."

"What does that mean?"

"Nothing. I didn't say a word."

"You're up to no good." Stanton's eyes narrowed. "Drink up so I can go back for refills."

"I'm sorry, I cannot chug this glass of wine. Words cannot describe how bad it is. Honestly, I could get a better Chianti at a pizza parlor on Coney Island."

"You said it was lovely."

"I was being polite. There must be some queen on this sandbar with a bottle of good Bordeaux. That's my mission this weekend—to find that bottle."

"He's hot, right?"

Marvin turned around and looked at Hutch again. "Not my type, of course, but he's an immortal."

"What's that?"

"The highest spot on the gay food chain, above the tens. Gods that walk amongst us mere men."

"Who told you that?"

"I know my gay history. I've read *Dancer from the Dance*. This place where we're standing, it's legendary. The Fire Island Pines can transform your life, but it can also destroy it. If you fall in love with an immortal, there's no turning back. You will never be able to love another man for the rest of your life."

Stanton threw back his head and laughed. "That is the stupidest, most melodramatic thing I've ever heard come out of your mouth."

"We both know that's not true, Apollo."

Stanton swallowed the last of his beer and said, "I need a refill." He crossed the patio toward Hutch, who had a fresh, cold bottle of Heineken waiting for him on the bar when he stepped up.

"Is this for me?" Stanton asked.

"Yes, it is. Was I too forward?"

"What do you mean?"

"Before, when I asked if you needed a tour guide."

"No, you weren't too forward. It's my gatekeeper test. Any guy who doesn't ask twice is not someone I'm interested in."

Hutch smiled and raised an eyebrow. "Good test. So, what's with the sidekick?"

"Marvin?"

"Yes."

"He's my roommate at NYU. Great guy. We're both in the music school."

"Music?"

"Yeah."

"Groovy," Hutch said.

"Groovy? You do realize it's 1981, don't you?"

"I'm done here at seven. Would you like to take a walk on the beach?"

Stanton laughed and said, "Oh, God."

Hutch threw up his hands. "How many times am I going to have to ask?"

"It's not that. Some things just strike me as funny."

"A walk on the beach is funny?"

"Maybe funny is the wrong word. It's just not what I'm used to. We don't even have beaches where I'm from—and if we did, two guys would definitely not be taking a walk there."

"Where are you from?"

"Ohio."

"Don't they have Great Lakes in Ohio?"

"Not the part I'm from. They have cloudy skies and soybean fields."

"Not even any amber waves of grain?"

"Not even."

"So is that a yes or a no?"

Stanton paused.

"Excuse me?" It was the man standing behind Stanton. "Are you two going to talk all day, or would it be possible for me to get a drink?"

"Sorry," Hutch said to the man, and then he quickly looked back at Stanton. "So?"

"Sure. Where do I meet you?"

"Right here."

"Okay. I'll be back at seven."

TWO hours later, after he had dropped Marvin off at the house, Stanton returned to the Blue Whale and waited near the entrance. Hutch stuck his head up from behind the bar and yelled, "I'm almost finished." After a few minutes, he came around the corner and Stanton got his first unobstructed view. Hutch was about Stanton's height, but his shoulders were broader. In the light, his blond hair had streaks of white, the natural effect of salt water and sun, and it was long enough that Hutch had to push it out of his slate-blue eyes. He wore a pair of white shorts and a blue Columbia University tank top that accented his tan skin. While Hutch lacked the glossy shine of a *GQ* model, he made up for it with a stunning matte finish that Stanton preferred.

A group of men sat at a nearby table and whistled as Hutch strode across the deck. One of them called out, "Hey, Hutch, who's the lucky boy?" Hutch didn't answer, but instead blew the men a kiss as he passed their table.

He waltzed up to Stanton and asked, "You ready for your first gay walk on the beach?"

Stanton noticed a ring hanging on a chain around Hutch's neck. "What's that?"

Hutch looked down and quickly repositioned the chain so it hung inside his shirt. "Nothing. Follow me." He led them through the small harbor and onto one of the main boardwalks that bisected the island and led to the beach. "Where are you staying?"

"With some guy," Stanton said.

"Some guy? Are you trying to be vague?"

"No. He's kind of my boss. I started this new work-study job at the bursar's office last month. We both decided to stay in the city and go to summer school."

"Who's we?"

"Me and Marvin. I went back to Ohio last summer, but I just couldn't do it this year. So our plan is to pick up some extra classes and graduate in three and a half years. Anyway, I got this part-time job and my supervisor is this old queen—his name is Colby. He invited us out for the weekend."

"I know Colby. He and his lover come to tea sometimes during the week. Did you know they met in Australia during World War II?"

"Yes, we've heard all the stories. They're both pretty nice and not too creepy, so that's a relief. I like Archy's accent."

"Yeah, I think he's sexy."

"Really? Isn't he in his fifties?"

"You wouldn't sleep with Paul Newman?"

Stanton thought about it. "No. Maybe back in the seventies, when he was in *The Towering Inferno*. Certainly when he was in *Cool Hand Luke*. I don't know—I'd have to see what he looks like now. I like Steve McQueen better anyway, if you're going for a hot, older guy."

"Steve McQueen is dead."

"Oh. When did that happen?"

"Last year."

"Hmm. Guess I won't be sleeping with him anytime soon." The two men walked for a moment in silence, and then Stanton said, "Marvin told me you asked him if I like German or Italian opera. What was that all about?"

"It's one of those things that tells you a lot about a person. You know, like crunchy or smooth peanut butter?"

"Smooth."

Hutch grinned. "Me too."

"I was told not to try and bullshit my way through any discussion about the opera. Sorry, I'm not very sophisticated."

"That's okay. He answered for you."

"What do you mean?"

"He told me what kind of opera you would like, if you went."

"What did he say?"

"Italian. He was pretty sure about it too. He said when you finally listen to Wagner, there's no way you're going to hear it as anything other than noise, which I have to admit cracked me up. How is it that a music major has never been to the opera?"

"There's more to music than dead white guys."

"I know that, but don't you have to know a little bit about everything?"

"You'd be surprised what you can get away with at NYU."

"What instruments do you play?"

"I'm not a musician anymore."

"What happened?"

"I found out I wasn't very talented."

"Ouch."

"Yeah. So now I'm trying to figure out why I'm still majoring in music."

"It's a big industry—producers, studio people, talent scouts. Lots of jobs. People are always going to buy records."

"Marvin thinks I should become a critic."

"A critic? You're kidding, right?"

"No, I'm not. He's got it all mapped out. He's going to be the classical music critic for the *Times* and I'm going to cover pop music."

"I didn't know anyone actually wanted to be a critic. I thought it was just something people fell into."

"Well, Marvin doesn't fall into anything."

They reached the beach and walked down the steps to the sand. Hutch stopped and took in the sight of the ocean. "This is my favorite place on earth." They kicked off their shoes and began to stroll. Hutch waved at two men heading toward them and called, "Fuzzy."

"Hi, Hutch," one of the men answered. "Did you finally meet your Starsky?"

"This is Stanton. He won the cute-boy contest at tea today."

Fuzzy laughed. "What cute-boy contest?" He reached out and shook Stanton's hand. "This is Willy. We just met at tea too."

"Must be something in the air," Hutch said.

"Something other than gay cancer."

"Right?" Hutch said. "I saw that in the paper today. Crazy, huh?"

Fuzzy nodded. "Sure is. Well, you two have a nice evening."

The men said good-bye as Stanton and Hutch continued on their way.

"Tell me something about yourself," Hutch said.

"Like what?"

"I don't know. Most music majors were band nerds in high school. You don't strike me as a former band nerd."

"I'm not. I played football in high school."

"Quarterback?"

"No, but I sucked his dick."

"Really? You were out in high school?"

"No, I'm barely out now. It was an unfortunate incident. Brendan Baxter was his name. I was a sophomore and he was a senior. I worshiped him. He was the varsity quarterback—everyone on JV worshiped him. He gave me a ride home one afternoon after practice. He was so much smarter than your typical jock. We became friends after that, until one night we were drinking and talking about sex. I guess I was being a smartass because he said, 'Blow me,' and I said, 'Whip it out.' I thought we were both joking until he...."

"Whipped it out?"

"Something like that."

"Where did this happen?"

"In the front seat of his car."

"What did you do?"

"I went down on him. What was I supposed to do?"

"Did you talk about it afterward?"

"No way. We just pretended it never happened."

"What do you mean by barely out? Do your parents know?"

"No. I haven't gotten to that point yet."

"You're still uncomfortable with it?"

Stanton laughed nervously. "A little. I know my parents would be extremely uncomfortable with it, and they're paying my tuition bill, so I have no intention of rocking that boat right now. I'm getting comfortable with it, but I still don't get the feminine, queeny part. I like sports, I'm not flamboyant, I don't like musicals, I don't call guys 'she'. And trust me, I get crap about all this on a daily basis from Marvin."

"Did you guys know each other before you started college?"

"Me and Marvin? No. We were thrown together our first year at Weinstein."

"What's that?"

"The freshman dorm at NYU. I didn't know anyone coming from Ohio, so I had to take my chances in the roommate lottery. They at least try to put people together from the same school—like music majors with other music majors. The first week was hysterical. Marvin hated me so much he asked for a transfer. He thought I was this stupid goyish jock from Iowa. I kept correcting him, but he got it into his head that I was from Iowa."

"But you didn't correct him about the stupid or the goyish part?"

"I'm afraid I played right into those stereotypes. Unintentionally, of course, but still. I made the mistake of pronouncing Chopin like it's spelled."

"You mean chopping? Like choppin' wood?"

"Yes."

Hutch laughed and Stanton couldn't really blame him.

"I told you," Stanton said, "not very sophisticated. I felt like an idiot, but I didn't know any better. Besides, that's why I came to New York: to learn about that kind of stuff. Anyway, on top of that, there are no Jewish people in the town I'm from, so I was naturally curious and probably asked too many questions."

"So you are a little goyish?"

"I eat pastrami on white bread."

"Aw, come on. That's just—"

"I hate rye bread."

"What changed his mind?"

"He walked in on me making out with a guy. When he saw that, I guess he figured maybe I wasn't such a lost cause after all. So he sat me down and we had a long talk over a bottle of good red wine." Stanton stared out at the ocean. Since the water was calm, he asked, "Do you want to skip some stones?"

"Sure."

They walked to the edge of the water and squatted down. Stanton quickly found several suitable stones and began skipping them across the water. His first attempts yielded three or four solid skips.

"You're good at this," Hutch said.

"I've had a lot of practice. My parents took us to Michigan for vacation every summer. Me and my brothers and cousins went down to the lake every night to skip stones. On a calm night, I could pull out six or seven skips on a single throw."

Hutch stood up and tried his hand, but his stone didn't skip at all and sank instead. "I guess it's harder than it looks. What's the trick?"

"Flat stones. And throw underhand, parallel to the water. Like a curveball."

Hutch tried again. He managed one solid skip and then a second, less spectacular one.

"Watch this," Stanton said. He placed three stones in the palm of his hand and angled them over the water. They fanned out and each skipped four or five times.

"How did you do that?"

"I told you," Stanton said. "Practice."

As they talked, they continued to rummage through the sand and toss their finds across the surface of the water.

"I noticed you ordered for Marvin without asking," Hutch said. "This afternoon at the Blue Whale, I mean. He only drinks red wine?"

"He only drinks good red wine. He almost gagged on that crap you served him. And he drinks Tab. The fridge in our room is always stocked with Tab."

"My, he's a little JAP, isn't he?"

"Can you believe I didn't know what that meant when I first moved here? I literally thought everyone was talking about Japanese people. Finally, Marvin told me it meant Jewish-American Princess. Then he started telling me all the jokes."

"How many JAPs does it take to screw in a light bulb?"

"Two. One to call Daddy and one to pour the Tab." Stanton threw a stone out over the water. "How do you know when a JAP has an orgasm?"

Hutch chuckled and skipped another stone. Stanton noticed that he was getting better. Then Hutch said, "She drops her nail file. What's a JAP's favorite wine?"

"I haven't heard that one."

"I wanna go to Miami! I wanna go to Miami!"

The two men cracked up.

"Good one," Stanton said. "I'll have to tell that to Marvin. He'll get a kick out of it."

"You do know those jokes are offensive, don't you?"

"You're the one that started it."

Hutch's next throw skipped three times. "So you and Marvin became friends after that?"

"Yeah. That night we sat on the floor of our room and listened to Carly Simon's *Hotcakes*. Do you know that album?"

"Yes, I think so. It's the one she recorded when she was pregnant, right?

"Yeah, with her daughter Sally. There's something about it. She's in a really good place in her life, and it's just... I don't know, comforting. Too bad she couldn't stay there. Marvin came out to me that night, and I told him I was still struggling with it. It was the first time I ever acknowledged to another person that this was actually happening to me, and even then I couldn't say the words."

"What words?"

"I'm gay." Stanton stopped skipping stones and brushed his hands together to remove the sand. "I just couldn't say it at the time. So I changed the subject and we started talking about music. It's ridiculous how much he knows about practically every genre—classical, jazz, rock, pop. You name it, he seems to be an expert on it. I'm like a sponge around him."

Hutch faced him and asked, "Do you think he's in love with you?"

Stanton shook his head. "No. Everyone asks me that, but I know the truth. Marvin likes his men the way he likes his coffee."

"Strong and black?"

"Ding ding," Stanton said as he touched his index finger to his nose. "You picked the correct door."

"What's my prize, Monty?"

"You have won an all-expense-paid trip for two to…. Where do you want to go?"

Hutch paused. "I'm thinking."

"Paris? London?"

"No, it's summer. Let's go somewhere cold. Like Alaska."

"You're taking me?"

"Sure, why not? We could go all the way north to the arctic circle."

Stanton didn't respond. They stood at the edge of the water as the sun sank toward the horizon. It was a postcard moment, and Stanton wanted to appreciate it. "Let's keep walking," he said. They headed away from the water and farther down the beach. "How old are you, by the way?"

"Twenty-four," Hutch said.

Stanton pointed toward Hutch's tank top. "I take it you went to Columbia?"

"Yes. Prelaw."

"And now you're tending bar on Fire Island? What happened?"

"I don't want to talk about that right now. Let's talk about music some more. How do you feel about good old rock and roll?"

"It's not really my favorite genre."

"Not even Springsteen?"

"Especially not Springsteen. His voice is like sour wine over gravel."

"I know that words are coming out of your mouth, but I can't believe what I'm hearing."

"Rock should not be an excuse for bad singing. He's just like Dylan."

"You don't like Dylan, either?"

"I might like him if I could understand some of his lyrics. Singing through your nose is a bad idea, no matter who you are."

"What Springsteen have you listened to?"

"Born to Run."

"That's it? One album?"

"One song."

"You've only heard one Bruce Springsteen song and you're basing your entire judgment on that?"

"How long are you going to keep this up?"

"Sorry, but you should at least give me one chance to change your mind. One Springsteen song and one Dylan song. You listen to each of them, and if you are unmoved, then I'll never bring it up again."

Stanton stopped walking. "You have the records out here?"

"Yeah, back at my house."

"Okay, then, let's go." As the two men changed direction, Stanton asked, "Do you maybe have the new Air Supply album too?"

Now it was Hutch's turn to stop walking. "You like Air Supply?"

"Yeah, why?"

"I don't know anyone who admits to liking Air Supply."

"Then everyone you know has a serious problem."

Hutch laughed and his whole demeanor changed. "Okay, that decided it. I want to give you something." He undid the clasp and removed the chain from around his neck. He pulled the ring off the links and said, "All year, I've been waiting for someone to show up. I could feel him out there, getting closer." He held up the ring. "This is a Claddagh ring. I was in Nantucket over Memorial Day, hanging out with some friends from Boston. They all had these rings. They explained that it's an Irish tradition for women, but the gay guys up there have co-opted it, and since my mom is Irish, I bought one."

"And you've been wearing it on a chain around your neck?"

Hutch smiled. "Yes. I don't think it's the kind of ring you're supposed to give to somebody, but I don't care. It's two hands clasping a heart, with a crown on top. See?" Hutch held up the ring so Stanton could examine it closer. "The heart symbolizes love, the hands are friendship, and the crown is loyalty."

"Loyalty? I like that."

"When you wear it with the point of the heart facing out toward your fingertips, it means you're available and open to love. The other way means you're taken. You're single, right?"

"Yes. Very."

"Groovy tunes," Hutch said. "Relax, Stanton…. What's your last name?"

"Porter."

"Relax, Stanton Porter. I'm not asking you to go steady with me."

"Then what are you asking?"

"Are you open to love?"

Stanton paused and thought it over. Then he looked at Hutch and said, "You're intense."

Hutch nodded. "Yes, I am."

"So you're saying I'm the someone you've been waiting for?"

"I'm saying let's find out."

"But why me?"

"What do you mean?"

"I don't know. This place is crawling with hot guys, and you could have your pick of any of them. So why me? It seems like a fair question."

Hutch grinned. "You do realize you're super hot, don't you?"

"So it's just physical?"

"No, that's not what I meant. But what kind of answer are you looking for? Do you want me to tell you that it's because you have the presence of a man twice your age? When you stepped onto the deck of the Blue Whale today, you turned heads. Did you even notice that?"

"Marvin said something, but I didn't notice."

"Of course you didn't, so maybe that's why you. Or maybe it's because you told me a story about giving the quarterback a blow job, which is not like anything I've ever heard on a first date before. You were telling me who you really are, instead of doing your impersonation of a perfect person. That alone is remarkably refreshing out here." Hutch paused, but then he laughed and shook his head. "Or maybe it's because of Air Supply."

"You like Air Supply too?"

"I love Air Supply. I just bought their new album, and I've gotten nothing but grief about it."

"Do you have it out here?"

"Yes."

"Whoever's giving you grief needs to lighten up."

"It's all in fun, really." Hutch held out the ring and said, "I could give you a thousand reasons why, but none of them would really matter. The only thing I'm asking is, are you open to love?"

Stanton looked into Hutch's slate-blue eyes and knew there was only one true answer. He held out his right hand and Hutch placed the ring on his finger, with the heart facing out.

"It fits," Hutch said.

"Gee, I feel like Cinderella."

"Maybe, just maybe, I'll get you to turn that around someday."

Stanton liked the thought. "Take your best shot, Hutch. Now, can we go jump in your Gran Torino and tear up the streets of Bay City?"

Hutch laughed. "You're on, Starsky."

THEY left the beach and walked to Hutch's house west of the harbor. When they entered, three men sat at the table, eating dinner. The first floor seemed typical of a Fire Island rental, though Stanton based his observation entirely on the inside of Colby's house and that of his next-door neighbor. The kitchen and dining room took up half of the space, while the living room occupied the other.

"We waited until eight," one of the men said.

"I know the rules. Hey, guys, this is Stanton. These are my housemates and best friends—Paul, Robert, and Michael."

"Nice to meet you," Stanton said. Hutch's friends stood up and shook his hand. Robert possessed the coveted combination of dark hair, blue eyes, and fair skin. He looked like a casual Prince Charming in shorts and a Columbia T-shirt. He was one of the most beautiful men Stanton had ever seen in his life, and before he could stop himself, he blurted out, "Wow. You're really good-looking."

Robert grinned like a young Kennedy, and Michael said, "Thank you for that. Because he didn't get his ego stroked enough at tea today."

Michael was no slouch in the looks department either. He had strawberry-blond hair, cut conservatively. The sun had tinged his pale skin red, but it looked good on him. He wore blue jeans and a plain white T-shirt. He stood next to Robert as if they occupied the same space.

"Sorry," Stanton said. "I don't know why I said that."

Michael smiled and Stanton warmed to him immediately. "I was only joking. Welcome."

"Did you two enjoy your walk on the beach?" Robert asked.

"Yes," Stanton said. "I got a ring out of it, so I must be doing something right."

Paul sat up in his chair and asked, "You gave him the ring?"

"I did," Hutch said.

At first sight, Paul was the "gayest" of Hutch's friends. Stanton knew Marvin would kick him for thinking such a thing, but that didn't stop it from being true. Paul had feathered brown hair, a slight build, and mannerisms that could light up the sky. He wore Daisy Dukes and a T-shirt cut off to reveal his midriff.

"Interesting," Paul said as he looked Stanton over from head to toe.

"We're going to listen to some music," Hutch said. "I've got one chance to convert him over to the Springsteen side."

"What are you going to play for him?" Robert asked.

Hutch leaned over and whispered the answer into his ear.

Robert grinned. "Nice. Not taking any chances, are you? Well, if he has a soul...."

Stanton laughed. "What have I gotten myself into?"

"Let's go," Hutch said. He led Stanton across the living room and up the stairs into one of the bedrooms. He cleared a place on the bed, and Stanton took a seat. Hutch pulled an LP from one of the stacks sitting upright on the floor against the wall. He pulled the vinyl disc from the sleeve and handed the sleeve to Stanton.

"You'll want to read the lyrics as you listen."

Hutch dropped the record onto the turntable and poised the needle over the first track.

"This is a song about a choice," Hutch said. "Does she stay in her dead-end life, or does she cross the space between her front porch and his front seat...?"

As his voice trailed off, Hutch laid the needle on the record and Stanton heard "Thunder Road" for the first time.

TWO HEARTS

TOPHER parked his truck near the Texas History Museum and decided to walk the rest of the way downtown. No point in fighting with the festival crowds for parking. He walked through the Capitol grounds and continued south down Congress Avenue. He made his way to Second Street and then west to the Austin City Limits auditorium. After the heavy rains earlier in the week, it had turned out to be a beautiful evening. When he was about a block away, Topher took out his phone and called Stanton's number.

Hello.

"It's me."

Hi, Topher. I'm almost ready. I'll meet you on the street at the foot of the stairs in about five minutes.

"Okay, I'm almost there."

When Topher reached the block of both the ACL auditorium and the W Hotel, the atmosphere on the street was electric as people lined up for the concert. Stanton's idea of five minutes turned out to be more like twenty, but then Topher felt a tap on his shoulder and spun around.

"Hey," Topher said. "I was beginning to wonder if you were standing me up."

"Sorry about that. I had to stop by Marvin's room to check on him."

"Marvin Goldstein?"

Stanton smiled. "Yes."

"Who does he write for, anyway?"

"The Old Gray Lady."

"What's that?"

"*The New York Times.*"

"Wow. You two are strictly big league, aren't you?"

"He covers classical, though."

"What's he doing here?"

"Keeping me company. We've been friends for years, ever since our days at NYU. But the little troublemaker has been throwing up all afternoon. His loss is your gain."

"You went to school at NYU?"

"Yes, but back when that didn't mean anything."

"Classical, huh? He must know a lot about music."

"When it comes to music, Marvin is the second smartest person I've ever known."

"Who's the first? You?"

Stanton smiled again. "No. That's another long story. Shall we head in?"

"Sure." Topher followed Stanton as he led them up the stairs to the Porch, as the veranda outside the theater was known.

"Let's get a drink," Stanton said.

"Sounds good. Maybe that will give us enough time for you to tell me one of these epic stories you keep hinting at."

Stanton led them to one of the bars. "What can I get you gentlemen this evening?" the bartender asked.

"I'll have a vodka tonic," Stanton said. "No lemon, no lime, chilled but no ice." He turned to Topher.

"Just a Shiner for me, thanks."

The bartender executed Stanton's instructions perfectly. Stanton reached into his pocket and pulled out a credit card, and Topher handed him a ten-dollar bill.

"Put that away," Stanton said. "This one's on me."

Topher smiled and returned the cash to his wallet. He accepted the bottle of beer from Stanton and said, "Thank you. For everything."

Stanton held up his plastic cup in a toast. "L'chaim."

"What does that mean?"

"You said you had Jews in Texas."

"Well, okay, maybe not anyone I know personally."

"It means 'to life'. All the Yiddish I know comes from Marvin and his mother, although I've been told you can learn just as much from watching *Fiddler on the Roof.*"

Topher laughed and tapped the neck of his beer bottle against Stanton's cup. Then he took a swig and said, "Ah, that hits the spot."

"They really should not be allowed to serve alcohol in plastic," Stanton said. Topher took another drink as they stepped away from the bar and toward the edge of the Porch that overlooked Second Street. "One of the valet guys told me they recently renamed this street Willie Nelson Boulevard," Stanton said.

"I heard that. But I can't keep up with all the shit they rename in this town." He looked around at the crowd. "It's exciting. Being here, I mean. This is the hottest ticket at any SXSW in, like… forever, I think."

"So, tell me about your band."

Topher sighed. "Oh, man, I don't know. Are you actually friends with Brandon Flowers?"

"Friends is not the right word. At all. I spent a week with him and the Killers when I did that piece for NPR. He's a super nice guy, though. That's the thing about Mormons; they're all so damn nice. We still keep in touch. Twitter and things like that."

"Well, I don't know what I'm supposed to say about Judecca Rising compared to the Killers."

"Why do you have to compare yourself to them?"

"Because that's greatness, and I want to be like that."

"Brandon was just a kid once, you know, with dreams like you. What is your dream, anyway?"

"Not to be ordinary. I just want to write something that sticks. Do you know what I mean?"

"You're a songwriter, then?"

"I try, but most of it comes out sounding like crap. Sorry, I don't mean to be so down on myself. It's just that I've been frustrated lately."

"Frustrated how?"

"It's… I…. There are these songs in my head, but they're locked away, like in an attic or something." Stanton looked confused, so Topher tried to elaborate. "I can hear these songs, but they're just out of—I'm sorry, I'm not explaining it very well."

Stanton took a drink. "You're doing fine."

"Brandon Flowers was twenty years old when they started the Killers. I'm running out of time."

"That's nonsense."

"I'm not trying to be morbid or anything, but my dad got up one night to take a piss. He had a heart attack and dropped dead on the bathroom floor."

"I'm sorry to hear that."

"Thank you, but the point is he was thirty-nine years old. Any one of us could go at any minute, so excuse me if I'm a little impatient."

"Then what's your bar?"

"What do you mean?"

"For success? How will you know when you've made it? Every musician has a fantasy moment they dream about. You know, like winning a Grammy or playing at Madison Square Garden? Even I had one as a critic."

"What was it?"

"A byline in *Rolling Stone*."

"I take it that's happened?"

"Yes, it has. So what's yours?"

Topher felt his face turn red.

Stanton smiled and took a drink from his plastic cup. "Don't be embarrassed. If you're impatient, it might be a good idea to get specific about what you're trying to accomplish."

Topher didn't have to think about it. "You know how when you go on iTunes, and most of the homepage is stuff Apple is pushing that day, but then there are those top ten boxes on the right-hand side? I always look at the top ten singles—every day I look at them and think, that's what America is listening to. I want to see one of my songs there someday. After that, I think I could die a happy man."

Stanton took another drink and nodded. It looked like he was filing something away in his brain. He changed the subject, asking, "Do you remember the first time you heard a Springsteen song?"

Topher thought about the question. "My dad had all his CDs. I remember swiping them when I was about ten, so it must have been around then."

"My dad would have killed me if I had swiped his records."

"My dad didn't mind. At least at the time."

"What kind of music did he listen to?"

"All kinds. His favorites, though, were Springsteen, Buck Owens, and Otis Redding."

"That's an odd trio."

"He used to sing 'Sittin' on the Dock of the Bay' to me all the time."

"What about your mom?"

"Dolly Parton and Emmylou Harris. Yours?"

"The Mamas & the Papas and Herb Alpert and the Tijuana Brass."

Topher grinned. "I've never heard of that second one. I grew up surrounded by music. My mom and dad were always singing and changing out the discs on our CD player. I still don't understand how my dad loved music so much and still had so many problems with me making it."

"He didn't like the idea?"

"Nope. He thought it was a big waste of time."

"Well, fathers can be that way. I think it's part of their job description."

"When did you first hear a Springsteen song?"

"I was nineteen, almost twenty. I had heard 'Born to Run' on the radio and didn't get what all the fuss was about. I didn't like his voice, I didn't like the song—but then I moved to New York, where Springsteen is basically a god on both sides of the Hudson River. Someone sat me down and played 'Thunder Road' for me, and that changed everything."

"That's my favorite Bruce Springsteen song."

"Why doesn't that surprise me?"

Topher looked at him, puzzled. "What does that mean?"

"Nothing, really. Everyone's favorite is either 'Thunder Road' or 'Rosalita'. You just seem like a 'Thunder Road' kind of guy." Stanton turned away, and it looked as if he was remembering something.

Then Topher asked, "Do you know you get this look on your face sometimes? All wistful and shit."

"I guess Springsteen makes me all wistful and shit."

"Are you making fun of me again?"

"No, just the opposite. I think you're charming."

"Really? Well, you already know what I think of you."

"Coolest person you've ever met?"

"That's right."

"You need to get out more."

"By the way," Topher said, "did you know you can watch at least five different versions of 'Thunder Road' on YouTube?"

"Nothing beats it live, though."

"Do you think he'll play it tonight?"

"He would be a fool not to. Now, if he closes with 'Rosalita', that would be spectacular. But he won't."

"He should."

"Yes, he should. Word is he feels like he beat that tradition to death. He hasn't closed with it in years. I did my research."

"Then I'll pray for 'Thunder Road', at least, and hope I'm not disappointed. Tell me about the time you saw him. When did you say it was?"

"The summer of 1981, at the Meadowlands in New Jersey. Two days after I heard 'Thunder Road' for the first time."

"You said you were nineteen?"

"Almost twenty. It was the summer between my sophomore and junior year at NYU. That night, if you can believe it, he actually opened with 'Thunder Road'."

"And closed with 'Rosalita'?"

"Yes, plus four encores, one of which was 'Born to Run'."

"He saved 'Born to Run' for an encore? In 1981?"

"Yes. The people around us were going mental thinking he wasn't going to play it."

"What a cool memory to carry around with you—an early-eighties Springsteen live, in New Jersey."

"Yes," Stanton said. "On the floor."

"Who did you go with?"

Stanton's iPhone lit up in his hand. He swiped the screen and said to Topher, "Sorry, I'll just be a minute," before he turned and stepped away. "Hey, buddy, what's up?"

While Stanton talked on the phone, Topher finished his beer and did some people-watching, always a good pastime in Austin. A few minutes later, Stanton ended his call and they made their way into the theater, where the second of two opening acts was about halfway through its set. They took their seats in the mezzanine, and Stanton spent some time on Twitter instead of listening to the music, which at first irritated Topher to no end. But then he reminded himself that Stanton was working and they weren't here as friends.

When Springsteen and his band finally took the stage, Stanton turned off his phone and put it away. "Here we go," he said to Topher.

Bruce opened with a cover of Woody Guthrie's "I Ain't Got No Home," since the festival was celebrating the hundredth anniversary of Guthrie's birth. He followed that with a mixture of classic tracks as well as eight songs from the new album, *Wrecking Ball*. At just under three hours, it was a no-holds-barred, tear-down-the-ceiling kind of concert. They played "Badlands" and "The E Street Shuffle," but they didn't play "Born to Run" or "Born in the U.S.A."

Toward the end of the concert, Topher looked over at Stanton, who had that wistful look on his face again. When Topher turned back to the stage and watched Springsteen, he couldn't help but wonder what it would be like to hear throngs of screaming fans cheering his name. He questioned if being a mechanic and playing music on the side would be enough in the end. Would he grow to curse his dream like those other musicians Stanton told him about?

"Wondering what it will be like?" Stanton said as Bruce finished up "We Are Alive."

"Being up there, you mean?"

"Yeah."

"Are all musicians as predictable as me?"

"Pretty much."

"But it's like the lottery, right? That kind of success?"

Stanton nodded.

"So what happens to the rest of us?" Topher asked.

"Focus. Your dream is a lot more modest. Do you have your songs on iTunes?"

Topher shook his head.

"Well, then, how do you expect to win the lottery if you're not even buying tickets?" They looked at each other, and Topher saw Stanton's eyes widen and light up. "This is it!" Stanton yelled over the crowd, like a man half his age.

Topher turned toward the dark stage and saw Bruce Springsteen alone at the microphone, playing a harmonica riff, his face cast in shadow by the backlight. Topher didn't recognize the riff at first, but then it morphed into the opening bars of "Thunder Road."

"The rock-and-roll gods have answered your prayers," Stanton said as the crowd roared its approval.

Topher felt his phone vibrate in his pocket. He reached in and pulled it out as fast as he could, trying to prove to himself that he wasn't crazy. He flipped it open and looked down at the blank screen.

"Is everything okay?" Stanton asked.

"PVS."

"Phantom Vibration Syndrome?"

Topher nodded. His fingers began to tingle, and he felt like maybe his phone was trying to tell him something, but he ignored the feeling and put the phone away. Bruce Springsteen stuffed his harmonica into the back pocket of his blue jeans and sang the first line of the song. With only a simple piano accompaniment and showing little concern for the melody, exhausted and almost talking the lyrics, Bruce stood at the microphone in a lone spotlight, surrounded by darkness, gesturing with his hands. The rest of the band joined in, and with his electric guitar still hanging around his neck, he pulled the microphone off the stand and walked to the front of the stage. As if on cue, he stopped singing and the audience took up where he left off. A chorus of three thousand voices filled the auditorium as the crowd sang one of the song's most famous lines.

"That's a concert moment," Stanton said.

Topher's heart began to race. He saw rapid flashes of blurry pictures, and then everything distilled to a single point in front of him. His vision cleared and sharpened around the edges. He could hear every instrument on the stage distinct from every other instrument. And he could taste something.

Salt water.

When he was young, Topher used to go to Galveston with his parents and sister during the summer. He loved the taste of salt water on his lips when he swam in the Gulf and even wrote a song called "Saltwater Kisses."

The room began to spin, so Topher reached out and grabbed Stanton by the arm.

"Are you okay?" Stanton asked as he steadied him.

"Yeah, I'm good. I think."

Topher regained his footing and looked down at the edge of the stage. Bruce was clutching the hands of his adoring fans. Then he returned to the microphone stand and waved for his wife Patti to join him, but she seemed almost reluctant. Topher thought it was a sweet moment. The song kicked into gear, and he could feel himself transported. He realized what he wanted to do, even though he didn't understand it at all. He closed his eyes, took a deep breath, and then pulled on Stanton's arm and brought them face-to-face.

"What is it?" Stanton said.

Topher didn't answer; instead, he went up onto his toes, closed his eyes, and kissed Stanton. Instantly, he could tell he had caught the music critic off guard, which frankly Topher could understand because he had caught himself off guard too, but he kept his eyes closed and didn't stop. Stanton's lips were soft, and the stubble from his chin brushed up against Topher's grunge-inspired facial hair. He felt Stanton's hands on his hips and then wrapping around his waist. Before he knew what was happening, Topher raised his arms and his fingers made contact with Stanton's shoulders. He squeezed them, broad and solid, in his hands. Topher felt a tongue slide into his mouth. Stanton's hands dropped below his waist and cupped his ass cheeks.

Topher panicked and pushed Stanton away. "What are you doing?" he asked.

The look in Stanton's eyes betrayed his surprise and shock. "Kissing you back. Isn't that what you wanted?"

"I...." Topher looked around and saw two guys in the row behind them staring.

"Get a room," one of them said.

Topher looked back at Stanton. "I'm sorry. I don't know why I did that."

"Are you telling me it was an accident?"

"No. I'm telling you I'm not gay."

Topher watched as that wistful look disappeared from Stanton's face.

"Oh," Stanton said. He sneered and shook his head. "I get it."

"Get what?"

"Nothing. Never mind." Stanton turned back to the stage. "I need to finish watching the concert."

Topher glanced down. Springsteen and his band were taking their bows. "Is it over?"

"No. He still has the encores."

"How many?"

Stanton ignored the question. He crossed his arms over his chest and his face flushed red with an unpleasant emotion.

Topher felt sick to his stomach. He turned and saw Bruce switching out his electric guitar for an acoustic one. He introduced a woman named Michelle Moore, who Topher knew had sung backup on several of his tracks. That was when Bruce Springsteen did the strangest thing. He removed the guitar he had just strapped on and then handed it back to someone on the dark edges of the stage, as if it was simply too heavy for him to bear any longer. Then he began singing a new number called "Rocky Ground." It was a quiet song, filled with grace and forgiveness, and it brought all of Topher's buried sadness to the surface. He stole a furtive, sideways glance at Stanton, who continued to face forward and ignore him. Topher had just fucked up one of the best days of his life, and he knew it. Like Springsteen's guitar, Topher's grief was too heavy for him to bear. His shoulders began to shake and he did everything in his power to stop it, but the tears flowed despite his best efforts. He didn't know what to do. He wiped his face with his hands and rubbed his nose across the sleeve of his T-shirt. He tried to pretend nothing out of the ordinary was happening, and hoped Stanton hadn't noticed, but then Topher felt a sideways glance aimed in his direction and figured he probably had.

When the song ended, Stanton leaned over and asked, "Are you okay?"

"Yeah," Topher said. "Thanks."

Bruce played eight encores that night, and Topher watched and listened to all of them without saying another word to Stanton. To close, Springsteen brought several musicians onto the stage for a rousing sing-along of "This Land Is Your Land." Afterward, with his head lowered and his mind racing, more confused than he'd ever been in his life, Topher followed Stanton as he led them out of the auditorium, back to the Porch, down the stairs, and onto Lavaca Street. They stopped on the sidewalk and faced each other.

"Do you want to talk about it?" Stanton asked.

Topher looked down at the pavement. "I'm pretty embarrassed."

"Don't be."

Topher paused. "Are you gay?"

"You couldn't tell by the way I grabbed your ass?" Topher blushed and laughed a nervous laugh. "Yes," Stanton said, "I'm gay. I take it this is all new to you?"

"Yeah."

"Never kissed a guy before?"

Topher shook his head.

Stanton stepped back and mumbled, "You poor kid. I'm sorry I got angry and jumped to the wrong conclusion."

"You say that like there's a right conclusion. What did you think was going on?"

"Well, at first I thought you were kissing me because you wanted to, but when you said you're not gay, I thought maybe you were playing me."

"Playing you? How?"

"I don't know. You wouldn't be the first musician who thought I could do something for his career—introduce him around, maybe. You wouldn't even be the first musician who kissed me to make that happen."

"That's not what I was doing."

"I figured that out when you started crying." Stanton turned toward the entrance of the W and said, "I need a drink. Follow me."

He started walking. Topher hesitated for a second and then ran to catch up with him. When they reached the door, a young man in a white polo shirt held it open, and Stanton gestured for Topher to enter. He followed Stanton into a lounge called the Living Room. They passed several people with their shoes off, lying around on plush sofas and pillows. Stanton turned into another room on the right, and when Topher saw what was in it, he gasped.

"Holy shit."

On the far wall, from floor to ceiling, were shelves and shelves of records. Not CDs, but actual, honest-to-goodness vinyl records in their original sleeves. In the middle, over a fireplace, hung an orange, red, and pale-blue painting of geometric figures. Topher could see letters in the painting, but he couldn't fit them together. He definitely saw a backward "G" and maybe an "O" or two.

"Have a seat," Stanton said. "I'll be right back."

Stanton exited and Topher crossed to the only empty sofa in the middle of the room. There were three other couples present, but none of them paid any attention to him.

A few minutes later, Stanton returned with a bottle of Shiner and what was probably a vodka tonic, no lemon, no lime, chilled but no ice—and in a glass this time. He handed the bottle to Topher and sat down. "Let's start over," Stanton said. He raised his glass.

Topher clinked the neck of his bottle against it and drank three large gulps. He stared down at the bottle of beer in his hand and somehow resisted the urge to peel the label. "How does a person know?" he asked. "If he's gay, I mean?"

"I never had that problem. I always knew—my problem was admitting it. And coping with the fallout. Have you had these feelings before?"

"No."

"Then why did you kiss me?"

"Because I wanted to."

Stanton shook his head. "Sorry, that doesn't make any sense. Guys don't just wake up when they're twenty-six years old and want to kiss other guys."

"I didn't say I wanted to kiss other guys. I said I wanted to kiss *you*. There's a difference."

Stanton smiled. "Okay, but still."

"I don't know what's going on. It felt like.... God, it's going to sound so stupid."

"I promise not to judge. Much."

"It felt like a sci-fi movie. Like someone had planted a chip in my brain, and when I heard Springsteen sing 'Thunder Road', the chip activated. The next thing I knew, I wanted to kiss you. So I did."

Stanton remained silent.

"I told you it was stupid."

"That's not what I was thinking. How do you feel now?"

"Embarrassed. And..." Topher took a deep breath. "...strangely sad, like I did when my dad died."

"No, I mean, how do you feel about the kiss?"

"Oh." Topher thought it over. "I liked it, though it did freak me out a little when you...." Topher paused. He stared down at his bottle for a moment before he continued. "I've always put my music first and never had much use for dating. I've gone out with girls and even slept with a few of them. I'm not a twenty-six-year-old virgin. I've had guys hit on me before, but I've never hit on another dude, until—" Topher interrupted himself. "Sorry, I'm getting off track. I liked it. The kiss, I mean."

"I don't know what to say."

Topher stared into the fireplace and asked, "How long are you in town?"

"Until Sunday."

"That's three days away. Are you busy tomorrow?"

"No, but—"

"Then see me again. Please. I know I must seem like a train wreck, but maybe you could help me figure things out."

Stanton hesitated, but then said, "I don't think that's a good idea."

"Why not?"

"I—" Stanton stopped himself and took another drink. "Have you ever heard of the *I Ching*?"

"No. Why?"

"It's a book of Chinese philosophy. It explores the idea that everything happens for a reason, that nothing in the universe is random."

"I like that idea."

"So do I. Right now, pretty much every reasonable bone in my body is telling me to walk away from this, but then there's a tiny little part of me that says it's all so random that maybe—"

"—it happened for a reason?"

"Maybe. I'm still on the fence."

For a moment, it seemed as if Stanton was about to tell Topher something important, but then he shook his head instead. Topher glanced around the room. He took a swig of beer and asked, "How many records would you say are in here?"

Stanton looked at the shelves and considered the question. "Three thousand, give or take."

"What if I pulled out some records? Three, maybe. Let's say I randomly pull out three records."

"Why?"

"We both live through music, right? And since neither one of us seems to know what to do here, maybe we should ask the records. You know, look for a sign or something."

"Like the Oracle of Delphi?"

"Sure, whatever that means."

Stanton considered the proposal. "Are you willing to put our fate into the hands of the gods?"

Topher's phone vibrated in his pocket and he smiled, not bothering to check it. "Yeah, I'm willing."

"Okay, then," Stanton said. He gestured toward the wall. "Pick three off the shelf and we'll see what the oracle has to say."

Topher rose and went to the left of the fireplace. The room had filled up after the concert, and he could feel some people staring at him. He pulled two records at random and then crossed to the other side of the room. He looked up at the painting over the fireplace. He wished he could figure out what in the hell those letters were trying to spell. He pulled a third and final album from a shelf to the right. He returned to the sofa and sat down next to Stanton without looking at his draws.

"Let's see what you have," Stanton said.

Topher looked at the first record in his lap and grinned. He handed it to Stanton, who read from the cover, "Billy Joel. *Songs in the Attic.* Do you know this album?"

"Of course. Where do you think I got that expression? Remember when I was telling you about the songs locked in my head? I said it was like an attic somewhere. This is Billy Joel's first live album, and it has 'The Ballad of Billy the Kid' on it, which is the greatest Billy Joel song of all time."

"You have excellent taste."

"Thank you." Topher looked at the second album and couldn't believe his eyes. "No way."

"What is it?"

"Emmylou Harris. *Quarter Moon in a Ten Cent Town.* The first song is called 'Easy From Now On'."

"Miranda Lambert covered that a few years ago."

"That's right. The title of the album is a line from the song. Twice a month, on the nights of the quarter moons, my mom would wait 'til dark and then play it so loud the neighbors next door could hear."

"I don't get it."

"'Quarter Moon in a Ten Cent Town'. Twice a month, that was us. Ten cents is a dime, and we lived in Dime Box, which is literally a ten-cent town. So, twice a month, during the quarter moons, it was like Emmylou Harris was singing just for us."

Stanton's jaw dropped.

"You get it now?"

"Yes, I get it. You've got one more, though."

Topher looked down at the cover. He recognized a picture of John Lennon, but it was not a Beatles album. His heart sank. "Well," he said, "I don't know what your oracle is trying to tell us with this one, but it's a complete mystery to me."

"Let me take a look."

Topher handed Stanton the record and Stanton started to laugh.

"What's so funny?"

"It must be a comedy album," Stanton replied.

"You've never heard of The Firesign Theatre either?"

"No, but the pictures of Groucho Marx and John Lennon are a play on Karl Marx and Vladimir Lenin."

Topher sighed. "As usual, I don't have a clue what you're talking about."

"Karl Marx and Vladimir Lenin were the architects of modern communism. Marx wrote *The Communist Manifesto* in the nineteenth century. He's the guy who said religion is the opium of the people. Then Lenin put communism into practice during World War I, after the Russian revolution. It would be an understatement to say they were very serious men. Their names are often linked together, so to take that association and then play on it with pictures of a clown and a pop-culture icon is…. Funny."

"If you say so. Who's Groucho Marx?"

"He was a comedian. He made movies in the 1930s. You've never heard of the Marx Brothers?"

"Nope."

"How about the Three Stooges?"

"Yeah, my dad used to watch them."

"The Marx Brothers were kind of a precursor to the Three Stooges. Lots of physical comedy. Anyway, if you get all the references, it's a good laugh. But then you know what they say…."

"If you gotta explain a joke, it ain't funny."

"Exactly."

"You must read a lot. To know all that stuff, I mean."

"Not really. When I was in college, there was a movie called *Reds*, with Warren Beatty and Diane Keaton. It's the story of Jack Reed, the American who wrote *Ten Days that Shook the World*."

"What's it about? The book, I mean."

"The Russian revolution. I've never read the book, but I've seen *Reds* about four or five times."

"Who's Warren Beatty?"

Stanton rested his head against the back of the sofa and groaned. "How is it possible that Warren Beatty has been erased from the world? He was like the Brad Pitt of his day—a beautiful man and a great actor."

Topher set his beer down on one of the end tables and stared into the fire. "Well, I guess that didn't work. Some nice connections there, but I didn't see any signs, did you?"

Stanton did not reply, and Topher glanced back at him. He was staring down at the album. All the color had drained from his face, and he looked almost frightened. "What is it?" Topher asked.

"The title of the album. *How Can You Be in Two Places at Once When You're Not Anywhere at All.*"

"Does that mean something to you?"

Stanton took a long pause and then drank the rest of his vodka tonic in one gulp. He turned to Topher and said, "Where's your gig again?"

"Are you serious? You're going to come hear my band play?"

"As long as it's clear I'm not coming as Stanton Porter, the music critic. This is just Stanton, your... friend. Or whatever."

"That's fine. The Rooftop on 6th. Nine o'clock tomorrow. You're actually going to be there?"

"I'm going to try."

"No," Topher said. "I get that you're not coming as a critic, but you still are who you are. If I think you're coming to hear me tomorrow night and you don't show up, I'm going to be...." Topher paused. He almost said "heartbroken," but instead he said, "Disappointed. So either say you're going to come and mean it, or we'll shake hands right now and walk away, no hard feelings."

Stanton waited for a moment, but then he said, "Okay. I'll be there."

"Good." Topher stood up and Stanton did the same. "I'll see you tomorrow night, then. Nine o'clock. Don't be late."

"I'm always late."

"Don't be," Topher said. "Should we hug or kiss or something?"

Stanton reached out and pulled Topher toward him. He wrapped his arms around Topher's shoulders, and Topher surrendered to the embrace. Stanton felt sturdy and rock solid, like Topher could push and push and Stanton would never fall over. When he stepped back and looked up, Topher could see the wistful look had returned to his face.

After saying good night, Topher walked away and left Stanton Porter in the room of three thousand records. Topher returned to the street and felt his phone vibrate in his pocket.

"Yeah, yeah, I know," he said, ignoring it. "I like him too. He's kind of...."

And that was when it struck him—the word embedded in the painting over the fireplace. It was so obvious, he didn't understand why it took him so long to figure it out, but he smiled as he whispered it under his breath.

"...groovy."

INDEPENDENCE DAY

WHEN Stanton finished listening to "Thunder Road," he felt an uncomfortable ache in his stomach that told him he'd been wrong about Bruce Springsteen.

"Play it again," he said.

Hutch silently lifted the needle and reset it. They listened to the song a second time. It was not what Stanton expected at all. Springsteen had taken a single moment in time and turned it into something truly poetic and mesmerizing.

"Again," Stanton said as the song ended.

Hutch reset the needle, and they listened to it yet a third time. Afterward, the two men sat in silence, with Stanton on the bed and Hutch sitting on the floor.

"Well?" Hutch asked.

Stanton still said nothing, but looked at him and smiled.

"Is that…?"

"Okay, you were right. Are you happy?"

"Yes, but I'm not happy about being right. I'm happy that your previously held opinion was due to a lack of exposure, not—"

Stanton interrupted him with a laugh. "Because I'm stupid?"

"Something like that. Can we move on to Dylan?"

"Yeah, I suppose. As long as you're not going to play 'Blowin' in the Wind' for me."

"No," Hutch said. "Even I agree the Peter, Paul and Mary version is better, but don't tell Robert I said that. He thinks it's blasphemy." Hutch grabbed another album from against the wall and pulled the record from the sleeve. "Sorry, no lyric sheet for this, but I promise, you will understand every word."

"We are talking about the same Bob Dylan, aren't we?"

Hutch grinned. He set the needle onto one of the middle tracks and sat back. The sound of a harmonica and the strum of a guitar filled the room. Stanton listened, and once Dylan started to sing, he smiled. Hutch was right—he could understand every word. The name of the song was "With God on Our Side."

If pressed on the issue, Stanton would admit that he hadn't heard much of Bob Dylan's music except in passing, and he had certainly never heard this song. It sounded as if Dylan had walked into the studio and laid it down in a single take. The tempo was wildly inconsistent and often the guitar seemed out of step with the vocals, as if that was the point. Hutch didn't like this song because of the musical performance, or maybe he did, but he definitely liked what it had to say. So Stanton focused on the lyrics.

There was nothing groundbreaking about the song's structure—in fact, it had an almost childlike simplicity. Dylan introduced himself in the opening lines, but downplayed the importance of his identity.

"He's from the Midwest?" Stanton asked.

"Yes. Minnesota."

The song continued with an articulation of America's wars. It was more an observation than a critique, really, and Dylan kept coming back to his personal confusion juxtaposed with the historical justification for each war—a justification that stubbornly refused to change over time. Stanton had never been a fan of political or protest music, but Dylan found a hook that changed his opinion.

"It's smart," Stanton said as he listened and nodded. Hutch smiled, and Stanton added, "Wipe that smirk off your face."

"Can you blame me? I'm batting a thousand here."

Like "Thunder Road," the song had no chorus, something that would normally be unthinkable to Stanton. In the final stanzas, Dylan introduced Jesus Christ and Judas Iscariot, a bold move that caught Stanton's attention. As a Catholic, he appreciated the power of religious images and symbols. When the song ended, Stanton threw up his arms and lay back on the bed.

"Okay," he said. "I surrender. I love a song with a punch line."

"See, I told you."

Stanton sat back up. "It's the opposite of everything I ever thought about him. Simple, accessible—brave, even."

"You didn't think Bob Dylan was brave?"

"I lived a few hours from Kent State, so compared to that, no. Singing songs never struck me as particularly brave. But this is different—that's what I'm trying to say. He grounds it in such a personal point of view, not to mention the song is an open attack on religion in general."

"I'm glad you liked it."

"I did, but now can we listen to 'The One That You Love'?"

"Okay. But we have to keep the volume down. Robert can't know I'm listening to Air Supply."

"Is he really that much of a snob?"

"No, I'm kidding. Well, he is kind of a snob, but a really sweet one." Hutch pulled out the record and started the song. Then they lay down on the bed together.

"You know what this song reminds me of?" Hutch said, staring up at the ceiling.

"What?"

"*Romeo and Juliet.*"

"Really?"

"Yeah. Listen to the words. He's just spent the night with this incredible person, but now it's morning. He's asking for one more day. He promises to slow down time—anything to keep them together. It's like that scene from *R&J,* the morning after they're married."

"Parting is such sweet sorrow?" Stanton said.

"No. 'I must be gone and live, or stay and die.'"

"What would Robert think, comparing Air Supply to Shakespeare?"

Hutch laughed. "He'd have a field day with that one, wouldn't he?"

The two men listened to a few more songs, and then Stanton announced he should be getting back to the house to check on Marvin.

"Are you his friend or his babysitter?" Hutch said.

Stanton frowned and sat up. "Stop right there. Where did you grow up?"

"Manhattan."

"I thought so. You don't know what it's like to come to New York from somewhere else. When I moved here two years ago, I thought I had been dropped onto another planet. The culture shock hit me hard, and I told you how much I struggled with being gay. I would have done anything to not be this way."

Hutch sat up. "What were you so afraid of?"

"Going to hell."

"You really believed that?"

"I did at the time, yes. Some days I wonder if my parents wouldn't rather I be dead than gay. Where I come from, there's no such thing as being out. I had never seen two men holding hands before I moved here. New York is a bubble, and this place? They might as well call it Fantasy Island. You do know that the rest of the country isn't like New York, don't you?"

"What does all this have to do with Marvin?"

"After the night he and I talked, I tried to come out, at least to myself. But it wasn't easy. I got depressed that first semester and tried to kill myself."

Hutch lowered his head. "Oh."

"At the end of January, Marvin found me on our bathroom floor, overdosing on a bottle of sleeping pills I stole from my mom's medicine cabinet at Christmas. After they pumped my stomach, I was in the hospital overnight, and Marvin never left my side. Afterward, he did the one thing I needed more than anything else."

"What was that?"

"He treated me like an adult and told me the truth. He said everything I didn't want to hear. He was brutally honest with me. He told me I was spineless and that I expected everything to be easy. He told me that if I stopped feeling sorry for myself, I would see that being gay was actually my salvation—because without something to push against, without some kind of uphill battle, life has absolutely no meaning. He talked to me like no one has ever talked to me before in my life, and that was a turning point for me. He's a real mensch."

"What's that?"

"You mean I know more Yiddish than you?"

"I guess you do."

"It means an authentic person, someone who's there when you need them. So if you want to have any hope of ever turning this ring around, you will have to win him over, because he isn't going anywhere. Do you get what I'm saying here?"

"Yes, of course. I'm sorry."

"Don't be. I'm the one who should be sorry. This is why I'm single. I have no filter between my brain and my mouth."

"Are you still—"

"Suicidal? No, I'm not. I'm okay with things now. Am I jumping up and down about it? No. But I'm gay. I can say the words without choking on them. Believe it or not, I don't usually stir up this much drama. If you don't want to see me again, I'll understand. It's just... Marvin is a sensitive spot, so...."

"I get it," Hutch said. "I'll show you out."

They both stood up. Stanton looked at Hutch and knew this was the end. They made their way downstairs and through the living room, where Hutch's roommates had begun a game of Risk.

Michael waved and said, "I hope we'll be seeing you again, Stanton."

Stanton nodded and said, "I hope so too. Good night."

Once outside, Stanton wanted to make a quick getaway, but Hutch stopped him and asked, "Are you going to the Invasion tomorrow?"

"What's that?"

"Just a Fourth of July thing. About five years ago, some drag queen from Cherry Grove got refused service at the Botel. So she went back and gathered up a bunch of her sisters and then came back in a water taxi on the Fourth. I think they were secretly hoping for a confrontation."

"What happened?"

"Nothing. I mean, no confrontation, at least. The Pines guys threw open their arms and welcomed them. Everyone bought them drinks at the Blue Whale, so now it's become an annual tradition."

"Drag queens?"

"Yeah. Is that a problem?"

Stanton sighed. "Marvin says I don't understand the subversive power of gender swapping."

Hutch laughed. "He probably has a point."

"Maybe. I don't know. I'll talk to him about it. See if he wants to go."

"I hope you'll do that. Good night. It was great to meet you."

"You too." Stanton extended his hand.

"A handshake?"

"Sorry, I don't kiss on the first date anymore, if that's what this was."

"I gave you a ring. I'd say at the very least it was a first date."

"Okay, but still. I used to jump right into bed with guys, but then I noticed they all treated me like I was disposable the next day."

"I didn't ask you to jump into bed with me."

"I know that. I'm not a prude, I swear, but can I get to know you just a little bit better? I'm talking days, not weeks. That's all I'm asking."

Hutch smiled and opened his arms. "How about a hug, then?"

Stanton nodded and embraced him. It felt calm and safe. After a moment, he extracted himself and turned to walk away. "Good night," he said.

"The Invasion," Hutch called after him. Stanton glanced back, and Hutch blew him a kiss. "Tomorrow. Don't forget."

"Right," Stanton said. "I won't forget."

THE next morning, over breakfast with Colby and Archy, Stanton told Marvin about the Invasion. Archy made eggs Benedict, and they ate on the patio next to the pool.

Marvin laughed when Stanton relayed Hutch's description of the event. "Drag queens? Did you break out into hives when he told you about it?"

"It's fun," said Archy. "You should give it a look."

"You guys aren't going?" Stanton asked.

"No," said Colby. "At our age, we prefer quiet afternoons by the pool. We'd only ruin the scenery for the beautiful boys, but you two will fit right in."

"Are you supposed to meet him?" asked Marvin.

"No, he just asked if we were going. We didn't make any plans."

Marvin reached across Stanton to grab the butter, but then he paused when he noticed something. His eyes widened. "What is that on your finger?"

"What does it look like, buddy?"

"Did he…?"

"He did. But don't worry, I probably scared him off."

"Did you tell him about—"

"Yes."

"Feh!" Marvin slumped in his chair.

"Who's this we're talking about?" Archy asked.

"A guy I met at tea yesterday. One of the bartenders at the Blue Whale."

"What does he look like?" Archy asked.

"Tall. Shaggy blond hair. Gorgeous."

"Chris," Colby said.

"No, his name is Hutch."

"Ah, yes. I forgot about that nickname. He does look like that dreamy David Soul, don't you think, dear?"

Archy patted his lover on the arm and said, "You know I don't like blonds."

"You mean his name isn't really Hutch?" Stanton asked.

"Please, dear, who names their child Hutch? Even on the TV show, it was short for Hutchinson, or something like that. No, his name is Chris. People talk, of course, but I'm not one to gossip."

"What's there to gossip about?"

"Rumor has it that his family is very wealthy," Archy said.

"And," Colby added, "that they cut him off without a penny when his homosexuality was exposed. Scandalous, really."

"The plot thickens," Marvin said. "What's his last name? Rockefeller?"

"I don't know, dear. No one uses last names out here."

"*Mishegas*," Marvin said.

"What does that mean?" Archy asked.

"Insanity," Stanton replied.

"Well," Colby said, "of course, it's completely different for your generation. Everything is gay, gay, gay, all the time."

"Except the *Times* won't even use the word gay," Marvin said.

Colby waved his hand in dismissal. "And in light of that, can you blame people for being cautious? Some closet doors are nailed shut and will never be opened. Out here we can be free, but people still remember what lies north of Long Island Sound."

"Change requires courage."

"Do not lecture me about courage, young man. Archy and I have been lovers since 1944. I dare say that took a spot of courage, wouldn't you, dear?"

"How old were you two when you met?" Stanton asked.

"I was twenty," Colby said. "Archy was seventeen and absolutely the most beautiful thing I had ever laid eyes on."

"Let's get back to the ring," Marvin said. "On the first date? Really? What were you thinking?"

"I wasn't thinking anything. It's some Irish tradition. You turn it around depending on whether you're available or taken. Supposedly his mom is Irish—don't ask me to explain it."

Marvin shook his head. "This is what happens when tourists dabble in cultures they don't understand."

"Stop being so judgmental," Stanton said. "The way it is now means I'm available. And open to love. What's wrong with that?"

"Well," Archy said, "hopefully he'll get you to turn it around."

"I doubt it. Not after—"

Marvin interrupted him. "I think we should go, then. It'll be fun, and I'll get the pleasure of watching you squirm. Maybe one of the drag queens will even make a pass at you. Wouldn't that be exciting?"

Stanton scowled. "I'm breathless with anticipation."

"You forgot the pause."

"Archy," Colby said. "Do you sometimes feel as if they speak a different language to each other?"

"Sorry," Marvin said. "I took him to see *Rocky Horror* last month."

"And what, pray tell, is *Rocky Horror*?"

"*The Rocky Horror Picture Show*. A cult film that has midnight showings at the 8th Street Playhouse on the weekends. It's just a few blocks from our dorm. The audience participates and yells things at the screen."

"It sounds… ghastly," Colby said. "Why would anyone want to watch a movie with people yelling things?"

"Not to mention all the transvestites," Stanton said.

"Sounds like it's right up your alley," Archy joked.

"Anyway," Marvin continued, "when Tim Curry says, 'I'm breathless with antici—' he puts a long pause there, and the crowd is screaming, 'Say it! Say it!'"

"Say what?" Archy asked.

"Pation."

"Pation?"

"*Antici*—pause—*pation*."

Colby and Archy looked at each other, confused.

"Forget it," Marvin said.

"And how exactly do you find this entertaining?" Colby asked.

"Underneath his composed exterior," Stanton said, imitating Steve Martin, "is a wild and crazy guy. You should see Marvin in a corset. It's not pretty."

"My," said Colby, "having young people around is so educational, don't you agree, dear?"

Archy nodded as he finished his coffee. "It's certainly a different world out there these days."

LATER that afternoon, after spending some time by the pool, Stanton and Marvin got dressed and walked down to the harbor to take in the Invasion. It was the biggest crowd they had seen all weekend. Stanton kept looking around for Hutch.

"Don't worry," Marvin said. "He's got to be here somewhere. And if not, I'm sure he'll be working at tea."

"I blew it."

"Why did you tell him?"

"I don't know. It just happened."

"You need to roll these things out a little slower."

"I'm not in the mood to be lectured."

"You never are, but when has that stopped me?"

Stanton smiled. "I love you, buddy."

"You don't really have much choice in the matter."

"I know. I just wish I was more like you."

"You do not want to be a short Jew-boy in a sea of WASPy perfection."

"You know who you are and you never back down."

"I come from a people accustomed to adversity. It's in my genes."

"Well, I come from a people accustomed to denial and emotional constipation."

They stood on the edge of the harbor and waited for the Invasion to begin. When the boat finally arrived, bursting with garish, over-the-top drag queens, the crowd cheered and helped the ladies off one by one. Each got a formal introduction to the men of the Pines by the Cherry Grove Homecoming Queen.

Marvin elbowed Stanton in the ribs and said, "There he is."

"Where?"

"Over there, in front of the Pantry."

Stanton glanced over and saw him, standing with his shirt off, surrounded by his housemates. "Christ," he said. "Look at his body. Is he out of my league?"

"Not at all. You two were made for each other."

"What should I do?"

"Nothing. Let him come to you. Indifference is the greatest of the aphrodisiacs."

"But what if he hasn't seen me yet?"

"Wait until tea starts and he's working. Then you can casually saunter up."

"I'm no good at this. I just want to know if he's still interested. That's all. If he's not, at least I can move on."

"Patience, grasshopper. Anything worth your while is also worth the wait."

Late at night, alone in their room, Stanton and Marvin often watched old episodes of *Kung Fu* on TV.

"Old man," Stanton quoted, "how is it that you know these things?"

"Young man," Marvin quoted back, "how is it that you do not?"

Stanton closed his eyes and then opened them again. He glared at Hutch, willing him to look over in his direction, but all Hutch did was smile and laugh with his friends. Stanton didn't recognize one of the guys standing next to him, a handsome man in his early thirties who kept leaning over and whispering into Hutch's ear.

"That guy standing beside him is making his move," Stanton said. "Do you see how old he is? It's gross."

Marvin watched them for a moment. "Hutch isn't interested."

"How can you tell?"

"Look at the way he keeps turning to one of his friends after the guy says something to him."

"What do you mean?"

"Watch."

Stanton observed as the man put his arm on Hutch's shoulder and leaned over to say something. Hutch laughed at what the man said, but then turned to speak to Robert. That forced the man to drop his hand from Hutch's shoulder.

"He's being polite," Marvin said. "See? And that *shmendrik* can't take a hint. But that's beside the point. If you're going to pursue someone like Hutch—or Chris, or whatever his name is—you'll need to resign yourself to the fact that men will always be throwing themselves at him. You might as well get used to it."

"I've got to go over there. This is driving me nuts."

"Just wait a few more...."

Stanton had started to walk away when a piercing voice stopped him cold. It was the Cherry Grove Homecoming Queen, the one with the microphone, the one announcing all the participants as they stepped off the boat. She had called out Marvin's name.

"Is there a Marvin Goldstein in the house?" she repeated.

Stanton and Marvin looked at each other in horror.

"What's going on?" Marvin said.

"I have no idea."

"If I'm about to be publicly humiliated in front of all these men, I will never forgive you."

"You know I wouldn't do that."

"Marvin Goldstein?" the drag queen said again. "Oh, Marvin, come out, come out, wherever you are."

"What do I do?" Marvin asked.

The man standing next to them had clearly overheard their conversation, because he yelled out, "He's over here!"

"Shit," Stanton mumbled.

"Oh, God of Abraham, protect and watch over me in my hour of need."

"Marvin, honey, are you there?" the queen asked. "Don't be afraid. I don't bite... hard!"

Stanton pushed Marvin toward the pier and said, "Go. There's no way out of it now. Just bite the bullet and keep smiling."

Marvin pouted, but then reluctantly walked to the end of the pier. He slowly inched his way forward until he stood in front of the Cherry Grove Homecoming Queen. She reached out and pulled Marvin's face into her fake yet substantial bosom.

"Well, Marvin, aren't you a delicious little thing? We do love us a handsome Hebrew, don't we, girls?" Her fellow drag queens answered with a cheer while Marvin pulled away and stood in silence, his face purple with anguish. "Marvin, we brought you a surprise from the Grove today, at the request of our favorite hunky bartender at the Blue Whale. Hutch, do you want to join me and help with the honors?"

Stanton saw Marvin look his way and mouth, "I'm going to kill you." He looked toward the Pantry and saw Hutch break away from his friends and saunter down the boardwalk to the pier. The crowd parted for him like he was Moses.

"Last night," the Homecoming Queen said, "I got a call from Hutch. It seems Marvin here is a connoisseur of fine red vino, and since my wine cellar is legendary—"

"Lush!" one of her sister's screamed.

"Guilty as charged," the HQ said in agreement. When Hutch reached the pier, he walked up to Marvin and put his arm around him. "Hutch, would you like to take it from here?" she asked, handing him the microphone.

"Thanks, Patzi. Marvin, a little bird told me you were unhappy with the wine at the Blue Whale."

"I think the exact word the bird used was *crap*," Patzi bellowed. "But in the Blue Whale's defense, Marvin, no one orders wine at tea. And certainly not red!"

The crowd roared with delight.

"So," Hutch said, "I asked Patzi if she could bring over a bottle from her cellar."

Patzi held up a dark, dusty bottle for the crowd to see. Hutch handed the microphone back to her. "Marvin, I realize I could have grabbed practically any bottle and it would have been an improvement on what they serve at the Blue Whale. But Hutch introduced me to my husband last summer, so I owe him big-time. This, then, is a bottle of 1947 Chateau Cheval Blanc." Marvin's eyes nearly popped out of his head, and several of the men in the crowd gasped in shock. "I take it you know what that is?" Patzi asked. She grinned and lowered the microphone so that Marvin could speak into it.

"It's widely considered to be the finest Bordeaux, and possibly the finest wine of any kind, ever produced on the planet."

"Have you tasted it?" she asked.

Marvin laughed. "No. I wish."

"Well, that's what fairy godmother drag queens do, right, girls? We make wishes come true. From Cherry Grove to the Pines, from Patzi Klein to Marvin Goldstein, I bestow on you this bottle to share with your friends and loved ones." She handed him the bottle while Hutch reached over and playfully tousled his hair.

"I'm speechless," Marvin said. He accepted the wine from her and looked down at the label in disbelief. "Thank you. Both of you. This is...."

Stanton watched as Hutch bent down and whispered something into Marvin's ear. Marvin nodded and smiled. It was a great moment, but Stanton knew it could only mean one thing—Hutch was still interested. Stanton's grin widened as he watched Marvin walk back through the crowd. A gaggle of men greeted him and patted him on the shoulder as he passed.

When Marvin stood again by Stanton's side, he said, "If you don't date him, you have no sense in your head whatsoever."

"Oh, I know that, buddy. I'll be right back." Stanton walked over to the pier, where Hutch stood waiting for him. "Thank you," Stanton said.

"You're welcome. Did it work?"

Stanton laughed. "Trust me, it worked."

"I have to go sling drinks now, but will you and Marvin come by the house for dinner later? I don't want him to be on his own two nights in a row."

"Eight o'clock?"

"Make it seven thirty. I'm cooking, by the way. Nothing fancy, but it should be a nice meal."

"We'll be there." Stanton stepped forward and kissed Hutch on the cheek.

"Groovy," Hutch said, grinning.

"There's more where that came from." Stanton started to walk away, but then turned back. "Oh, and whoever that old guy was grabbing all over you, tell him to find someone his own age, please."

"You have nothing to worry about, Stanton."

"I know. I just want you to tell him that."

"I will happily pass the word along. By the way, that question you asked me yesterday. Why you?"

"Yeah. Sorry about that. You were right."

"No, I wasn't. You should know why I like you. Among all the other things, it's because of the way you stood up for your friend. Even when it meant sharing something uncomfortable about yourself."

"Love, friendship, and loyalty. That pretty much sums up what's important to me."

"You're a good man, Stanton Porter."

"Thanks. I like the way you see me. Seven thirty?"

"Seven thirty. Don't be late."

"I'm always late."

"Don't be. Not tonight."

Stanton turned and walked away. He rejoined Marvin, who stood in the shade of a dying oak tree.

"Everything kosher?" Marvin asked.

"Yep. We've been invited to dinner tonight at their house."

"Yes, I know."

"He told you?"

Marvin nodded. "Hutch and I have our own thing. I'm supposed to make sure you're not late."

"Good luck with that."

"What are we going to talk about with them?"

"What do you think we're going to talk about?"

Stanton started to walk away and could tell Marvin didn't get it at first. He smiled because he knew the answer would dawn on his friend eventually, which it did. Stanton could feel Marvin's excitement as he ran to catch up with him.

"It's music, right?" Marvin said. "We're going to talk about music."

BETTER DAYS

THE morning after the Springsteen concert, Topher dragged himself out of bed and into the bathroom. He looked in the mirror. Were those bags under his eyes? Sleep had been hard to come by after the events of the previous night.

Once he finished his shower and got dressed, Topher made his way into the kitchen. Since he and his three bandmates shared a house, mornings tended to be a little chaotic. The twins, Robin and Maurice, were packing lunches, while Peter sat at the table eating a bowl of cereal.

"How was the concert last night?" Peter asked.

"It was groovy."

Robin raised an eyebrow and said, "Groovy?" He opened the fridge and pulled out two small containers of yogurt, then handed them to his brother.

Peter finished his cereal and drank the remaining milk straight from the bowl. He stood up and gestured to the box. "You want any of this before I put it away?" he asked Topher.

"No, I'm not hungry."

"What was he like?" Robin asked. "It's not very often you get to hang out with a big-time music critic like Stanton Porter."

Topher went to the coffeepot on the counter and poured himself a cup. Then he turned to the others and said, "He's coming to our gig tonight."

"What?" all three exclaimed together.

"How did you swing that?" Robin asked. "Did you blow him or something?"

Topher cleared his throat and said, "No, it was his idea."

"We'd love to hear all about this," Maurice said as he handed one of the brown-bag lunches to Robin, "but we're late as it is." The twins both worked at the airport—Maurice for a rental car company and Robin on the ground crew. Robin drove around one of those carts with the checked baggage.

"We'll see y'all tonight at seven," Robin said, and then they disappeared out the back door.

"You off today?" Topher asked Peter.

"Yeah, I switched shifts with one of the other guys." Peter worked in the lumber section of Home Depot, which was a natural fit since Peter's father owned the lumberyard in Dime Box. "I'm going to head downtown and check out some of the outdoor stages."

Peter had started toward the kitchen door when Topher stopped him and asked, "Can I tell you something?"

"Sure, what's up?"

"I kissed Stanton Porter last night, in the middle of 'Thunder Road'."

"Seriously?" Peter said. "Bruce played 'Thunder Road'? I hate you."

"Didn't you hear what I said?"

"Yeah, I heard you. What kind of reaction are you looking for?"

"I don't know. Aren't you surprised?"

Peter looked like he was thinking it over. Then he said, "Not really. I've talked to two guys in the past year, both of them supposedly straight, both of them telling me the same story. They met a gay dude they really hit it off with, they decided to try out the sex part, and they liked it. A lot. Way more than they ever imagined. One of them even told me his boyfriend gives him blow jobs when they watch college football on Saturday afternoons."

"Sounds like Travis."

"You want to hear my theory?"

"No. It's too early for you and your theories."

"Too bad. In four or five generations, sexual orientation will disappear and we'll all just fall in love with people."

"Would you ever consider banging a dude?"

"I don't rule it out," Peter said, "but I'm sticking with the ladies for now, thank you. I wouldn't mind a blow job while I'm watching the Longhorns, though, if she's offering. How old is this Stanton Porter, anyway? I remember reading his articles in *Rolling Stone* ten years ago."

"He's fifty."

"Good Lord, dude. Let the jokes begin."

"He's a really hot fifty."

"Right. Maybe you should take him to Luby's for your first date. I think he can get the senior's discount on the early-bird special if he shows them his AARP card."

"You're hysterical. I haven't even thought about a date."

"Why not? If you kissed him, there must be something going on there."

"Maybe. I don't know."

"Sounds like you need to figure things out."

"You're probably right."

"I'm always right. If there's one thing I've learned from my time in the dating pool, it's that the window of opportunity only stays open for a short time. Carpe diem, my friend. We're not getting any younger." Peter started to leave, but then he stopped himself. He turned to Topher and asked, "So, did you blow him?"

"No!" Topher said. "Not yet, at least."

WHEN he got to the shop, Topher began a service check on a Dodge Durango. It was a simple job—an oil change and multipoint inspection—but Topher was so distracted by his thoughts of the night before that he replaced the spark plugs with the original, used ones.

"Shit," he mumbled under his breath when he realized his mistake.

Travis stuck his head out from underneath the hood of a Chevy Silverado and asked, "What's got you so out of sorts this morning? I thought you'd be all high on life after seeing the Boss last night."

"I don't know." Topher realized if he could talk to anyone about what had happened the night before, Travis was that person. Last year, Travis had fallen head over heels in love with a guy after being straight his whole life. "What are you doing for lunch today?" Topher asked him.

"The usual. Going back to the house and making a sandwich. Why?"

"You want to grab a bite across the street? I could use the ear."

Travis lit up at the prospect. "Sure thing. Can we go to Jason's? I like their French onion soup."

"Sure. I'll let Darrell know we're taking lunch at the same time."

Shortly after noon, the two men washed their hands and headed across the street to Jason's Deli. Once they got their food and sat down at one of the window booths, Travis immediately grabbed his spoon and speared the cheese of his soup. He twirled it around and then shoveled it into his mouth. "How was the concert?" he asked while still chewing.

"It was interesting. Stanton is a cool guy. He's lived quite a life."

"That's his name? Stanton?"

"Yeah. Stanton Porter."

"He's hot."

"Yeah, you already mentioned that. He's a music critic for NPR. You've heard him on the radio."

"Did you two sit together?"

"Yeah."

"What's the problem, then?"

Topher decided to dodge the question for the time being and instead said, "I'm curious. What happened to you last year? With Ben, I mean. You know I think the world of him, and I don't have any problems with you being gay now. It's cool to say that, right?"

"Yes, I have a boyfriend. It's okay to call me gay."

"Okay. So you never really told me the whole story of how that went down."

Travis struggled with the stringy cheese for a moment longer and then swallowed. He looked out the window and said, "I can't explain it."

"I'm not asking you to explain it. I just want to know how it happened."

"Well, I reckon it all started at the funeral, after his parents were killed in that car crash. His daddy had already taken me under his wing at that point, and me and his brothers were as thick as thieves, but of course Ben still lived in New York. I'd seen pictures of him, and even then I noticed how handsome he was. I mean, you can look at someone like Brad Pitt and tell he's a good-looking guy, can't you?"

"Yeah, I suppose."

"Well, I saw him for the first time at the funeral. There he was, in the flesh, sitting in the front row with his brothers. Still, I didn't meet him 'til later, at the cemetery."

"Did you know something was up then?"

"Looking back, I reckon I did, but it wasn't until about a week later, on New Year's Eve, that I knew for sure. But good golly, that was just the beginning of the drama. You know what I went through with—"

Topher interrupted him. "Had you ever been attracted to a guy before that?"

"Nope. Never. But Ben is no ordinary guy. He's a force of nature. I go down to his office sometimes, and you should see the way those other lawyers fawn all over him—like they're in love with him too! Everywhere we go, people are just naturally attracted to him, and I was no different. From that very first day, well, maybe I wasn't in love with him at that point, but I already loved being around him. When he took me back to the cemetery to pick up my truck, you should have seen the sparks fly. He said something about me not wanting to be a mechanic for the rest of my life, and I went off on him about how I can fix anything, thank you very much, and then he smiled the Ben smile for the first time, and I melted right there on the spot. At one point, he reached across the seat to get some gloves out of the glove box and brushed across my knee. I swear I about jumped out of my skin. The whole day, it was like... I don't know."

"Like you remembered something you had forgotten."

"Yeah, exactly. He made me feel like I was the most important person in the world. The next day he came by and asked for my advice. Isn't that the craziest thing you ever heard? He's a lawyer and he's asking my advice about his brothers. Turns out he even listened to me too."

"How did it turn... you know?"

"Physical?"

"Yeah."

"Well, after a few days, I started thinking about what it would be like to kiss him."

Topher choked on his roast beef sandwich.

"You okay?"

"Yeah. It just went down the wrong pipe. Keep going."

"Well, I don't know why I started thinking about it. Maybe because he has such nice lips."

"Did you just up and do it one day?"

"Nu-uh, I wish I could say I was that brave, but I wasn't. He kissed me first."

"And?"

"My dick got hard. A man's erection never lies. I guess that makes me bisexual, but I never felt bisexual before then. After that kiss, though, I couldn't think about nothing else, and by the time we finally had sex a month later, I was bursting out of my skin with excitement."

"A month later? What took you so long?"

"Like I said, I was a coward. I give Ben credit for moving that along too."

"Do you look at other guys now?"

Travis hesitated. "Since then, I've kind of opened my eyes a bit. I recognize a hot man when I see one—like that Stanton Porter guy. I even watch some gay porn now, looking for sex tips and role-playing scenarios."

Travis leaned forward and lowered his voice. "There's this one dude, Spencer Reed, good golly, he's hot. But that's just between you and me. If you ever tell Ben that, I'll slap you upside the head, you hear? He still thinks I'm only gay for him."

Topher laughed. "Do you miss sex with women?"

Travis shook his head emphatically. "Good Lord, no. Ben is the love of my life and the best sex I've ever had—hands down, no contest. I got no reason to look elsewhere, male or female. Not to mention, he'd kill me. Why you asking about all this, anyway?"

Topher paused and took a drink of his Dr Pepper. He watched as Travis spooned some more soup into his mouth, then he said, "I kissed Stanton in the middle of 'Thunder Road'."

Travis froze mid-slurp. "Oh, shit," he said.

"Yeah. My thoughts exactly."

Travis put his spoon down and rubbed his scalp. "Do you think Darrell puts something in our water?"

Topher laughed again. "I thought the same thing. I've never been so confused in my life."

"Well, you came to the right place, at least. I know exactly where you're coming from, my friend."

"So give me some advice. What do I do?"

"First, tell me what happened."

"I don't really know what happened. It was toward the end of the concert, when Bruce finally sang 'Thunder Road'. That's my favorite Springsteen song. First, I'd been feeling my phone vibrate all day, but every time I checked it, there was no call or text."

"Weird."

"Yeah, that's what I said. Stanton called it Phantom Vibration Syndrome. Says he read about it on the Daily Beast."

"What's that?"

"I don't know. So Springsteen starts to sing 'Thunder Road', and I feel my phone vibrating in my pocket. When I pull it out, there's no call or text, and I think maybe my phone is trying to tell me something."

"Topher...."

"I know, it sounds crazy. Then, it was like somebody flipped a switch in my head. That's the only way I can describe it. The room started spinning, and then bam!"

"Don't tell me you puked or nothing."

"No, just the opposite. All my senses went into overdrive."

"Like Peter Parker when that spider bit him?"

"Exactly. I could see every color and hear every note, and I swear to you on my father's grave, I could taste salt water."

"Wait a minute. Didn't you write a song called 'Saltwater Kisses'?"

"Yes, and don't think that wasn't the first thing that popped into my head. Anyway, I'm watching Bruce Springsteen and his wife Patti sing 'Thunder Road' into the same microphone, and it hit me. I realized I wanted to kiss Stanton Porter. I didn't understand why, but I knew that's what I wanted to do. So I did it."

"What was his reaction?"

"He liked it, but then—"

"Did you freak out?"

"Kind of. He kissed me back and grabbed my ass, so I pushed his hands away and told him I wasn't gay."

Travis began to laugh uncontrollably.

"It's not funny," Topher said.

"Oh, it's funny, all right. One minute you got your tongue down his throat, and the next minute you're telling him you're not gay? I bet Stanton was having a laugh riot at that point. He is gay, isn't he?"

"Yeah."

"I figured. Most straight guys don't grab your ass when you kiss 'em."

"He didn't seem too happy about it, I admit. He gave me the cold shoulder after that. I thought I had ruined everything. I was tired and confused and running on emotional fumes...."

"Don't tell me you started crying?"

"I couldn't help it, and the more I tried to stop, the worse it got."

"How did he react to that?"

"Well, it seemed to melt the ice a bit, but then we had to stand there through eight encores."

"What happened after the concert?"

"We went into the hotel where he's staying—the W, real fancy—and he took me to this room that has tons and tons of records, from floor to ceiling. We had a drink and talked. The next part I can't really explain, but long story short, he's coming to my gig tonight."

Travis sat for a moment in silence.

"No advice?" Topher asked.

"Did you like kissing him?"

"Yeah, I did, but that's about as far as I've gotten—processing all this, I mean."

"Have you been thinking about him today?"

"I haven't thought about anything else."

"I noticed you hardly touched your lunch. You kind of sick to your stomach?"

"Yes."

"Sleep last night?"

"Not really."

"You ever had those symptoms before?"

"After meeting someone, you mean?"

"Yeah."

"No. I've never felt this discombobulated the next day."

"Where in the hell did you get that word?"

"My mom uses it all the time."

"And you're going to see Stanton again?"

"Yeah. Tonight."

"Do you want to talk about second and third base?"

Topher took another drink of his Dr Pepper. "I hadn't really thought about it, but I guess we should."

"Well, first off, it don't sound like you're one of those guys who gets instantly grossed out by the thought of sex with another dude."

"No, not at all. I liked kissing him, and I've thought about sex with a guy before, just not with Stanton specifically."

"But nothing's ever happened?"

"No. But not because it grosses me out. I just haven't had a lot of sex, period."

"Have you ever watched gay porn?"

"No, but then I'm not a big porn guy."

"Has a dude ever made your dick hard?"

Topher thought about the question. Then he said, "Not that I recall."

"Ever taste your own come? After you jack off?"

Topher could feel himself turn red.

"Never mind, the look on your face just answered for you. I think we need to do a little test, just to see where we stand. Close your eyes."

"Now?"

"Yes, now."

Topher looked around the dining room. "This is stupid. We're in a public place."

"Don't be a wuss. I'm not going to tell you to whip your cock out. Besides, trust me, it's not stupid. I'm the sexpert here. We're missing a crucial piece of information. Now close your eyes."

Topher did as instructed.

"You remember what Stanton looks like?"

"Of course."

"Then picture yourself undressing him." Topher started to chuckle, and Travis said, "You're not going to score any points by laughing when he takes his shirt off."

"Okay, okay."

"Now, look at him. Picture yourself undoing his belt and sliding his pants down."

"This is getting—"

"Then you take it from here. Drop to your knees and see what happens. In your head, I mean, not here in the booth."

Another silence fell over the table. In his mind's eye, Topher could see Stanton in front of him. His sturdy and rock-solid chest had a light coat of hair that tapered into a trail leading downward. Topher followed the path and then saw himself pull Stanton's cock out of his briefs. It was a nice size—bigger than his own—and cut. He dropped to his knees and took Stanton's smooth balls into his hand. He leaned forward and licked a drop of come from the slit. He took the whole of Stanton's cock into his mouth and tasted a man in a way he had never—

Topher's eyes shot wide open.

"You got a rise in your Levi's?" Travis asked.

Topher nodded and Travis laughed.

"Welcome to the club, Toph. That's the crucial piece of information we were missing. Now, do you want things to go in that direction or not?"

"I think so."

"Sorry, none of that. You can't be wishy-washy about sex with a gay guy. If you string him along and then decide you don't want to go through with it, well... there's a name for guys like that."

"Cock tease?"

"Bingo. You don't want to be one, trust me, so I'm going to ask you again. Do you want things to go in that direction?"

Topher's cock was still hard from thinking about blowing Stanton. "Yes."

"And if it does, you're not going to freak out or nothing, are you?"

"No, I'm not going to freak out."

"You sure? It's not like sex with a woman. There are cocks and mouths and assholes everywhere you turn. It can get sweaty and rough too. Hell, I got bruises half the time from the way Ben fucks me. Are you ready for that?"

"I can handle myself just fine."

"Okay, then. My advice is, stick to blow jobs the first time. And no teeth. Ben and I can make a night out of oral sex, and you can too. If butt-fucking comes up, just put it off 'til next time. We can talk about that later."

The two men sat in silence for a moment, and then Travis said, "What's going on in your head?"

"He feels... I don't know. Familiar. I can't explain it any more than that."

Travis stared down at his empty bowl of soup.

"What?" Topher asked.

"Nothing. Just one of Ben's crazy theories. How old is Stanton?"

"He wouldn't tell me exactly, but he's fifty. He said he first saw Springsteen in 1981, and he was just about to turn twenty at the time. I can do the math. Besides, I Googled him."

"Wow, he looks mighty fine for fifty. Are you sure this don't have nothing to do with your daddy issues?"

Topher stiffened his spine. "What's that supposed to mean?"

"Now, calm down there, partner. We both know you've never forgiven yourself for what happened, even though you were acting like any other boy at that age. I'm just asking if maybe you suddenly being attracted to a man who's old enough to be your daddy don't maybe have something to do with your actual daddy?"

Topher set his jaw and turned his head away. "This has nothing to do with my father."

"Fine, fine, step away from the ledge, I'm backing down. So you got no problem with his age?"

"You just used Brad Pitt as the standard for male hotness—and he's almost fifty. Come on, I know you see what I see. Stanton's super hot. If anything...."

"What?"

"Am I good-looking enough for him?"

Travis stared at Topher with that protective glint he usually reserved for Ben's brothers. "You are a smoking-hot piece of ass. Not like I want to tap that or nothing, but don't let nobody never tell you otherwise."

Topher turned red again. "Thanks. And no, I don't have a problem with Stanton's age. And I don't have a problem with him being a guy." Topher wiggled around in his seat and readjusted his pants.

Travis looked at him and his mouth fell open. "Do you still got a boner?"

"Maybe. I'm kind of horny all of a sudden. That thing you did made me—"

"Be careful. If you pursue this, it could change your life forever. I know that sounds like something out of *Dawson's Creek*, but look at what happened to me."

"All of that was good."

"Not all of it," Travis said. "Sure, everything worked out in the end, but it got mighty bad along the way. I had a song called 'Losing My Mind' on repeat when I was in Alaska. I never told anyone this, but while I was up there, Ben called me on our birthday. I saw the number. I knew it was him. But I let it ring anyway. I never told him that. I never told him I sat there and cried for two hours after. I just wasn't ready to face him. Love cuts both ways. That's all I'm saying."

Topher took a deep breath before he said, "I've got to see where this goes."

"Okay. Tell me what's going to happen tonight."

"He's coming to the Rooftop for my gig."

"The gig is fine and dandy, but you got to get some time alone with him, just the two of you. You'll also need a follow-up, though. Give me a second to think about it." Travis took a gulp of his Coke and stared out the window. Then he turned to Topher and looked him straight in the eye.

"I got a plan."

BLOOD BROTHERS

AFTER the Invasion, Stanton and Marvin decided to skip tea dance and spend the rest of the afternoon by the pool. Colby and Archy had left for a day at the beach. Stanton didn't mind having them around (after all, it was their house), but he was glad to have some time alone with Marvin.

"Did you see his friends?" Marvin asked as he stretched out under an umbrella. "I'm not used to being around men who look like that."

"What are you talking about?" Stanton said. He was lying on a towel next to the pool, his face turned toward the sun for optimal tanning. "You tell me I look like that all the time. Are you just blowing smoke up my ass?"

"No, but you're different. You're a mess."

Stanton moaned. "If people heard the way you talk to me, well, they would not have nice things to say about you."

"You know what I mean."

"What? Once you found out how fucked up I am—"

"It made you a real person."

"Then once you get to know them, they'll become real people too. Give it a chance, please. I'm sure they've got problems just like everybody else."

"I didn't say I wasn't going. Of course I'm going. Especially if we're going to be talking about music."

"What are you wearing?"

"My mother bought me a nice pair of linen shorts and a matching shirt."

"What's linen?"

Marvin started to giggle.

"What did I say this time?" Stanton asked. "Where I come from, linens are something you put on a bed."

"It's also a fabric that people wear in the summer. It wrinkles a lot and is very popular in these beach communities."

"Why do people wear it if it wrinkles?"

"I don't know, because it's expensive."

"Gee," Stanton said. "Haven't they heard of polyester? It doesn't wrinkle."

"It also doesn't breathe. Besides, the seventies are over. The eighties are all about natural fabrics. What are you wearing?"

"Some shorts and a T-shirt. I didn't check the label, but I think they're just regular old fabric. Are you going to bring your bottle of wine to share?"

"Yes, I am. It's the least I can do."

SHORTLY before seven thirty, Stanton and Marvin made their way across the island to Hutch's house, which sat directly behind the Pantry on Lone Hill Walk. They went up the winding path to the screen door and saw Hutch and his housemates gathered in the kitchen, preparing dinner. Stanton knocked.

"Come in, guys," Hutch called.

Stanton opened the door and led Marvin inside. Hutch wiped his hands and walked over to greet them. His housemates stopped what they were doing and prepared to introduce themselves.

"Five minutes late," Hutch said. "Not too bad."

Marvin threw up his free hand in resignation. "It was the best I could do."

"You did great, Marvin. These are my friends and roommates." Hutch turned and introduced Marvin to Robert, Michael, and Paul. "You guys met Stanton last night. This is his roommate at NYU."

"Please," Michael said. "Everyone on the island knows who Marvin Goldstein is."

"At least they do now," Paul added. Marvin turned several shades of red. "Don't be embarrassed. There are queens out here who would kill for that kind of exposure."

"I'm not really looking for exposure," Marvin said.

"Is that the bottle?" Robert asked.

"Yes," Marvin said. "Good wine is meant to be shared, so I thought we could all have a glass."

"Groovy. Let me get a corkscrew."

"What's it called again?" Michael asked.

"Chateau Cheval Blanc, 1947. It was a great year for Bordeaux."

"Why is it called blanc if it's a red wine?" Michael said. "That's French for 'white'."

"That's the name of the winery," Marvin explained. "It means White Horse Castle."

Michael nodded. "Of course. It's tragic what's become of my French."

"What's so special about it?" Paul asked. "From the look on some of those guys' faces, you'd have thought she brought you Harrison Ford's jockstrap."

"Some wines are legendary," Marvin said as he held up the bottle. "It's all about weather. Supposedly, it was a hot summer and a rainy September. They call this wine a happy accident."

Hutch gave up on his search through the drawers and announced, "I can't find a corkscrew."

"We're not wine drinkers," Robert said.

"That's okay." Marvin set the bottle down on the kitchen counter and carefully removed the red foil from around the neck. He set the foil aside and asked, "Do you have a wooden spoon and a kitchen mallet of some sort?"

"Sure," said Hutch. He reached into a drawer and produced a long wooden spoon and a lobster mallet. Hutch handed them to Marvin, who placed the end of the spoon handle against the cork and lightly tapped on the other end with the mallet. After a few seconds, the cork pushed through and disappeared into the bottle. The men in the room applauded.

"It pours kind of wonky," Marvin said, "but it went down in one piece, so it won't affect the taste. Glasses?"

"Very resourceful," Michael said. "I like that. And we do have proper stemware." He went to the cupboard and began to pull wine glasses from the top shelf. "Don't ask us why we have glasses but no corkscrew. We're just renting this place for the summer."

Marvin poured the wine, glass by glass. "It's just like they say," he said.

Stanton stared in shock. "It looks like motor oil."

"Yes," Marvin said. "It's almost like port." He handed each man a glass, and they lifted them in a toast.

"To the summer of '81," Hutch said.

"Hear, hear," Robert seconded.

They clinked glasses and drank. Marvin and Paul took the time to swirl the wine and appreciate its bouquet.

"I didn't expect it to be so sweet," Stanton said.

"Or so strong," Michael said as he started to choke. "Sorry, I'm not much of a drinker. Where's my bong?"

"I put it in the cupboard over the sink," Hutch said.

"You guys don't mind if I smoke a bowl, do you?" he asked Stanton and Marvin.

"Not at all," Stanton said. "We're cool. Right, Marvin?"

"Oh, yeah. We're cool."

Robert laughed and tousled Marvin's hair like Hutch had done that afternoon on the pier. As Michael retrieved his bong from the cupboard, Robert and Paul moved a large bowl of salad and a plate of corn on the cob to the table, while Hutch went outside to pull salmon and vegetables off the grill. The six of them sat down, with Robert and Michael at either end of the table. Hutch and Stanton sat together on one side, facing Marvin and Paul on the other.

"What's your story?" Stanton asked as everyone began to fill their plates. "The four of you, I mean." He slathered butter onto his corn and showered it with salt.

Hutch started to laugh. "You having a little corn there with your butter and salt?"

"Wait until you see me put ketchup on my scrambled eggs."

"Or milk on his apple pie," Marvin said.

"That's how we do it where I come from. So, how do you guys know each other?"

"We went to Columbia together," Robert said.

"All four of you?" Marvin asked.

"Yes," Michael said as he held in a hit of smoke. He exhaled and set the bong on the windowsill behind him. "Robert and Hutch were roommates, so they were friends first."

"Wrong," Paul said.

"Oh, right. I always forget you knew Hutch at prep school. Anyway, Hutch and Robert were roommates, and then Robert and I tricked one night after a dance."

"We've been to your dances," Stanton said.

"Really?" Hutch asked.

"Yes," Marvin said. "Several times. We NYU boys love the Columbia dances. The notice is always on the back page of the *Voice*, like you're reaching out to us or something. The first Friday of every month. You should see the Number 1 train going uptown from our neighborhood. It's packed."

"Are you two dating, then?" Stanton asked Michael and Robert.

"No," Robert said. "The trick fizzled, but the three of us started hanging out together."

Michael looked at Robert from across the table and shook his head. "Fizzled? That's how you describe it?" Then he turned to Stanton and said, "The trick did not fizzle. When we woke up the next morning in his dorm room—Hutch had slept on the couch in the floor lounge—Robert told me he wasn't interested in a boyfriend, but his roommate had an extra ticket to see Frank Sinatra at Madison Square Garden, and did I want to go with them? This was 1974. Legendary concert. Twenty thousand people. Televised live. Who all was there, Robert?"

"Rex Harrison. Carol Channing."

"Robert Redford," Hutch said.

"He closed with 'My Way'. That cemented our friendship, and Robert and I dated for two years. Then he went back to being a whore, and *that's* when it fizzled."

"I do not apologize for my healthy sexual appetite," Robert said.

"No," Michael replied, a note of sadness in his voice. "You do not apologize."

"So where do you come in?" Stanton asked Paul.

"Like Michael said, I knew Chris at prep school."

Stanton turned to Hutch and asked, "You're Chris, right?"

"How did you know that?"

"Colby told us."

"Sorry," Paul said. "He's always been Chris to me."

"The TV show came out our freshman year," Hutch explained. "Robert started calling me Hutch because he said I look like David Soul."

"You do," Michael said.

"I don't," Hutch insisted, "but they say no one gets to pick their nickname, and it stuck. I never liked Chris anyway, so I didn't really mind."

"I wasn't around when they were freshmen," Paul said. "I started my first year at Cornell, but I hated it up there in the middle of fucking Ithaca nowhere. So, I transferred to Columbia when I was a sophomore."

"He's our Ringo," Robert said. "Everything fell together when he came along. After that, the four of us were pretty much inseparable."

"And now what do you do?" Stanton asked.

"I work on Wall Street," Robert said, "for an investment firm. I'm the one with a real job."

"I'm an actor," Paul said.

Stanton looked at Michael. "As little as possible," he said.

Paul silently mouthed to Stanton, "Trust-fund brat."

"You should talk," Michael mumbled.

Robert intervened, saying, "Hutch told us that you're both music majors."

"That's true," Stanton said.

"Marvin's going to be the classical music critic at the *Times* someday," Hutch said.

Marvin nodded. "Also true."

Robert leaned over to Marvin and asked, "What about contemporary music?"

"What about it?"

"Aren't you interested?"

"Of course I'm interested," Marvin said, "but it doesn't exactly lend itself to criticism and analysis in quite the same manner as, say, Mozart."

"You don't think the Beatles are as complex and layered as Mozart?"

"Robert," Hutch interjected, "ease up, man."

Marvin laughed and said, "There is no need to ease up. If we're going to talk about music, then we can take the gloves off."

Stanton smiled. "Watch out, Robert."

"No," Marvin said. Stanton watched as Marvin returned his attention to the food on his plate, as if that was the last word on the subject.

"No, what?" Robert asked.

"No," Marvin repeated, "I do not think the Beatles are as layered and complex as Mozart. I'm not calling the Beatles dreck, but Mozart was a genius, like Shakespeare or Picasso. His is the musical mind against which all others are compared. He never revised. He simply transcribed what he heard, fully formed, in his head."

"You don't think John Lennon was a genius?"

"Was he composing symphonies when he was eight years old? You're talking about an extremely talented man who wrote great music. I'm talking about someone who was touched by God. There's a difference."

"What did Shaw say?" Paul said. "I think it was Shaw. 'Talent does what it can—genius does what it must.'"

"For the record," Michael said, "Edward Bulwer-Lytton said that, but let's not get—"

Stanton interrupted and said to Marvin, "You're giving them the impression that you're a classical music snob."

"I'm doing no such thing."

"You are and you know it. He talks a big game," Stanton said to Robert, "but one of the reasons we're friends is because we both share a deep and abiding love for bubblegum pop."

"I have an idea," Robert said. "Let's play the Greatest Game."

"Oh, no," Michael groaned. "That game makes my head explode."

"What's that?" Stanton asked.

"You don't want to know," Paul said. "Trust me."

"Deep down inside, you love it," Hutch said. "And it's a good way to get to know people."

"Let me guess," Marvin said. "You pick a category and everyone has to name the greatest example in that category."

Hutch and his friends all laughed. "You don't miss a beat, do you?" Robert said. "We each get to pick a category, but it has to pertain to music. That's the only rule."

"No repeats," Michael said.

"Sorry, there is a second rule. No repeats."

"Ultimate final category rule," Paul added.

"Three rules," Robert said. "Anyone else want to add a rule? Good. Hutch, you go first."

Michael reached around for his bong and muttered, "I'm not stoned enough for this."

Robert pointed across the table and asked, "Hutch, would you pass me the salad, please?"

Hutch passed him the bowl of greens and said, "Okay, let me think. Greatest Springsteen song for twenty-five dollars, Art."

Stanton, aware of his limited knowledge of the subject, yelled out, "Thunder Road." Hutch smiled and Stanton felt a hand rest on his knee under the table. "Sorry, it's the only one I know. And like."

"Rosalita," Robert said.

"Darkness on the Edge of Town," Michael followed.

"'Backstreets', I guess," Paul said. "This is why I hate the no-repeats rule. Everyone knows that the only real contenders are 'Thunder Road' and 'Rosalita'."

"Marvin?" Hutch asked.

"I'm thinking."

While they were waiting on Marvin, Paul looked at Stanton and said, "Do you realize that every man on this island has tried to pick Chris up this summer and you're the first one to succeed?"

"That's because he didn't try to pick me up," Hutch said.

"That's right," Stanton said. "I won the cute-boy contest yesterday."

"The what?" Michael asked.

"The cute-boy contest," Stanton repeated. "Every day the bartenders pick the cutest boy on deck and give him free drinks." Michael, Robert, and Paul broke out into laughter. "What's so funny?"

"Hutch," Robert said. "Come on, now, I know you can do better than that."

"Oy vey," Marvin said to Stanton. "When you say it like that, of course it sounds ridiculous. I'm mortified that we fell for it."

"You mean...?" Stanton slapped Hutch on the arm. "That was a pickup line?"

Hutch blew him a kiss. "It worked, didn't it?"

"What is it with you and blowing kisses?"

"That's my thing."

"Your thing? Like saying 'groovy'?"

"Yeah. Everybody needs a thing or two, don't you agree?"

"Tenth Avenue Freeze-Out," Marvin said.

"Nice one," Hutch added. "Then I'm going to say 'Born to Run'."

"Hutch," Robert said, "who goes next?"

"Paul."

Michael shook his head and said, "Get ready to roll out the show tunes, girls."

"I shall not disappoint," Paul said. "Greatest show tune of all time. Ready, set, go."

Stanton shook his head. "Sorry, I'm out."

"No," Marvin said, "you're not." Stanton looked at him, puzzled. "I play it all the time, and I've even heard you singing it in the shower."

Stanton remembered. "Oh, right! That song about the boy with the bugle."

"If He Walked Into My Life?" asked Paul. "From *Mame?*"

"That's it," Stanton said. "That's a great song."

Paul nodded. "Indeed it is. A little Jerry Herman eleven o'clock number in the house tonight. Angela, step up and take a bow."

"Whatever that means," Stanton said under his breath as he finished off his salmon. He disliked fish in general, but this was pretty delicious, especially with the large slabs of grilled summer squash.

A silence fell over the table as everyone considered their answers.

"This is impossible," Michael said.

"Rose's Turn," Robert yelled. "It's the mountain that every great female star has to climb at some point."

"Home," Hutch said. "From *The Wiz*. Because I love the way Stephanie Mills sings it, like she can't contain her joy."

Marvin chimed in next and said, "Sondheim must be represented, so it's between 'Losing My Mind' and 'Being Alive'."

"Or 'Send in the Clowns'," Paul said. "It's the only show tune of the last decade that was also a radio hit."

"I'm going with 'Being Alive'. He's at least trying to deal with love as it's actually lived."

"I had such a crush on Larry Kert when I was fourteen," Paul said.

Marvin looked confused. Then he turned to Paul and said, "Larry Kert wasn't in *Company*."

"Yes, he was."

"No. Dean Jones sang on the original cast recording."

"I know, but right after it opened, Dean Jones left because of a messy divorce or something, and Larry Kert took over. He got the Tony nomination that year, not Dean Jones."

Marvin looked like he was going to burst with excitement. "I had no idea. It's so nice to meet someone who knows more than I do."

"Oh, Marvin," Paul said, clearly flattered, "you and I are going to be such good friends. Maybe even sisters someday."

"Finally. Someone I can swap gender pronouns with."

Stanton glared at them both.

"Michael," Paul said, "do you have an answer?"

"How about 'Don't Rain On My Parade'? Isn't that iconic Streisand?"

"Very," Paul said. "And an excellent choice. You can never go wrong with Barbra." Paul scratched his nose and took a bite of bread. He looked at Stanton and Hutch across the table as he chewed. "It's all about you two tonight. Don't you agree, Marvin?"

"It's always about Stanton."

Paul laughed and said, "Marvin, I'm very intrigued by this sudden romance between our two friends, and I want to pick the perfect song for the soundtrack. At first I was thinking 'Tonight' from *West Side Story* or maybe even 'Meadowlark' from *The Baker's Wife*. Do you know that show?"

"Know it?" Marvin said. "I worship the ground Patti LuPone walks above."

"But it looks like you two could dance all night, so that's my answer. 'I Could Have Danced All Night'."

"Predictable," Michael said. Paul ignored him.

"Are we going to the Pavilion later?" Robert asked.

"Stupid question," Paul said. He pointed to Marvin. "You're next."

Marvin put down his fork and took a deep breath. "Greatest song by Carly Simon."

"Now we're talking," Stanton said.

"You're So Vain," Hutch said. "It's got to be about Jagger, don't you think?"

Marvin shook his head. "Mick Jagger sang backup on the song. It can't be about him."

"That's why it's so cool. He was in on the joke."

"No way," Stanton said. "It's definitely about Warren Beatty."

Robert followed and said, "'Anticipation'. It works even as a ketchup commercial." Then he looked across the table and frowned. "Michael, you only ate half your salmon."

"I'm not hungry."

"Then pass it down to me. I'll eat the rest of it. I hate to see good fish go to waste."

Michael handed his plate to Paul, who reached across Marvin and passed it to Robert, as if this was a well-established ritual.

"Sorry," Robert said. "I didn't mean to interrupt. Where were we?"

"Carly Simon," Paul said. "I'm going to say 'The Carter Family'. I love that it's about not knowing what you have until it's gone."

"Excellent choice," Marvin said.

Stanton looked at Paul and asked, "Why do you want to be an actor? In case you haven't noticed, there are a lot more actors in New York than jobs."

"He's a natural storyteller," Michael said.

"When I was a freshman up at Cornell," Paul explained, "my roommate was a drama major, and he had this book on his desk all semester. *Act One*, by Moss Hart."

"Oh my God," Marvin said, "I love that book!"

"Of course you do," Stanton said.

"One day before Thanksgiving," Paul continued, "I picked it up and read the first page, then the second, and after that, I could not put it down."

"What's it about?" Stanton asked.

Marvin jumped in and answered the question. "It's about how Moss Hart meets George Kaufman, and how they wrote the play *Once in a Lifetime* together, and how it was such a huge hit that it changed Hart's life forever."

"I did my first play a year later," Paul said, "after I moved back to New York. What can I say? I'm hooked on the theater."

"Wasn't Moss Hart married to Kitty Carlisle?" Robert asked.

"Yes," Paul said, "but before that he was Gordon Merrick's lover."

"Who's Gordon Merrick?" Stanton asked.

"He writes trashy gay romance novels," Paul said. "Deliciously trashy, I might add."

"Do you have one I could borrow?" Marvin asked.

"Of course, Martina."

"Michael," Robert said, moving the game along, "it's your turn."

"What's the category again?"

"Carly Simon."

Michael grinned and said, "His Friends Are More Than Fond of Robin."

Marvin nodded his approval and then gestured across the table. "Go ahead, Stanton."

"Thanks, buddy. 'Boys in the Trees'. The whole album is perfect, but the song itself is one of the greatest things I've ever heard."

"Which means it's my turn," Marvin said. He thought it over for a moment as he finished chewing some squash. "'In Pain', from *Come Upstairs*. It's her rawest, most gut-wrenching moment by far. It's the opposite of *Hotcakes*."

"Marvin," Paul said, "you are so deep."

"Who's next?" Michael asked.

"Robert," Marvin said.

"Greatest Beatles song."

"Talk about impossible," Michael said.

"Hey Jude," Hutch said.

"I Want to Hold Your Hand," Stanton followed. Under the table, Hutch intertwined his fingers with Stanton's.

"Yesterday," Paul said.

"Can we stop for a moment and sing that?" Hutch asked.

Paul shook his head. "My mother always used to say, 'No singing at the dinner table.'"

"Come on," Hutch pleaded, "it takes two minutes." He sang the first word and everyone else joined in. The song's melancholy filled the room like an omen, and Stanton couldn't help but wonder if these were the good times they would long for one day.

When they finished, Marvin said, "Let It Be."

Stanton watched as Robert strummed his fingers against his head and then looked at Michael. The two men stared at each other across the table, as if they were in a dual, each waiting for the other to draw.

"While My Guitar Gently Weeps," they said at the same time.

"Jinx!" Robert yelled. "Owe me a line of coke."

"No repeats!" Paul screamed.

Stanton was about to correct Robert and tell him it was a bottle of Coke and not a line of coke, but then he realized the word swap was intentional and stopped himself.

"That wasn't a repeat," Michael said. "That was a simultaneous answer. Those are allowed."

Stanton chuckled and asked, "Do you guys make up these rules as you go along?"

Paul glared at Michael and said, "It does seem that way sometimes, doesn't it? Stanton, it's your turn."

"Okay. Well, so far this has been way too highbrow for me. So let's go with the greatest song from the seventies that's so bad it's good."

Hutch squeezed Stanton's hand under the table and said, "I love it."

"I Think I Love You," said Marvin. "Can't out-bad the Partridge Family."

"Yeah," Stanton agreed, "that's a good one."

"Any song by the Carpenters," Robert said.

"Excuse me?" Stanton objected. "First, if we're making up rules, then you must pick a song—not a band, duo, or singer. And second, I said so bad it's good, not so good it's good."

"You do not seriously think—"

Stanton interrupted him. "You have to separate the music from the voice. Pipes like Karen's only come around once in a generation. It's not her fault that her brother got ahold of them."

"Have you heard her cover of 'Don't Cry For Me Argentina'?" Marvin asked.

"She recorded that?" Paul said.

Marvin nodded. "You simply must give it a listen. It's by far the best version I've ever heard, and I wouldn't even know about it if Stanton hadn't played it for me. It's even better than Patti's."

Paul gasped and said, "Blasphemy."

"I know, but my mother once told me that blasphemy was what got Dorothy Parker a seat at the Algonquin Round Table, so embrace it."

Stanton looked at them and asked, "What's the Algonquin Round—?" But then he stopped himself. "Never mind. Years from now there will be a Carpenters renaissance and a complete overhaul of their critical reputation. Mark my words."

"Okay," Robert said. "I'll go with 'Seasons in the Sun', then. Is that acceptable?"

Stanton smiled and said, "Yes. Thank you. I like that one."

"I got it," Paul shouted. "'Don't Cry Out Loud'. No, wait. I can do better than that. 'You Light Up My Life'."

"That's just bad," Stanton said.

"Then what's that song from *The Poseidon Adventure*?" Paul asked.

"The Morning After," Stanton and Marvin said.

"Yes! That is splendid trash." Then Paul looked over at Marvin's plate and asked, "Aren't you going to eat your salmon skin?"

"No, I hate that part."

"It's supposed to be good for you. Puts hair on your chest or something."

"I've got plenty of hair on my chest."

Stanton turned to Hutch. "Any ideas?"

"Of course. 'Brandy (You're a Fine Girl).'" The table erupted into laughter and the opening verse of the song.

"This is fun," Stanton said. "Although anyone listening right now would wonder if we've all lost our minds."

Michael sighed. "Now I've got to top that." He thought it over for a moment, then said, "Why didn't I think of this before? 'The Night the Lights Went Out in Georgia'."

"Thank you, Vicki Lawrence, for that gem," Marvin said.

"That song," Paul agreed, "is the very definition of so bad it's good. "

Michael smirked. "Okay, Stanton, let's see you out-bad that."

Stanton laughed and looked across the table at his best friend.

"You got this," Marvin said.

"I know that." Stanton paused for a moment, and then he said, "Billy, Don't Be a Hero."

The cheers at the table were so loud they shook the house.

"My mom loved Bo Donaldson and the Heywoods," Paul screamed.

The six men broke out into a complete a cappella rendition of the song's chorus. After the chaos had subsided, everyone turned to Michael for the final category.

"Greatest song ever," he said. "Who wants to go first?"

"Ah," Marvin said. "That's what you mean by ultimate final category rule."

No one responded at first, but then Paul raised his hand and announced his pick. "Imagine."

"Okay," Robert said, "if we're going to go with sweeping greatness, then there's only one choice for me. 'What's Going On'."

"No one can argue with Marvin Gaye," Michael agreed. "Hutch?"

"Dylan has to be in the mix somewhere, so I'll go with 'The Times They Are a-Changin''."

"Oh," sighed Stanton. "I like that one you played for me last night."

"I know, but it's not his greatest. It's just my favorite."

"How can you separate the two?"

"That," Robert said, "is a discussion for another time. Marvin?"

"'Redemption Song'. Bob Marley."

"You are full of surprises, aren't you?" Michael said. "And I mean that in a good way." Marvin grinned. "Stanton?"

"This one's easy," Stanton said. "Bridge Over Troubled Water."

Everyone nodded with appreciation. Hutch leaned over and whispered into his ear, "I'm going to sing that for you someday."

"You sing?"

"Yeah. I'm a musician, kind of a singer/songwriter type deal."

Stanton pulled back and smiled. "Did you know musicians and mechanics are my two weaknesses?"

"Sorry," Hutch said. "I can't help you with that second one. I don't even own a car."

Paul laughed and said, "You could always buy a pair of coveralls and smear some grease on your face."

"Very funny," Hutch said.

Everyone turned to Michael and waited for the final answer to the final category. He pushed his plate away and said, "There's no Elvis yet, which is almost un-American. But we also have zero women represented."

"Greatness is not a democracy," Robert said.

"Aretha?" Paul suggested.

"I know 'Respect' is the obvious choice, but no. For me, the greatest song ever is still Billie Holiday's version of 'My Man'."

"Come on," Hutch said. "He cheats on her, beats her, disregards her, and still she comes back on her knees? That is your greatest song ever?"

"I think she sounds funny," Stanton said. "She's got a weird voice."

"She's got an expressive voice," Michael insisted. "It's an honest song. Not all of us get the fairy-tale boyfriend, Hutch. Not all of us get to sit back and watch our dreams come true. Some of us get the guy who thinks monogamy is a four-letter word. Those are my people, and 'My Man' is our song."

An awkward silence fell over the table.

"I'm sorry," Hutch said. "I didn't mean to—"

Robert put up his hand and interrupted him. He glared at Michael across the table. "Why do you have to go all *Who's Afraid of Virginia Woolf* on me every time we have guests?"

"I think Barbra's version is better anyway," Paul said.

"So," Stanton said, "you two are boyfriends."

"No," Robert said. "We're not. Isn't that right, Michael?"

Michael did not respond. Instead, he turned around and grabbed his bong off the windowsill. He picked up his antique gold lighter and took a hit.

Marvin raised his hand and asked, "Hey, guys, do you know the story behind 'While My Guitar Gently Weeps'?"

"No, Marvin," Michael answered abruptly. "I've never heard it."

"Me neither," Robert said.

"Since it's both your favorite Beatles song, I thought maybe...." Marvin looked to Stanton for help.

Stanton nodded his encouragement and said, "Tell the story."

"Well, when George Harrison wrote it, he was into the *I Ching*. That's a book of Eastern philosophy."

"We know what the *I Ching* is," Michael said. "We have these big-time Ivy League educations, remember?"

Stanton thought Michael was making an ass of himself, so he raised his hand to butt in. "I tend not to know stuff like that, so if Marvin explains something, it's probably for my benefit. He's nice enough to make sure I don't look like too big of a fool."

Michael's face softened, as if he suddenly realized he was taking his frustrations out on the wrong person.

Marvin continued. "Anyway, the whole Eastern concept that Harrison was into at the time was this idea that everything is meant to be. There are no accidents—no coincidences. Everything is part of this giant, perfect tapestry."

"Like Carole King," Paul said.

"That's right. So, one day Harrison went to his parents' house in northern England and pulled a random book from the shelf. He said he would write a song based on the first words he read. He opened the book, and the first words he saw were *gently weeps*. He started to write a song with those two words, and that became your favorite Beatles song."

No one spoke for several moments after that. Then Michael said, "Robert, do you remember when you wanted to volunteer for the Big Brother program and they turned you down because you're gay?"

"How could I forget?"

"We should adopt Marvin as our little brother. What do you think?"

"I think it's an excellent idea."

Marvin blushed.

Michael grabbed the bong and pushed it across the table toward Marvin. "Care to partake?" Michael asked.

"I don't know how," Marvin said. "Will you show me?"

"Are you sure?" Stanton asked.

Marvin rolled his eyes. "I do not intend to go through my entire life without ever smoking marijuana. Don't be such a prude. We're in college. Try it with me."

Stanton laughed and said, "Okay, buddy." Michael gave them a lesson in bong carburetors and smoking etiquette, and Stanton got high for the first time. He didn't know what to expect, but he liked it, especially when Hutch and his friends produced a chocolate cake for dessert. The six of them continued discussing music for several hours. They finished off Marvin's bottle of wine and passed around the bong a few more times. Later, they moved to the living room and Hutch got out his guitar, a beautiful black Fender acoustic with mother-of-pearl inlays around the sound hole. The burgundy leather strap had *Hutch* branded on it in a script that reminded Stanton of the Old West.

"Any requests?" Hutch asked.

Marvin considered the question before he said, "What's your range?"

"I'm a tenor."

Marvin nodded. "How about 'Che Gelida Manina'?"

Everyone laughed except Stanton, who asked, "What's that?"

"Rodolfo's act one aria from *La Bohème*," Robert said.

"What does the title mean?"

"What a frozen little hand," Paul said.

"You asked for requests," Marvin said. "An acoustic version of 'Che Gelida Manina' could be lovely, assuming you have the voice for it."

"Ohhhh," Robert called out. "Little brother has thrown down the gauntlet now. Will Hutch take up the challenge? The crowd waits with breathless antici—"

There was a pause in the room.

"Say it!" yelled Marvin and Paul.

"—pation."

"Okay," Hutch said. "I will take up the challenge." He strummed his guitar to find a few chords.

Stanton looked at Marvin suspiciously, and then he said, "Wait a minute, I'm not buying this at all. You just happen to know an aria that Marvin pulls out of his ass?"

"It's a very popular aria," Marvin said.

"You two set this up, didn't you? Today on the pier, after you gave him the wine? You whispered something to him, and Marvin nodded. You told him you were going to invite us for dinner, but you also told him to request this song."

"I thought we had him," Hutch said to Marvin.

"He's not the naïve farm boy from Iowa anymore."

"I was never a farm boy, and I'm still not from Iowa." Stanton could see Hutch and Marvin did indeed have their own thing, complete with its own confidences. He turned to Marvin and asked, "So, is this my first exposure to Italian opera?"

"Yes. And if you don't like it, then there is no hope for you."

Stanton closed his eyes. "Okay, I'm ready."

The room fell silent as Hutch sang the first line, the same note hopping in quick succession, then a lift. The song opened up and Hutch's voice revealed itself, not trained in opera, but pure in tone and rich with emotion. He sang:

"Che gelida manina,

se la lasci riscaldar.

Cercar che giova?

Al buio non si trova."

Stanton's eyes sprang open and he looked at Marvin. They both grinned as Robert, Michael, and Paul nodded their heads in appreciation and basked in the expansive melody created by Hutch's spectacular set of pipes. Stanton could tell Marvin appreciated the classical form infused with Hutch's near-pop sensibility. The aria contained some of the highest notes Stanton had ever heard, but Hutch managed them effortlessly, especially the big splashy one toward the end. Instead of blowing them into the next room, though, Hutch pulled back and allowed his voice to quietly soar and break, but only for a second. When he came to the end, Hutch's final, sustained note pierced the night air and then faded away into nothingness. A moment of complete and utter silence followed that final note. Stanton knew it was the kind of moment every performer dreams of, the silence before the ovation.

"Bravo!" Marvin cheered. The room erupted into thunderous applause. "That was magnificent."

"That was… amazing," Stanton said. "I guess I do like opera after all—Italian opera, at least."

Michael poked Hutch in the foot and said, "When are you going to ask him?"

"Stop it," Hutch said.

"What are you talking about?" Paul asked.

"You didn't hear?" Michael said.

"Hear what?" Stanton asked.

Hutch got up and went over to the side table next to one of the sofas. He opened up the drawer and took out an envelope. He sat back down next to Stanton and handed it to him.

"What's this?"

"Look inside," Hutch said.

Stanton opened the envelope, took out two tickets, and read, "Bruce Springsteen and the E Street Band. July 5, 1981. The Meadowlands." He looked up at Hutch. "That's tomorrow night."

"Do you want to go?" Hutch asked.

"With you?"

"Of course with me. It'll take a few trains to get over there, but I took off work and everything. You have to see him in person. It'll be amazing."

"How did you get these?"

"We know a guy," Michael said.

"We know a lot of guys," Paul added, laughing.

Stanton looked at Marvin, who said, "We're going back to the city tomorrow anyway. Say yes."

"They're great seats," Hutch said enticingly. "On the floor."

"Yes," Stanton said. "I would love to go. This is so exciting."

The men sat back, and Hutch took a few more requests. Afterward, Paul tried to convince Marvin and Stanton they had to experience a Saturday night at the Pavilion. Marvin hesitated at first but finally agreed, and Stanton delighted in watching Hutch's friends drag him onto the cavernous dance floor, where the six of them stayed for several hours. They danced to classic tunes from Abba, Donna Summer, and other disco favorites. When Stanton heard a female cover of Gordon Lightfoot's "If You Could Read My Mind," he followed Hutch's lead and took off his shirt. He nodded with glee and raised his hands into the air.

Hutch grinned and said, "Now you're a proper homosexual."

"Who is this?"

"Her name is Viola Wills."

"I love it."

At around three o'clock, Marvin began to yawn and Stanton indicated it was time for them to go. Hutch left his friends on the dance floor and walked them out of the club. Once they were on the main path, Hutch asked, "You two can find your way back in the dark, right?"

"We'll be fine," Stanton said. "The full moon helps. Thanks, it was a great night."

"It's not over for them," Hutch said. "They'll be there until after the sun comes up. Morning is the best part."

"I'd like to see it," Stanton said, "but we need to get some sleep."

"I know. I'm heading to bed now myself. Big day tomorrow."

"Thank you for a wonderful evening," Marvin said. "Your friends are nothing like what I expected."

Hutch smiled. "I think they would say the same thing about you. And I mean that in a good way."

"What's the story with Robert and Michael?" Marvin asked.

"Marvin," Stanton warned. "It's none of our business."

Hutch laughed and said, "Don't worry, Starsky. It's not like it's a big secret. Everyone on the island knows the story."

"Are they lovers?" Marvin said.

"They used to be. But then Robert couldn't keep his dick in his pants and finally insisted on a little bit of sexual freedom."

"What happened?" Marvin said.

"Michael broke up with him. Except that he didn't."

"What does that mean?" Stanton said.

"They still live together and sleep in the same bed. Their lives are completely enmeshed, and they don't date anyone else. They just don't have sex with each other anymore."

"Do they have sex with other people?" Marvin said.

Hutch laughed. "Of course. They're both regulars down at the Meatrack. That's what makes the whole thing so ridiculous. They're like two peas in a pod, but Michael can't see that. To him, when you have a lover, that means no sex with other people. So they've negotiated this twisted compromise that even I don't understand."

"See?" Stanton said to Marvin. "I told you they had problems like everybody else."

"Anyway," Hutch said, "I'll stop by Colby and Archy's place tomorrow around noon. We should probably catch the one o'clock ferry."

"We'll see you then," Stanton said. He hugged Hutch and closed his eyes in deep satisfaction.

Hutch turned to Marvin and pulled him into a hug as well. He lifted Marvin off the ground and said, "I'm so glad Stanton has such good taste in friends."

As Stanton and Marvin walked away, Marvin whispered under his breath, "I could have gotten home on my own, you know?"

"I know that. It's better like this, though. I like a slow burn."

They walked a few more steps. Then Marvin said, "I told you people would call you Starsky."

I'M A ROCKER

"WHAT kind of plan?"

Travis took one last bite of the sandwich in front of him and set his tray to the side. He wiped his face with a napkin and said, "First, before the show, ask your buddies if they can pack up afterward without you, just this once. Tell 'em it's a special occasion. Then take a walk with Stanton down Sixth Street, but go east. It'll be quieter as you move away from the crowds, so you'll have a chance to talk. There are some cool bars on the other side of I-35, so take him for a drink and let him get to know you. Turn on the old Topher charm. Be honest with him about what you want. If you're interested in something more than friendship, for God's sake, tell him that. Don't make the same mistake I did, sitting on your hands, saying nothing."

"I don't know. I've already kissed him. Seems like I should let Stanton make the next move."

"Hmm." Travis paused. "You might be right. If only we knew how gay guys think."

The two men sat in silence for a moment. Then Topher got an idea. "What about Ben?"

Travis's eyes lit up. "Why didn't I think of that?" He pulled his iPhone out of his pocket and swiped at the screen.

"I should get one of those," Topher said.

"This was a Christmas present. Ben said enough with the disposable phones." Travis put the phone on speaker and set it down in the middle of the table. Ben picked up after two rings.

Hey, stud, you calling for a nooner? I'm not due in court until two.

"I'm here with Topher, Hotshot. You're on speaker."

Topher could hear Ben chuckling.

Sorry about that. Hey, Topher, what's up?

"Hey, Ben."

"We have a question," Travis began. He looked at Topher and signed, *How much can I tell him?* Travis had briefly dated Topher's sister, Trisha, before he met Ben. Trisha was deaf, and the three of them used sign language when they were together.

Topher leaned forward and spoke into the phone. "Ben, there's a guy I met yesterday, and I kind of like him."

Topher waited for a response, but Ben said nothing.

"You there?" Travis asked.

Yes, I'm here. I'm focusing on the words "guy" and "kind of." I thought you were straight, Topher.

"So did I, until I met Stanton."

What's going on at that shop, anyway? Are Ed and Royce next?

"Ben," Travis said. "This is serious."

I'm just saying. It's not like that would be a bad thing. Do you like him or not, Topher? None of this "kind of" bullshit.

"Yes," Topher said. "I kissed him."

Then what's the question?

"Since Topher's already kissed him," Travis said, "he thinks Stanton should make the next move. I think Topher should be upfront about what he wants."

How old is this guy?

"Fifty," Travis and Topher said.

Fifty? Well, that makes the answer easy. If you want something to happen, you're going to have to throw yourself at him.

"Really?" Topher asked.

Any guy that age would love to have a boyfriend like you, Topher, but most guys your age are not into fifty-year-olds, and they know it. If he pursues you, he risks looking like a creepy old man, but if you pursue him, well... he feels like a stud. Get the picture?

Topher nodded and said, "That makes sense."

Who is this guy, anyway?

"His name is Stanton Porter."

Stanton Porter, the NPR music critic?

"Yeah," Topher said.

Invite him over for dinner at our house. I'd love to meet him. Sorry, I have to run now. Dan is giving me the signal.

"I'll see you at home," Travis said.

You're picking up Cade and taking him to practice?

"I got it covered. I love you."

I love you more.

"How sweet," Topher said.

Travis ended the call and put the phone back into his pocket. "You heard him, even though I had already thought of that 'dinner at our place' idea, and Ben just beat me to the punch. You two come over tomorrow night. Stanton will see that you hang out with cool gay people. And frankly, if he can resist my family, then you don't want to have nothing to do with him."

Topher smiled. "I like that plan."

When they returned to the shop after lunch, Topher's inability to concentrate only worsened. Now he thought about the kiss *and* the picture Travis had planted in his head at lunch, the one with Topher on his knees and Stanton's cock crossing his lips for the very first time. After work, he rushed home and ran into his room. The house was empty, but he locked the door anyway. Topher stripped off his clothes and lay down on the bed. He took his dick in his right hand and closed his eyes. Stanton's cock was waiting for him in the dark. He spit on his hand and imagined what that cock would feel like hitting the back of his throat. The thought alone made his dick throb and stiffen up. Topher started to stroke, and before long, he shot a healthy load onto his stomach and chest. He ran two fingers through the pool of come between his pecs and tasted it, the corners of his mouth turning up as he remembered Travis's question. He jumped into the shower and washed away any doubts he had about pursuing Stanton Porter.

THAT night, at five minutes after nine, Stanton still hadn't shown up at the Rooftop. Topher talked the set over with his bandmates as a way to stall for a little more time.

"Do y'all mind if I skip the strike tonight?" Topher asked them. "I'm going to see if Stanton wants to hang out afterward."

Peter winked and said, "We don't mind."

"Are you sure he's coming?" Robin asked.

"He said he would be here, and I don't want to start without him," Topher said.

"Do you think he's going to talk about us on *All Things Considered?*" asked Maurice.

"No," Topher said. "He's not coming as a critic."

"What do you mean, he's not coming as a critic?" Robin said. "What's the big fuss for, then?"

Topher hadn't gotten the chance to tell Robin and Maurice about the kiss yet, and he didn't have time to go into it right then and there, so he looked to Peter for help.

"Let's drop it," Peter said, pointing toward the wall. "Is that him over there?"

Topher turned around and saw Stanton coming up the stairs. He looked as handsome as ever in jeans and a blue NPR T-shirt, which Topher noticed he filled out nicely. Topher reminded himself of Ben's advice and then ducked over to say hello. "You made it," he said. "Almost on time too."

"Hi," Stanton said. He reached out to shake Topher's hand, but Topher laughed and hugged him instead. He made sure to run his hands up and down Stanton's back.

"I think we're past the handshake, don't you?" Topher whispered into his ear before releasing him.

Stanton smiled and looked uncomfortable. "Sorry about being late, but we weren't expecting the crowds on the street." Stanton turned to the short man standing next to him and introduced Topher.

Topher offered his hand and said, "It's great to meet you, Marvin. Thanks for the Springsteen ticket. I hope you're feeling better."

Marvin shook his hand. "Yes, I am. And you're welcome. It's a pleasure to meet you as well. I'm looking forward to hearing your band."

"I hope we don't disappoint you. By the way, did Stanton tell you I kissed him last night?"

Marvin grinned and said, "Oh, yes. He told me all about it. You pushed a few of his buttons."

"Excuse me," Stanton said. "I'm standing right here."

Topher laughed and grinned at him. "Anyway, we're going to start now. Would you like to hang out after the show?"

"Hang out?" Stanton asked.

"Yeah. Walk around, take in the sights, maybe grab a beer. You know, a date? You do go on those, don't you?"

Stanton turned to Marvin, who raised his hands. "Don't look at me."

"You can come too," Topher said.

"No, thank you. I didn't get much sleep last night, so I'm heading back to the hotel afterward. Say yes, Stanton. A handsome young man is asking you out. Don't be a *yutz*."

Stanton looked a little surprised, but not in a bad way. He nodded and said, "Okay, I'll wait for you."

Topher grinned and walked back to the edge of the bandstand. The open-air Rooftop was one of his favorite venues, as it literally meant they got to play under the stars. The crowd had swelled to about a hundred and fifty people. Dressed in tattered blue jeans and a work shirt, with his name embroidered on one side and a patch that read "Home of the Groovy Mechanics" on the other, Topher strapped on his guitar and stepped up to the microphone. "We are Judecca Rising," he said in a low, grumbling voice.

Topher hesitated for a moment. He waited for the crowd to quiet before he began their opening number. Topher sang the first line solo and a cappella, and on line two, Peter added his voice. The twins, Robin and Maurice, joined them on the third line. Their harmonies blended perfectly and rose into the night sky above their heads. They held the final note of the first verse until Topher thought he might run out of air. Then Maurice tapped his drumsticks together four times and they launched into "Beaches on the Moon," a rousing anthem Topher had written a few years earlier. He'd been hanging out at home watching TV with Maurice, who was reading a book for school. When Maurice went into the kitchen to get something to eat, Topher had glanced over and saw the author's name, Anne Tyler, and a chapter title, "Beaches on the Moon." *That would make a great song*, he had said to himself, and he went into his bedroom that night and wrote it in a single sitting.

As Topher began their second number, a ballad called "Surrender to Love," he wondered what his father would think if he were still alive, or if he would have even bothered coming to hear Topher at all. How long would they have fought over his decision to pursue music instead of college? He liked to think his dad would have been okay with it eventually.

As he finished "Surrender to Love," Topher took a swig from his bottle of Shiner Bock and glanced over at Stanton. Topher's heart began to race a bit, because he knew the next song was "Saltwater Kisses." Topher put his newfound resolve into action and locked his gaze on Stanton. He used his own lyrics to convey the thrill of kissing him for the first time. Topher felt excited and playful and hopelessly in tune with his instrument. He was in the pocket, a phrase he had heard before but never understood.

That was when Topher realized he was getting hard. He grinned at Stanton and looked down at his crotch. Topher had never performed horny before, and he couldn't believe what a difference it made. His skin was on fire, and he finally felt like a rock star. As they approached the final bars of the song, Topher reached down his pants and wiped the sweat off his balls. He pulled out his hand, kissed it, and on the last note, blew the kiss to Stanton.

The crowd erupted.

Topher knew anyone who said time was constant had never been a singer. Sometimes at four o'clock in the afternoon, he couldn't get the second hand to move fast enough on the shop clock. But now he couldn't slow it down to save his life. There was no other place where the melody surging through the marrow of his bones made him feel this alive. Time raced forward, and before he knew it, Topher was finishing up their last original song. He glanced at Stanton again and wondered where the hour had gone.

After finishing their penultimate number, Topher stepped up to the microphone and said, "I want to thank everyone for coming out and supporting local bands." The crowd applauded, and Topher slung his guitar around so it rested against his back. "Everything you heard tonight I wrote myself. We have some free CDs for everyone. I see Peter recruited some beautiful young women to pass those out for us. Thank you, ladies. We also have free downloads at our website, judeccarising.com. And now that it's time to say good night, we're going to continue our tradition of closing with a cover. I think you'll recognize this one. It's an oldie but a goodie."

Topher looked at Peter, who began to play the first chords of the song. Topher heard a few gasps in the room. He took off his guitar and leaned it against one of the speakers. He stepped up to the microphone and wearily sang the first words of "Bridge Over Troubled Water." He'd been singing this song since high school, but tonight he finally connected with it, and he didn't need to ask himself why. He stood with his hands in the back pockets of his jeans, his vocal style simple and straightforward, as if he was talking to a friend. Or maybe a boyfriend.

Out of the corner of his eye, Topher thought he saw Marvin grasp Stanton by the elbow. He considered each lyric as he sang it, his voice breaking at one point when he thought about what it might mean to lay himself down for someone like Stanton. He pulled himself together as he approached the song's final bars and reached effortlessly for the famous troubled high notes. His voice swelled and filled the night. It reached beyond the rooftop and onto the street below. That night, Topher had the entire city at his feet. He finished the last note and closed his eyes. The crowd went silent and he held his breath. He stood still for several moments, knowing he'd killed it. When he opened his eyes and exhaled, the crowd went wild, and he saw Stanton's face wet with tears. When the applause ended and the set was over, several people came up to congratulate him, and a few girls even slipped Topher their phone numbers. By the time he made his way over to Stanton and Marvin, Stanton had dried his eyes and was smiling again.

"Are you okay?" Topher asked.

"Yes, I'm fine. That song is just—" Stanton stopped himself for a moment, but then he laughed. "Out of all the songs in all the world, you had to pick that one?"

"You're a very talented young man," Marvin said.

"You really think so?"

"I really think so. Your voice, especially. That's a gift. I've only heard a voice like that once before in my life."

"Really?" Topher said. "Who was that?"

Marvin looked at Stanton. "We'll leave that for another time, won't we? Right now, I must head back to the hotel and call my husband. You two have a lovely evening. Topher, it was a pleasure to meet you. Mazel tov."

"It was nice to meet you too, Marvin. I hope I'll be seeing you again sometime."

"Nothing would make me happier." Marvin stepped forward and wrapped his arms around Topher. He held him close for a moment. Then Marvin pulled back, turned away, and rushed down the stairs without saying another word.

"That was weird," Topher said.

"That's Marvin. Do you need to strike first?"

"No. I asked the guys if I could skip tonight and hang out with you instead. Special occasion, and all."

"I'm special, eh?"

"You're the most famous person to ever hear us play."

"Famous? I am not famous. Besides, I told you I wasn't here as a critic."

"I know. You ready to take that walk?"

"Sure. Lead the way."

Topher led them down the stairs and onto Sixth Street. The festival crowd had turned into a sea of people in a carnival atmosphere. Street performers broke out into impromptu dances in the middle of the throng. Topher and Stanton stopped to watch a puppet show with a small skeleton who sang Frank Sinatra songs. They checked out the Doritos stage, over which had been built a three-story replica of a vending machine, with giant bags of Doritos inside.

"Let's walk down to Cheer Up Charlie's," Topher said. "Travis told me about it. He calls it Queer Up Charlie's."

"Is it a gay bar?"

"It's an Austin bar. You'll see all sorts, probably."

"And I probably won't be able to tell which is which."

Topher laughed. "Does my generation puzzle you?"

"Something like that."

They began walking east, the crowds thinning as they went.

"You seem different," Stanton said.

"Different how?"

"More confident, sure of yourself. Not exactly the confused kid from last night. I wasn't expecting to be blown a kiss soaked in sexual innuendo."

"Now, see, when you turn a phrase like that, I know you're a writer. Did you like it? The kiss, I mean?"

"That's beside the point. How did you get from last night to here?"

"I have good friends who helped me sort through it all."

"And what did you and your friends decide?"

"It wasn't a group decision. Travis just asked me a few questions and I answered them. He used to be straight too, and now he has a boyfriend."

"Is this some kind of epidemic in Austin?"

"Very funny. Anyway, he put a certain picture in my head and.... Let's just say my reaction cleared up any confusion, to the point where I had to rush home after work and take care of business."

"What picture?"

Topher grinned. "We'll hold off on that until later. You're not the only one who can be all mysterious and—"

"What exactly are you saying?"

Topher stopped walking and turned to face Stanton, who tried to look composed but didn't do a very good job of it. "I'm saying, watch out Stanton Porter, because I'm coming after you."

"Excuse me?"

"I don't stutter. I know you won't make the next move because you think I'm too young and inexperienced. I get it. But according to the rules, at least as I understand them, I can pursue you, and there isn't a damn thing you can do about it."

"I live in another city."

"So?"

"So, that means this has nowhere to go."

Topher shook his head. "Look, I don't know why this is happening to me. Or us. But I saw your face when you read the title of that third album last night. I don't know what it was, but you got a sign, didn't you?"

Stanton paused. "Maybe."

"What did it mean?"

"I don't want to go into it. Not right now."

"Then answer me one question, truthfully. Did you jack off last night thinking about me?"

Stanton looked away.

"I thought so," Topher said. "Because I jacked off thinking about you too, and it was hot. So what do you say we go get a drink and see how this thing plays out?"

Stanton took a long pause, but then nodded his assent. Topher's phone vibrated in his pocket. He grinned but ignored it. He tilted his head toward the east and led the way. They continued walking until they crossed under the interstate and found the bar. They made their way to one of the picnic tables on the patio, and Topher went to get them beers. After a minute, he returned to the table with two cans of Lone Star.

Stanton stuck up his nose. "They didn't have anything in a bottle?"

"Nope. Sorry, princess."

Stanton laughed. "You know just which buttons to push, don't you?"

"It seems I do." Topher took a swig of his beer. "So, what did you really think of our set? Do I suck?"

"No, you don't suck at all. Marvin was right. You've got a voice that…. I mean, to match Art Garfunkel is no small feat, and you did it. I was in tears.

That's the greatest compliment I can give you. The original stuff is a little pedestrian, except for that opening. What's it called?"

"Beaches on the Moon."

"Yes. That's the kind of thing that can dominate iTunes these days."

Topher smiled. "Thanks."

"It reminds me of FUN."

"Fun?"

"The band."

"Oh, right. The guys who did 'We Are Young', you mean?"

"Yes, and their new one is fucking brilliant. It's called 'Some Nights'. That down-tempo song you did, though, right after it, what was that called?"

"Surrender to Love."

"That's it. 'Surrender to Love'. Just awful. One of the worst things I've ever heard in my life. Have you ever surrendered to love?"

"No, but—"

"Do you even know what that means?"

Topher shook his head.

"I didn't think so. Never sing that song again, and if anyone asks, deny you wrote it."

"Don't hold back or anything. Tell me what you really think."

"Would you rather I sugarcoat it?"

"No. Never do that with me."

Stanton took a drink of his beer. "I couldn't even if I wanted to."

"That's what makes you a good critic."

"I suppose, but sometimes it makes me a terrible human being. Enough about me, though. I want to hear about Dime Box, Texas."

Topher grinned. "What do you want to know?"

"Everything."

"Well, like I told you, it's about seventy miles east of here. Population of around 370 or so, depending on if anyone was born or died that day."

"That's small. What about your family?"

"My mom still lives there. I told you my dad died."

"How old were you?"

"Seventeen."

"Wow. That must have been rough."

"You have no idea."

"Any siblings?"

"I have a sister who lives in Houston. We don't talk much, really, mostly 'cause she's deaf. She loves texting, though. She dated Travis before he met Ben, but now she's engaged to a new guy. I try to get home and see my mom at least once a month. They say John Lennon called his mother every week. What about you?"

"I'm from a small town in the Midwest, but more like forty thousand small, not 370. My parents still live there. My mom has Alzheimer's now, and my dad is the most amazing man I've ever met. And if you had told me twenty-five years ago that I would be saying that, I'd have said you need to get your head out of your ass. He is just so cool now—the greatest example of what it means to be a man, the way he's taking care of my mom."

"Any brothers or sisters?"

"I have two brothers and a sister. They all still live in Ohio. I'm the prodigal son who goes home twice a year, but I do call my mom every week. I'm following John Lennon's example and I didn't even know it."

"How did you become a critic?"

"I got my first job out of college at the *Village Voice*. That was a time before websites and blogs—when newspapers still mattered. I started at the bottom and wrote my way up. Marvin helped me a lot. I kind of made a name for myself when boy bands hit in the nineties."

"Made a name for yourself how?"

"I had the audacity to compare the Backstreet Boys to the Beatles. I was crucified by several other music critics, even though Marvin was the one who encouraged me to make the comparison. He always says nothing gets people's attention like blasphemy."

"So what happened?"

"He was right. Sure, some people hated me, but suddenly everybody knew my name. That's when *Rolling Stone* called, because they love controversy. I wrote for them for about ten years before I jumped ship to NPR."

"Do you like the Wanted?"

"I love the Wanted."

"Me too."

"I can understand that people like some songs and don't like others. What I don't understand, even after all these years, is when one person, or a group of people, pretend that they know which songs are better than others. All critical yardsticks are bullshit."

"So where does that leave you? As a critic, I mean?"

"I don't know. I understand the concept of musical sophistication. I can hear the difference between 'Hey Jude' and 'Backstreet's Back', but I can't really hear the difference between 'I Want to Hold Your Hand' and 'Tearin' Up My Heart'."

"You just mixed up the Backstreet Boys and 'N Sync."

"They're interchangeable. Even when I can hear the distinction, I still think it's primarily a matter of taste, because otherwise everyone would agree about everything, and we don't even agree on the good stuff. I like writing about music as a fan, describing what works for me and what doesn't. Where does my life intersect with the Killers? Or Judecca Rising? And how do they intersect with each other? You were amazing up there tonight, but you have no idea what experiences I brought to the table. If other people brought different experiences, then they probably had a different reaction. And to take it one step further, I think I have different reactions on different days. Every time I hear a new song, the circumstances of that moment have an enormous impact on how I respond to it. Criticism is really just the articulation of that response, in that moment."

Topher felt his face getting warm. "You thought I was amazing?" he asked.

"Yes. I would never bullshit you about that. You get the good with the bad. But why do you do it?"

"What do you mean?"

"Why do you get up on stage and sing songs?"

"Because I like it."

"Oh, come on. Can't you come up with something better than that? If my job as a critic is to articulate my reaction, then certainly your job as an artist is to articulate your motivations and feelings. Try again. Why do you get up on stage and sing songs?"

Topher fumed for a moment but then thought it over. He told himself Stanton did this for a living and probably enjoyed it. He knew if he took it personally, Stanton would clam up and stop talking about music altogether, and there was no way Topher was going to let that happen.

"I know that I go through my life as Topher Manning. I know I'm having an individual experience, I get that. But I also know there's something out there bigger than me, and you can call it God, or the collective unconsciousness, or the goddamned smoke monster for all I care. Everything that I do and everything that you do—and everything that any one of us ever does—is ultimately an attempt to connect our puny little lives to that bigger something. Nothing makes that connection like music—not a painting or a sculpture or even a book or a play—so that's why I get up on stage and sing songs. I'm trying to plug into the universe."

Stanton held up his hands. "Now, do you see the difference between that answer and the other one?"

"Yeah, I suppose I do."

"Do you think that music can change the world?"

"No, I don't think that, but can you imagine a world without it? That sounds like just about the worst possible place imaginable."

"You and Nietzsche."

"Who's that?"

"A nineteenth-century German philosopher. He said, 'Without music, life would be a mistake.'"

"That would make a great tattoo." Topher lifted his right arm. "Maybe here, on the side of my torso."

"When did you get the sleeve?" Stanton asked.

"After my father died. But let's back up a minute. If all critical yardsticks are bullshit, then why did you just tell me that 'Surrender to Love' is bad?"

"I didn't. I never used the word bad, because I never use good or bad. I said it was awful and one of the worst things I've ever heard in my life. That was an honest reaction."

"You do realize that worst is the superlative of bad, don't you? Bad, worse, worst."

Stanton looked chagrined. "Damn, you're right. See, even I'm full of shit half the time. Nice job. I like a man who can hold his own."

"This is fun all of a sudden."

"As for that song, though, you really should listen to me. It's bad. There, I said it."

"I appreciate your honesty. I don't have anyone else in my life who talks to me like this."

Stanton took a drink from his can of beer and grimaced. "This tastes like Pabst Blue Ribbon," he said. "Just awful. So, I'm guessing music is what brought you to Austin?"

"Kind of. We followed Maurice here when he came for college. It's a great place to live. It's so different from the rest of Texas."

"That's what you told me. It does seem very liberal for Rick Perry country. How did you become a mechanic?"

"There's a little automotive shop in Dime Box, right across from the lumberyard. I worked there part time during high school. The guy who owns it knows Darrell, so when I moved here, I got hooked up with Groovy Automotive."

"That's where you work? It's called Groovy Automotive?"

"Yeah, didn't you see the sign?" Topher pointed to the patch over his heart. "Or the logo on my shirt?"

"No, sorry. I'm not very observant."

"Did you also miss it in the painting last night?"

"What are you talking about?"

"The word *groovy*, in the room of three thousand records. The one inside the hotel."

"The painting over the fireplace?"

"Yeah."

"It said *groovy*?"

"Yep, it sure did. All the letters are there."

That wistful look on Stanton's face returned. "I guess I missed that too."

"You'd better wake up and pay attention. Anyway, Darrell's a good man to work for, and the other mechanics are super cool. Especially Travis. I told you he has a boyfriend now. He lives with Ben and his three brothers."

"Travis has three brothers?"

"No, Ben does. The five of them live in a house together. The brothers are still teenagers."

"Ah, I see. What happened to the parents?"

"They died last year, in a car accident."

"Oh, sorry."

Topher nodded and said, "I'm sure they'd appreciate your sympathy, but that family has bounced back pretty nicely, like the phoenix rising from the ashes. Every time I go over there, I learn something new."

"Sounds like a fascinating setup."

"They invited us over for dinner tomorrow night. If that's something you'd be interested in."

"You already have our second date planned?"

"Third, actually. I'll always think of Bruce Springsteen as our first date."

Stanton laughed. "Why do I feel like you're driving this ship and I'm just a passenger?"

"Is that a yes or a no?"

Stanton paused. Then he said, "Sure. I need to spend the day with Marvin, though. He has a couple of bands he wants to see in the afternoon."

"Groovy."

"Are you going to start saying that now?"

"Maybe. I'm trying it on for size."

Stanton took another drink of beer. "Tell me about the other guys in the band. How long have you known them?"

"My whole life. We're all from Dime Box."

"Two of them are identical twins?"

"Yeah. Robin and Maurice."

"Was their mom an E. M. Forster fan?"

"I don't think so. She was a Bee Gees fan."

"Oh, that's right. Robin and Maurice Gibb were twins."

"Yep. Robin plays bass. Maurice is the drummer, and Peter is the guy on keyboards and guitar. The four of us have been friends since we were kids. I'm a year younger, but in a school that small, it didn't really matter. All twelve grades are in the same building."

"How many students were in your graduating class?"

"Seven."

Stanton shook his head in disbelief. "Where did you learn to play the guitar?"

"We had a music teacher, Mrs. Gephart, who came once a week. She did what she could, and the rest we picked up on our own."

"The four of you blend together very nicely."

"Thank you. We practice a lot, and it helps that we live together."

"All four of you?"

"Yeah. We rent a house up on Eleventh Street, just a few blocks from here. Want to see it?"

"Are you flirting with me?"

"I'm trying."

Stanton frowned. "Look, if I were ten years younger and you were ten years older, I'd be all over you like a cheap suit, but as it is—"

"Then good thing I don't have to wait. For a cheap suit, I mean. Let's face it, I need my youth advantage in this situation. Otherwise, you would be way out of my league, Don Draper."

Stanton tilted his head back. "You are fucking adorable, do you know that?"

"You think so? Travis said I'm a hot piece of ass."

"I would say that's an accurate description. Look, I'll admit, it freaks me out a little that people probably think I'm your—"

"Don't say it. And they wouldn't think that if you kissed me. At least I hope they wouldn't. This isn't Mississippi."

"Usually I'm up for this kind of adventure, but you seem like dangerous territory to me."

"Aw, come on. Dangerous? I think of myself as a lot of things, but dangerous isn't one of them. Although I did feel like a bad boy singing up there tonight."

"You mean you're not always like that?"

Topher grinned and replied, "No, something special happened."

"You plugged into the universe."

"Maybe. Or maybe it was because I've been thinking about kissing you again all day."

"Music and sex. Marvin says they're the same thing."

"So, are you going to kiss me? Or do I have to crawl across this picnic table and do it for you?"

"Here?"

"Why not? It's a gay-friendly crowd. Besides, Travis and Ben make out all over town. Are you afraid you're not a good kisser?"

"I'm a great kisser."

"Then prove it."

"No, I can't. People will think...."

Topher stood up and crawled on top of the picnic table.

"What are you doing?"

"I warned you." He swung his legs around and sat down in front of Stanton, bringing them face to face. "This is kind of cool. When I sit up here, I'm a little taller than you." He trapped Stanton between his knees.

"People are staring," Stanton said.

"So? Do you care what they think?"

"Yes, I told you that yesterday. I'm not interested in being a spectacle. I like my private life to stay private."

"I hate to burst your bubble, but no one in this town cares who you kiss."

Stanton paused and looked like he was thinking that over. Then he said, "You're probably right. I don't know what's wrong with me."

Topher put his arms around Stanton's neck. "Look at me, handsome." Stanton tilted his head up, and Topher gave him a peck on the lips. "I know you're worried about the age difference." Topher kissed him again. "And the long-distance thing." Topher kissed him a third time. "And the fact that I've never had sex with a dude. But you don't have to worry about any of those things."

"What am I getting myself into?"

"I don't know, but what do you say we find out?"

And with that, Topher pulled Stanton toward him and pressed their lips together in a hungry kiss. Stanton moved his hands up Topher's legs and around his waist, as he invaded Topher's eager mouth with his tongue. Topher felt a lifetime of passion in that kiss, but he couldn't explain where it came from. He pushed his fingers through Stanton's lush hair and then slowed things down. He ran his tongue across the smooth enamel of Stanton's teeth and ended with a tender kiss on his lips and nose.

"You're right," Topher said quietly.

"About what?"

"Being a good kisser."

Stanton tightened his grip around Topher's waist. "You're intoxicating."

A woman walked up to their table and said, "That was hot."

"Thank you," Topher replied. "Isn't he something?" The woman nodded and walked away as Stanton buried his face in Topher's chest. "See?" Topher said. "People aren't staring because you're older than me—they're staring because you're fucking sexy."

"They're staring because I'm with you."

"I'll take it either way," Topher said. He kissed Stanton again and then asked, "You ready to head back to your hotel?"

"I thought we were going to your place."

"You want to? I cleaned up and everything."

"No… well, maybe another time. Let's head back to the W for now."

They left Cheer Up Charlie's and retraced their steps down Sixth Street. Topher's phone vibrated in his pocket, and he got an idea. "What's your favorite Beatles song?"

Stanton paused and gave Topher one of his blank stares. "'I Want to Hold Your Hand', why?"

"Okay," Topher said as he reached out and intertwined his fingers with Stanton's. "If you insist."

Stanton tensed for a moment, but then he relaxed, like he was resigning himself, and they continued walking hand in hand. "How did you know that was going to be my answer?"

"You're way more predictable than you realize, Stanton Porter, the music critic. By the way, I've been meaning to ask you an important question. It might be a little personal, though."

"That's okay. We were making out, and now we're holding hands, so I'd say we've crossed the personal line. What's the question?"

"Do you like crunchy or smooth peanut butter?"

Stanton stopped walking.

"What's wrong?" Topher asked. "I was trying to be cute. I thought you'd laugh."

Stanton blinked. "Nothing's wrong. I'm just exhausted, that's all. You're very cute. And smooth. I like smooth peanut butter."

"Me too. Don't you think little things like that tell you a lot about a person? I mean, really, the whole point of peanut butter is to take peanuts and turn them into something smooth, like butter. Have you ever seen crunchy butter?"

Stanton laughed.

"That's more like it," Topher said.

They made their way back to Stanton's hotel. They held hands and checked out the many musical offerings along the way. When they arrived back at the W, Stanton stopped on the sidewalk. "What time is dinner tomorrow night?"

"You're not going to ask me up?"

Stanton looked down at the pavement. "It's complicated."

"You have your own room, right?"

"Yes, but—"

"Do you have a boyfriend back in New York?" Topher slapped his forehead. "Jesus, I didn't even think to ask that."

"No, I wouldn't be standing here if I had a boyfriend. I'm not that guy."

"Then what is it? I want to do this. You know that, don't you? I'm not a cock tease."

"I know that. And I understand it's not fair to you, but... meeting you has been... unusual for me."

"What does that mean?"

"Maybe we can spend tomorrow night together?"

"Really? After dinner?"

"Maybe. I need to talk to Marvin again."

"What does he have to do with it?"

"Like I said, it's complicated."

"What's going on? Does this have anything to do with the title of that album last night?"

"No. Maybe. I wish I could explain it, but.... Can you trust me for now?"

"Yes, but you can trust me too."

"I know that, it's just... I haven't figured out how to talk about this yet."

"Talk about what?"

"Can we please—"

"Yes, yes, okay, I'll back off. More than anything else, I want tonight to end on a solid note, so this is me backing off. I had a great time with you, thanks for coming to our gig, and I'll call you tomorrow about dinner." He stepped forward and kissed Stanton in full view of the W valet staff. Topher wanted that kiss to convey everything he was feeling, so he held nothing back. When he pulled away and looked up, Topher could tell he had left his mark, because all Stanton could say was "Wow."

"You going to jack off tonight thinking about me?"

"Do you mind?"

"I'd mind if you didn't. Good night, Stanton."

"Good night."

Topher grinned and began to walk away, but Stanton stopped him. "One more thing. This may be out of line, but hear me out. The name of your band, it's a little pretentious. You should really think about changing it, especially since the perfect alternative is staring you right in the face."

"What's the alternative?"

Stanton paused for effect.

"Dime Box."

Topher's eyes widened. "I love that."

"Just an idea."

Topher wrapped his arms around Stanton. "It's a great idea. Thanks again for everything. I'll see you tomorrow." Topher paused for a moment with his head resting against Stanton's chest. Finally, he untangled himself, turned around, and walked away. Topher could feel Stanton watching him and he smiled, but he didn't look back.

WHEN Topher arrived at home, Maurice, Robin, and Peter were sitting in the living room. Topher grinned and asked, "Is there anything to eat in this house? I'm starving."

"Let's go into the kitchen," Robin said as he jumped off the sofa. "We'll make some pancakes."

"Yes!" Maurice yelled.

The four men scrambled into the kitchen, where Robin began pulling ingredients from the pantry and Maurice got eggs and milk from the fridge. Topher loved watching the twins work together in the kitchen. When people asked him what it was like being around identical twins, he always said the biggest surprise was how little they needed to talk to each other.

Maurice pulled his long, curly hair into a ponytail before he began to crack the eggs. When they were little, Peter had a horrible time telling them apart and insisted one of them grow his hair out. Maurice volunteered and had liked it so much he kept it that way.

Topher grabbed a package of Chips Ahoy cookies and then joined Peter at the table.

"How did it go?" Robin asked as he measured Bisquick into a bowl. "With Stanton Porter?"

"Groovy," Topher said. He bit into one of the cookies and passed the bag to Peter. "He loved 'Beaches on the Moon'. He said it could dominate iTunes."

Peter passed on the cookies but said, "We've always known it was our best song. When are you going to write something like that again?"

"I'm sorry, guys. I know I'm supposed to be the songwriter here, and lately I haven't been delivering. I swear to God, there are songs being held hostage in my head. Great songs. I just haven't figured out how to get to them yet."

"What did he think of the rest of the set?" Robin asked.

"He wasn't too kind about it. He called it pedestrian, whatever that means."

Maurice ducked behind his brother to grab a whisk from the drawer. "He's a critic. It's his job to be an asshole. But pedestrian means commonplace. Ordinary. Uninspired."

"I figured it wasn't a compliment. He told me 'Surrender to Love' was one of the worst things he'd ever heard."

Topher's three bandmates suddenly fell silent. All Topher could hear was the sound of whisking batter. "What's the matter?" he asked.

Peter got up and went to the cupboard. He pulled down four plates and set them on the countertop. He opened a drawer and gathered up forks and knives, then set them on the plates. He crossed back to the table and put the stack down in front of Topher. "Set the table."

"What are you guys not telling me?"

"Jesus," Maurice said, "I'll say it. Stanton Porter is right. It's one of the worst things I've ever heard too."

"Seriously? Why didn't you say something to me?"

Robin retrieved a portable griddle from underneath the sink and plugged it into the wall to heat up. Then he turned to Topher. "Sometimes, it's hard to find the words."

"Cliché-ridden?" Peter suggested.

"Saccharin-coated?" Maurice added.

"Celine-Dion-inspired?" Robin said with his usual shit-eating grin.

Topher surrendered. "Okay, I get the picture. Geez."

Maurice handed the batter to Robin and said, "Look, Topher, we're not trying to kill your buzz. Speaking of which, Peter, would you go get my bong out of the living room, please?" Peter left the kitchen and returned moments later with the water pipe. He handed it to Maurice, who pulled a disposable lighter from his pocket and took a hit. "Here's the thing," he said in a squeaky voice. He turned his head and exhaled. "Sorry about that. If you had asked me yesterday what I really thought of Judecca Rising, I'd have told you we were a mediocre rock band on the fast track to obscurity. But after tonight, I'll come right out and ask the question on everybody's mind. What in the fuck happened to you, Topher?"

"What do you mean?"

"You slayed 'Bridge Over Troubled Water'."

"You kicked ass on everything tonight," Peter said.

Robin started to ladle pancake batter onto the hot griddle. "Greatest vocal performance by the Topher ever. You were in the danger zone."

"I have never heard you sound so good," Peter said. "It was more than that, though. You were like a young Mick Jagger up there. How many girls slipped you their phone number afterward?"

"I didn't count them. I just threw them away."

Robin and Maurice stopped what they were doing and looked at Topher. "Are we missing something here?" they asked.

Topher nodded. "Sorry, guys. I haven't had a chance to tell you what's going on. I was on a date tonight. With Stanton."

Maurice threw up his hands and started dancing around.

"Fuck," Robin muttered.

"What's going on?" Topher said.

"I just won a hundred bucks," Maurice exclaimed.

Robin flipped the pancakes and then said, "I am deeply wounded, Topher."

Peter started laughing and asked, "Did you two bet on whether Topher was gay or not?"

Maurice giggled. "Yes."

"And you bet that I was?" Topher asked.

Maurice laughed even louder and answered, "Yes! Sorry. I just had a feeling."

"How could you keep something like that a secret?" Robin asked. "I told Maurice there was no way you could be gay and me not know about it."

"I'm sorry," Topher said. "It all happened kind of quickly."

Maurice stood next to his brother with a large platter in his hands, ready to receive the pancakes as they came off the griddle. Then he asked, "What am I going to do with my hundred bucks?"

Robin began to transfer the golden-brown pancakes to the plate. "I just don't like being out of the loop with my best friends."

Maurice kissed his brother on the cheek. "Oh, poor baby. You're just pissed you lost a hundred bucks. Give Topher a break. He said it just happened, okay?"

"I heard him. Get those over to the table before they get cold."

Maurice did as he was told. "Can someone get the butter and syrup, please?"

Topher got up and crossed to the fridge for the butter and then pulled a bottle of syrup from the pantry. "Now I see what all this romance crap is about," he said. "I just met the guy, and I'm already crazy about him. I mean, who acts this way? He brings up stuff in me that—"

Peter raised his hands. "Be careful, dude. Whatever you're about to say, I can tell right now, it's going to make you sound like Bella Swan."

"Who's Bella Swan?" Maurice asked.

"The chick in *Twilight*," Peter replied.

"Jesus," Maurice said. "How can you watch that shit?"

"Girls love it, and I love girls."

Robin turned off the griddle, and the four men sat down around the table. They piled their plates high with buttermilk pancakes and began to eat.

"I was happy tonight," Topher said as he shoveled food into his mouth. "I mean, completely and deliriously happy, and now I'm just bummed that I'll be sleeping alone, and I've never felt this way before."

"Why are you sleeping alone?" Peter asked.

Topher shrugged and said, "I don't know. He's into me, I can tell. But at the same time, he's acting all weird. I think the age difference bothers him."

"Does it bother you?" Maurice asked.

"No, but for some reason he didn't want me to spend the night. He said maybe tomorrow."

"I always knew this day would come," Robin said.

"What day?" Topher asked.

"You're just like your parents," Robin said, and Maurice shook his fork in agreement. Together, the twins said, "You're only going to love one person in your life."

Peter nodded. "We've always known that."

"Do you think Stanton is that person?"

"Well," Peter said, "if you ask me, all the signs are there. I mean, so far it's played out like a classic romantic comedy."

Topher and the twins groaned.

"Peter," Robin said, "don't pretend Topher's life is like one of the chick flicks you watch in order to get laid."

"Hear me out," Peter said. "Really, I mean it, let me have my say. First, there's the ridiculously improbable chance meeting. I mean, come on, his borrowed car breaks down in the H-E-B parking lot? And his friend just happens to get sick so he has an extra ticket to the Springsteen concert? Like I said, ridiculously improbable, because if this were an episode of *Breaking Bad,* we'd call that lazy writing, yo. But this is a romantic comedy, so we accept it. Remember *Notting Hill*? Never mind, of course you don't. The whole movie begins when Julia Roberts, playing a fictional version of Julia Roberts, walks into Hugh Grant's bookstore. That's the setup. She just walks in. Anyway, back to you and Stanton. Scene two: the DNA-altering first date, complete with a kiss during the greatest Bruce Springsteen song of all time, which just happens to be the closing number before eight encores."

"Sorry," Topher said to the twins. "I didn't tell you about that part yet."

"Oops," Peter continued. "Sorry. My bad. Then, the romantic date on Sixth Street after the gig tonight. Tell me, did you grab a Shiner Bock at one of our city's colorful watering holes?"

"It was a Lone Star," Topher said with a grin.

"Of course it was. Take that, Tim Riggins. Did you make out or hold hands?"

"Both."

"You need to stop," Robin said to Peter. "You're creeping me out."

"In case you haven't noticed, I'm the only one who ever dates in this house, so excuse me if I'm a little excited to have another human being around for a change."

Maurice chuckled. "He's got a point, bro. Besides, boy meets boy has been the setup for some of the greatest stories ever told. Like Achilles and Patroclus."

"Or Walt and Jesse," Peter added.

"Or Starsky and Hutch," Robin said. "Owen Wilson still cracks me up in that movie."

"There's one more thing," Topher said as he poured syrup onto his last bites of pancake. "Stanton thinks we should change the name of the band."

"What?" Maurice said. "What's wrong with the name of the band? It's classic! Rising from the lowest circle of hell, tipping our hats to Dante. It shows we have brains."

"He said it was pretentious."

"Pretentious? I'd like to see him do better."

"He said we should name the band after our hometown."

Peter and the twins stopped eating.

"You mean...?" Robin asked.

"...Dime Box?" Maurice finished. "As the name of the band?"

Peter speared the last bites of pancake with his fork and popped them into his mouth. "I got to hand it to this Stanton Porter dude. He's old, but he's good."

"Fuck," Robin muttered. "And we just paid a three-year contract on the Judecca Rising domain."

"Shall we put it to a vote?" Peter said. "All in favor of changing the name of the band to Dime Box, say aye."

DOWNBOUND TRAIN

STANTON woke up to someone knocking on his bedroom door. He rolled over and rubbed his eyes. "Come in, buddy."

Marvin opened the door a crack and asked, "Are you decent?"

"Does it matter?"

Marvin came into the room and sat down on the bed. "It's almost ten."

"So? We're not leaving until one."

"Aren't you excited?"

"Yes, I'm excited. Can't you tell?"

"He really likes you."

"You think so?"

"Springsteen tickets? On the floor? Yes, I think so."

"Maybe this is it."

"What do you mean?"

"I mean, maybe he's the one. Let's face it; I have a lot of first dates but not many second ones. And this is number three."

"You're an acquired taste."

"It's like he gets me."

"I'm excited for you. Really. But a little caution wouldn't kill you."

Stanton thought it over. He knew this could be a turning point. He had the opportunity to put all the crap of the past two years behind him, but he would have to embrace who he was if he wanted any kind of future with Hutch. He decided to take the plunge. "I'm sick and tired of caution," he said. "I'm done hating who I am and hiding it. I feel safe when I'm with him, and if he turns out to be the love of my life, I'm not going to run away from that. It's time to step up."

"I like this new side of you."

"So do I. Did I miss breakfast?"

"Yes. Archy made blueberry waffles. They were *batampte*."

"Damn, I love waffles."

"You love breakfast."

"That's true. It's the most important meal of the day. Why didn't you wake me?"

"You have a big date tonight. We got in late, and you needed your beauty sleep."

Stanton laughed and sat up. He grabbed Marvin and wrestled him onto the bed. "Stop it!" Marvin screamed in protest. "You know I'll pee my pants if you tickle me." Stanton released him and Marvin rolled onto his back, resting his head against Stanton's shoulder. "Do you think it will ever happen to me?" Marvin said.

"What?"

"You know. Do you think I'll ever meet someone and—"

"Of course it will happen to you, but you're not doing yourself any favors by being a niche player."

"We do not need to have this conversation for the fiftieth time."

"Okay, fine," Stanton said. "See what I care. Keep beating off to your Lando Calrissian action figure, because I have not seen one black guy since we've been out here. Not even a token."

"There's more to the world than Fire Island."

"Please, you don't have to tell me that. But we go to Uncle Charlie's every weekend, and every weekend it's the same."

"Yes," Marvin said, "but we go there because you won't go anywhere else."

"We go to Julius sometimes, when I don't want to pay for drinks. And you know how I feel about the Ninth Circle."

"There are bars uptown that would be better for me."

"Not in any neighborhood that would be safe for us. Besides, I hate going above Fourteenth Street."

"How did you become a downtown snob in two years? You're from Iowa."

"I'm from Ohio."

"Boz Scaggs and Eric Carmen are from Ohio," Marvin said. "And Devo. Don't forget Devo."

"It's my goal in life to try and forget Devo. If they play 'Whip It' at one more dorm party, I'm going to shoot myself."

TWO hours later, Hutch arrived at their door, ready to go. They said good-bye to Colby and Archy and made their way back to Manhattan via a ferry, a shuttle bus, and two trains. When they arrived at Penn Station, Marvin took the subway downtown to their dorm, while Stanton and Hutch grabbed something to eat. After their meal, they caught the New Jersey Transit to Secaucus. Once they were seated and the train had pulled out of the station, Hutch reached over and took Stanton's hand.

"Thank you," Stanton said.

"For what?"

"The weekend. The tickets. The new lease on life."

Hutch grinned. "I didn't know it was that momentous, but you're welcome."

"So, who are you, anyway?"

"What is that supposed to mean?"

"People talk, you know."

"People? You mean Colby and Archy?"

"Yeah."

"What did they say?"

"That your family is wealthy and that they cut you off when they found out you're gay."

"Well, they're half right at least."

"Which half?"

"Yes, my family is wealthy. All four of us—Robert, Michael, and Paul too—we were raised on the Upper East Side, so money's not a big deal to us. But my father did not cut me off. I did that myself."

"Why?"

"I didn't want his money, because it would have given him a say in how I live my life. And me being gay was only part of the problem. He wanted me to be a lawyer, and I wanted to be a musician. That's what really pissed him off."

"What about your mom?"

"The only thing my mother cares about is her bottle of vodka. I haven't seen life behind her eyes in years."

"Really? I'm sorry to hear that."

"It doesn't matter. I don't see them much these days. Robert, Michael, and Paul are my family now. We take care of each other."

"That must be nice, like having three Marvins. You finished college, though, right?"

"Yes, but I'm not interested in going to law school or working in business or real estate."

"So you're a bartender instead?"

"Yes. That's what actors and musicians do. They wait tables and sling drinks."

"Don't get so defensive. I'm just asking. You gave me the twenty-question drill at the beach on Friday, so now it's my turn. How do you afford a place in the city and a share on Fire Island?"

"I don't have a place in the city."

"Oh. You live out there full time?"

"For now, I do. I work six days a week, but only five-hour shifts, so I have a lot of free time to write. It's a nice way to spend the summer. I'll move back in with Michael and Robert after Labor Day. Michael has a three-bedroom apartment in the Village."

"A three-bedroom? In Manhattan?"

"I know. It's spectacular. His grandmother gave it to him when he graduated from Columbia."

"Jesus. And here I thought I was hot stuff when my grandmother left me $1,000 in her will. What kind of songs do you write?"

"Bad ones, mostly. I'm no Paul Simon, but I like to think of myself as an undeveloped talent. I have all these songs in my head, but I'm the opposite of Mozart."

"What does that mean?"

"You remember what Marvin said? Mozart heard everything fully composed and just wrote it down. I'm the opposite. I can hear these songs in my head—every day I can hear them—but I can't get to them. It's like they're locked away somewhere."

"Maybe you just need to find the key."

"I don't think it's that simple."

"You never know. It could be a place or a person, or even an experience. Something could be out there waiting for you, something that will unlock those songs in your head."

Hutch glanced sideways and smiled. "You're hot and smart, do you know that?"

"I'm full of shit half the time," Stanton said. He looked out the window as the train surfaced from its Hudson River tunnel. "I'm glad I'm not a musician," he continued. "I wouldn't want the life. I'm looking forward to some stability after college. Health insurance. A pension. Knowing where my next paycheck is coming from. You know, a real job."

"There's nothing wrong with that."

"It sounds like we're different, that's all."

Hutch squeezed Stanton's hand in reassurance. "Different is good."

"This is the first time I've held hands with a guy in public."

Hutch got a surprised look on his face. "Should I not?"

"No, you should. I'm turning over a new leaf. All I've ever experienced is the downside of being gay, and this is a chance to see the other half. The good stuff."

"You mean you haven't had a boyfriend in two years?"

"Nope. Plenty of dates but no boyfriend. Too uptight, I guess. At least that's what Marvin says. That's why the new leaf. Have you had lots of them?"

"Boyfriends, you mean?" When Stanton nodded, he continued, "Let's say I've had my share of short-term relationships. But I wouldn't call them boyfriends. I like sex but not one-night stands, so I developed a bad habit of dating boys for the wrong reason."

"I get the picture. I don't mean to come off like a prude, but sex still makes me nervous."

"That's okay. I think we should wait too."

"You do?"

"Absolutely. At least a few weeks. Maybe even a month or more."

"A month? But I said a couple of days."

Hutch crinkled his nose and grinned. "Who said you get to decide these things? My virtue is at stake here too, you know?"

"Your virtue?"

"Indeed. My virtue."

"But—"

"No, you started this, Stanton Porter. Now, we're going to see just how long you can hold out. I predict that by the end of this concert, you'll be begging for a piece of my ass."

"You're enjoying this, aren't you?"

"Maybe. You're cute when you squirm."

"Where are we sleeping tonight, anyway?"

"I don't know. I haven't thought that far ahead."

WHEN they arrived at the Meadowlands, Stanton and Hutch grabbed a beer and talked some more before taking their seats. They joined the throng of avid Bruce fans on the floor, and Hutch kept finding reasons to brush up against Stanton or lean over and whisper things into his ear, things like, "Do you think I'm sexy?"

Stanton shook his head. "Really? Is that a rhetorical question? Because God help you if it's not."

"Have you jacked off thinking about me?"

Stanton blushed and kept his eyes on the stage. "Maybe."

"That turns me on." Hutch faced forward as well and continued talking. "I've jacked off thinking about you too. More than once. Last night, when I got home from the Pavilion, I went up to our rooftop deck and took off all my clothes. Did you know our house on the island has a deck on the roof? I lay down under the stars and imagined what it's going to feel like when you're inside me. Deep inside me. I came so hard I shot myself in the face and tasted my own come. I didn't mean to, but it landed on my lips, and the next thing I knew, I was licking it off and—Well, you get the picture."

Stanton felt his cock harden in his pants. Hutch moved his left arm to the back of Stanton's seat. He leaned over and said, "What did you think of the Greatest Game?"

"I liked it."

"It's kind of stupid, I know."

"It wasn't stupid. I had fun."

"I liked your answers, by the way. 'Billy, Don't Be A Hero'. That's when I knew you were the one for me. That and Air Supply, of course. What's your favorite Carpenter's song?"

"Only Yesterday."

"I'll have to check that one out."

"I'm warning you. It's shamelessly sentimental."

"Then good thing I'm feeling all warm and fuzzy inside."

Stanton turned his head and looked into Hutch's eyes.

"You know what I mean?" Hutch asked.

"Yeah," Stanton said. "I think so. My dick is hard."

Hutch laughed from deep in his chest and reached over with his right hand. He squeezed Stanton's crotch. "Okay," he said, clearly impressed. "Maybe a month is unrealistic given the size and girth of what I'm feeling down there."

"I'd say a few hours is unrealistic."

Hutch continued to rub Stanton's erection. "Think about pink bunnies and unicorns and maybe it will go away. But whatever you do, don't think about what it's going to feel like when it crosses my lips for the very first time. And definitely don't think about spreading my firm asscheeks and sliding your cock into my insatiable fuckhole, because if you think about that, your erection will never go down."

"And if you don't stop rubbing my dick, I'm going to come in my pants."

"Oh," Hutch said as he snatched his hand away. "Sorry about that. I forgot you're still a teenager."

"I'm going to be twenty next month." They straightened up and composed themselves. "I really like your friends," Stanton said. "Marvin raved about them all the way back from the Pavilion."

"Sorry about all the Robert and Michael drama."

"Nah, it was fine. I liked Michael. Marvin's mom always says life naturally wants to be messy. He's an only child, so he thinks he missed out on having brothers."

"Robert is an only child too."

"What about you?"

"I have an older brother."

"Two brothers and a sister here."

The opening act took the stage while Hutch continued talking over the music. "You should come back out to the island next weekend. You and Marvin both."

"Really? Where would we sleep?"

"You can sleep with me, and Marvin can have the pool house. It's got a bed, its own bathroom, even a stereo. We're going to stock it with records, red wine, even some Tab."

"You've talked to your housemates about this?"

"Yes."

"And I'll be sleeping with you?"

"Yes. You don't like the idea?"

"I like it just fine, but we haven't even had sex yet."

"Don't worry. I have a feeling that won't be true for much longer." Hutch kept his gaze fixed on the stage and said, "This opening act is terrible."

At around nine o'clock, the stadium went dark and the people on the floor began stomping their feet. Then an announcer said, "Ladies and gentlemen, tonight the Meadowlands proudly welcomes back to New Jersey a true native son. Put your hands together for the greatest rock-and-roll superstar in America, Bruce Springsteen and the E Street Band."

The crowd erupted as the lights on the stage flared up and immediately went dark again. Stanton and Hutch waited as the spectators gradually fell silent.

"There's no way he's going to open with it," Stanton whispered.

"Show a little faith, Starsky."

Bruce stepped into a lone spotlight center stage. When they heard the familiar piano and harmonica riff, Stanton and Hutch turned to each other in amazement.

"Do you know what this means?" Hutch said. "The rock-and-roll gods are smiling down on us tonight."

"I can't believe it. It's like—"

Stanton never finished his thought. Instead, Hutch took his hand, and they turned back to the stage, not wanting to miss a single second of "Thunder

Road." They sang along and danced with the people around them. Stanton knew it was a singular experience that would never be repeated in his lifetime.

Bruce sang the last line, and as the band played out the instrumental closing, Hutch pulled on Stanton's arm, bringing them face to face. Stanton's heart began to pound and he felt something like clarity. He could hear every instrument on the stage distinct from every other instrument.

"Close your eyes," Hutch said.

"Why?"

"Because I'm going to kiss you now."

Stanton closed his eyes and waited, but when he didn't feel anything right away, he said, "What's wrong?"

"Nothing. I'm just memorizing your face."

Stanton opened his eyes as Hutch leaned in. They looked at each other, and Hutch hesitated. "Okay," he said, "we'll do this with our eyes open."

Hutch tilted his head and touched their lips together. It seemed to Stanton as if one of them expected the other to stop, but that didn't happen. In fact, Stanton had reached his breaking point. He threw his arms around Hutch's neck and pulled him in close. He locked their lips together and shut his eyes. Hutch tasted like beer and sex and salt water. Stanton could only think of one word to accurately describe it.

Intoxicating.

Hutch's lips were soft and the stubble from his chin brushed up against Stanton's smooth face. Stanton felt Hutch put his hands on his hips, and then wrapped them around his waist. He raised his arms and his fingers made contact with Hutch's shoulders. He squeezed them, broad and solid, in his hands. He felt a tongue slide into his mouth. He reached around and grabbed Hutch's ass with both hands, cupping his buttcheeks.

"What are you doing back there?" Hutch asked.

"Checking out the merchandise."

"Does it pass inspection?"

"I'm going to need a closer look at some point."

Hutch kissed him, without hesitation, and they forgot about Bruce Springsteen on stage. They forgot about the crowd around them. They forgot about things like jobs and college and an uncertain future. All that existed was this single point in space and time.

Hutch pulled away. "This is our touchstone," he said. "If something happens and we get thrown off course, we'll use 'Thunder Road' to find our way back. Don't ever forget this moment. Promise me."

"Yes, okay. I promise."

Hutch kissed him again, and Stanton couldn't resist asking, "Did you know your kisses taste like salt water?"

"I swim in the ocean every day. My mom used to say I'm half fish."

"Like *The Incredible Mr. Limpet?*"

"Exactly."

They turned back to the stage. Stanton took Hutch's hand and said, "It feels like my life has finally begun."

Hutch squeezed and said, "Our life, Starsky."

THREE and some odd hours later, when the concert ended, Stanton looked at Hutch and said, "That was one of the most amazing experiences of my life."

"Springsteen in Jersey, baby. That's a notch on your belt they can never take away."

"Thank you for that."

"You're welcome," Hutch said as they filed out of the stadium with the rest of the concertgoers. "Do you think we can sleep in your dorm room tonight?"

"Yeah, that'll be fine. We're going to wake up Marvin, but he'll go right back to sleep. No funny business, though, not with him there. I don't want to be one of those creepy roommates."

"Just sleep. I promise."

They took their time catching a bus back to the Secaucus station. Stanton thought he would be tired, but it was just the opposite. He felt energized and hornier than ever. Bruce Springsteen wasn't just a music god, he was a sex god. On the bus, Hutch kept touching the back of his neck and running his fingers along the inside of his thigh.

"We need to do something about my boner," Stanton said. "It's not going down. It's like just being next to you makes me hard."

"I have an idea."

By the time they reached the platform, it looked like a previous train had taken away most of the crowd, leaving only a handful of passengers behind. As they waited for the next train, Hutch stood in front of Stanton and kept pressing his ass against his crotch.

"You're not helping," Stanton said. When the second train arrived, they got onto one of the center cars, and Stanton took a seat next to the door.

"Follow me," Hutch said.

"What's wrong with this car?"

"I told you, I have an idea."

Hutch began walking, and Stanton followed. Hutch reached back and took Stanton's hand. They made their way from one car to the next, the crowd thinning as they went. When they got to the fourth car back, it was dark and empty.

Stanton stopped and turned Hutch around. "I can't wait any longer. My balls are blue and my dick is ready to explode."

"What about my virtue?"

"Fuck your virtue. You didn't drag me all the way back here so you could play hard to get."

Hutch laughed. "But don't you want our first time to be special?"

"You don't think this is going to be special? Years from now, when we're old and gray, we'll tell this story about how we went to see Bruce Springsteen, and I got so turned on that I couldn't wait—I just had to fuck you right here on the New Jersey Transit."

"So we're going to grow old together, eh?" Hutch asked. "You promise to hold up?"

"You know I'm still going to look great when I'm fifty."

Hutch reached out and put his hand on Stanton's bulge. "Your dick is as stiff as a surf board."

"I've never had sex in public, but I'm actually less nervous than I would be if we were in bed."

"You've had sex in public. You went down on that quarterback in his car."

"That doesn't count. There was no danger of getting caught."

Hutch squeezed Stanton's cock and said, "I think they call that autofellatio."

"Kiss me," Stanton said. Hutch leaned in and their lips met, but then Stanton stopped him. "No, I mean, kiss me like you mean it. Like I'm the one you've been waiting for." Hutch looked at him and grabbed Stanton by the waist. The violence of their kiss threw Stanton off balance and he almost fell into the seat. While they kissed, Stanton felt his pants being undone and Hutch sliding a hand into his briefs.

"Thank God for well-hung boys from Iowa."

"Ohio," Stanton said. "Now shut up and blow me."

"That's more like it, Starsky."

"I don't think Starsky ever said 'blow me' to Hutch."

"Oh, I disagree."

"Can we not get into the homoerotic underpinnings of a television show right now? I said, blow me."

Hutch dropped to a squat and pulled Stanton's thick cock from his pants. Stanton closed his eyes as Hutch's warm mouth engulfed his shaft. He reached down and ran his fingers through Hutch's hair. He relished the blow job until he felt the rise of an orgasm, then he stopped. Stanton reached down and pulled Hutch to his feet. They stood in the empty aisle, still close to the car's end door. Stanton pulled his pants up. "Over there," he said. "Those four seats facing each other." Hutch followed instructions and walked halfway down the car to the open space. "Put your hands against the wall," Stanton said. Hutch did as he was told, and put his hands up as if he were about to be arrested. Stanton reached around and undid his shorts. He let them fall to the floor of the train and looked down at Hutch's bare ass, plump like two ripe melons and framed by Speedo tan lines.

"No underwear?" Stanton asked.

"Nope."

"Did you plan this?"

"Maybe." Hutch stepped out of the shorts and placed his right foot on the seat. Then he reached back and pulled his ass cheeks apart, which Stanton interpreted as an invitation to fuck. He pushed his jeans down to his ankles and reached out to caress Hutch's pale white ass. Hutch spit on his hand and slicked up Stanton's cock, then he said, "Come on, slide it in. We don't have all day. The conductor is going to get to this car eventually."

"This is so romantic," Stanton sneered.

"Shut up and fuck me, stud. We'll have plenty of time for romance later."

Since Stanton and Hutch were about the same height, the tip of Stanton's dick lined up perfectly with the pucker of Hutch's ass. They both groaned as Stanton entered him. "Oh, fuck, that feels good," Stanton said.

"Don't worry about going slow at first. I can take it."

"Shut up and let me do the fucking. I'm in charge now."

"Yes, sir."

Stanton pulled the front of his T-shirt over his head, and then concentrated on the sensation of his dick sliding in and out of Hutch's butt crack. He looked down, mesmerized by what he saw. The car was lit by random flashes that filtered through the smoky glass of the train windows. Those flashes left Stanton with only short glimpses of their fucking, but they were enough for him to realize he wanted more of this.

Stanton pulled out and sat down. "Ride me," he said. Hutch turned around and lowered himself onto Stanton's dick. "A little reverse cowboy action," Stanton said. "I like that."

"I hope so," Hutch said as he bobbed up and down, "because you're going to be doing a lot more of it in the future."

"Sometimes it's like you read my mind."

"Sometimes it's like you read my soul. Shit, I'm getting close already. The head of your cock is hitting that spot."

Hutch reached down and stroked himself until chunks of semen began spurting from his dick. Stanton withdrew his cock, and in a few quick strokes, added his own spattered load to the pool of come gathering on the grimy floor. Hutch collapsed onto the seat next to Stanton, then reached down and put on his shorts.

"That was incredible," Stanton said. He stood and pulled up his jeans, buttoned his fly, and flipped his T-shirt back over his head.

"Your dick is amazing," Hutch said as he stood up and zipped his fly. "How big is that monster?"

"I don't know," Stanton said, sitting back down. "I've never measured it."

"Liar." Hutch sat next to him and laid his head on Stanton's shoulder. "Where did you pick up a phrase like 'homoerotic underpinnings'?"

"Where do you think?"

"Oh, right. Marvin. He's a groovy cat."

"Yes, he is."

"You two are coming out to the island next weekend, right?"

"I need to talk to him, but I'm pretty sure the answer will be yes. You and your friends made quite an impression."

"It's going to be the summer of our lives, Starsky."

Stanton shifted to the right and rested his cheek against the top of Hutch's head. A few moments later, he heard the sound of heavy breathing and smiled. Stanton liked the fact that Hutch felt comfortable enough to fall asleep. He faced forward and stared down the length of the empty car. The train slowed to a crawl as Stanton looked down at his hands. He thought about doing it. Too soon? He didn't care. Without disturbing Hutch, he pulled the ring off his finger, turned it around, and then slid it back on. The end door flung open and a tall, looming figure stepped into the shadows.

"Tickets," the conductor announced. "Have your tickets ready. Tickets, please. Next stop Penn Station, New York City."

IF I SHOULD FALL BEHIND

ON SATURDAY afternoon, as he stood in his kitchen, Topher called Stanton's number to confirm their plans for the evening. When Stanton answered, Topher had to shout over some music in the background to be heard.

Hey, Topher.

"Where you at?"

I don't know. We crossed the river.

"You mean Town Lake?"

That is not a lake, that's a river. Where are we, Marvin?

Topher faintly heard Marvin answer, *South Congress*. Then Stanton said, *We're just walking around. We had lunch at a food court made of trailers.*

"That's a cool part of town. We still on for dinner tonight?"

Yes. Don't start with me, buddy.

"Excuse me?"

Sorry, I was talking to Marvin. He enjoys watching me squirm.

"Why are you squirming?"

I'm still uncomfortable with your age.

In the background, Topher heard, *That's because you're still uptight.* Then Stanton said, *Don't listen to him. What time is dinner?*

"I'll come down and pick you up at seven thirty. How's that?"

I can take a cab, really. I don't want you to feel like you have to chauffeur me around.

"Shut up. I'll call you when I get there."

Topher closed his phone. He laid it down on the table as Robin came into the kitchen. Robin glanced at him on his way to the fridge and said, "Look at you, all glowing and shit."

"Don't make fun of me. I'm nervous enough as it is."

"You got plans tonight?"

"We're going to dinner at Travis and Ben's place."

Robin grabbed a beer from the fridge and turned to Topher. He screwed off the cap and took a swig.

"I'm sorry," Topher said. "That I didn't tell you about Stanton, I mean."

Robin took another swig of beer. "You didn't think I was going to be a dick about it, did you?"

"No, that wasn't it at all. There just wasn't time."

"You could have called me."

"I know. It won't happen again."

Robin smiled and said, "It better not. When are you going to bring him here for dinner? We'd like to meet him too, you know."

"If I see him after this weekend, this will be our next stop, I promise. Travis thought dinner at their house would be a good follow-up to our date last night."

"Well, he's probably right. There's something about that Ben Walsh."

"You got a little man crush, there?"

"Stop it. I'm just saying, it will give this Stanton guy a good impression, unlike introducing him to trailer-park trash like me and Maurice."

Topher shook his head. "You know I hate it when you talk that way."

"Sorry."

Topher picked up his phone and put it in his pocket. "I'm going to take a nap and then get ready. Hopefully I won't be home tonight."

"What are you wearing?"

"Jeans and a T-shirt."

"Classy. Which T-shirt?"

"The one with the row of dice that says 'Choose Your Weapon' underneath."

"Geek-chic. Nice. You going to shave?"

"You don't like my facial hair?"

"I don't know. Maybe go all boyish on him, even put some product in your hair."

"Product?"

"It wouldn't kill you to show a little effort, dude. There's some in our bathroom."

WHEN Topher pulled up to the W promptly at seven thirty, Stanton stood outside the hotel waiting for him. "Look at you," Topher said as Stanton opened the door and climbed into the truck. "You're on time."

"I'm making an effort."

"Do I get a kiss?"

Stanton leaned over and planted a big one on Topher.

"You don't seem too uptight to me," Topher said.

Stanton kissed him again, this time like they hadn't seen each other in years.

"I missed you."

"Really?" Topher said. "It hasn't even been twenty-four hours. Does that mean you're surrendering to my swagger?"

"It's kind of hard to resist."

Stanton kissed him a third time, and Topher felt his cock thicken inside his briefs. He reached down to adjust himself. "It's not the only thing that's hard."

Stanton flashed a devilish smile and said, "You'd better drive."

Topher pulled onto Lavaca Street and headed north. "I like seeing you three days in a row."

"You look great, by the way. I like the clean shave. What does your T-shirt say?"

"Choose Your Weapon."

"I don't get it."

"They're dice. In a role-playing game, you use dice to fight your opponents."

"Like *Dungeons & Dragons*?"

"Yeah."

"I thought that was for fourteen-year-old boys."

Topher laughed. "Very funny. I guess the charm of the T-shirt is lost on you."

"Perhaps, but not the charm of the man wearing it."

Topher grinned and could tell something had changed, but he didn't want to spoil the moment by asking what had caused it. They passed the Capitol, and Topher turned right. He headed east toward Red River Street and held Stanton's hand as he drove. "You know what song I love?"

"Tell me," Stanton said.

"'True Blue'. Madonna."

"That's one of her best—and most underappreciated. Did you know she wrote that for Sean Penn? 'True blue' was one of his favorite expressions."

"Really? I didn't know that. Do you like to camp?"

"You mean the tent kind or the drag-queen kind?"

"The tent kind."

"It doesn't matter. I've never done either one."

Topher snorted a laugh. "Are you serious? You've never been camping? Not even when you were a kid?" Topher turned left on Red River and headed toward North Campus, where Travis and Ben lived.

"Not even when I was a kid," Stanton said. "We took family vacations to a place called Crooked Lake in northern Michigan, which is not to be confused with the northern peninsula. We rented a cottage, but never tents."

"You weren't a Boy Scout?"

"No. I was a Cub Scout, but we never went camping."

"I bet you've never ridden a horse either. Have you?"

Stanton laughed. "I have never ridden a horse."

Topher stopped at a red light on Thirty-Second Street. He turned to Stanton and said, "Tell me you at least know how to play pool."

"Sorry. I do not know how to play pool."

"Well, princess, we're going to have to teach you a thing or three one of these days. Maybe even how to two-step."

"I've been to the Round-Up in Dallas. Two men in Wranglers spinning around to Reba McEntire. Strangest thing I ever saw. So that's what you do in Dime Box? Go camping, ride horses, and play pool?"

"And basketball."

"Why basketball?"

"It's the sport that requires the fewest number of players. Small school, remember?"

"Oh, right. Sorry."

"But I wasn't very good at it. Too short."

"Do you have a movie theater?"

The light turned green, and Topher shifted his focus back to the road. "No. We had to drive to Taylor or Brenham for that. Speaking of Dime Box, I told the boys about your idea. Renaming the band, I mean."

"Did I ruffle any feathers?"

"Well, Maurice threw a small fit, but when he heard your suggestion, he ended up caving in. The vote was 4-0 in favor, but now we have to change our website and everything. Robin wasn't too happy about that." Topher turned off Red River and onto Ben and Travis's block. "I wanted to ask you something. Have you ever heard anyone else talk about music locked in their head? Honestly, I can't write anything these days. I don't remember being this frustrated, ever. Seems to me there's got to be a key of some sort." Topher glanced over and noticed Stanton wasn't paying attention. "Hello? Are you listening to me?"

Stanton didn't respond, but instead stared blankly out the window. Topher pulled into the driveway of the Walsh house and Stanton muttered, "Holy shit" under his breath.

"What's wrong?" Topher asked.

"Nothing. It's just that… I've been here before."

"To this house?"

"Yes. It's no big deal, just one of those random universe things."

"Except the *I Ching* says there are no random universe things."

"Did you read the *I Ching*?"

"Wikipedia. So, you've been here before? When you were in Austin the first time?"

"Yes."

Topher raised his eyebrows. "Weird."

The two men got out of the truck and walked up the porch steps to the front door. Topher knocked, and seconds later, Ben's seventeen-year-old brother Quentin answered. "Hey, Topher, come on in," he said as he opened the screen door. "Who's the grown-up?"

"This is Stanton. Stanton, Quentin."

Stanton extended his hand and said, "Nice to meet you."

"You too," Quentin said. He stepped out of the way so Topher and Stanton could enter the house. They were greeted immediately by Ben and Travis, who came through the dining room from the kitchen.

"Ben Walsh."

"Stanton Porter."

Travis stepped forward. "Travis Walsh."

"You have the same last name?" Stanton asked.

"We do now," Travis said.

Stanton turned back to Ben and said, "I met your parents years ago, when your mother was about a week away from giving birth to you."

Topher watched as Ben pulled back in surprise. "You've been here before?"

"Yes," Stanton said. "However many years ago it was that you were born. It was in July, I think."

"Yeah, 1983. I was born on the twenty-second."

"Right. It's just one of those coincidence things."

"Unless it's not," Topher said.

Stanton chuckled. "I came to visit a friend of mine who lived in your garage apartment at the time. He was going to law school."

"And you actually met my mom and dad?" Ben asked.

"Yes. Your dad was a remarkable man. Topher told me they died in a car accident. I'm sorry to hear that."

"Thanks for the sympathy," Ben said.

"I remember him talking about what they were going to name you. Did you know you were going to be Caddy if you were a girl?"

"Yes, I know that. My youngest brother eventually got that one. Cade?" he yelled into the living room. "Topher's here."

Cade, the youngest Walsh brother at thirteen, came around the corner. "Hey, Topher, what's up?"

"Nothing much, dude. This is my friend, Stanton."

"Hey," Cade said, shaking his hand.

Stanton stared at the three of them. "You're like a good-looking version of the Baldwin brothers."

"We've only heard that one about a million times before," Cade said, after which he left and returned to the living room.

"Ignore him," Ben said.

"Where's Jason?" Topher asked.

"He's spending the weekend at Jake's house," Ben said. "His boyfriend," he explained to Stanton.

"You have a gay brother?"

"Yes. One gay, two straight." He put his arms around Travis's neck and pulled him close. "And I recruited my boyfriend."

"Topher told me. You dated women before you met Ben?"

Travis smiled. "Yeah, but those days are over. I think I was just killing time 'til this one came along. Can I get you something to drink, Stanton?"

"I'll take a beer, as long as it's not in a can."

Topher laughed.

"We have Shiner in a bottle," Travis said.

"That would be great."

"Topher, you want to come into the kitchen and get the beer?"

"Sure." Topher said as he followed Travis.

Once they were out of earshot of the others, Travis whispered, "This is fate, him having been here before. It's like y'all were destined for each other."

"Dial it back just a bit, please."

"Did you have a good time last night?"

"We had a great time. He's an amazing kisser."

"You rascal. But no sex?"

"No. He said maybe tonight. I'm keeping my fingers crossed."

Travis sighed and continued. "Okay, then, here—let me pull some beers from the fridge so you can get back in there." Travis went and retrieved four bottles, then used a small opener to uncap each of them in quick succession.

Topher gathered three of them up in his hands and made his way toward the kitchen door.

"I got to go out and check the grill," Travis said. "Tell everyone dinner will be ready in ten minutes."

"Will do."

Topher returned to the living room and handed one of the beers to Ben. "Travis said ten minutes." He sat down on the sofa next to Stanton and handed him the third bottle. "L'chaim."

Stanton smiled and clinked the neck of his bottle with Topher's. "You're taking up the Yiddish now?"

"Isn't that what you said Thursday night?" Topher asked.

"Yes, but I'm an honorary Jew."

"There's no such thing."

"There is. Marvin's mother made me one."

"I think you might offend people saying that."

"Maybe. Wouldn't be the first time."

Without thinking about it, Topher leaned over and kissed Stanton. When he turned back, Ben and his two brothers were staring at them.

"I see you followed my advice," Ben said.

Quentin rolled his head back and exclaimed, "Oh. My. God. Topher too?"

"Seriously?" Cade said. "You can't even visit this house anymore without turning gay."

"What advice?" Stanton asked.

"Ben said I would have to throw myself at you if I wanted anything to happen."

Stanton laughed and turned to Ben. "So I have you to thank."

"You could say that."

"What do you do, Ben? For a living?"

"I'm a trial lawyer."

"The best in town," Topher added.

"Thanks for that," Quentin said. "Like his head isn't big enough already."

"It's not as glamorous as being a music critic," Ben said, "but it suits me. I've heard a few of your features on NPR. You've rubbed shoulders with a lot of the greats."

"Yes, but I've never thought of it as glamorous. I'm more of a parasite, really."

Topher put his hands over his face and said, "Parasite?"

"I've never actually accomplished anything in my life. All I've done is write about other people's accomplishments."

"That's hogwash," Topher said. "Music is like those trees falling in the forest. It doesn't exist if no one is listening. You represent the listener."

Stanton took a swig of his beer. "I like the way you see me."

Travis entered from the dining room. "I hope you like burgers and dogs from the grill. We had a real turd floater earlier in the week, and the weatherman said more was coming. Now, normally, we wouldn't complain, because we always need the rain, but no one wants a soggy music festival. After all, this is our city's big showcase. And then Thursday night, turns out the weatherman was wrong, and it clears up like a SXSW miracle. I said to Obi-Wan, we gotta get out the grill."

"Who's Obi-Wan?" asked Stanton.

"Me," Ben said. "Obi-Wan. Ben Kenobi. Ben Walsh."

"Oh, I get it." As everyone headed for the dining room, Stanton grabbed Topher by the elbow and asked, "What's a turd floater?"

"A heavy rainstorm."

Stanton laughed. "Priceless. I can't wait to tell my father that one."

"You enjoying yourself?"

"Yes, very much. It's good to be back in this house. Ben reminds me of his dad. Thank you for inviting me."

"You're welcome, but it was kind of selfish. I thought they'd make me look good."

"You don't need any help with that."

Topher grinned and decided he liked this side of Stanton. When they joined the others in the dining room, Topher sat at the head of the table opposite Travis, with Stanton in Jason's vacant chair next to Ben, and Quentin and Cade facing them. A large platter of cheeseburgers and hot dogs sat in the middle of the table, along with corn on the cob, some potato salad, buns, a plate of sliced tomatoes and onions, another plate of lettuce leaves, a bowl of chips, three jars of pickles, and an assortment of condiments.

"So, Stanton," Ben began as he piled tomatoes and lettuce onto a cheeseburger, "if you need some advice on how to handle a guy that goes gay for you, I could probably squeeze you in."

Stanton laughed and shook his head. "Is that what you think is going on here?"

Topher winked at him. "If I'm going to go gay for somebody, I'm glad he looks like you."

"It does baffle me," Stanton said. "My generation thought of bisexuality as a joke. It was nothing more than a way to break our fall as we stumbled out of the closet. So I'm skeptical."

"It baffled me too," Ben said. "But I've got to admit, I've changed my tune." Ben leaned over and kissed his boyfriend. "This one's the best thing that ever happened to me."

"You're a proper homosexual, though, right?" Stanton asked.

Topher found Stanton's choice of words funny, and it seemed Ben did too, because he said, "I like that—proper homosexual. Yes, I am. For the most part. The usual high-school stuff."

"That doesn't count. So you two," Stanton said, pointing to Topher and Travis, "do you think you were gay the whole time? Or is this just a quirk?"

"I was not gay the whole time," Travis said.

"I don't know," Topher said. "You're the first guy I've ever kissed. Would I have eventually kissed another guy if you hadn't come along? I don't know."

"Okay," Stanton said, "what do you think triggered it, then? Why me?"

Topher couldn't help but notice that Stanton had a strange look on his face, like he already knew the answer.

But before Topher had a chance to respond, Ben said, "I have a theory." He put down his cheeseburger and wiped his face with a napkin.

"Here we go," Travis said.

"Jesus," Quentin sneered. "Now you've got him all wound up."

"Be quiet, little brother. You know it's a good theory, especially since you helped me come up with it."

"What are you talking about?" Topher asked.

Ben began. "The question we're asking is: What's going on when a straight guy falls in love with another man? I'm not talking about a Kinsey three or four here, but someone who is a solid number one. I think what's going on in those circumstances is—"

Ben paused.

"A continuation," Quentin suggested.

"Exactly," Ben said. "Thank you, Q. A continuation of... of a previous relationship."

"*Little Buddha*," Cade said.

"What's that?" Topher asked.

"A movie," Quentin said. "One of our favorites. It's about the search for the reincarnation of a Buddhist teacher."

"Is that the one with Keanu Reeves?" Stanton asked.

"Yes. Do you know that the whole Tibetan state, before it was taken over by China, was founded on the belief that the Dalai Lama reincarnates over and over again?"

"I told you I learn something new every time I come here," Topher said to Stanton. "How do you know about all this?"

Quentin hesitated, but then he said, "I looked into it after our parents died, thinking maybe they'd come back. It's not unusual for kids like me to dabble in these things after.... Well, you know."

"How does it work?" Topher asked.

Quentin chuckled. "It's not like there's a rule book somewhere. My guess is we can do whatever the hell we want after we die. We can come back or not come back. We can wait awhile or not at all. I read that people who die suddenly or who have an urgent need to finish something can do it within weeks or even days."

"Don't you need at least nine months?" Topher asked.

"No," Quentin said. "The soul joins the body at first breath. If the need is great enough, a soul could pass from the dying words of an old man straight into the lungs of a newborn child."

"Travis and I were born on the same day," Ben said. "July 22, 1983. I think something happened. There was an accident, like my parents. Our lives got cut short and we came back that exact same day. So when we finally met twenty-seven years later, it didn't really matter that I was gay and Travis was straight."

"I was just so happy to see him again," Travis said. He reached out and took Ben's hand. "We picked up right where we left off. I've never been able to explain it, but it felt as natural as breathing."

Ben looked at Stanton. "Maybe that's what's going on with you and Topher too."

Stanton put down his hamburger and asked Ben, "Did your father ever tell you about Brendan and Trent?"

"No, I don't think so. He never mentioned anyone by those names. Who were they?"

Stanton didn't answer, but he got that white and frightened look on his face again.

Topher took Stanton's hand and turned to Ben. "Are you saying that Stanton and I maybe knew each other in a previous life?"

Stanton attempted a weak smile and said, "Previous for you, at least."

"What does that mean?" Topher asked.

"When is your birthday?"

"Why?"

"Just humor me."

Topher paused. "November 6, 1985."

Stanton closed his eyes. "Six days."

"What are you talking about? What does six days mean?"

Stanton took a deep breath. "I had—" He stopped himself, hesitated, and then shook his head. "I shouldn't do this."

"Don't say that," Topher said. "If something's going on, it's time for you to tell me what it is."

Everyone at the table stopped eating. Topher waited for Stanton to explain just what in the hell was going on.

"I had a boyfriend," Stanton said.

"Okay. And?"

"He died of AIDS six days before you were born."

"Stanton," Ben said.

"What?" Stanton asked.

"No, I'm sorry. I remember hearing Colin's mother talking about a guy named Stanton. Your boyfriend, what was his name?"

"Chris Mead."

Travis and the Walsh brothers looked at each other, their disbelief stretched across their collective faces.

"Fuck me," Ben said softly.

"Would somebody tell me what's going on here?" Topher said.

"Are you shitting me?" Quentin asked. "You were boyfriends with Joseph Mead's dead son?"

"Well, he wasn't dead at the time, but yes. Do you know Joseph Mead?"

"Do we know him?" Quentin looked at Ben from across the table. "Do you think that Topher could be…?"

Ben shook his head. "This was supposed to be for fun, not—"

Topher interrupted him, asking, "Who is Chris Mead?"

Ben didn't respond, but turned to Stanton instead. "I went to Columbia Law School with Colin Mead, Chris's nephew."

"Carl and Norma's son?"

"Yes."

"The last time I saw him he was two years old."

"I was working at Wilson & Mead when my parents were killed, and I had to move back to Austin," Ben said. "We spent last Thanksgiving with the Meads."

"They're like our second family," Cade said.

"Chris was in this house," Stanton said. "He came with me that weekend. We stayed in one of the rooms upstairs, the one facing west."

"That's my room," Quentin said.

"What were you doing here?" Topher asked Stanton.

"It's a long story. Ben, I'm trying to tell you that Chris Mead met your mom and dad."

Ben shook his head. "That's not possible. My father would have mentioned it to me when I met Colin."

"Not necessarily. Chris didn't talk about his family while we were here. There's no reason your father would have connected him to Colin twenty years later. I don't even remember if we told him our last names."

"Would you two stop it?" Topher said. "You're not making any sense." He squeezed Stanton's hand under the table and asked him, "So, you were in love with this guy?"

"Yes. I was."

"And his name was Christopher too?"

"What do you mean, too?"

"My name is Christopher."

"What do you—?"

"Chris*topher*. I hated being called Chris when I was a kid, and then the guy from *That '70s Show* came up with Topher, so I ran with it."

"I can't believe I never put those two things together."

Under the table, Topher pulled his hand away. "Is that why you've been acting all weird this weekend? Because I remind you of a dead guy?"

"Topher," Quentin said, "you might be that dead guy."

"Excuse me? I'm not somebody else. I'm me. So what if I was born six days after he died? That's called a coincidence."

"What about the *I Ching*?" Stanton asked.

"Fuck the *I Ching*. Do you think I'm acting on someone else's feelings for you from twenty-five years ago? What's wrong with you people?"

Topher's phone vibrated furiously. He looked down at his pocket and yelled, "Shut up!"

"Topher," Ben said. "I didn't mean to—"

"I don't want to be mixed up with your feelings for somebody else. Is that what's been going on this whole time?"

"Maybe we should go," Stanton said.

But Topher had no intention of going anywhere until he got some answers. "It is, isn't it? Do I look like him?"

"No, not at all."

"Are my eyes the same?"

"No."

"Then what is it? What is it about me that makes you think this way? I want to know."

Stanton remained silent.

"Tell me!"

"Your voice," Stanton said. "It turns out the eyes are not the window to the soul. It's the voice."

"Interesting," Quentin said.

Stanton continued. "There are a lot of things, little things, that would take way too much exposition to explain. But if I close my eyes and listen to you talk or sing, especially when you sing, your voice is exactly like his." Stanton paused. "I can almost imagine he's here."

Topher stood up so quickly his chair fell over behind him. "You've been using me this whole time, so that you can pretend you're with him. What kind of an asshole does that?"

"Topher," Travis said. Ben reached out and took his hand to silence him. "Never mind. I'll keep out of it."

"I should take you back to the hotel," Topher said.

"You're right." Stanton pushed his chair back and reached out to shake Ben's hand. "Thanks for dinner, guys. I'm really sorry about this."

"No," Ben said. "It's my fault."

Topher stood silently while Stanton shook Travis's hand and said, "If I ever see you again, and I hope I do, remind me to tell you the story of Brendan and Trent."

TOPHER and Stanton left the house and drove back to the hotel. They said nothing. When Topher pulled into the driveway, a valet worker stepped up to the truck and opened Stanton's door.

"Give me a minute," Stanton said to the valet. He turned back to Topher. "I'm sorry. I thought I was doing the right thing. I wanted to get to know you without—"

Topher raised his hand and stopped him. "I asked you last night. You could have told me about this then. I trusted you, just like you asked. Too bad you didn't trust me."

"Please, I—"

"Have a nice trip back to New York. Tell Marvin thank you again for the Springsteen ticket."

"Don't do this to me. Tell me I will see you again."

Topher shook his head and looked at Stanton. He could see the pain in his eyes, but it didn't change Topher's mind. He couldn't give Stanton what he wanted. "I'm sorry," he said. "I can't tell you that right now."

Stanton remained seated for another moment, but then he stepped out of the truck. "Okay. Good luck, Topher. I hope things go well for Dime Box." He closed the door.

Topher put his truck into gear and drove away. He glanced into his rearview mirror and saw Stanton alone on the sidewalk. He didn't even try to fight the tears. When he got home, Robin, Maurice, and Peter were in the living room, watching an episode of *Breaking Bad*. They must have seen his blood-shot eyes as he walked silently down the hallway and into his bedroom, because as Topher closed the door, he heard Peter saying to the twins, "Worst thing about the 'boy meets boy' scenario? It's almost always followed by 'boy loses boy'."

Part 2:
Homesick

BOOK OF DREAMS

TOPHER stood on a beach. He looked to the left and saw two men walking toward him. He turned to the right and saw two men walking away. This wasn't Galveston. The water that trickled through the sand and reached his toes was too cold to be from the Gulf of Mexico. No, this was an ocean. Topher had recently developed the ability to figure out when he was dreaming, even while still inside the dream. It didn't strike him as anything miraculous, except that this beach reminded him of something. But he didn't recognize the two men walking toward him, and he couldn't see the faces of the two men walking away.

"Hey," he called to the back of their heads.

Then he woke up.

It was Monday morning. He would follow through on his resolve. He would go back to work and pretend the whole thing with Stanton Porter had never happened. When Peter and the twins asked him about it on Sunday, Topher had shut them down. He had no idea how to even begin that conversation, and thankfully they didn't press him.

Travis, however, was a different story. About an hour after Topher arrived at work, Travis wiped his hands and stepped into Topher's bay. "What happened after you left the house?" he asked.

"We said good night and he caught a plane back to New York yesterday. I'd say that about pretty much sums it up. Another SXSW has come and gone."

"Has he called you?"

"Yeah, but I haven't picked up."

"I know Ben told me to mind my own business, but don't you think that maybe you overreacted just a tad?"

"I don't think so. He was using me, and all because I sound like his dead boyfriend. The whole time we were together and I was babbling on, he was sitting there pretending I was some other guy."

Travis huffed. "Hogwash. He don't strike me as that kind of person. Besides, he said there were other things too. Did you at least give him a chance to explain?"

"I gave him a chance Friday night. I knew that something was going on, but he didn't want to tell me. I asked him to explain it. 'Trust me,' he said. How long was he going to wait?"

"Just what was he supposed to say? I think you might be the reincarnation of someone I was in love with twenty-five years ago? No one in their right mind would ever say that to a person they just met. So you tell me, how was he supposed to pull that rabbit out of his hat? What exactly was he supposed to say that would explain everything and not make him sound like a total nut job?"

Topher fell silent and realized Travis had a point. "I don't know."

"Yeah, neither do I. He didn't tell you because he was afraid you'd react exactly like you did, and frankly, I don't blame him one bit. Ben brought the whole thing up, and Stanton probably felt like we backed him into a corner. If you want to be mad at somebody, be mad at us."

Topher suddenly felt small. "What am I going to do?"

"The next time he calls, pick up the damn phone. Get past this. And don't toss something aside just because you don't understand it yet."

"You mean the whole reincarnation thing?"

"Yes, I mean the whole reincarnation thing. Maybe it's just a coincidence, you sounding like him, but then again, maybe it's not. I've known you for two years. I know the one thing you're afraid of is that you'll die an ordinary man. You're just like Ben. But guys like Stanton and me, we're the opposite. All we want is to be ordinary."

"Stanton is not ordinary."

"That's not what I meant. All we want is to be happy and for no one to notice us. Give me a little corner of the world with Ben and our boys and I'm good to go. But you're different. You want people to listen to you, to pay attention, so here's your chance. Wake up." Travis clapped his hands for emphasis. "Because if this is really happening to you, then that would make you the most extraordinary person I've ever met."

"You believe it's possible?"

"I don't know what I believe, but what I know is, when I met Ben it was just like you said at lunch the other day—like I was remembering something I'd forgotten. What was I remembering? What were you remembering when you kissed Stanton in the middle of 'Thunder Road'?"

Topher rubbed his forehead, and Travis's phone rang. He pulled it out of his pocket and looked down at the screen. "It's Ben. He wants to apologize to you." Travis swiped the screen and answered the call. "Hey, Hotshot."

Travis nodded and handed his iPhone to Topher, who put it to his ear and said, "Hello."

Hey, it's Ben. Sorry about Saturday night. I was a real moron.

"No, you weren't. Not at all. You did me a favor, and Travis got me looking at things from a different angle this morning."

He has a way of doing that. You should listen to him.

"Honestly, though, I didn't understand anything you and Stanton were talking about. Who are the Meads, and what do they have to do with Stanton and your parents?

I met Colin Mead my first year of law school, at Columbia. His grandfather is Joseph Mead, half of Wilson & Mead. That's where I worked after I graduated. Colin was my best friend, and I worked for his family. The firm is a very big deal.

"What does that have to do with Stanton visiting your parents?"

Joseph Mead had two sons, Carl and Chris. Carl is Colin's father. Chris died of AIDS in 1985. Stanton was his boyfriend during the last four years of his life.

"So Stanton and Chris Mead visited your parents?"

Yes and no. It was back in 1983, just before I was born. Stanton and Chris were actually visiting the guy living in the garage apartment, Brendan. But knowing my father, they probably spent a lot of time in the house. No way could my dad have resisted two visitors from New York City.

"What do you know about Chris Mead?"

Not much. Joseph doesn't talk about him. I know Chris and his father weren't on good terms when he died. That's why there's an empty chair at the table during Thanksgiving dinner. Colin said the old man has never forgiven himself.

"The old man?"

That's what we call Joseph Mead.

"Ben, I gotta run. The apology wasn't necessary, but thanks all the same. Travis is a lucky guy."

Aw, shucks. Go on. More of that, please.

"Here's Travis."

Topher handed the phone back, and Travis crossed into his bay. He liked watching Travis's face when Ben called. He even knew what that felt like now, with Stanton.

Topher went to work on an oil change for a 2009 Acura. He tried to digest all the information Ben had just thrown at him. Topher admitted to himself that maybe he had overreacted a little. Did he really believe Stanton was using him, or was that just a first response to hearing Stanton talk about someone else he had been in love with? And then there was Chris Mead. Who was this guy, and what did it mean that Topher had his voice? Did it have anything to do with the phantom vibrations coming from his cell phone all weekend? Topher realized he had more questions than answers, and he decided to pick up the phone next time Stanton called. He poured a carton of oil into the engine, and that was when it hit him. Topher stood up so quickly he banged his head on the open hood.

What if learning about Chris Mead unlocked all the songs in his head?

Ed, one of the other mechanics in the shop, called his name across the bays. "Hey, Topher, it's that guy who took you to the Springsteen concert. He's on the radio."

Topher and Travis rushed over to Ed's work bench. "Turn it up," Travis said. Ed reached over and raised the volume on the shop receiver.

—*It's* Morning Edition *from NPR News. Good morning, I'm Steve Inskeep. I'm talking to NPR music critic Stanton Porter, who returned last night from Austin, Texas and the twenty-sixth annual South by Southwest music festival. Good morning, Stanton.*

—*Good morning, Steve.*

—*So tell us, how is Austin looking these days?*

—*It's quite a scene. I'm not a big fan of festivals in general. I'm always afraid I'm not at the hot show or maybe I'm missing the buzz on something, but I went primarily to see Springsteen and hear his keynote.*

—*How was he?*

—*The concert was amazing. He still puts on a fantastic show, even at his age.*

—*At any age, don't you think?*

—*True, but he's legendary for his live performances. We already knew that. What we didn't know is that he can also give one hell of a speech.*

—*The keynote. We have that on our website, correct?*

—*Yes, you can watch it for free at npr.org/music. I urge everyone who loves pop music to give it a listen. It's an inspirational history lesson.*

—*Did you see any local bands or make any new discoveries while you were there?*

—*I did come across one local band.*

—*Tell us about that.*

—*When I heard them Friday night, they were calling themselves Judecca Rising, but I understand they've changed their name to Dime Box since then.*

—*Did you have anything to do with that, Stanton?*

—*Maybe. Dime Box is the small town near Austin where all four of the guys in the band are from. I might have suggested a name change. What do you think, Steve?*

—*I like it better than Judecca Rising.*

—*They've got a very radio-friendly sound, and the lead singer, Topher Manning, has the kind of voice that can bring an audience to its knees. They did mostly original stuff, and I would encourage our listeners to go to their website and download one track in particular.*

—*Which one is that?*

—*It's called "Beaches on the Moon." It's been getting a lot of heavy play on my iPhone. The one thing I will have to say about these festivals is you will hear performances you can't hear anywhere else, like Springsteen closing with "This Land Is Your Land," or a local band like Dime Box doing a cover of "Bridge Over Troubled Water."*

—*That's a big song to tackle.*

—*Steve, they brought the house down with it. Or roof, I should say. Austin is the kind of city where bands routinely play on the roof. Those of us lucky enough to have been there will be talking about it for years to come.*

—*Where can people download their music?*

—*I just posted a link on the NPR music blog. If you follow me on Twitter, you've probably already checked them out.*

—*I don't follow you on Twitter, Stanton.*

—*It pains me to hear that, Steve, because you would have missed out on a band like Dime Box.*

—*Do you think you'll return to SXSW next year?*

—*I'm not committing one way or the other.*

—*I see. Stanton Porter, keeping his options open. We're going to be talking to several other NPR music critics this week about SXSW, and we'll play out this segment with "Beaches on the Moon" by Dime Box. This is* Morning Edition *from NPR news. Thank you, Stanton.*

—*Thanks, Steve.*

Topher's face felt hot as he heard his voice burst through the radio, singing the chorus from "Beaches on the Moon."

"Holy shit," Travis said. "You're on national NPR radio!"

Topher's phone rang. He took it out of his pocket and flipped it open. Robin. He pushed the answer button and put the phone to his ear.

Did you know about this?

"No, I didn't know anything about it."

I got a call from the place that hosts our website. That segment aired an hour ago on the East Coast. The traffic has already crashed our site. We had five thousand downloads of "Beaches on the Moon" in one hour.

"Robin, can I call you back?"

Sure. You okay?

"Yeah, I just gotta call Stanton and apologize."

I know you told us you didn't want to talk about it, but seems like whatever he did, he's trying to make up for it.

"I got my feelings hurt, that's all. It's just… I didn't handle it very well. I got to go."

Topher ended the call and his phone rang again. He looked down. Peter. Everyone would be calling, he knew that. He sent Peter to voice mail. Then he tapped through his contacts and found Stanton's name. He stepped out of the bays and into the sunlight. He pressed the call button, and Stanton picked up after two rings.

Hey, Topher, it's good to hear from you.

"Did you say all that just to get me to call, or did you really mean it?"

A long pause.

Yes.

Stanton's answer rankled Topher at first, but then Stanton laughed and that seemed to melt the ice between them. What Stanton said on the radio was the coolest thing anyone had ever done for him, and Topher had no intention of picking a fight over it. "We got five thousand downloads of 'Beaches on the Moon' in one hour. Our website crashed."

That's great news. Well, sort of. Not the website crashing part.

"I've never heard myself on the radio before. I owe you one."

You don't owe me anything. I was only doing my job.

"I didn't know you sent out a tweet about us too."

I tweet about bands I like all the time. It's the only reason people follow me.

"But I thought you weren't coming to our show as a critic."

And I thought you said I still am who I am. I liked what I heard. I told you that.

"You liked some of what you heard."

And that's the part I talked about.

"Okay, fair enough. I'm sorry about Saturday night. Maybe I overreacted a little."

You didn't overreact, and you have nothing to apologize for. I'm mortified by my behavior. Even suggesting that you might be—Never mind. I only hope you can forgive me.

"So you don't believe it?"

No, I don't, and I'm sorry if I suggested I did. I had all day yesterday to think about it. Yes, there were a few things that reminded me of him, but really, I haven't heard his voice in twenty-five years. I got swept away. I saw what I wanted to see. It was selfish, and the worst part is, I hurt you in the process.

"I don't break, you know?"

That doesn't excuse what I did.

"So you won't tell me anything about him?"

No, I would rather not do that.

"Why not?"

Because on Saturday night, when you called me an asshole and thought I'd been using you, that was one of the saddest moments of my life. I really like you and I fucked it up. I liked talking with you about music and kissing you on the picnic table. I liked the way you crawled on top and said, "I warned you." But then I dragged him up from the past and ruined it. I'm an idiot.

"You liked talking about music with me?"

Yes, very much.

"It won't be that way next time, I promise. I want you to tell me about those other things, because one of them might unlock—"

There was nothing that can't be explained by simple coincidence. Look, let's be clear about something. I'm not sorry that I didn't tell you earlier—I'm sorry that I told you at all. It was irresponsible.

"So it's not true?"

No, it's not true. It was just my delusion.

Topher thought it over and decided he'd let it go, even though he wasn't ready to accept no as the final answer. He turned around and raised his hand to his forehead, blocking out the morning sun. Travis looked at him and signed, *Are you talking to Stanton?* Topher nodded. Travis smiled and gave him a thumbs-up.

"Okay, I'll drop it. For now. Can I come visit you?"

Topher had to wait a moment for an answer.

Why?

"What do you mean, why? Isn't it obvious?"

I talked about "Beaches on the Moon" because I think it has potential. I'm glad you called so that I could apologize. Profusely. But now that I'm back in New York, I don't see the point of pursuing this.

"Humor me."

Stanton laughed on the other end of the phone, and Topher took that as a good sign, so he pressed on.

"I'm coming to New York. If I have to, I'll call the *New York Times* and ask to speak to Marvin Goldstein. I'll say to him, 'Marvin, please, I'm coming after Stanton Porter, so can I stay with you for a week while I convince him to go out with me?' And if you think for a Texas minute that I won't actually call him up and say those things, then you got no idea who you're dealing with, Warren Beatty."

You found out who Warren Beatty is?

"I watched *Reds* yesterday. See how I'm listening even when you think I'm not? I bawled my eyes out at the end, thank you very much. I needed that like a hole in the head."

You think I'm as hot as Warren Beatty in Reds?

"You know I do."

Topher waited. After about a ten-second pause that felt more like ten minutes, Stanton finally popped the question.

Would you like to come visit me in New York?

"I thought you'd never ask."

I'm leaving for California in a few days.

"For the feature on Linkin Park?"

Yes. I'll be there for two weeks. You can come visit when I get back.

"I can't wait." Topher turned around and saw Darrell glaring at him. "I'm getting the evil eye, so I'd better get back to work. Can I call you tonight?"

Yes. You can call me anytime you want.

"I'm glad Saturday night wasn't the end for us."

Me too, Topher. I'm glad it wasn't the end.

THAT evening, the members of the band now known as Dime Box gathered in the kitchen of their house on East Eleventh Street.

"This business meeting is officially called to order," Peter said.

"What happened today?" Maurice asked. "I haven't heard the whole story yet. All I got was a text from Robin."

Peter used his NPR app to play the segment for Maurice, whose eyes bulged out when he heard the part about Topher bringing an audience to its knees. "Who is this guy?" he asked. "I thought he broke your heart."

"No," Topher said, "he didn't. It was just a road bump. I talked to him on the phone this morning. He's going to be in California for the next couple of weeks doing a feature on Linkin Park's new album, but I'm going to visit him when he gets back to New York."

"Linkin Park?" Robin and Maurice said.

"Can we get back to business?" Peter asked.

Maurice turned to Robin. "What's going on with the website? Your text said it crashed."

"They got it back up, but not until this afternoon."

"It was a huge missed opportunity," Peter said.

"Don't you think I know that?" Robin barked.

"You're the one who was in charge of the website," Peter barked back. "Who knows how many downloads we would have gotten if—?"

"It's not like we had any extra money to spend, dickwad. We got what we paid for."

"Calm down," Topher said. "Let's face it. Up until today we've been strictly bush league."

"So what do we do now?" Maurice said.

"I don't know. I guess I thought that if I wrote music and we played our gigs, then eventually someone would come along and offer us a record deal. Isn't that how it's supposed to work?"

"How in the fuck am I supposed to know?"

"Chill," Robin said.

Topher heard the next-door neighbor's dog barking up a storm. Then Peter asked, "What about Stanton Porter?"

Topher glared across the table. "What about him?"

"He started all this. Don't you think he could give us some advice?"

Topher balked at the suggestion. He remembered how prickly Stanton got when he asked him for advice the first day they met. "I don't think that's a good idea."

"Why not?" Robin asked.

"Because I'm trying to get him to date me, not be our manager."

"That's bullshit," Peter said. "He told you he wasn't coming to our gig as a critic, and then he goes and does something like this?"

Topher raised his hands. "What do you mean, something like this?"

"Did he even tell you he was going to say those things?"

Topher bowed his head. "He probably would have if I hadn't ignored his calls."

"We're not ready for this," Peter said with a huff. "He put the spotlight on us too soon."

Robin raised an eyebrow. "Too soon? Seriously?"

"We've been doing this since high school," Maurice said. "We're twenty-seven years old. If this is going to happen, it needed to happen yesterday."

"I know that," Peter said. "I'm sorry. It just seems like it wouldn't hurt to ask him if he could give us some advice."

Topher couldn't stomach disappointing his friends, so he caved. "Okay. I'll see if he's free to talk."

"Tell him to call me," Peter said. "I can put him on speaker. You have that crappy phone."

Topher took out his phone and found Stanton's name. He punched a button and waited for Stanton to pick up, which he did after the first ring.

Hey, Topher. Did I tell you that I'm using "Beaches on the Moon" as your ringtone?

Topher grinned and said, "That's sweet. I'm here with the boys. They want to talk to you."

Am I in trouble?

"No. They want to ask your advice."

Silence.

Don't ask me to do this. I want them to like me.

"Why do you think they wouldn't like you?"

Because I've had these conversations before, and I always come off like a bully. I don't sugarcoat things. You know that firsthand.

"Hold on a sec." Topher put his hand over the mouthpiece. "If he talks to us, you can't take it personally, no matter how harsh it gets. You understand? Like Maurice said, it's his job to be an asshole. He's not going to treat us like schoolboys or worry about hurting our feelings."

"We got it," Peter said. "I think we'd all welcome someone talking to us like adults for a change. Right, kids?"

The twins nodded enthusiastically, and Topher returned to the phone. "They understand how it's going to go. I promise they won't hold anything against you."

Okay, but I warned you.

"I understand that, and I take full responsibility for whatever happens. Can you call Peter's number so we can put you on speaker?"

Does he have an iPhone?

"Yeah. Here's the number."

Hold on, let me get a pen.

Topher read out the numbers and then hung up his phone. A few seconds later, Peter's began to vibrate and he swiped the screen to answer the call. He pushed the speaker icon and brought Stanton into the room.

"Hey, Stanton, it's Topher. You there?"

I'm here.

"I know this is an awkward way to meet the band, but let me introduce you to Peter, Robin, and Maurice. Boys, this is Stanton Porter, the music critic."

"Hey, Stanton," they all said.

Hello.

"Where do you want to start?" Topher asked Peter.

"Stanton, this is Peter Moses. I feel like you created an opportunity for us—which we are really grateful for, don't get me wrong—but I'm not quite sure how to capitalize on it."

Another silence.

"Stanton?" Topher said quietly.

I don't know where to begin.

"Stanton, this is Robin Ackerman. I just want to say thank you. Frankly, no one's ever noticed us before, so you've earned the right to say whatever the hell you want. We've been through a lot of shit in our lives. We all have thick skin."

Topher relaxed, because he knew that Robin giving Stanton permission to be himself was the smartest thing any of them could have done.

Okay....

Topher whispered, "Here we go."

Why in the fuck are you giving your music away for free? I handed you five thousand customers and you failed to monetize that? And what was up with the CD giveaway at your gig Friday night?

"We thought it was a good way to promote ourselves," Robin said.

To who? My father? I defy you to find one teenager in Austin who owns a CD player. I don't even have an optical drive in my laptop anymore. How much did those CDs cost you?

"Three hundred bucks."

That was Peter again, right?

"Yeah."

I thought so. Peter, the next time you want to piss away $300, give it to me instead. I can make better use of it, because that's what you did. You flushed it down the toilet. You're acting like it's 1995 and the only way to launch a music career is with a record deal. The smart musicians are not waiting for that anymore. Haven't you ever heard of social media?

"Stanton, this is Maurice Ackerman. We'll be the first to admit we're not all that tech savvy."

Maurice, how tech savvy do you have to be to Google, "How do I get my music on iTunes?" Do you have any idea how easy it is? Not to mention how lucrative?

Stanton paused, and Topher noticed the next-door neighbor's dog had stopped barking.

Okay, I'm going to take a deep breath now. It's important to understand the mistakes you've made in the past if you're going to lay out a road map for the future. Is everyone still on board? Anyone hate me yet?

"We're good," Robin said. "And I'm authorized to speak for all of us."

Good. So, obviously, what's the first order of business?

Topher knew the answer. "Get 'Beaches on the Moon' on iTunes and Amazon."

Yes. You'll need to sign up with an aggregator. You pay them a fee and you retain all the rights. They deal with Apple and everyone else directly. The two that everybody uses are TuneCore and CDBaby. Look over their terms and pick the one that's best for you. Next, and I can't stress this enough, go mobile. All four of you should be on Twitter, but not to promote yourselves. Promote what you love. Become part of the conversation. Upgrade and redesign your website, but more importantly, hire someone to build you a phone app, because that's where people live these days. Your whole purpose in life should be to get your music onto people's phones. But make them pay for it. To do that, you need content. Fans want to see you, and even though MTV abandoned the M long ago, kids still watch videos on their phones. You need to make one for "Beaches on the Moon," post it on YouTube, and then e-mail the link to every music blog you can find.

"Isn't a video going to be expensive?" Robin asked.

Yes.

"We don't have any money," Topher said.

If you don't do this now, Dime Box will go cold and the moment will pass. I would give you the money, but I know Topher would never agree to that.

"You're damn right I wouldn't."

Robin looked at him. "Come on...."

"We are not taking money from Stanton. Period."

"I can ask my parents," Peter said. "How much are we talking?"

About $10,000. You have a huge student population there with an entire crop of budding filmmakers. One of them is going to love making a music video for you. Ask people to work for cheap and then remember to reward them later.

"I think they could swing ten Gs," Peter said.

I'll talk to them on the phone if you think it would help.

"You would do that?" Peter asked.

Yes, as long as you three convince Topher to let me pay for his plane ticket to New York. I want him spending his money elsewhere.

Topher instantly objected. "Now, let's hold on one second—"

"Done," Robin said with a glare of finality in Topher's direction. "I'll take care of that."

Topher threw up his hands in resignation.

Excellent. Now that the harsh part is out of the way, here comes the good stuff. I'm a fan, guys. You have a very tight sound. You look great together. The set of identical twins doesn't hurt. And you have a lead singer with one of the most unique voices I've ever heard. Your weakness is the material. You have one great song and the rest....

"Pedestrian," Maurice said.

At best. Topher, I'm afraid it's all on you. Given the buzz from this morning, I believe you can launch Dime Box using "Beaches on the Moon." It's that good, but you're going to have to follow it up eventually. If you can't top it, then you should consider other songwriters.

"No," Maurice said. "The whole point of this was to play Topher's songs."

Sometimes all you get is the voice, Maurice. Art Garfunkel could never have written "Bridge Over Troubled Water," but Paul Simon couldn't have sung it, either. If Topher's voice goes to waste because you insist on clinging to mediocre material, then I will consider that the equivalent of a musical crime.

"So that's it?" Topher asked. "We put the song on iTunes, make a video, and hope it goes viral?"

I have other ideas, but that's enough to get started and keep you busy for the next month. You can't really monetize the video, but the video will drive the digital sales. By staying independent, you actually make more money from your iTunes sales than an artist with a label. You can pocket up to sixty-nine cents a download. Does anyone have a calculator handy? That means you need to sell fifteen thousand downloads to pay Peter's parents back. You had one-third of that this morning. Do you see now why I'm a little hot under the collar?

Topher had no idea they could have been making that kind of money.

"I get it," Peter said. "But how many of those five thousand people who downloaded it for free would have paid for it?"

We'll never know that, Peter, now will we?

"Yeah, yeah, okay. We were idiots."

You were green, so consider this your wake-up call. People know your name now, guys. Follow your instinct to capitalize on that.

"What other ideas?" Maurice asked. "You said you had other ideas for things we could do."

There are ways to reach millions of people at once. FUN. didn't break out into the mainstream until Glee *used one of their songs. It's too late for this season, but—*

Robin scoffed at the suggestion. "How in the hell do you expect us to get the people at *Glee* to listen to our music?"

You forget who I am, Robin.

That pretty much struck the boys speechless. After a moment, Topher asked, "You're going to help us?"

If you'll let me. I have ten thousand followers on Twitter, and at least a thousand of those are in the industry. It's my job to promote bands I like. I'm not saying Glee *will use it, but it's right up their alley, and I can certainly get someone to listen to it. Same situation with* So You Think You Can Dance. *I went to college with one of the musical directors. "Beaches on the Moon" would be fantastic for one of the group numbers that open the show, and that's coming up this summer. If you can combine either one of those with putting a song in the top ten on iTunes, then* Saturday Night Live *will come calling next season.*

"This is surreal," Peter said.

"This is still a dream," Topher reminded them.

There is one more thing you can be working on right now.

"What's that?" Robin asked.

Go back to Dime Box and play a concert. Start planning it now. Get a thousand people to show up. Turn the town into a parking lot. Film the concert, project it onto giant screens, and then post the whole thing on YouTube. Is there any kind of distinctive landmark or visual in the town?

"There's a water tower," Peter said.

Does it say Dime Box on it?

"Yeah."

Boys, that's your first album cover right there.

LUCKY TOWN

STANTON sat silently next to Marvin and stared down at his hands. It had already been four days, with three left to go. They were sitting shivah for Marvin's father, who had been diagnosed with brain cancer their senior year at NYU. Stanton looked across the Goldstein living room at his boyfriend. Hutch frowned and glanced over at Robert, Michael, and Paul. All three of them were having difficulty sitting still in their dark suits and skinny ties. They had visited Marvin and his mother each of the four days, but an hour was about all they could handle.

Three of Marvin's cousins sat with them. With Mrs. Goldstein's permission, one of the relatives began to tell a story about Mr. Goldstein, and that naturally put Stanton in a reflective mood.

He sat up straight in his chair and thought about everything the six of them had been through since they met on that July night fifteen months earlier. Stanton smiled as he remembered that weekend with Hutch, the Greatest Game, and sex on the New Jersey Transit. Stanton and Marvin had made the trip to Fire Island every weekend for the rest of that summer. The six men spent their days at the beach and their nights cooking and listening to music. Marvin and Paul would drink wine and talk for hours next to the pool, but in public, when they went dancing at the Pavilion, or to tea at the Blue Whale, it was Robert and Michael who took Marvin under their wing and introduced him to all the popular men.

Stanton remembered how he'd focused his own attention on Hutch during those months. Their courtship had been the stuff of island gossip and envious stares. They took a walk on the beach every day after Hutch got off work, and stayed up every night making love on the rooftop deck. Hutch would wrap them in a blanket just before the sun rose, and Stanton would fall asleep that way, nestled in his boyfriend's arms. Somehow, he always woke up around noon in their bed, and he figured Hutch must have carried him there every morning. They usually fucked before lunch, and even then, Stanton always craved more.

"Whenever you want a blow job," Hutch said repeatedly, "all you have to do is blow me a kiss, and I'll know what that means. I take my responsibilities as a boyfriend very seriously."

When that first summer ended, the center of their lives shifted back to Manhattan. Marvin tacked pictures of their new friends on their wall in Brittany, one of the NYU dorms for upperclassmen. Marvin had taken dozens of photos of Hutch, Robert, Michael, and Paul, dressed in drag for a house party (Stanton had adamantly refused to participate), or standing on the beach with their backs to the ocean. In one of the beach shots Stanton took, he remembered Hutch had blown him a kiss instead of saying cheese.

As he continued listening to the cousin's story about Mr. Goldstein, Stanton couldn't help but feel nostalgic about their idyllic junior year. He and Marvin had spent most of their time at Michael's apartment in the West Village, or Paul's on St. Marks Place. The six of them also met for dinner at restaurants like The Empire Diner, Kiev, Ray's Pizza, Cafe Figaro, or Gene's Patio. Hutch insisted they stop for dessert at Rumbles at least once a week.

Stanton thought about the first time the six of them took the train to Queens. It had been Robert's idea to meet Marvin's parents. So, one Sunday afternoon, they dressed up and made the trek to Astoria, and after that it became a weekly ritual. Mrs. Goldstein served the boys lavish meals and tried out different recipes from Julia Child's PBS cooking show. She discussed the latest Broadway musicals with Paul and her son, that being the year of both *Dreamgirls* and *Nine*. Robert and Michael talked about jazz with Mr. Goldstein. Hutch could jump into either conversation and Stanton into neither, but he didn't mind. It was enough to see Marvin so happy.

At the end of each Sunday, as they were about to leave for the train back to Manhattan, Robert, Hutch, Michael, Paul, Marvin, and Stanton would quietly ascend the stairs to Marvin's boyhood room. There, they would close the door and smoke a joint, an enhancement that made the return trip decidedly more entertaining. Mr. and Mrs. Goldstein, who conveniently looked the other way, often sent the boys back to the city with sincere hugs and a bag of chips.

On these subway rides home, Robert would inevitably launch a discussion about the current state of music in America. Each week, he would announce a different topic, like "New Wave and the theoretical justifications for why we hate it" or "The rise of MTV and the fall of the singer/songwriter." Marvin called these the Stoned Subway Seminars. The discussions usually covered a spectrum too wide for Stanton to follow, but he always made an effort, asked questions, and learned from this remarkable band of friends he had somehow stumbled into.

They managed to get tickets to just about every major musical event in the city. They went to the Simon & Garfunkel reunion concert in Central Park. They saw the Go-Go's at the Palladium and the Police at Madison Square Garden. They went to the opera and the symphony, and even saw a woman play Hamlet at the Public Theater. Stanton knew he would always think of his junior year as the time when his life truly began.

As he sat in Marvin's living room, Stanton thought about the summer that had just ended. At Hutch's suggestion, he worked as a bartender at the Blue Whale, and even though he hated the job, it meant another summer on the island with his boyfriend. Marvin got an internship at the *New Yorker*, but had still been able to join them almost every weekend.

The Goldsteins' front door opened, and Stanton snapped out of his daydream. A frigid October wind blew across the wood floors. The rabbi from Marvin's synagogue stepped into the house, followed by several elderly women. Hutch and his friends rose and gave up their seats. Paul looked at Stanton and nodded upward, a gesture that meant they were going upstairs to Marvin's room.

Stanton looked at Marvin, who silently gave him permission to follow the boys. The five men quietly ascended the steps and filed into Marvin's small room. Robert, Michael, and Paul piled onto the twin bed. Hutch sat on the desk chair, and Stanton took a seat on his lap. Paul opened the window, and Michael pulled a joint out of his blazer pocket.

"Winter's almost here," Robert said.

Michael handed the joint and his antique gold lighter to Paul, who lit the blunt and passed it back to Michael.

"All this death makes me mental," Paul said.

"Did you hear about John Monroe?" Michael asked.

Robert took the joint from Michael, saying, "No, I haven't seen him at the gym in weeks."

"That's because he's dead. His funeral was last weekend. They're calling it AIDS now."

"What does that stand for?" Stanton asked as he accepted the joint from Robert and took a hit.

"Who knows?" Michael said. "We're in a high-risk group with Haitians, can you believe it? I heard a joke the other night at Uncle Charlie's."

"Must we?" Robert pleaded.

"What's the hardest part about telling your parents you have AIDS?" Michael said, ignoring him.

"What?" Stanton asked. He held the joint up to Hutch's lips so he could take a puff.

"Don't encourage him," Hutch squeaked, holding the smoke in.

"Trying to convince them you're Haitian."

The more Stanton thought about that joke, the funnier it got.

"Well," Paul said, "I've stopped sleeping around."

"Like that's going to make a difference," Robert said.

"Why wouldn't it?" Hutch asked.

"Because it's a disease," Robert said. "Eventually they're going to discover it has a cause and an incubation period. It's probably a virus or a new strain of bacteria, which means you get it from someone who's already infected. You don't get it from being a slut."

"But doesn't being a slut increase your chances?" Stanton asked.

"Any one of us could have it," Robert continued. "It could be years before we find out. Some people will have slept with a thousand guys and some people will have slept with one. Don't turn this into a moral argument against sexual pluralism."

"That's not what I was doing," Paul said. "I was simply stating that right now getting laid is not worth dying for."

Robert shook his head. "I don't want to live in a world where I can't get laid."

"Can we talk about something else?" Hutch asked.

"Please," Stanton said.

The door opened and Marvin walked in. "Hey, guys."

"Get in here and close the door," Robert said. Michael reached out and pulled Marvin onto the bed.

"How are you doing, buddy?" Stanton asked.

"My ass is sore," Marvin kvetched as he nestled into his comfort zone between Robert and Michael. "I'm sick and tired of sitting."

"Are you allowed to be up here?" Hutch said.

"I don't care. I need a break. Somehow I think God will forgive me."

Stanton held out what remained of the joint to Marvin. "Want some?"

Marvin looked at him with suspicion. "Sitting shivah stoned?"

"You're a very high-functioning pothead," Paul said.

"And everyone will assume your red eyes are from crying," Michael said. "It's the perfect cover."

Marvin paused, but then accepted the joint and took a hit.

"What's going to happen to your mom now?" Paul asked. Marvin handed the roach to him, and Paul put it out on the windowsill.

"She'll join the widow's club at the synagogue and start begging me for grandchildren," Marvin said. "She believes gay people will be allowed to get married and adopt someday, so she wants me to have a boyfriend lined up and ready to go."

Paul slapped his knee and rolled his head back in laughter. "Your mother is a trip sometimes."

"That's what I said. We still have sodomy laws to get rid of, I told her."

"When are you going to break the news that you're into black guys?" Michael said.

"As soon as I meet one. Until then, I'll allow her to have her fantasy of me falling in love with a nice Jewish boy, preferably a doctor, of course, and us moving in across the street."

"There are black Jews," Michael said.

"And black doctors," Robert added. Then he looked at Michael, and together they said, "But I bet there aren't any black Jewish doctors!"

Marvin started laughing a stoned laugh, and Stanton could tell they would have to wait a few minutes before heading downstairs.

"I think it's possible," Hutch said. "Gay marriage, I mean."

"Are you kidding?" Stanton asked. "You need to get out of Manhattan more. We will never see gay marriage in our lifetime. West of the Hudson River, the world is a different place. None of you realize that."

"Why would gay men want to get married anyway?" Robert said. "That is an institution created and run by women."

"No one expects you to believe in settling down," Michael said.

"I feel very settled. Do I wish you would have sex with me again? Sure, but I understand why you won't. Other than that, look around us, boys. This is what it's all about. The six of us."

"Speaking of the six of us," Paul said to Robert, "did you get our tickets to *Torch Song Trilogy* yet? It opened in June, for Christ's sake. I feel like we're the only proper homosexuals in Manhattan who haven't seen it."

"I got them," Robert said, "so you can stop your bitching, Janet."

Stanton felt a hand poking his shoulder.

"It's almost five," Hutch said. "We need to head back into the city if we're going to make it to my parents' place by eight. We have to shower and change first."

"You're meeting the family tonight?" Robert asked Stanton.

Stanton nodded. "Yes. Any advice?"

"Nothing can prepare you for Joseph Mead," Michael said. "Even my father isn't that bad."

"Don't listen to him," Hutch said as he squeezed Stanton. "I will be right by your side, and afterward you can fuck me until my ass is sore. How does that sound?"

Stanton thought it over. "That sounds like a fair trade. It would be even better, though, if you threw in a trip to the Saint this weekend."

Only Hutch, Robert, and Michael were members of the nightclub, but Paul, Stanton, and Marvin could go as guests.

"Twist my arm," Hutch said. "Why don't we all go? Is it too soon for you, Marvin?"

"No. The whole point of sitting shivah is to get it out of your system and then move on. We should definitely go dancing."

"Excellent," Stanton said as he kissed Hutch. "Just don't forget that I have no pretense to sophistication, so if I embarrass you in front of your family, you were given fair warning. Your boyfriend is a hick."

"At least he's honest," Robert said to Hutch.

"It's bullshit," Hutch said. "His father has a college degree and a white-collar job. He's hardly Jethro Clampett."

"Maybe not," Stanton said. "But that doesn't mean I'm prepared for what's in store tonight. And his name was Jethro Bodine."

THREE hours later, when Stanton and Hutch arrived at the Mead residence on Fifth Avenue, overlooking Central Park, they exited a private elevator and a maid greeted them.

"Hello, Anita," Hutch said. He took his coat off and handed it to her. Stanton did the same. "This is my boyfriend, Stanton."

Anita nodded and disappeared down the hallway to Stanton's left. Ahead of him, the room opened up into a massive living space with a floor-to-ceiling view of the park.

"Jesus Christ, preppy. Nothing you said prepared me for this."

A man in his fifties, who Stanton assumed must be Hutch's father, entered from the hallway on the other side of the room.

"Chris," he said.

"Hi, Dad. This is Stanton. This is my father, Joseph Mead."

Mr. Mead shook Stanton's hand but did not speak to him. He turned to Hutch and said, "I just got off the phone with your grandfather. There's an opportunity up in Newport. I told him to call you."

"Dad, you know I'm not—"

"Would it kill you to listen to him, son?"

Stanton watched as his boyfriend shrank in his father's presence, a feeling he understood all too well.

"No, it wouldn't kill me. I'll call him next week."

Mr. Mead slapped his son on the back. He led him out of the room and down another hallway, leaving Stanton behind. Hutch glanced over his shoulder and silently pleaded for forgiveness. Stanton didn't know if he should follow or wait, but soon it was a moot point, because Hutch and his father disappeared around the corner. Stanton turned toward the windows and welcomed the chance to catch his breath. Maybe they would forget about him and he could stay here, all by himself. The trees in the park screamed their brilliant autumn colors. Then a light over the elevator went off and a buzzer sounded. Anita appeared from the first hallway and froze when she saw Stanton alone in the room.

"Don't worry," he said. "I'm not going to swipe a candlestick or anything."

The elevator doors opened and a woman stepped out. She looked to be in her late twenties, with beautiful brown hair and eyes. She wore a smart and stylish outfit that was tasteful without being extravagant. She smiled when she saw Stanton.

"Are you Chris's boyfriend?" she asked.

"Yes. I'm Stanton Porter."

A man followed her off the elevator. He removed her coat and handed it to Anita. "What are you doing in here alone?" the man asked.

Stanton hesitated at first, but then said, "I don't know. His father came in, and then they just… left."

The woman shook her head. "Good Lord. That man has no manners whatsoever."

"Norma, please…."

The woman stepped into the room and introduced herself. "I'm Norma Mead. This is my husband Carl, Chris's older brother."

"It's nice to meet you both," Stanton said as he shook their hands.

"I'm sure they're in the study," Carl said to Norma. "I'm going to go rescue Chris." He kissed his wife on the cheek and exited down the second hallway.

"Come here," Norma said to Stanton, "let's take a load off before we face the firing squad." She crossed to one of the white sofas, sat down, and then patted the seat next to her.

"Thank you," Stanton said as he joined her.

"Don't take it personally."

"What do you mean?"

"He's like that to everyone."

"You mean their father?"

"Yes. He's not a monster, but you wouldn't know it by the way he acts sometimes. If you're going to survive in this family, you'll learn to laugh it off, like I do. Carl and I have been married for two years, and the ice is only now beginning to thaw. And I said thaw, mind you, not melt."

"Why? Look at you, you're perfect. What problem could he possibly have with you?"

"I like you already, but I'm common."

Stanton chuckled. "What is this, England?"

"No, but it's the Upper East Side, which is pretty much the same thing."

"Well, I was just telling Hutch this afternoon that I'm pretty common myself, so maybe we can keep each other company at family gatherings."

Norma reached out and grabbed his hand. "I would like that very much. Now, the good news is, I'm going to take the pressure off you tonight."

"How do you plan to do that?"

"By announcing that I'm pregnant."

"Wow, congratulations."

"Thank you."

"No, thank *you*," Stanton said. "This is going to be great. We can ignore the whole 'gay son and his boyfriend' business. What's their mother like, by the way?"

Norma gasped. "Wait until you meet her. She's like Nancy Reagan, only less animated."

THAT night, after a round of intense fucking lasting well over an hour, Stanton and Hutch lay intertwined on the bed. Stanton spent at least half his nights here, at Michael's apartment, and liked that it was just a short walk from his dorm. Hutch had his own room, Michael and Robert slept in the master bedroom, and the third room sat empty.

"Such a weird day," Stanton said.

"I know."

"It makes you wonder, doesn't it? Marvin's dad is gone, and your dad... never mind. How would you feel about moving in together when I graduate next year?"

"Where did that come from?"

"You don't like the idea?"

"I love the idea. Except...."

"Except what?"

"You have to tell your parents first. I'm not living with a closet case. You know that."

"I'm not—"

"You are. You've come a long way, and I love you for that, but you have to take the final step. I'm not hiding you from my family."

Stanton pulled away. "You're going to hold up your family as an example of why I should come out to my parents? Your father pretended I wasn't even in the room tonight, and your mother—"

"Be careful. Don't go there."

"Sorry." Stanton paused and took a breath. "I'll tell them after I graduate. I promise."

"You do realize I can never take this relationship seriously until you do, right?"

"Yes, I realize that. It's just... I'm not ready for the fallout. It's going to be bad."

"You don't know that."

"Yeah, I kind of do. Maybe someday, in like twenty years, things will be different, but at first, it's going to kill them. Especially my father."

"They'll love me once they get to know me."

"You don't get it. They'll never let me bring you home. I don't know if you'll ever meet them. I don't even know if I'll be welcome after I tell them."

"Are you serious?"

"Yes. As uncomfortable as I was tonight, at least your dad let me through the door—or the elevator. We will not be welcome in my father's house. I'm certain of that."

"Oh. I didn't know it would be that bad."

"It will be. So can you just give me a few more months? I promise I will give you a reason to take this relationship seriously."

Hutch pulled him close. "It's a big responsibility being the love of your life, Starsky. Do you know how hard it is to say no to you?"

Hutch wrapped himself around Stanton, who lay on his back and stared up at the ceiling. He watched the shadows play across the white plaster canvas.

"What's your favorite Beatles song?" Hutch asked.

"You know what it is."

"Say it."

"I Want to Hold Your Hand."

"Okay, if you insist." Hutch reached out and took Stanton's hand into his own. Stanton turned onto his side and faced him. "I'm sorry I left you alone tonight," Hutch said. "When we got there, I mean."

"It's okay. I liked talking to Norma."

"My brother really liked you too. And my father will come around. Give him time."

"You're too good for me," Stanton said.

Hutch shook his head.

"You know it's true."

"I don't know anything of the sort."

"I love you, Hutch."

"I love you too, Starsky. We need to think of something really groovy for Marvin and his mom, when they're finished sitting."

"We should bring her into the city and cook them dinner."

"Thanksgiving! We'll have them here for Thanksgiving, so she won't have to think about it at all. They can just show up. It'll be perfect, because it's the one holiday we all share. We have a lot to be thankful for this year."

"What about your father's Thanksgiving? At the St. Regis? This was supposed to be my first one."

"We'll skip it this year. We should spend this Thanksgiving together, as a family."

"What's going on?"

Hutch fell silent for a moment, and then he said, "He told me I couldn't bring you."

"What?"

"He doesn't want to deal with my grandparents."

"I guess our fathers are cut from the same cloth after all."

"I told him I wouldn't be there."

"You shouldn't do that."

"Yes, I should. At some point that's exactly what we need to do. Nothing is going to change if we keep going to Thanksgiving dinner and leaving our lovers behind."

Stanton smiled. "Okay. We'll start our own traditions, then. Now, can I ask you a favor?"

"What?"

"It's been a rough day. Will you sing me a song? Your voice always makes me feel—"

"You don't have to explain. What do you want to hear?"

Stanton had been thinking about it all day. "Do you know what song was released the year I was born?"

"What?"

"Can't Help Falling In Love."

"You want me to sing Elvis? I don't know. My voice never fit with his music."

"It's one of the greatest love songs of all time."

"Okay, okay. I'll give it a shot. For you. This should be interesting, though. Let me get in the mood."

Stanton closed his eyes as Hutch began to sing about wise men and fools. He liked to believe Hutch loved him that way. He liked to believe, like the song, that Hutch's love was inevitable.

IN EARLY November, Stanton, Marvin, and Hutch resumed their Saturday morning breakfasts, which had been put on hiatus during Mr. Goldstein's illness. They met at Sandalino's on Barrow Street, a warm and inviting cafe with slender, swinging doors and no sign above the door, speakeasy style. In Stanton's opinion, Sandalino's had the best waffles in the Village. On one particular Saturday, Marvin and Hutch began arguing violently about a piece of music, while Stanton ate quietly and absorbed as much as he could.

"What do you mean when you say '4'33"' is a joke?" Hutch asked. "Are you being serious or just playing devil's advocate?"

"I'm being serious," Marvin said. "I am not going to devote my entire life to music, only to be told that four minutes and thirty-three seconds of silence qualifies as a composition. You're a songwriter. You should be insulted."

Stanton raised his hand, which signaled that he required a footnote.

"It's your turn," Marvin said.

Hutch turned to his boyfriend and explained. "Okay, '4'33"' is a composition by John Cage. It consists entirely of durations, during which the musician is supposed to sit on stage and not play his instrument. It is not, as Marvin contends, four minutes and thirty-three seconds of silence. It is four minutes and thirty-three seconds of the ambient sound in the room. It is a brilliant articulation of the most important question in our lives."

Stanton nodded. "What is music?"

"Exactly. We spend our whole lives making and singing and talking about and dissecting music, but we almost never attempt to define it or ask what distinguishes it from noise or even silence. Is music defined by its content or by the response of an audience to it?"

"Like the tree falling in the forest?" Stanton said.

"Yes, that's a fair question. Does music exist if no one is listening? But Cage is actually interested in a more complex question. If we remove the content, can the response alone be considered music? Can you write a song during which the musician doesn't play his instrument? Turns out, you can. Will a sophisticated symphony audience sit and listen to four minutes and thirty-three seconds of nothing? Turns out, they will."

"That doesn't make it music," Marvin said.

"Then what does? If you want to talk about a joke, let's talk about your notion of authorship. You think a composer writes a song and then somehow controls it. You think music is fixable, like pinning fog to the side of a building."

"Of course music is fixable," Marvin said. "That is why man invented things like scales and notes. I'm not going to abandon common sense in order to appease your postmodern sensibility. We can all listen to Toni Basil's 'Mickey' and say, 'That's Toni Basil's 'Mickey',' even if someone else sings it. And I only use that as an example because Stanton will not stop listening to it."

"Hey," Stanton said in his own defense, "that's a slice of pure pop heaven."

"So," Hutch said, "if I start to change the lyrics and alter the melody, when is it no longer Toni Basil's 'Mickey'?"

"They did," Stanton said.

"What do you mean, they did?" Marvin asked.

"The song used to be called 'Kitty'. It was about a girl and they changed the name for Toni Basil, so that it would be about a guy. But the same songwriters got credit."

"See," Marvin said to Hutch. "Common sense."

Stanton decided to jump into the fray. "I see both sides. Come on, Hutch. Four minutes and thirty-three seconds of nothing? Does he get royalties for that? On the other hand, Marvin, the idea that composers can control what other people do with their music is absurd. I'm sure Beethoven didn't anticipate a disco version of the Fifth Symphony, but there it is on the *Saturday Night Fever* soundtrack, plain as day. And it seems to me that silence is the thing that makes music possible. It's like what darkness is to the light. So clearly this John Cage guy isn't trying to pull an 'Emperor Wears No Clothes'."

Marvin shook his head in frustration. "You of all people must understand my point. Don't you see how pretentious this is? Paying twenty-five dollars so that you can watch someone not play the piano?"

"I said I see both sides. It's kind of ridiculous, I admit, but it's also one of the things you admire most."

Hutch pointed at Marvin from across the table. "Blasphemy! That's exactly what it is."

"Damn," Marvin said. "You know if you sell it to me as blasphemy, I won't be able to resist. But it doesn't change my argument. Cage is asking important questions, I concede that, but they are questions better explored in the realm of theory and criticism. There is no need to make a mockery out of the very thing you're trying to understand."

"So the fundamental questions are off-limits to artists?" Hutch asked.

"I did not say that. All I'm saying is, if you want to write a song about the nature and definition of music—and really, how boring would that be?—then write a song. But don't piss on my head and tell me it's raining. That's what Cage is doing here, and even he agrees with me. He's all but disowned the piece."

"He hasn't disowned it."

"Enough," Stanton said. "Let's talk about something else."

"He doesn't like to argue the way we do," Marvin said.

"I know." Hutch put his arm around Stanton. "It's fun, Starsky. And you did great when you jumped in there."

"I'm getting used to it," Stanton said. "But I still don't know enough to keep up with you two."

"You know things we don't," Marvin said with a wave of his hand.

"Yeah, right. I know trivia about one-hit wonders."

"And there's no reason you can't spin that into a career," Marvin said. "We've had this conversation a thousand times. You have the musical sensibility of a thirteen-year-old girl."

Stanton brimmed with anger. "Do you hear how he talks to me?" he asked Hutch, who was having a hard time suppressing his laughter.

"Stanton," Marvin said, "who do you think buys music? I didn't say you had the *intellect* of a thirteen-year-old girl. You're smart; I know that. I think you could bring a unique voice to music journalism, if only you would filter your sensibility through a critical lens."

"Why can't my sensibility *be* my critical lens?"

"Because it doesn't work that way."

"Says you. The idea that best and favorite aren't the same thing is just you two fooling yourselves."

"You're sounding remarkably like John Cage," Hutch said.

"You know I love you," Marvin said to Stanton. "Don't take this personally, or we'll stop talking about music around you."

"When you call me a thirteen-year-old girl, it's hard not to take it personally."

"I'm sorry. I will try to refrain from those comparisons in the future."

"Don't you dare. If you start sugarcoating things, I'll never get anywhere."

"Make up your mind," Marvin said. Then he turned to Hutch in a huff and asked, "What are we going to do with him?"

"I don't know. He's too adorable to return to the pound."

Stanton elbowed his boyfriend in the ribs. He secretly enjoyed it when they teased him this way, which they both knew.

Sitting with Marvin and Hutch at their regular table inside Sandalino's, Stanton couldn't help but wonder what the future might hold. He'd never had ambitions to greatness, but he could see glimmers of it in Hutch and Marvin. This neighborhood had been the stomping grounds of Allen Ginsberg and Jack Kerouac, so Stanton figured anything was possible.

He lifted his glass of orange juice and said, "I would like to propose a toast." Marvin and Hutch raised their glasses. "Here's to the comforting fact that the road ahead is longer than the road behind."

"Hear, hear," Marvin said. "To the future. May we burn bright or not at all."

Hutch grinned at Stanton. "The sky is the limit."

LIVING PROOF

"IF YOU get on the subway by yourself," Travis said as he drove Topher to the airport, "make sure you know if you're going uptown or downtown. I made that mistake and paid for it dearly, my friend. Are you nervous?"

"I am when you keep asking me that," Topher said.

"Sorry, Mr. Famous Rock Star."

"I am not a famous—"

"One hundred thousand hits on YouTube—"

"Is a drop in the bucket. Practically nothing these days."

"So you're not nervous?"

Topher thought it over and then said, "I'm more excited than nervous. I can't believe it's taken so long for this trip to finally happen."

Five weeks had passed since he and Stanton met at SXSW. He looked out the window at the bluebonnets along the highway and thought about everything that had happened since that fateful weekend in March. During those five weeks, the men of Dime Box had worked the longest hours of their lives, averaging as little as four hours of sleep a night. They followed Stanton's advice and hired a young filmmaker Maurice had gone to UT with. His name was Kai Jackson. Kai's concept was to showcase Austin by shooting at iconic sites around the city. The boys liked the idea, but they'd had no idea it would mean such long hours.

Topher looked over at Travis, who was driving with the window down and singing some Rascal Flatts. When Travis had heard about the music video, he suggested they hire Jason's boyfriend Jake as an assistant director. Topher remembered him saying, "All that boy ever talks about is going to Hollywood and making movies. It would be the thrill of his life, not to mention he's your target demo. He can bring some good ideas to the table, I bet."

They ended up hiring Jake, Jason, Quentin, and several of their friends to help out, since they were basically willing to work for pizza. The young crew had labored tirelessly to make sure things got set up on time and ran smoothly.

Travis took a break from his singing and asked, "Are you gonna talk to Stanton about Quentin's project?"

"I'm going to try, but don't get your hopes up."

Quentin's project was something that had come up around the beginning of April, at the end of a particularly long day of location shooting. Quentin had approached Topher and asked if they could talk. He'd stuffed his hands into his pockets and said, "I wanted to ask you a favor. Travis told me you're going to see Stanton again."

"Yeah. I'm going to New York in a couple of weeks."

"I wondered if you two would help me out. I want to do a project for school."

"What kind of project?"

Quentin paused for a second and then said, "About reincarnation."

"Oh. I'd ask what that has to do with me, but I think I already know the answer."

"I want you to do a Dalai Lama test. And I want to film it, make a short documentary. Jake is going to do all the camera work and help me with the editing. I think it could be really cool."

"What's a Dalai Lama test?"

"Stanton puts three items in front of you, but only one of them belonged to... him."

"And I have to pick the right one?"

"Yeah. You okay with that?"

"I am, but Stanton's not. I wish I could help you, really I do, but he doesn't believe any of it."

"What do you mean he doesn't believe any of it? He's the one who brought it up."

"I know that, but after the way I reacted, he refuses to talk about it now."

"Jesus, don't you want to find out about him?"

"Yeah, I do. But Stanton says he doesn't want me thinking his feelings for me are mixed up with his feelings for Chris Mead. I'm the one who accused him of that, so I kind of shot myself in the foot there."

"But this could be proof, if you get it right."

"Nah, not to Stanton. He'd just say I had a one-in-three chance, and those are pretty good odds."

"So you're going to leave it at that?"

"Hell, no. I'm not leaving anything. I'm going to get to the bottom of this, one way or another. My whole future might depend on it. But I can't guarantee Dalai Lama will have anything to do with it."

"It's *the* Dalai Lama. It's a title."

"What?"

"Forget it. If he changes his mind, would you let me know? I think you're making a huge mistake."

"I'll let you know. I promise."

Back in the truck, Topher looked over at Travis and could tell he had pissed him off a little.

"What do you mean, don't get my hopes up? I always get my hopes up when it comes to those boys."

"I told you, Stanton's like a brick wall on the subject."

Topher smiled and looked back out the window. He thought about the five weeks of phone calls he had shared with Stanton. They had talked almost every night, even when Stanton was in California. Then they would talk for hours on Sundays, when Topher had the day off. He would ask Stanton endless questions, determined to mine his encyclopedic knowledge of pop music. Topher listened to every feature story Stanton had ever done on NPR, and then peppered him for behind-the-scenes scoop. Stanton taught him how to unpack a song and understand its structure. He warned Topher against using a single word to describe any idea or concept, because otherwise it would get trapped by the limitations of that word.

One night, Stanton surprised Topher and put Chester Bennington on the phone to say hello and wish Dime Box good luck with the video. Topher laughed when he remembered how he had nearly peed his pants.

"What's so funny?" Travis asked.

"Nothing," Topher said, but then he went back to thinking about Chester Bennington.

"I love your job," Topher had said to Stanton, once they were back on the phone together. "I just talked to Chester Bennington. I feel like a teenage girl. Had you ever met him before?"

No. I'd met Mike Shinoda once, but none of the other guys. The new album is off the hook. Just stunning. Wait until you hear it.

"When does it come out?"

June, but the piece is going to air next month, in five parts, on All Things Considered.

"Robin and Maurice were so jealous when I told them where you are. *Hybrid Theory* is their story, and they always say that Linkin Park saved their lives."

They had a rough childhood?

"Their parents were a nightmare—meth heads, both of them. They lived in a trailer park over near the arena."

Dime Box has an arena?

"That's what we call it. It's where they have the rodeo every summer. Anyway, one day when they were seniors, Mom and Pops Ackerman decided to just up and disappear, literally. One morning the twins woke up and their parents had packed everything while they were sleeping. Just left town without them."

What happened to them?

"No one knows."

No, I mean, what happened to Robin and Maurice?

"My mom took them in. My dad had passed at that point, and my sister Trisha had moved to Austin, so we had the extra room. Maurice still managed to get all As and a scholarship to UT. Anyway, that's why they worship Linkin Park, especially Chester Bennington, and that's why they're going to be as green as lizards when I tell them who I just talked to."

Hey, I've been meaning to ask you. Are you still having phantom vibrations from your phone?

"No," Topher said. "That's stopped. Why?"

No reason. Just wondering.

Travis snapped his fingers in front of Topher's face and said, "Hello? You there?"

"Yeah, sorry. I was just thinking about talking to Chester Bennington."

"You're supposed to be thinking about Stanton, or didn't you know that?"

"I haven't been thinking about anyone else for five weeks. Leave me alone."

"All right," Travis said. "Go back to your daydreaming."

Topher looked out the window and thought about how Stanton had acted after he finished in California and returned to New York. He had sent a YouTube link to Topher for Oleta Adams's "Get Here." Topher broke down into a puddle of sobs when he listened to it. He wanted to jump on a plane right then and there, but instead he responded with a nineties song he found called "It's Written All Over My Face," by Banderas. Stanton answered with the Dave Aude remix of One Direction's "What Makes You Beautiful," and Topher followed that with Carly Rae Jepsen's "Call Me Maybe."

Back in the truck, Topher reached into his pocket and pulled out his phone.

"Who you calling?" Travis asked.

"No one. I just want to read a text Stanton sent me one night." He tapped through their many conversations until he found it:

The sky is the limit.

Topher had called him that night and asked, "Where did that come from?"

The guy in the video for "Call Me Maybe." The tattoo on his chest. It says, "The sky is the limit."

"Did you freeze the frame to read that?"

Maybe. I'm glad you called, though. Let's talk about dates for your visit.

The trip had to be pushed off further than Topher wanted because of the filming schedule, but they finally settled on late April. One week before the trip, Dime Box posted their finished video for "Beaches on the Moon" to YouTube. A hundred thousand hits in seven days. That translated into roughly ten thousand downloads between iTunes and Amazon, which translated into $6,900. They were over halfway finished paying back Peter's mom and dad.

Travis exited the freeway and asked, "Did you watch any of that gay porn I told you about?"

Topher pulled his attention back to Travis. "Excuse me?"

"You heard me."

Topher frowned and nodded. "Yeah, I watched some of it. I don't think I want to be taking tips from those guys, though. I mean, who has sex with another dude for the first time on camera? And what happens when their moms find out? The thing that really drove me bat-shit crazy, though, was all the problems they had taking off their clothes. Seriously, I'm watching this one scene, trying to get into it, and this guy is struggling to get his jeans off while he's on his knees, giving this other dude a blow job. And I'm screaming at my laptop, 'Stand the fuck up and take your pants off, you idiot!'"

Travis laughed and slapped his knee. "And why do they keep their socks on? Ben is always screaming at the screen too, saying, 'Take your damn socks off.'"

"And who knew there was so much sex going on in auto shops?"

"Right, I know. Ben and I have done it in the bays."

"Are you serious?"

"Hell, yes, I'm serious. We go over there late at night, since we all got keys. Turns him on. I wear my coveralls, and he fucks me on the workbench. It's a hot scene. The whole mechanic thing is a fantasy for these gay boys. We got to use that to our advantage when we're wooing 'em. Ben and Stanton are both smart and sophisticated, but you and me, we come home with grease splotched on our foreheads. Ain't nothing sexier than that."

When Travis dropped Topher off at the departure curb, his parting words were, "Don't forget to relax your jaw when you deep-throat. And when you're on your knees sucking Stanton's cock, remember to look up at him. Ben loves that."

THE flight from Austin to New York passed quietly. Topher had only been on a plane once before, when he took a weekend trip to Las Vegas with his mother and sister. On the phone the previous night, Stanton had told him to take a cab and he would pay for it.

The bus or train is too much hassle. It's either take a cab or I'm coming out there to meet you.

"Why am I flying into Newark?" Topher had asked.

Because it's right across the river. It's not like Texas, where you have to drive six hours just to get to another state.

When he arrived at the Newark airport, Topher found a cab and sent Stanton a text as soon as he was on his way into the city. When the taxi exited the Holland Tunnel and Topher saw Manhattan for the first time, he felt a quiet exhilaration.

He pulled out his phone and called Robin. "Dude, I'm in New York City."

How is it?

"It's pretty damn groovy."

Tell Stanton we can't wait to meet him in person. We talk to him so much he already feels like one of the family.

"I'll tell him. How many downloads yesterday?"

Twelve hundred. If everything holds steady, we'll be able to pay Peter's mom and dad back, with interest, by next week.

"We're not getting rich, but we're having fun."

It's more money than I make in three months. Did you ever imagine?

"That's all I've done for years. We're ready for this."

I know. You're going to have to pinch me every once in a while, though.

"I gotta go. I'm almost there."

Text me later.

Topher ended the call as the cab pulled up to Stanton's building. He lived on the west side in Hell's Kitchen, near Forty-Third Street and Eleventh Avenue, even though that didn't really mean anything to Topher.

Stanton stood waiting for him. His hair had grown out a little, and he looked sexier than ever. He wore shorts and a sleeveless NYU T-shirt that showed off his arms. Stanton opened the car door and said, "Welcome to New York. Sorry I didn't dress up. I just came from the gym. This weather is crazy warm for April."

Topher stepped out, but he didn't start with words. Instead, he wrapped his arms around Stanton's torso, closed his eyes, and exhaled. After a moment, he stepped back and looked up into Stanton's smiling face. "Damn, I forgot how good-looking you are."

"Stop it. Where's your bag?"

"Oh, in the backseat." Stanton paid the cab driver while Topher reached in and pulled out his duffel bag, then closed the door behind him. "I just got off the phone with Robin. They can't wait to meet you in person."

The taxi pulled away and Stanton asked, "Are you hungry?"

"I'm starving."

"Let's get you settled upstairs and then we can get some food."

Stanton led him into the building, past the doorman, and up the elevator to the thirty-fourth floor. Topher sensed an awkward formality between them. They walked down a hallway and into Stanton's apartment, a beautiful two-bedroom with panoramic views of the city.

"Wow," Topher said as he looked out the window, "this is a big step up from Dime Box, or Austin, even. I suddenly feel like a hick."

Stanton smiled and shook his head. Then he gestured to the guest room on the right. "You can put your bag in here. You have your own bathroom if you want to take a shower or something."

"I'm good," Topher said. He stepped into the room and dropped his bag on the bed, even though he had no intention of sleeping in the guest room. He slipped past Stanton and back out into the living room, where he went immediately to the large window. Stanton followed and stood next to him. "What am I looking at?" Topher asked.

"The Hudson River."

"So that's New Jersey on the other side?"

"Yes. Where Springsteen's from."

"Now I see why they call it a concrete jungle. What's that building with the red letters?"

"The New Yorker."

"Very cool. I can't believe people actually built this. It's the most spectacular thing I've ever seen in my life."

They stood for a moment in silence, and then Stanton said, "I'm glad you're here."

"Me too." Topher wanted to kiss him, but decided to hold back. "Food?"

"Food, right. What are you hungry for?"

"Pizza," Topher said.

"Well, one thing we've got in New York is great pizza."

"I'll be the judge of that."

"I'm sure you will. Let's walk over to Claudio's. It's about a block away."

"Okay, then. Lead the way."

Walking the streets of NYC for the first time, Topher could barely take it all in. The sights, the smells, but most of all, the sounds. "It's so loud," he screamed to Stanton.

Once they got their slices and sodas at Claudio's, Stanton immediately brought up the video for "Beaches on the Moon."

"I have to admit," he said, "I have the YouTube page open all the time, and I'm constantly hitting refresh. At least a thousand of those hundred thousand are mine."

"Robin said we'll be able to pay Peter's parents back by next week."

"And soon you'll be able to afford your own plane ticket, rock star."

"You sound like Travis. Maybe I'll take you somewhere when I'm rich and famous."

"Like where?"

"I don't know. Hawaii, maybe. I've always wanted to visit Hawaii. Somewhere with beaches."

"Speaking of beaches, I've noticed you started using an acronym for 'Beaches on the Moon' in your texts. BotM. Don't do that."

"Why not?"

"Didn't Travis explain to you what a bottom is?"

"Yeah, but—" The point dawned on Topher, and he said, "Oh, I get it. That's funny. The acronym for my first big song means getting fucked in the ass."

Stanton changed the subject. "How's the songwriting going?" Topher rolled his eyes in response. "That bad, eh?"

"I could write another 'Beaches on the Moon', but I don't think we want to become Sum 41."

"You're not interested in churning out one skate-park anthem after another?"

"See? You get it."

"So write something different."

"I'm having a hard time."

"Are the songs still locked in your head?"

"Yeah. When I sit down to write, what comes out are fragments or unfinished phrases. Splintered lyrics. I can hear a melody so sweet it would break your heart, but it sounds like it's coming from another room down the hallway, and I can't find that room."

"Chris had the same problem." Stanton froze when he realized what he'd said. "Shit," he mumbled. He finished chewing the food in his mouth and swallowed. "I am so sorry. I had every intention of not bringing him up this weekend."

Topher thought about what he had just heard. Chris Mead had the same problem? What if this could be the key? He took a drink of his Coke and decided to play it cool. *Don't push*, he told himself. "It's okay," he said. "I want to talk about it. If you do."

Stanton did not reply.

"Are you just going to shut down on me?" Topher asked.

"If you insist on doing this, at least let's not do it in public."

"You're the one who brought him up. I didn't insist on anything."

"I'm sorry, but you just got here. Can we focus on us for a while? Stanton and Topher."

Topher backed down. "You get top billing, eh? It's not Topher and Stanton?"

"You know what they say: age before beauty."

Topher laughed and finished up the last of his pizza. As they walked back to Stanton's building, Topher asked him what he thought of Gotye's "Somebody That I Used to Know." Stanton's mood shifted immediately, and he launched into a speech about the birth of a pop-cultural moment and the power of social media to transform a relatively unremarkable song into a global phenomenon.

Once they were back in Stanton's apartment, Topher stood in front of the gigantic window and stared down at the city. The sun had set, and he got an eyeful of Manhattan at night.

"Would you like a beer?" Stanton called from the kitchen.

"Do you have Shiner up here?"

"No, sorry. I asked, but no Shiner. I got Heineken instead. Is that okay?"

"Sure. I didn't come here for the beer."

Stanton joined him at the window with two bottles. He handed one to Topher. "L'chaim."

Topher raised his and said, "Cheers." He took a swig and swished the beer around in his mouth before he swallowed it. Stanton grew still beside him. "I need to tell you something."

"Okay," Stanton said. "What is it?"

"I don't have much experience."

"With… what?"

"I've only had sex with four girls in my life. If you put a gun to my head and forced me to tell the truth, I'd say none of them were all that. I never thought it might mean I'm gay, although why that didn't cross my mind seems a little odd, even to me. I guess I thought it meant I didn't like sex very much. I've also never been in love. I've dated girls, but never called any of them my girlfriend."

"Why are you telling me all this?"

"Because I have a feeling you've got a shitload of experience in all those areas—except maybe the 'sex with girls' part. So it dawned on me that you might find this a lot to take on."

Stanton took a swig of his beer, then looked out the window and said, "You're right. I have reservations."

"I know that. But it's been so long since I've seen you. I thought maybe you changed your mind."

Topher could see the corner of Stanton's mouth curl upward. "I admit these past few weeks have been a blast. I've really enjoyed talking to you about music, but we can't keep this up forever. I have roots here and you have roots in Austin. And then there's the age difference. Sorry, but I'm just going to say it."

"Don't, please."

"I'm old enough to be your father."

"I couldn't care less about how old you are."

"The younger one never does, because people will not be making fun of you. You will always be Ashton Kutcher, and I will always be Demi Moore."

"Anyone who makes fun of you is an asshole, and you shouldn't give a shit what they say." This wasn't going at all like Topher expected. He figured they'd leap into each other's arms and the clothes would naturally fly off by themselves. He turned away from the window and crossed to the sofa. He sat down and took a drink from his bottle of beer. "Tell me about the other stuff."

"What other stuff?"

Topher quoted Stanton's words back to him. "'There were other things, little things, that would take way too much exposition to explain.' That's what you said at dinner that night."

"I told you I didn't want to talk about him."

"Who do you think you're protecting at this point? Because it isn't me. I hope I've made that clear. And why are you standing over there? Come here and sit down."

Stanton went to the sofa and sat next to Topher. "Why are you pursuing this? I told you there's nothing there."

"Says you. You seem to be on the fence about everything, so the way I see it, I got nothing much to lose. So tell me about the other stuff and let me decide. Because if there is even the slightest chance that something you tell me could unlock these songs in my head, then I need to hear it."

"Fine," Stanton said. He sat back into a corner of the sofa and took a deep breath. "Air Supply. You both like Air Supply. Then there was that saying you used, 'the devil is in the details'. He used to say that a lot too. The kiss during 'Thunder Road'. Chris was the person who took me to the Springsteen concert thirty years ago, and he kissed me for the first time during 'Thunder Road'."

Topher's jaw dropped. "And you don't think that means something?"

"Yes, I think it means something, but not what you think it means. What you had during 'Thunder Road' was a moment of clarity. That's all it was, because I'm pretty certain that if I put an end to this right now, you would not go back to dating women. I have been where you are. You have no idea how much I empathize with what you're going through. But eventually you're going to have to say the words."

"What words?"

"I'm gay."

"You think I'm acting like I'm special or something? Like I can't handle being gay?"

"I think you should have listened to your first instinct to reject this connection with Chris Mead. There's nothing there except a series of coincidences."

"Was there anything else?"

"Maybe. A few more things."

"Like what?"

Stanton paused. Topher could tell he was getting frustrated and didn't want to continue. But then he said, "Groovy."

"Groovy?"

"Yes. It was his catchphrase. And blowing kisses. That was another one of his things. He asked people if they liked smooth or crunchy peanut butter.

He said he was going to sing 'Bridge Over Troubled Water' for me, but he never got around to it before…. I think he was saving it for our five-year anniversary. You sang a song called 'Saltwater Kisses', and his lips tasted like salt water when I first met him. He claimed it was because he was half fish and swam in the ocean every day."

"Claimed?"

"Yes. I found out later it was just a fad saltwater-flavored lip balm he used that summer."

"I tasted salt water just before I kissed you."

"So what? People taste salt in their mouths when they get dehydrated. It's very common."

"Do you have an explanation for everything?"

"Yes. That's my point. Lots of people like Air Supply. Lots of people say 'groovy'. Lots of people blow kisses. The smooth or crunchy peanut butter thing isn't exactly original. 'Bridge Over Troubled Water' is a very popular song, even after all these years. Yes, I have an explanation for everything, and as long as that's the case, then this story you're telling yourself is nothing more than a fantasy."

"So you've considered all that, and you've come to the conclusion that it's a series of coincidences?"

"Yes."

"I could understand one or two things—hell, maybe even three—but you just rattled off about nine different similarities there, princess."

"Don't you see? Those are nine dots. Nine things that so many people share, and the only reason they mean anything to you is because I gave you a reason to connect them. That was my mistake, and I'm sorry for it."

"I think you're being ridiculous. Do you need me to paint it in the sky for you?"

Stanton's face turned red, and Topher knew it was time to back off.

"I'm sorry," Topher said. "What do you need? To believe, I mean?"

"Proof."

"Proof?"

"Yes. There isn't one thing you know about him that you haven't heard from me or maybe Travis and Ben. If this is real, then why is it all conveniently circumstantial? Why don't you remember even one detail?"

"Because people don't remember that way. I don't understand how you can look at everything you just told me and not see what I see."

"Because I would have to abandon reality in order to do that. I admit, during that first weekend in Austin, I got swept away too. I thought it had to be true. But then your reaction snapped me out of it."

"I wish you wouldn't keep beating me over the head with that. It was just my initial reaction, for Christ's sake."

"No, it wasn't. It was a reality check. This is your life we're talking about. I don't know what I was thinking, suggesting such a thing. I plead temporary insanity. Losing him was painful beyond my wildest dreams, but it's in the past, where it belongs."

Topher stopped. He heard the wail of a siren down on the street. He hadn't really thought about the fact that Chris Mead had died of AIDS, and Stanton probably held his hand through the whole thing. "So that's what this is about?"

Stanton shrugged. "Maybe. Please don't ask me to do this. I don't think I could handle losing him a second time."

That shut Topher up for several minutes. Then he said, "I think I'm going to sleep in the guest room tonight, but not because I got my feelings hurt or anything like that. I'm just exhausted, and I think we got off on the wrong foot."

"I agree. It's been a long day."

Topher got up. "I get it. I'm sorry I pushed you. I don't know what I was thinking, barging in here without a clue. It'll be just you and me from now on."

"Thank you."

"Let me get some sleep and I'll feel better in the morning."

"I think that's a good idea."

"Good night." Topher stumbled to the guest room and quickly undressed. He pulled back the covers on the luxurious bed, which was stacked with soft pillows. He nestled between the sheets, closed his eyes, and immediately fell asleep.

WHEN he woke up, the room was dark and quiet. Topher lifted his head. In the corner he could see red neon numbers: 3:15 a.m. March 15. The day he met Stanton. He tried to swallow, but his mouth was dry. He got out of bed and pushed his bare feet into the carpet. He went to the bathroom and washed out his mouth with cold water. He went back into the bedroom and attacked the zippers on his bag. He found his toothbrush and toothpaste, brushed his teeth, and then lay back down on the bed.

In the silent apartment, he heard Stanton walk through the living room toward the kitchen. He got off the bed and crept to the doorway. He heard Stanton opening the fridge and saw a light pierce the darkness. Stanton took a drink of something. Topher guessed it was probably orange juice, but he couldn't see, so there was no way to know for sure. Then the refrigerator door closed and the light was gone.

Topher stood in the doorway and watched as Stanton walked through the living room toward the master bedroom. "Hey."

Stanton stopped with a shock. "Shit, you scared me."

"Sorry." Topher noticed they were both wearing nothing but white briefs. "At least we answered that boxers-versus-briefs question right off the bat."

Stanton laughed.

"Can't sleep?" Topher asked.

"I wake up a lot in the middle of the night."

"I've never seen you with your shirt off."

"Embarrassing, isn't it?"

"Hardly. You have more muscles than me."

Topher stepped into the room and walked over to Stanton. He stood in front of him, about a foot away. "It's strange," Topher said. He could hear Stanton's breathing increase slightly.

"What's strange?"

"The confidence I have when I'm around you."

"You mean you're not always like this?"

"No. Never."

"I'm sorry about earlier," Stanton said.

"It's not important. I think you're wrong, but it doesn't matter. We'll do it your way."

Topher looked down. He could see Stanton's cock pressing against the cotton of his briefs. Now that his eyes had adjusted to the dark, Topher could see the outline clearly. "How big is that thing?" he asked.

"I've never measured it."

"Liar."

"I don't think we should do this," Stanton said.

"Do what?"

"Aren't you seducing me?"

"You're walking back and forth to the kitchen in your underwear, and you're accusing me of seducing you? Come on, princess. This might be my first time at the rodeo, but even I've seen *The Graduate*."

"I've never met anyone who could use that rodeo metaphor and sound authentic."

"Let's face it: you've never met anyone like me."

"That's certainly true. You do know that sex will take things to the next level?"

"Know it? Hell, I'm counting on it. You got a problem with that?"

"I'm not all in yet. Like you said, I'm still on the fence."

"Are you saying that if I reach out and start rubbing your dick through those white cotton briefs, you're going to push my hand away and stop me?"

"I don't have that kind of willpower. Especially not around you."

"Are you saying I could pretty much have my way with you?"

"That's pretty much what I'm saying."

Topher grinned. "Can I ask you a question?"

"Of course."

"Okay, but before I ask it, you need to know that it makes absolutely no difference to me whatsoever how you answer. I understand the risks, and we can use protection."

Stanton nodded. "You want to know if I'm HIV positive."

"Yeah."

"No, I'm not. The test came out the same year Chris got sick. At Marvin's insistence, I got one right away, and it came back negative. I didn't understand how it was possible, except that he never fucked me."

"Never?"

"Not in our four years together."

"You say that like you weren't too happy about it."

"I wasn't, but he had no interest. Turns out it may have saved my life, though. It never occurred to us to use condoms with each other."

Topher grinned. "Do you see what you just did, how cool that was? You talked about him like it was the most natural thing in the world."

"I'm sorry, I—"

"Let's not spend the whole weekend apologizing."

"Okay. I'm sorry," Stanton said, which made them both laugh. Topher reached out and rubbed Stanton's thickening cock, and Stanton let out a muffled gasp.

"I have an interest," Topher said.

Stanton closed his eyes and asked, "What do you mean?"

"In fucking you." Topher continued to stroke Stanton's dick as he talked. He could feel it getting stiff in his hand. "It's pretty much all I think about. I wonder what your ass will feel like in my hands—and then when I'm inside you, I wonder what that will feel like too. And sucking your cock. I think about that a lot." Topher let go of Stanton's dick and stepped forward. "I'm negative too," he said.

"I figured."

"I used condoms every time."

"Good boy."

Topher grinned and said, "That's sexy as hell."

"What is?"

"You calling me 'boy'."

"We're still using condoms, though. You know that, right?"

"So you've resigned yourself to the fact that this is going to happen?"

"Maybe."

"Say it."

Stanton hesitated, but then he whispered, "This is going to happen."

The dim light from the windows hit just right so Topher could see a tiny reflection of himself in Stanton's brown eyes. "Touch me," he said.

Stanton reached out and slowly ran his fingertips up Topher's arms. It made him shudder.

He leaned forward and kissed Stanton without touching him back. "I was right."

"About what?"

"Orange juice. I guessed orange juice."

Topher kissed him again, but this time it was like someone opened up all the floodgates on the Mansfield dam. Their bodies pressed together, and Topher threw his arms around Stanton's neck as he ground their erections together.

Topher pulled back. "Your bedroom or mine?"

Stanton didn't answer, but instead leaned down and threw Topher over his shoulder. He carried him into the master bedroom and tossed him down on the bed.

Topher howled with laughter and yelled, "You think that just because I'm smaller than you, you can throw me around like some plaything?" He looked up and watched Stanton, a towering figure in his life, silent and strong and singular. Topher reached his arms out and said, "Come here. Kiss me."

Stanton did, but then he moved down to kiss Topher's nipples. He swirled his tongue around each one so they hardened and peaked. Topher closed his eyes and felt Stanton's lips descend his torso. He knew he didn't have much meat on his bones, but he was toned. They looked good together this way. Topher was sure of it. He propped himself up on his elbows and watched as Stanton slid toward the elastic band of his briefs.

"Big moment," Stanton said.

"I'm not worried."

Stanton pulled back the briefs, and Topher's uncut cock jumped out, already at full attention. Topher liked his rather average seven-inch dick, which wasn't too thick and had a slight mushroom head.

"I can see why." Stanton took it in his hand and stroked it.

"Is that a tattoo on your shoulder?" Topher asked.

Stanton glanced backward and to the left. "Yeah," he said. "I forget it's there most of the time."

"You got one lonely tattoo? Let me see." Stanton hunched forward so Topher could inspect his ink. "A flying horse?"

"Pegasus."

"There was a flying horse named Pegasus?"

"Yes," Stanton said as he continued to stroke Topher's cock. "In Greek mythology. He was the offspring of Poseidon and Medusa. When Perseus cut off her head, Pegasus came out of her body with his brother, Chrysaor."

"You know a lot about that stuff, don't you?"

"Not really. I've seen *Clash of the Titans*. The one with Harry Hamlin, who also had amazing nipples, just like you. Anyway, Pegasus went straight to Mount Olympus and was loyal to Zeus after that."

"Why get a tattoo of a flying horse?"

"I don't know. I liked the story. I value loyalty. I know it's not one of the seven virtues, but it should be. Love, friendship, loyalty. That's what matters to me. Now, are you ready for a blow job?"

Topher nodded. "I think so. I've never had one before."

"Never?"

"Nope. All the girls I slept with said, 'No way, Jose.'"

"I hope I do a good job, then."

"I hope so too."

Stanton looked at Topher's dick in his hand, then leaned over and wrapped his lips around it. Topher threw back his head and choked on his cry. In his head, church bells rang, lights began to flash, and a host of other clichés followed. Topher had always believed he didn't like sex, but now he laughed at the absurdity of the idea. Stanton's warm tongue felt awesome as it swirled around his cock. He lay back on the bed and allowed himself to drift away for a moment. When he felt Stanton kissing him again, he took control and rolled on top. He pinned Stanton's hands above his head and planted his face in one of Stanton's armpits. "I love the way you smell," he said.

Topher released Stanton's arms and ran his hands down the sides of Stanton's torso. He moved south and grabbed his briefs. He pulled them down and away, off Stanton's feet and onto the floor. Topher stared at his exposed cock. It was big. Really big. It must have been nine inches at least, cut and thick. Topher spread Stanton's legs and knelt between them. He reached out and grabbed Stanton's monster with both hands, one on top of the other, and squeezed—not hard enough to hurt, but enough that Topher could get a real feel for this thing he was about to put into his mouth. He released his left hand and pulled the dick toward him. He licked the head and Stanton quivered, so he did that again.

Then Topher realized everything was all wrong, and he jumped off the bed.

"Stand up," he said.

"Why?"

"Because I've been fantasizing about this moment, when your cock crosses my lips for the very first time, for five weeks. And in that fantasy, I'm on my knees and you're standing in front of me."

Without further discussion, Stanton jumped to his feet. His cock jutted out like a tree branch. Topher dropped to his knees and looked at it. He took it in his hand and stroked it a few more times, then leaned forward and opened his mouth as wide as he could. It tasted musky. The first half slid in easily, but then it hit the back of his throat and stopped. Topher closed his eyes and released his jaw. He followed Travis's instructions, allowing Stanton's cock to continue past the sticking point and down his throat. *Don't panic*, he told himself. Topher's eyes started to tear up and his dick got rock hard. Damn if this wasn't turning him on. He pulled off Stanton's cock in one motion. He threw back his head and gasped for air. "Jesus Fucking Christ!" he yelled.

"You're telling me that's the first time you've sucked a dick?"

"Yes."

"No one would ever believe it. And certainly not me."

"Look how hard I am." Topher leaned back on his knees so that Stanton could see, then he took Stanton's cock back into his mouth. Topher started stroking himself as he slurped and licked with unbridled enthusiasm. He looked up and saw Stanton smiling down at him, running his hands through Topher's hair.

Stanton pulled away and walked over to the nightstand. He opened the drawer, pulled out a condom and a bottle of lube, then walked back to Topher. "Stand up."

Topher rose to his feet, and Stanton wrapped the condom around Topher's cock. He dabbed it with a few drops of silicone.

Stanton lay down on the bed and said, "Come here."

Topher pounced on top of him. "What do I do?"

Stanton lifted his legs and reached underneath. He grabbed Topher's cock and guided it toward his asshole. Topher felt his dick press against the opening and tried to push in, but Stanton resisted.

"What's wrong?" Topher asked.

"I haven't done this in a while. You're going to have to be patient with me."

Topher laughed. "That's funny. Me being patient with you, I mean." He kept the head of his cock against Stanton's hole and leaned down to kiss him.

Topher tasted salt water as soon as their lips touched. "Do you taste that?" he asked.

But before Stanton could answer, Topher felt a pop and his dick slid in. Stanton pressed against Topher's thighs and said, "Slow, slow, slow."

Topher had to muster every ounce of control he had, because all he really wanted to do was slam his cock deep into Stanton Porter—to connect with him in a way that required no explanation. But he didn't do that. Instead, Topher entered him one inch at a time. Stanton stroked the back of his head as he ran his other hand down his spine. The room fell quiet and still.

Topher felt blood rush to his dick. He started to fuck Stanton with a soft rocking motion. They kissed as their rhythm increased. Topher pulled his dick out to the head and then thrust it back in. Stanton tried to throw his head back, but Topher grabbed him by the scruff of the neck and kissed him hard on the mouth. He put Stanton's legs onto his shoulders.

"Fuck me," Stanton said.

That was the invitation Topher had been waiting for. He unleashed the last of his pent-up horniness, all five weeks of it. He pounded away at Stanton's ass until he could feel his balls tighten and begin to explode. Topher came with such force he momentarily blacked out. He saw flashes of a life that was not his own—pictures, faces, and music. Everywhere, all around him, hundreds of songs still locked away, half melodies that would—

Topher collapsed on top of Stanton and gasped for air. Stanton eased his legs down and Topher slid his cock out. He nestled into the hollow of Stanton's arm. When Topher ran his hand across Stanton's chest, he felt something sticky. "You shot your load?"

"Yeah."

"I guess that means I did okay?"

"Yes, that means you did great."

"Good," Topher said. Then he promptly closed his eyes and fell asleep for the second time that night.

TOPHER and Stanton spent most of the next day in bed. They did get up to take a shower at one point, but that only gave them another reason to fool around. Topher soaped up Stanton and said, "I've never had sex for more than ten minutes at a go. This is pretty groovy."

"I'm glad you're having a good time."

After their shower, they returned to the bed and Stanton started playing a game. He narrated his movements like a character from a cheesy romance novel. "Then Stanton explored every curve and contour of his new lover's body. He traced the line of Topher's powerful abdomen muscles, lightly caressing the smooth, alabaster skin. The older man, more experienced in the ways of l'amore, took the youngster's engorged member into his hand and stroked it."

"Youngster? You're no good at this. Let me show you how it's done." Topher flipped Stanton onto his back and pinned him to the bed. "Then Topher, the stud mechanic who fucked like a rock star, pressed his raging manrod into the space between Stanton's quivering legs. Stanton moaned and said...."

"Take me, Topher. Ravage my pink, hairless hole. Fill me up with your seed. That's it. Tease me with it. Make me beg."

"Topher reared up and said, 'Good golly, you're a hot piece of ass.'"

"Good golly? No one says 'good golly' in bed. I would have stopped reading right there."

"I bet Travis says 'good golly' in bed."

"Well, Travis can get away with it. You can't."

"Okay. Then Topher leaned down and stared into his future's eyes."

Stanton laughed. "His future?"

"Shut up. There was so much Topher wanted to say, but he couldn't find the words. Not yet, at least. So he kissed Stanton and collapsed on top of him, quietly molding himself around his lover's body." Topher listened to their hearts beat together in unison, and it reminded him of why he liked cheesy.

"You okay?" Stanton asked.

"Yeah. You want to fuck again?"

"You're going to wear me out."

"I hope so."

An hour later, they took a break and Topher asked questions about Stanton's life, and Stanton did the same. They talked about where they'd been headed before all this. Topher's stomach started to growl, so Stanton went into the kitchen and came back with a plate of food.

"Have you ever had lox?" he asked Topher, still naked.

"I don't even know what that is."

"Neither did I before I moved here. It's salmon. You eat it on bagels with cream cheese. It's really good—try it."

Stanton fed him a bite, and Topher's mouth sang with delight. "Damn, you mean people eat that every morning?"

"Yes, can you believe it? You and me, we're so much more alike than you'll ever realize."

After they ate all the bagels, they raided the kitchen for more munchies, then Topher took what he thought was a well-deserved nap.

When he woke up, he found Stanton reading next to him on his iPad. "Are you waiting to be kissed?" Topher said as he rubbed his eyes.

"Yes, I am."

Topher pulled Stanton down and they started to make out, which naturally led to more sex.

Toward evening, Stanton went into the bathroom and closed the door. Topher jumped off the bed and caught his reflection in the sliding closet doors, which were made of mirrors. He looked at himself standing there, completely naked. He thought maybe he should start going to the gym. He flexed, and then chuckled at how stupid he looked. He saw a couple of shirts covered in plastic bags from the dry cleaners. One of the doors stood open a crack, and the shirts were sticking out. He stepped closer and opened the closet door. Stanton's shirts were on hangers and arranged by color. He could also see four or five suits and a tuxedo.

"I bet he doesn't even do his own laundry."

Topher reached out and touched the shirts, then moved them along the steel rod one at a time. He wasn't snooping, he told himself. He looked down and spotted something in the corner. He panicked and turned around, afraid that Stanton would catch him. The bathroom door was still closed. Topher pushed the shirts to the side and saw a guitar case sitting upright in the back corner. Without thinking, he reached for the case and pulled it out of the closet. He set it down on the bed and flipped up the latches. He raised the lid and gasped. It was the most beautiful guitar he'd ever seen, a black Fender acoustic with mother-of-pearl inlay around the sound hole.

The bathroom door opened and a naked Stanton stepped into the room. Topher looked at him and froze. "I...." That was all Topher got out. He watched Stanton's face. He looked for a sign of forgiveness, but mostly what he saw was frustration and disappointment.

Stanton crossed to the closet, pulled out a pair of briefs, and put them on. "Please put that back where you found it."

"I'm sorry. I promise I wasn't snooping. I was just looking in your closet and I saw it. I can't help myself around guitars. Can I play it?"

"I asked you nicely to put it away. Let's get dressed so we can go to dinner."

"Was it his?"

"Don't press me on the guitar. What happened to this being about you and me going forward? Remember?"

"Okay. It's just...." Topher closed the lid and fastened the latches. He returned the guitar to the corner of the closet and walked out of Stanton's room. He went to the guest room and rummaged through his duffel bag. He pulled out some underwear, socks, a pair of jeans, and one of his work shirts. He knew he shouldn't have been poking around in Stanton's stuff, but that guitar was calling to him. What if the black Fender was the key to everything? Topher got dressed and met Stanton in the living room. "Are you mad at me?" he asked.

"No," Stanton said. "I'm tired of the way he keeps poking his nose into everything we do. It's like there's three of us in this apartment. I hate it."

"I don't feel that way."

"I know you don't. That's why I wonder if this is going to work."

"Oh."

"We had three dates in Austin, and then we haven't seen each other for five weeks. I nearly ruined it all by bringing up a ghost, and now that ghost is everywhere I turn. I'm trying, really I am, but then something like that happens and it pisses me off. I'm not mad at you. I'm mad at him."

Topher couldn't believe what a mess he'd made of things. "If I lose you over a guitar, I'll never forgive myself."

"That's not what's happening. I'm still here, but can we get back to you and me and go get some dinner? There's a great Italian place I wanted to take you to. Do you like Italian?"

"I like anything with red sauce."

Stanton laughed and pulled Topher into his arms. "How you're navigating your way through all this, I will never know."

FOR Sunday brunch, Topher and Stanton had plans to meet Marvin and his partner, Tyrese, at their place in the Village. Topher took his first subway ride and thought it was fun enough, even though he wanted to see what it was like during rush hour.

When they arrived at Marvin and Tyrese's apartment, a three-bedroom on Christopher Street, Marvin embraced Topher like an old friend. Tyrese was a tall, handsome black man in his early forties, with a friendly look about him that Topher warmed to immediately.

They served made-to-order omelets, and Topher had his with Swiss cheese and mushrooms. As they sat down to eat, Marvin placed a bottle of ketchup on the table in front of Stanton.

"What's that for?" Topher asked.

"Watch," Marvin said.

Stanton picked up the bottle and poured ketchup liberally over his omelet.

"Whoever heard of such a thing?" Topher said.

The four men laughed and started to eat.

"I like your video," Tyrese said to Topher. "You're a natural in front of the camera."

"Do you think so? It's tough to watch myself. I think I look kind of goofy."

"Oh, no," Tyrese assured him. "'Goofy' is not the word I would use."

"Are you a music critic too?"

"Lord, no. I'm an investment banker."

"You work on Wall Street?"

"Yes. I'm one of the evil ones that people are trying to occupy."

"You don't seem evil to me." Topher took a bite of his omelet. "Tell me about Stanton's other boyfriends."

Stanton choked and took a drink of his orange juice.

"What other boyfriends?" Tyrese asked.

Topher turned to Stanton. "You mean you've been single this whole time?"

Stanton glared at Tyrese. "This is not an appropriate conversation for brunch."

"Topher," Marvin said, "how is the songwriting going?"

"Not too great. I'm working on this one song, but I keep coming up short."

"Is it a love song?" Tyrese asked.

"I'm not sure. I got this idea to write a song about home, but of course that's such a cliché. I mean, how many times has that been done?"

"It's also static," Marvin said.

"What do you mean?"

"Home is a place, even if it's a metaphorical place. It's a destination. But the best songs are about a journey."

"So you're saying, don't write a song about home. Write a song about—"

"Missing home. Being separated from home, maybe even against your will. Write a song about trying to get back."

"Like being homesick."

Marvin smiled. "Exactly. Now you're dealing with longing and desire—a need to return to a place of comfort. Now you're Odysseus, far away from Ithaca, and literally sick from your grief."

"Or Dorothy," Tyrese added, "trying to get back to Kansas."

Topher looked at Stanton, who wore an increasingly irritated expression on his face as he ate his ketchup-covered omelet in silence.

"I liked the video too," Marvin said. "You sound great. Your voice is— Sorry, I was instructed not to bring that up."

"That's okay," Topher said. "I got the same instructions."

Stanton glared at them both. From the look on Marvin's face, Topher guessed he didn't agree with Stanton's dismissal of the whole reincarnation thing. Topher admitted to himself it was probably a stupid thing to do, but he decided to do it anyway. So he took a deep breath and asked Marvin, "Did you know Chris Mead too?"

"Yes. I was there the day Stanton met him."

Stanton stood up. "Marvin. Outside. Now."

"But our omelets will get cold," Marvin said.

"Now."

Stanton walked to the front door. Marvin got up and said, "Excuse us for one minute." Then he followed Stanton out the door and closed it behind him with a loud bang.

Topher looked at Tyrese, who forced a pleasant smile onto his face and said, "Dessert?"

"What are they talking about?"

"What do you think?"

"So he's told you about Chris?"

"Topher, there are three things you need to know if you are going to date Stanton. First, he tells Marvin everything. Second, Marvin tells me everything. And third, the two of them are completely dysfunctional when it comes to each other. They can say the most vicious things and it doesn't affect their friendship one bit. So they are out on the street right now fighting about whether or not Stanton should tell you about the other three."

"What other three?"

"Oops," Tyrese said with a chuckle. "Isn't that what you say in Texas these days?"

"Don't hold Rick Perry against me, please. What other three?"

"Come here." Tyrese got up from the table, and Topher followed him into the living room. They went to a long bookshelf on the wall next to the window, where about forty pictures were scattered haphazardly. Topher bent down and examined the photos carefully. He pointed when he recognized a twenty-something Stanton and said, "Look at him."

"I know," Tyrese said. "He was like a young god, wasn't he?"

"Is that Marvin?"

"Yes."

Topher looked closer and noticed that many of the pictures were of four young men. "Is one of these guys—?"

"The one with the shaggy blond hair."

For the first time, Topher looked into the slate-blue eyes of Chris Mead. He was beautiful, but they looked nothing like each other. Nothing at all. "He sounded like me?"

"I never knew him," Tyrese said. "Marvin and I have only been together for twelve years. Everything I know is hearsay."

"Who are the other guys?"

"Chris's best friends." Tyrese pointed to each one as he spoke their names. "Robert, Michael, and Paul."

"Oh, no," Topher said.

"Oh, yes."

"Robin, Maurice, and Peter."

"Stanton met Chris one summer on Fire Island. Marvin was out there with him, so Chris invited them both to dinner with his friends. Every once in a while, we still pull out the weed and get a little stoned, and they tell the story of that dinner like it's a Greek myth."

"They like Greek stuff, don't they?"

"It's one of the things that makes them proper homosexuals. Anyway, the six of them became like a family. When Marvin talks about the four of them, the way they took him under their wing like brothers and gave him confidence, and then the way they disappeared, one after the other.... It's enough to break your heart."

"They all died?"

"Yes, within about eighteen months of each other."

"How did Stanton and Marvin survive that?"

"Who said they did?" Tyrese looked through the books on the shelf below. "Now, you need to develop a sudden interest in either *Bach and the Baroque* or *Jazz in Twentieth-Century America.*"

"Why do I need to develop a sudden interest in either—" Topher stopped talking as he watched Tyrese take apart one of the picture frames. He removed the back panel and slipped out the photograph. He handed it to Topher. It was a picture of the four young men, without Stanton and Marvin, standing on a beach somewhere with their backs to the ocean, their arms draped around each other's shoulders.

"Because those are Marvin's two books. You saw them on the shelf and begged if you could have one to read for the plane ride back to Austin."

"Marvin has written two books?"

"Yes."

"What does the book have to do with the—?"

"Just pick one!"

"Okay, okay. *Jazz in Twentieth-Century America.*"

Tyrese took one of several copies of the book from the shelf and snatched the photograph from Topher. He placed it between the pages, then he handed the book to Topher. "It's how you're going to smuggle the picture out of this apartment."

"Won't Marvin notice it's gone?"

"No. He's not that observant."

"What if Stanton looks inside? I have to carry this book around for the rest of the day."

"Trust me, he will not look inside. Stanton hates jazz."

"He does?"

"He says it makes him sick to his stomach."

"How can an American music critic hate jazz?"

"Sister, your guess is as good as mine."

Topher and Tyrese returned to the table, and Topher sat down in front of his cold omelet.

"Why did you tell me all that?"

Tyrese filled their cups with fresh coffee. He sat back down and said, "I don't know what you're talking about. We have pictures in the living room. You asked who's in those pictures. I told you." Tyrese winked at him.

"Thank you."

"Marvin and Stanton have a twisted loyalty bond. They fight all the time, but they would never betray each other. I love them both, but I don't feel that obligation. You have a right to know what's going on. Or at least to decide for yourself what's going on."

They heard the front door open. Tyrese leaned over and said, "Let's not tell them about our conversation right now, though. They've already ruined the omelets. I have a lovely blueberry tart for dessert, and I don't want them to ruin that too. Deal?"

"Deal."

Stanton and Marvin rounded the corner, and Tyrese asked them, "Is everything okay?"

Stanton smiled. "Yes. Everything is perfectly kosher now. I apologize for the cold eggs."

Topher could tell from the look on Marvin's face that everything was not perfectly kosher.

"Forget about it," Tyrese said to Stanton. Marvin sat down and Tyrese leaned over and gave him a kiss. "At least you made it back in time for dessert."

AFTER brunch, Stanton and Topher took another subway uptown to Central Park and ended the day at the Metropolitan Museum of Art. They spent an hour with the Impressionists, Stanton's favorite part of the museum, and Topher came to understand why. The Monets and the Manets nearly knocked his socks off, the way they suggested light and shadow instead of directly representing it.

As they left the museum and were walking down the long, sweeping steps, what looked like two fourteen-year-old girls approached them, dressed in a fashion even Topher recognized as upscale.

"Excuse me," one of the girls said to him. "But are you the lead singer of Dime Box?"

Topher blushed and turned to Stanton, who shook his head and said, "Don't look at me."

Topher nodded at the girls and said, "Yeah, I'm Topher."

"I told you," the second girl whispered to the first. Then she turned to Topher and said, "We've watched the video for 'Beaches on the Moon' about a hundred times on YouTube."

"What's your Twitter name?" the first girl asked. "We couldn't find you."

"I don't have one yet," Topher said. He kicked himself for not taking care of that. "I'm working on it."

The two girls looked at each other, puzzled. "Well, we liked your Facebook page," one of them said, "and think those twins are totally hot." Then she noticed Stanton. "Is this your father?"

Stanton's face fell and his smile disappeared.

Topher stuttered, "I... no... this is...." He paused, and then he said, "This is my boyfriend."

"Your what?" one of the girls asked.

The other girl started laughing. "Oh, I get it. It's like a redneck incest joke, right? He's my dad *and* my boyfriend. Does everyone from Texas have that kind of twisted sense of humor?"

"Do you hang out with Adam Lambert?" the other girl asked.

Topher shook his head and said, "No. I've never met him."

"I heard he's a total douchebag," the first girl said.

"Get a Twitter account and we'll totally follow you," the second girl said. "Can we get a picture to tweet?" She handed her phone to Stanton. "Do you mind, Dad?"

Topher stopped them. "Wait a minute. He's not my dad. My dad is dead. This is Stanton Porter, and he's a very famous music critic. I'm lucky enough to be spending the weekend with him here in New York."

The two girls looked at Stanton, who stared back in pale-faced horror. One of the girls said, "But he's so...."

"Old," Stanton said. "Yes, I know."

"It's kind of creepy," the second girl said. "Really. Cradle-rob much?"

Before Topher realized what was happening, Stanton grabbed the girl's phone and snapped a picture of them with Topher. He handed the phone back to the girl and said, "Good day, ladies."

"Thanks," the girl said as she took the phone. "Have fun in New York. I think." As the two girls turned and walked away, one of them said, "What just happened?"

Stanton sat down on the steps and lowered his head. Topher joined him, with Marvin's book in his lap. "How did I not see this coming?" Stanton said.

Topher didn't want to downplay what had just happened. He knew that being called "Dad" and "creepy" was Stanton's worst nightmare.

"You're about to break out. Our romance is one tweet away from becoming public knowledge. Once that happens, the gossip columns won't be far behind."

"Gossip columns?" Topher said. "Are you crazy?"

"Do you think the tabloids don't follow the private lives of pop stars?"

"I'm not a pop star."

"Not yet, but it's only a matter of time. You were just recognized by strangers."

"How bad will it get?"

"It's not Gawker I'm worried about. It's the comments section. Once the first picture of us hits online, it will be open season. And what those girls just said to me will sound like compliments in comparison."

"Then don't read the comments section."

"I know I'm not supposed to care what people think, but I do. Things are going to change, and people will be paying attention to who you're kissing. We're not on the patio of some bar in Austin anymore. I don't want my colleagues laughing at me behind my back."

The thought chilled Topher. "Could this affect your career?"

"I don't know."

"Are you out at work?"

"Of course. I'm not talking about whether or not I'll lose my job. I'm talking about my reputation."

Topher felt his breathing quicken as a wave of anxiety rushed over him. "I'm sorry, Stanton. I had no idea."

"It's not your fault. Like I said, I should have seen this coming. And avoided it."

"What does that mean?"

"Nothing. It's getting late. Let's head back to the apartment."

"Do you want to get some dinner while we're out?"

"No," Stanton said, his shoulders hunched over in a defeated posture. For the first time since Topher had met him, Stanton looked his age. "I'm kind of beat. Do you mind if we just go back and watch a movie or something?"

"No," Topher said. "I don't mind."

THAT night, Stanton made them sandwiches and they watched the latest *Mission: Impossible*. They slept in the same bed, but they didn't have sex. Topher figured that wasn't a good sign. By the time he flew back to Austin the next day, Stanton had pretty much stopped speaking to him. It wasn't a mean silence. In fact, Stanton was very polite. But Topher couldn't change what had happened on the steps of the museum, and he couldn't change how Stanton felt about it. For the first time, Topher admitted to himself that maybe this wasn't going to work out. He wondered if things might have been different if Stanton hadn't helped Dime Box launch "Beaches on the Moon." The irony stung him. In order for one of his dreams to come true, he might have to let go of the other. As Stanton put Topher into a taxi, they said a cursory good-bye that included a hug, but no promises of future contact.

While his plane sat on the Newark runway, before the flight attendants told everyone to turn off their cell phones, Topher called Peter.

Hey, Topher, what's up? How's NYC?

"It didn't work out too good, Pete."

Shit. I'm sorry about that, dude.

"Yeah, me too."

Did you break up?

"I think so. He never said the actual words, but I doubt I'll be seeing him again."

Oh, I see. It sucks that we never got to meet him in person.

"I know," Topher said, and then he started to tear up. "Dammit."

Are you crying again?

"Yes."

You really need to get that under control.

"I can't help it. I did everything I could, everything I knew how. What more could I have said to him?"

It's not your fault. Maybe it wasn't meant to be.

Topher looked up and saw the flight attendant motion for him to put his phone away. "I need to hang up now."

Okay. We'll take care of you, man. You know that, right?

"Yeah, I know that."

Okay, then. Come home to Texas. Where you belong.

Topher ended the call and stuffed the phone into his front pocket. He pulled Marvin's book out of his backpack and found the photograph Tyrese had given him. He looked at the four men and the unbridled joy on their faces. He noticed that Chris was laughing and blowing a kiss to the person taking the picture. Probably Stanton.

Topher's phone vibrated in his pocket, and he nearly jumped out of his seat. It had been five weeks since he last felt the phantom vibration. He reached in and pulled his phone out. He flipped it open and stared down at the blank screen. He didn't know if he should laugh or cry some more. He put the phone back into his pocket and returned the photo to the pages of *Jazz in Twentieth-Century America*. Then he rested his head against the airplane window.

"Boy trouble?"

Topher glanced over at the old woman sitting next to him. "Something like that."

"Don't fret. You'll be fine, once you start listening."

"I listen to him all the time."

The woman smiled. "I wasn't talking about him."

KINGDOM OF DAYS

AFTER they graduated from NYU, Stanton and Marvin moved into Michael's apartment. Stanton shared Hutch's room, and Marvin took the empty bedroom. Although Marvin found himself unemployed, Stanton's senior internship at the *Village Voice* had turned into a job. A few days after the move, Paul stopped by with a proposal. He was tired of living alone, so he offered to switch with Stanton and Hutch. "It's a fantastic apartment," he said. "It would be perfect for you two."

Stanton huffed. "Why didn't you say something before we moved all my stuff?"

"Sorry," Paul said. "I didn't think of it until yesterday."

"Well, it's a perfect location," Stanton said, "At least if you forget about the bathhouse two doors down. It's a block away from the *Voice* offices." He looked at Hutch and understood why he wasn't saying anything. Stanton hadn't written the letter yet. "Can we talk about this and get back to you?"

Paul sighed. "Of course."

Stanton and Hutch decided to take a walk, so they left the apartment and headed west toward the piers. The warm May day was sunny and the sidewalks were crowded.

Stanton took his boyfriend's hand. "I'm ready to tell my parents. You said we could get a place together if I told them. So I'm going to write a letter, and then we can take Paul up on his offer."

"I've been thinking too."

"About what?"

Hutch ducked around a couple of Clones and said, "Let's face it. If the music thing was going to happen for me, it would have happened by now. Paul Simon was twenty-four when he hit it big. James Taylor was twenty-two when he released 'Fire and Rain'. I'm twenty-six and I've been at it for four years, hustling for every gig I can get my hands on and playing to five people who aren't even listening half the time. I don't want to be a starving artist anymore. I think I'm done. If I were talented, someone would have told me by now."

"But your voice—"

"—is not enough. I don't want to be known for my singing."

"Why not? Art Garfunkel is just as famous as Paul Simon."

"No, he's not. He barely has a career since they split up. Everyone knows Paul Simon was the talented one, and that's what I'm interested in—the talent, not the fame."

"But—"

"I'm not going to sing other people's songs. Period. End of discussion. I'd rather refocus my life and think about our future together. I want you to be comfortable. You have a job now. It's time I got one as well."

"You have a job," Stanton said. "You're a bartender and you make decent money."

"So, you want a boyfriend who works until 4:00 a.m. every night?"

"But that's what musicians do. I knew what I was signing up for. What happened to the sky is the limit?"

"Nothing happened to it. It's just not going to involve a music career anymore. I'm allowed to give you what you want. I told the guys at the Blue Whale that I won't be coming back this summer. I'm going to talk to my brother about working for him."

"Don't do that, especially not for me. It's not what I want."

"I can't keep chasing a dream in hopes that one day I'll find the key that unlocks these songs in my head. I'm tired. I'm worn out. A man can only take so much rejection."

"Chris...." And that was the first time Stanton called his boyfriend Chris.

"I guess it's time I give up the stupid nickname too, eh?"

"I don't know why I called you that."

"You hear it from Paul and my family all the time."

"I suppose. So, are we going to take the apartment? Do you want to shack up with me?"

Hutch nodded. "I love you, Stanton. More than my friends, more than my family, more than music itself. You are the simple truth of my happiness. Yes, I want to shack up with you. We're going to have a place of our own, and I'll sing for you whenever you want, and it will be everything we always hoped for."

Stanton kissed him, and they returned to the apartment to give Paul the news. That evening, they scheduled the switch for August 1.

"WHAT are you so engrossed in?"

Stanton looked up from his magazine and saw Robert and Michael coming through the door. The six of them had rented their usual house on Fire Island for the summer, though Stanton had learned the year before that Michael was the only one who did any actual renting. That was his thing. Michael paid for the vacation house and never charged his friends rent to live in his apartment. Such were the perks of hanging with the trust-fund crowd, though now that he had a job, Stanton could finally contribute to the meals jar.

"*Time*," Stanton said. "I picked it up before we got on the ferry."

"What's on the cover?" Robert asked.

Stanton turned the pages back and read out loud, "July 4, 1983. Disease Detectives. Tracking the Killers. The AIDS Hysteria."

"Fantastic," Michael said as he sat down on the sofa across from Stanton. "Happy Fourth of July to you too, *Time* magazine."

"I wasn't even reading that article."

"What were you reading about?"

"Mary Hart and *Entertainment Tonight*."

"I'm glad you have your priorities straight. Why didn't you go to tea?"

"I don't know," Stanton said. "Not in the mood, I guess. How was it?"

"Let's face it. The glory days are over."

"Still haven't heard back from your parents yet?" Robert asked as he rummaged through the kitchen for something to eat.

"No, not yet."

Michael tensed up. "How long has it been?"

"Two weeks."

"That's not bad for a coming-out letter," Robert said, a little louder than usual. "I'll bet you money they went and talked to their priest about it."

"Who's probably a goddamned fag himself," Michael added.

"Where's Hutch?" Stanton asked.

"Hanging out with his old Blue Whale buddies," Michael said. "This is the first summer he hasn't tended bar there since we graduated. He misses them."

Stanton set his magazine aside. "Do you think he's doing the right thing?"

Robert laughed, but it sounded more like a bark. "Ha! Sometimes I like to laugh like that just to sound like Bea Arthur in *Mame*. Ha! I would make a spectacular Vera Charles."

Stanton leaned forward and whispered to Michael, "Is he high?"

"Very."

"I am not very high," Robert said. "I am only pot-brownie high, which is higher than pot-smoking high, I admit, but not as high as Quaalude high. God, wouldn't I kill for a Quaalude right now."

"Come sit down," Michael said.

Robert settled on a bag of Famous Amos cookies and came into the living room. He plopped down on the sofa and laid his head on Michael's lap. "Ha!" he said before he munched down on a cookie. "Do I think he's doing the right thing? Asking his brother for a job? Ha!"

Michael ran his fingers through Robert's hair. "Calm down, Bea. We get the point."

"He's making the biggest mistake of his life," Robert said. "And all because he loves you, Stanton. I hope you know that."

Michael shook his head at Stanton. "Ignore him."

"I will not be ignored, dammit!"

Michael rolled his eyes.

"Why won't you have sex with me?" Robert said. "And call me your boyfriend in public?"

"This is neither the time nor the place to have that well-worn conversation. Stanton is not interested in the twisted contours of our relationship."

"Actually, I'm fascinated by it."

Michael shot Stanton a few eye daggers and mouthed, "Don't encourage him."

Robert curled up into the fetal position and said, "It's because I can't keep my dick in my pants, isn't it?"

"That's right," Michael confirmed.

"One of these days, I'm going to change."

"Or maybe I will," Michael said, shaking his head again. "In the meantime, you don't see me going anywhere, do you?"

"No. You deserve better, though."

"You're right," Michael said. "And so do you. But here we are."

Robert sat up and said to Stanton, "Hutch can still back out, you know."

"I don't think he will. We're having dinner with Carl and Norma next week."

"To meet the little nephew?" Robert asked.

"Yes," Stanton said. "Hutch is so excited. They named him Colin. But he's also going to talk to Carl about the job idea."

Michael sighed. "I don't know why he doesn't call his father. His trust fund is just sitting there, waiting for him. If he's going to become a Mead, he might as well—"

Robert interrupted him. "Not everyone is content living off their family's money."

Stanton saw Michael's face redden with anger. He wanted to change the subject anyway, so he said, "Thank you guys for taking Marvin in while he looks for a job."

"Are you crazy?" Robert said. "We'd do anything for that boy, wouldn't we, Michael?"

"He's not exaggerating."

"Besides," Robert continued, "it's only been six weeks since you two graduated. He'll have better luck with the job hunt after Labor Day. Now that he lives with us, though, we're never letting him move out, even after he gets a job. I only wish we had another bedroom so that all of us could live there together."

The door swung open and Paul entered, followed by Marvin.

"How many more times must I be subjected to 'Gloria'?" Paul bellowed.

"Oy vey," Marvin said. "I hear you, sister. If they don't stop playing that thing, I'm the one who's going to be hearing voices in my head."

"Hello, Stanton," Paul said. "We missed you at tea."

"Thanks. I'll come with you tomorrow."

"You should have seen Paul dishing this piece of chicken to filth," Marvin said.

"What happened?" Stanton asked.

"You encouraged me," Paul said to Marvin. "Don't pretend you didn't."

"I am totally innocent," Marvin maintained, and then he continued with Stanton. "Robert started talking to this young kid who didn't know who Montgomery Clift was. I didn't think it was that egregious, but Paul got all verklempt about it."

"The three of you were laughing and egging me on," Paul said. "You know I am not responsible for my behavior when you do that."

Stanton turned to Michael. "You were in on this too?"

"I observed," Michael said. "The kid actually reminded me a lot of you."

"Oh my God," Paul gasped. "You're right. Oh, now I do feel bad."

"What did you say to him?" Stanton said. "And in my own defense, I did know who Montgomery Clift was when I moved here."

"First," Marvin began, still laughing, "Paul gets that really condescending look on his face, you know the one, and then he asks the kid if he's ever seen *From Here to Eternity?*"

"I was not condescending," Paul insisted. "Unlike Stanton, he was simply not cute enough to be that stupid."

"I don't know if I should thank you or hit you."

"The kid, of course, says no, he's never seen it," Marvin said, "so Paul asks him if he knows who Elizabeth Taylor is? And the kid, of course, says yes. So Paul tells him that Montgomery Clift was the name of her horse in *National Velvet*, and that he should use that little bit of trivia to impress at his next cocktail party."

"Paul," Stanton said, "that was mean. And I'm surprised by you, Marvin."

Marvin took a seat next to Stanton. "This is what happens when you don't come to tea. Paula over there corrupts me."

Stanton grinned and put his arm around Marvin. "So now it's my fault you've all turned into vicious queens?"

"Yes, it is. Everything's your fault. Right, Paul?"

"Yes," Paul said from the kitchen. "Everything is Stanton's fault. If he hadn't turned that damn ring around, none of us would be sitting here. Well, we would probably be sitting here, but you two wouldn't."

Marvin whispered into Stanton's ear, "See how important you are."

Paul came into the living room and sat down with a glass of wine. Marvin stared at him and asked, "You didn't pour one for me, bitch?"

"Do I look like the help?" Paul said. "Stanton, have you started packing yet?"

"No, but we still have a month, almost. What about you?"

"I'm doing one box a day, but I can't wait to move. Marvin, once we're roommates, I'm going to introduce you to towel drag."

Stanton laughed. "Trust me, he needs no introduction."

The door opened and Hutch sauntered in. "Where's my boyfriend?" he asked in a loud voice.

"Over here," Stanton said.

Hutch went to the sofa and gently wedged himself between Stanton and Marvin. "Sorry, Marv, but I have to tell my own little Warren Beatty here that I missed him."

"Do not call me Marv. Please."

"Are you drunk?" Stanton asked.

"A little sauced, yes, sir, I am. The boys kept buying me shots, what was I s'pposed to do?"

"If they went and jumped off the Brooklyn Bridge, would you follow them?"

"Of course not, Starsky. You mad at me?"

Stanton softened immediately. "No. I'm just on edge."

"The letter?"

Stanton nodded. "Let's talk about something else while we start dinner. Who wants to shuck corn?"

AN HOUR later, while a substantially sobered-up Robert was on the patio minding the grill, Stanton stepped outside and asked if he needed any help.

"No, I think we're set. Just have to turn the steaks one more time. I like 'em bloody, but you know Michael." Robert flipped the meat and foil-covered garlic bread. "Sorry about earlier. Maybe two of those brownies was one too many."

"It's okay."

"I don't want you to think I blame you for Hutch giving up on his music. I have no business criticizing other people's relationships."

"You weren't doing that."

"Michael's right. I should keep my nose out of it."

Stanton paused and thought about what he was about to ask, but he decided to ask it anyway. "Why can't you give him what he wants?"

Robert poked the steaks with his tongs. "It's a little more complicated than that. Don't forget we had six years of history before you and Marvin showed up. But I admit, I'm weak. One time I made it a whole seven months. Then a really hot Italian man cruised me on the subway, and it was all over. I'm not going to make him a promise and then break it again. I might be an asshole, but I'm not that kind of asshole."

"I just know how much he loves you."

"And you don't know how much I love him? Besides, stop acting like he's some sort of gay saint. He may have been Snow White once, but then he drifted."

"Mae West, right?"

"I was paraphrasing, but yes. Very good."

"Give me another one."

"What a story," Robert quoted. "Everything but the bloodhounds snapping at her rear end."

"*All About Eve*. Again."

"But there are things that happen between a man and a woman in the dark—that sort of make everything else seem—unimportant."

"*A Streetcar Named Desire*."

"You're ready for the world, Stanton. Look, Michael says one thing and does another. I didn't bring down our beautiful romance single-handedly. Grab that plate."

Stanton picked up the platter and held it while Robert transferred the food from the grill. "I'm sorry," Stanton said. "It's none of my business."

"Don't apologize. I know I practically beg for the attention, the way I air our dirty laundry in public. But no one can understand a relationship except the two people in it. You get that, don't you?"

"Yes."

"Someday I'll figure the rest out. I just hope it's not too late."

WHEN they returned to the city, Stanton found a letter from his parents waiting for him in the mailbox. He sat down with Hutch on their bed and held the envelope in his hands.

"Whatever it says," Hutch said, "just remember that I love you."

Stanton tore at the seal and took the pages out. Two were in his mother's handwriting, one in his father's. He began to scan the words.

Disappointed.

Cannot support.

Don't understand.

Not the same as your brothers and sister.

Maybe someday.

Chris not welcome.

P.S. We still love you.

Stanton passed the pages to Hutch as he read them. It was exactly as he had expected. "I feel sick to my stomach," he said. He looked at Hutch and saw the shocked expression on his boyfriend's face.

Hutch took a deep breath. "I don't understand how parents can say things like this to their own child."

"It's too much for them. I'm all alone now."

"No, you're not. You have me and four other guys who love you to death."

"Don't forget Marvin's mom. I'm afraid she's going to call them up with a few choice words."

"Somebody should."

"No. Now's not the time. I don't know why I was holding onto the hope that they would accept it. At least it's done now. And it's better than hiding. I've got a job and we're moving into a new place. Life is good, so to hell with them."

Stanton tried to smile, but he knew Hutch could see right through his facade. He couldn't even begin to process the pain of being rejected by his parents, so he put the letter into a drawer and focused on packing for the rest of the day.

That night, after Hutch fell asleep, Stanton lay awake for more than an hour. For some reason, he thought about Christmas. What would happen if Hutch broke up with him? Where would he go for the holidays? Would he sit alone in his apartment and eat Chinese takeout? Whatever the case, Stanton felt like a bridge was crumbling behind him. He tried to push the doubts out of his mind, but he also wondered if Hutch was worth it.

And Stanton hated himself for that.

FOUR days later, while they were packing, the phone rang and Hutch picked it up.

"Hello? ... Yeah, who's this? ... Okay, one sec." Hutch covered the mouthpiece with his hand. "It's a Brendan Baxter. Where have I heard that name before?"

"Holy shit," Stanton said. "Brendan Baxter is the quarterback I gave a blow job to. Remember? I told you about him the first day we met."

"What's he calling you for?"

"How am I supposed to know?"

"Well, talk to him and find out. But you have a boyfriend now, so if he asks for another blow job, the answer is no."

"Very funny." Hutch handed him the phone. "Hello?"

Stanton? It's Brendan. Brendan Baxter. You remember me? It's been a few years, I know.

"Of course I remember you. How did you get this number?"

I called your mom.

"My mom? You talked to my mom?"

Yeah. She said you put this number on your last letter and it might work. She was really nice about it. Your dad even remembered me.

Hutch looked at Stanton and held up his hands, as if to ask, "What's going on?"

Stanton mouthed, "I don't know," and then he went back to the phone. "Do you still live in Houston?"

No. I live in Austin now. I'm going to law school at the University of Texas.

Like Stanton's father, Brendan's dad worked for Marathon, an oil company with headquarters in Ohio and an office in Houston. The Baxters had moved to Texas right after Brendan graduated from high school, and that was the last Stanton ever heard from him.

"It's been five years, man. Don't get me wrong, it's good to hear from you, but what's this about?"

Brendan cleared his throat. *I'm sorry. I didn't know who else to call. Can I ask you a personal question?*

"Sure."

Are you gay?

Stanton didn't reply.

Hello?

"I'm here. And yes. I'm gay."

Stanton could hear Brendan sigh with relief.

Thank God. I know you gave me that blow job when we were in high school, and it seemed as if you liked it. Not that I didn't like it too, but I never did anything with a guy after that. At least, not until a couple of days ago.

"What happened a couple of days ago?"

I met Trent Days.

"You mean, *the* Trent Days? The baseball player?"

That one.

Stanton paused while he connected the dots. "Are you telling me the Eskimo Slugger is gay?"

Hutch's eyes popped out of his head.

This is confidential. You can't tell anyone.

"Too late. My boyfriend is standing right here. He's the one who answered the phone."

I'm freaking out. I don't have anyone to talk to about this.

"Are you two—?"

Doing it? Yeah, as of last night.

"You've had sex with Trent Days?"

I had amazing sex with Trent Days. Eight isn't just his jersey number. I think I'm falling in love with him.

"What? You said you just met him a couple of days ago."

I didn't say it made any sense. Didn't you know when you met your boyfriend? After a couple of days, didn't you realize what was going on?

Stanton thought about that first weekend with Hutch. "Yes, maybe. But you can't just date Trent Days. There's no such thing as a gay pro athlete. He would have to leave the sport, and you'd become the Wallis Simpson of baseball."

I don't know who that is, but that's why I'm calling you. I'm all alone, man. I don't know what to do. I don't have any gay friends. I'm in over my head and I'm drowning here.

Stanton considered his options. The letter from his parents was the kind of thing that made him impulsive. He looked at Hutch. "How would you feel about a trip to Texas?"

Hutch raised his hands like he was on a roller coaster. "I would be very much in favor of it."

Stanton turned back to the phone. "Would you like a couple of visitors? My boyfriend gives the best advice of anyone I know. Whenever I need to sort through a mess, I always ask him."

That would be so great. When can you make it?

"Any reason why we can't go this weekend?" Stanton asked Hutch.

"Not that I can think of. We have dinner with my brother tomorrow night, but after that we're free."

"We can come in on Friday," Stanton said to Brendan. "Does that work?"

That's perfect.

"This is kind of cool."

It will be good to see you. I'll call tomorrow. And please, don't mention this to anyone. I hope I can trust you.

"Don't worry, Brendan. You can trust us."

THE next evening, Stanton and Hutch caught a cab to Carl and Norma's new brownstone on the Upper East Side. As a young man, Carl Mead had rejected the law in favor of a career in real estate, and his first investments in Chicago had lined his pockets handsomely. Now, at thirty-two, he was poised to repeat that success in New York. Stanton liked Carl well enough, but Norma had easily become his favorite Mead.

The taxi pulled up to the brownstone and the two men got out. "What's the apartment number?" Stanton asked as Hutch paid the driver.

"What do you mean? He bought the whole thing."

"The entire brownstone? Are you kidding? Was that really necessary?"

"Norma has about twenty-five brothers and sisters. She's hoping this way they'll come and visit if they can stay with her. But it's hopeless."

"Why?"

"They hate New York."

"Twenty-five? You're exaggerating, right?"

"Not by much. There are over ten of them, I think. Maybe not; I couldn't keep track. I only met them once, at the wedding. They're Quakers or Amish or something like that. The entire family still lives in a small town in South Dakota. Blue River? White River? I don't remember, but I'm pretty certain of one thing—none of them will ever visit the evil New York City."

"Did they say that?"

"Pretty much. They talked about it like it was Sodom and Gomorrah rolled into one."

"That makes sense at least. She told me your father doesn't like her because she's common."

"Please. You've met my father. He doesn't need a reason to dislike someone."

Hutch rang the bell, and Norma answered the door. She threw open her arms. "Chris, Stanton!"

Stanton stepped in and hugged her. "This is some place you got here."

"It's a little much, I know, but I'm hoping to fill it with children."

"Where is my nephew?" Hutch asked.

"Right here." They looked up and saw Carl coming down the stairs with an infant in his arms. After completing his descent, he handed the baby to his wife and greeted Stanton and Hutch.

"It's good to see you both."

"You too, big brother. I'm sorry we didn't make it to the hospital when he was born. Stanton was graduating, and I had three gigs lined up back to back. It was kind of chaotic."

"I understand. I barely made it myself."

"Do you want to hold him?" Norma asked Hutch.

"Can I?"

"Of course," Norma said as she gently transferred the newborn into his arms. "Colin, I want you to meet your Uncle Chris."

The baby cooed, and Stanton grinned when he saw the look on Hutch's face. It dawned on Stanton that his boyfriend would make an amazing father. They headed toward the sitting room on the first floor, Hutch bouncing Colin and singing "Mockingbird" to him as he walked.

"I see you're keeping that C theme going with the names," Stanton said to Norma.

She pulled him in close and whispered, "I wasn't consulted."

"Are you serious? Your own child?"

"He's named after Uncle Colin, their mother's brother."

"The one who still lives in Ireland?"

"Yes."

"And you had no input at all?"

"None whatsoever."

"They're just like the Carringtons on *Dynasty*, right down to the gay son."

"Who does that make me?"

"Linda Evans, I think."

Norma laughed at the thought. "Oh, no. I'm not nearly glamorous enough to pull that off."

"Nonsense. You're the only one with any actual class around here half the time."

Norma placed her hand on Stanton's arm and kissed his cheek. "Thank God Chris met you. You are a real bright spot in this family."

"We're going to be the fun uncles and spoil your kid rotten. You know that, don't you?"

"I wouldn't expect anything less."

Over dinner, Hutch told Carl and Norma about their impromptu trip to Texas the next day but left out the part about Trent Days. The four of them talked about the Congressional page sex scandal that had hit the news that morning. Then Carl asked, "Have you talked to Dad lately?"

Hutch looked at him, as if he was hoping to avoid this conversation. "No."

"You have to make an effort too."

"We were there for Easter."

"So that's how it's going to be from now on? You plan to see your parents once a year? You should never have skipped Thanksgiving. You know how much that means to Dad."

"And leave Stanton at home?"

"He will come around eventually, but you have to meet him halfway."

"Asking me to show up alone and pretend I'm single is not meeting me halfway."

"Can't you see that you're being as stubborn and closed-minded as he is?"

"Carl," Norma said, "do we need to have this conversation right now?"

Hutch ignored her. "Dad pretends like Stanton isn't even in the room, just like you're doing."

Carl paused, clearly upset by the accusation. Stanton had never seen Hutch and his brother argue this way. Carl seemed to consider his words carefully, then turned to Stanton and said, "I apologize. I hope you know that

Norma and I support you two, but I'm trying to broker a peace here. Do you understand that?"

Stanton nodded. "I understand it more than Hut—I mean, Chris does. I'm on your side, Carl, but he's not doing this for me—he's doing it for himself."

Hutch smiled at Stanton. "Thank you."

Carl shook his head. "I still say, the more you come around, the more he'll get used to it."

Hutch took a bite of his pasta. He pointed at Carl with his fork and said, "I told you, I'm there when Stanton is welcome. Otherwise, I'm not. Those are the terms."

"At least I'm welcome some of the time," Stanton said. "That's more than my parents are doing right now."

"Did you hear back from them?" Norma asked.

"Yes, a few days ago. It wasn't pretty."

After dinner, Hutch asked Carl if they could speak privately. Norma looked at Stanton as they left the room. "What's going on?"

Stanton put his elbows on the table and folded his hands together. "Chris is going to ask your husband for a job."

"Oh, no. What about his music?"

"He's giving up. He says he's had enough rejection and he's done."

"Did you try to talk him out of it?"

Stanton sat back in his chair. "Yes, but his mind is made up. You can't force someone to follow their dream."

A few minutes later, Hutch and Carl returned to the dining room. Carl had a delighted look on his face. He sat down for dessert and said to his wife, "Chris and I are going to work together. Isn't that wonderful news?"

Hutch grinned and sat down too, but the hollowness lurking behind his eyes was a bad sign, and Stanton knew it.

THEY flew to Austin the next morning. From the moment they stepped onto Texas soil, the Lone Star State captivated Hutch. Even Stanton had to admit the sky was so big and blue it looked like someone had painted it. They took a short cab ride from the airport to Brendan's apartment north of the UT campus. When the taxi pulled up to a house, Stanton checked the address and asked the driver, "Are you sure this is the right place?"

"This is the address you gave me."

"But he lives in an apartment."

"There's an apartment over the garage."

"Oh." Stanton pulled out a five-dollar bill and handed it to the driver. "Keep the change."

They got out and walked up the driveway. Then a voice behind them asked, "You two visiting Brendan?"

They turned around and saw a man walking toward them. He looked to be in his late twenties. He was barefoot and wore baggy shorts with a University of Texas T-shirt. He had dark hair and eyes that were almost black. And he was hot. Really hot.

"Where did you come from?" Stanton asked.

The man laughed. "I live in the house." He had one of those deep, masculine voices that made gay men swoon.

"Oh," Stanton said. "Yes, we're visiting Brendan. I went to high school with him. My name is Stanton."

The man stepped forward and shook his hand. "Bill Walsh. You boys are from New York, right?"

"Yes. This is my...." Stanton faltered and he found himself retreating into the closet for a moment.

"Lover?" Bill Walsh said. "Or do you prefer partner?"

"Either one is fine."

"Brendan told me. You gay boys need to come up with something better. Lover sounds like it's all about sex, and partner sounds like it's all about business."

Hutch stepped forward and introduced himself. "I'm Hutch. Groovy to meet you, Mr. Walsh."

"Mr. Walsh? Shit, what am I, a year older than you? Please, call me Bill. Even my students call me Bill."

"You're a teacher?" Hutch asked.

"I'm a professor at the university, in the English department. Just getting started, though. My wife is expecting our first child soon. We were going to wait until I got tenure to start a family, but I guess my swimmers decided to boycott the rhythm method. You two should come into the house and rest for a spell."

"We haven't told Brendan that—"

"He's at work 'til four. He asked me to see to things until he gets back."
Bill Walsh turned around and walked away toward the front porch. "Follow
me, and we'll get you something to eat," he yelled over his shoulder. "You
like migas?"

Stanton and Hutch grabbed their bags and ran to catch up with him.
"What are migas?" Hutch asked as they climbed the steps to the front door.

Bill opened it for them and they stepped into the house. Stanton
dropped his bag on the floor and looked around. It was an old structure with
high ceilings, wood floors, and beautiful handcrafted molding. Stanton
couldn't put his finger on it, but there was something about the way the light
bounced off the walls that reminded him of Picasso.

Bill led them into the kitchen and explained, "Migas are a Tex-Mex egg
dish, with tomatoes and onions and peppers and tortilla strips. And cheese.
Lots of cheese, and salsa. Spicy salsa."

"It sounds great," Hutch said as they took a seat at the table. "I'm
starving. It was a long flight, and I couldn't eat that crap they served. Did we
even figure out what the mystery meat was?"

"I think it was Salisbury steak," Stanton said.

"It was disgusting."

"It was what most American school children eat every Wednesday."

"You'll be staying in one of the bedrooms upstairs," Bill said as he
pulled some eggs from the fridge. "It doesn't matter to me which one. They
both have a full bed."

"Oh," Stanton said. "We're not staying with Brendan?"

"No, he doesn't have room for you. That's just a one-bedroom
apartment over the garage. And mind you, he and Trent need their privacy
right now, if you understand my meaning, gentlemen, and I think you do."

"Can we...?" Stanton paused and felt himself retreating into the closet
again.

"Sleep in the same bed? Of course. I'm not my father, for Christ's sake.
My wife isn't going to like it, but you let me handle that part. Don't hold it
against her. To suddenly have four gay people in the house is going to be a
shock. She's small-town Texas Catholic, and that's a tenacious combination,
let me tell you."

"Thank you for your hospitality," Hutch said.

"You can take your bags upstairs and wash your hands. There's a
bathroom up there. I'm going to start the migas, so they'll be ready in about
ten minutes."

Stanton and Hutch grabbed their bags and ascended the staircase to the top landing. There was a bedroom on each side with a bathroom in between. They picked the one on the left, with the window facing west. They set their bags on the floor and sat down on the bed.

"This is so cool," Hutch said.

"I know. It's like we've stepped into someone else's story."

"Bill Walsh is a stud."

"You noticed that too, eh?"

"It's hard to miss. And his whole Texan thing?" Hutch lowered his voice in imitation of Bill. "Come in and rest for a spell."

Stanton laughed. "Don't get any ideas. We're not here to have a three-way with Brendan's landlord."

They washed their hands and then went back downstairs, where they found Bill in the kitchen serving up food. They sat down and each ate a large plate of migas. Stanton listened as Hutch and Bill got into a discussion about William Faulkner and Tennessee Williams and which one they thought was a better representation of Southern fiction. Hutch argued that Williams's characters, especially Blanche and Stanley, were more iconic than anything Faulkner created. Bill argued they were only more iconic because Vivien Leigh and Marlon Brando had played them in the movie, and he was under the impression they were talking about literature and not cinema.

The back door to the kitchen opened, and a very pregnant woman came in with a bag of groceries. "My goodness," she said. "The heat out there today. I don't think women were designed to give birth in Texas during the summer."

"Grace," Bill said as he stood up and took the bag of groceries from her. "These are our guests for the weekend, Stanton and Hutch. This is my wife, Grace."

Grace Walsh was a beautiful woman. Stanton thought she could easily pass for a dark-haired version of Grace Kelly in her *Rear Window* days.

Hutch stood up to shake her hand. "It's a pleasure to meet you, ma'am."

Stanton followed suit and asked, "When are you due?"

"Next week."

"Do you have names picked out yet?" Hutch asked her.

"Talk to Bill about that."

Bill Walsh set the groceries on the counter and said, "Benjamin if it's a boy, and Caddy if it's a girl."

Hutch laughed. "You're not going to name your children after the Compson siblings in *The Sound and the Fury*, are you?"

"I'm sure as hell going to try."

"I see my husband has already fed you," Grace said.

"Yes, ma'am," Hutch replied. "He makes a mean plate. Of these migas, I mean."

Grace joined them at the table while Bill unpacked the groceries. They talked for a while about what Stanton and Hutch should do and see during their visit. Then Brendan telephoned and told Bill he and Trent were on their way back to the house. Stanton and Hutch looked at each other and realized they were about to meet one of the most famous baseball players in America. Stanton turned to Bill and asked, "Can we go change?"

"Sure," Bill said. "But you do realize that Trent is just an ordinary guy, don't you? Don't dress up for him or he'll start making fun of you."

"Okay," Stanton said. "I just want to change my shirt."

He and Hutch went upstairs, but as Stanton was closing the bedroom door, he heard Bill and Grace Walsh downstairs in the kitchen. They were arguing.

"I'm not going to make a fuss about it. They are perfectly charming young men, but I'm not happy about them sleeping in the same bed while they're in this house. It's not right."

"You sound like your father. What happened to the woman I married?"

"We never discussed homosexuality before we got hitched. You know that. If you had asked me then how I felt about it, I would have told you. At least they're not my brothers. I can only imagine the grief their families must be going through."

"You're wrong about this. Shit, it's 1983. There are gay characters on TV now. Stanton and Hutch are sophisticated New Yorkers, and I'll be damned if I come off looking like a Texas hick in front of them."

"So that's what this is about? You're afraid of looking like some local yokel? Your lack of a backbone shocks me sometimes."

Stanton closed the door. "Did you hear that?"

Hutch nodded. "At least she thinks we're charming. That's a plus, isn't it?"

"Boy," Stanton said, "does he have me pegged wrong. Sophisticated New Yorker?" He chuckled at the suggestion.

"We were meant to come here. I can feel it. I don't know why, but someday it's going to make sense. I love Texas."

"You've only seen what's between here and the airport."

"It doesn't matter. We're going to see a lot more while we're here. Robert told me there's a music scene in Austin."

"It doesn't seem that much different from where I grew up."

"The devil is in the details," Hutch said. "What should I wear to meet Trent Days?"

Stanton could tell Hutch was barely able to contain his excitement. Stanton kissed him and said, "Go ahead. It's okay to act like a nine-year-old boy."

Hutch burst into a grin. "Okay, I admit it. I'm breathless with anticipation."

"You forgot the pause."

TWO days later, on Sunday afternoon, Stanton and Hutch stood in the driveway of the Walsh house and said good-bye to Brendan and Trent.

Stanton pulled Brendan into a hug. "This has been spectacular." Then he said to Trent, "I really hope you guys can work things out."

"Me too," Trent said.

Hutch hugged them both as well. "Thank you for inviting us. I can't tell you how much I am in love with Texas now. I feel like I'm leaving a piece of my soul behind."

Brendan laughed. "It has a way of grabbing you, doesn't it?"

"It sure does."

Trent looked uncomfortable, and Stanton wanted to reassure him. "We're not going to talk about this with anyone. We promise."

Hutch nodded. "I can't imagine what it's like to be you, Trent. We're here for you guys, no matter what you decide."

"Thanks," Trent said. "Don't forget what I told you, Hutch."

"I won't forget." As they piled into the taxi, Hutch waved to Brendan and Trent and said, "Y'all have a good evening."

The cab pulled away from the Walsh house, and Stanton turned to his boyfriend. "Y'all?"

"I'm practicing my Texan."

"What did Trent tell you?"

Hutch kissed him and said, "'Play the long game.' It's his motto."

"What were you talking about when he said that?"

"You. Baseball. Life stuff."

"Play the long game, eh? I like that."

"Me too."

They arrived back in New York late at night and hit the ground running the next morning. Between Stanton's job and the business of packing, it was only a matter of days before Texas felt like a distant memory. Then, on the morning of July 22, 1983, Hutch called Stanton at work and asked if he had seen the news. When Stanton said he hadn't, Hutch told him Trent Days had been killed in a plane crash the night before.

In the afternoon, when the passenger manifest was released to the press, it only confirmed what Stanton already suspected. Brendan had been on the same flight. He tried to call Bill Walsh several times, but there was no answer, and they didn't have an answering machine. It was a devastating blow to both Stanton and Hutch, but since they couldn't talk to any of their friends about it, they mourned in private and then moved on with their lives.

Hutch began his real estate job with Carl in early August. He and Stanton moved into their apartment on St. Marks Place and stepped into a new future together. At first, there was nothing but blue skies on the horizon. But as Labor Day passed and autumn arrived, Stanton began to realize that July's trip to Texas might go down as their last moment of real happiness together.

COVER ME

ON THE Friday night after Topher's return from New York, Dime Box closed their set at the Rooftop on 6th with a cover of Michael Jackson's "The Man in the Mirror." The crowds at their gigs had increased with their popularity, and the band found themselves getting more and more attention in the local press. Still, Topher and the twins were in a foul mood that night. Topher knew his vocal performance had been flat, but he could hardly bring himself to care. He had texted Stanton during the week and gotten one or two word responses. He knew it was over. Topher didn't hear from the phantom vibration again either. On top of all that, Robin and Maurice gave him the cold shoulder, because they were pissed about not getting to meet Stanton in person. They packed away speakers and amplifiers, while Peter chattered on about YouTube hits and search engine optimization. Topher and the twins just nodded and ignored him.

They got home well past midnight. Topher went straight to his room and crawled into bed. He was exhausted but couldn't sleep, and by morning, he felt downright hopeless. He dragged himself out of bed around eight and called in sick. Then he went into the kitchen, where Peter sat at the table eating a bowl of oatmeal.

"You look like—"

"Don't say it, Pete. Really, you think I don't know?"

Peter retreated to his phone and continued scrolling through something, probably his new Twitter account. He poured some more milk onto his oatmeal and took another bite.

"I'm sorry," Topher said. He took a glass down from the cupboard and filled it with orange juice. Anything that tasted like Stanton.

"Sit down," Peter said.

Topher put the carton of juice back into the fridge and joined Peter at the table.

"Have you ever heard of a musical called *The Fantasticks*?"

"No," Topher said.

"Do you remember that chick I introduced you to last week? Lacey?"

"Yeah. The really hot one with the button nose?"

"Yes. I was hanging out at her house last weekend with her roommates, Kenneth and Dan. We started talking about music, and they suggested Dime Box cover a show tune at the end of one of our sets. And I was like, what? Show tunes? Are you nuts? And so Kenneth pulled out his laptop and started playing me all these songs—amazing songs that none of us have ever heard. Melodies and emotions so big they'll make your head explode, tailor-made for your voice. Anyway, they played this song for me called 'Try to Remember'. It's from a show called *The Fantasticks*. And as I'm listening, I realized it's the same song as 'Yesterday'."

"You mean the Beatles?"

"Yes. Both songs are about heartbreak and looking back on a better time. They're both great songs—I mean, 'Yesterday' is one of the greatest ever—but guess what? They're not about love."

"They're about loss."

"Now you're with me. 'Yesterday' is filled with regret, but 'Try to Remember' looks at the loss and sees something almost necessary. Do you understand what I'm saying?"

"I think so."

"I don't know what's going to happen with you and Stanton, but don't be afraid to take what you're feeling and pour it into your music. You always talk about those songs locked away in your head. What if a broken heart is the key to unlocking them?"

"Do you really think that's possible?"

"Hey, it worked for Alanis Morissette." Peter finished his oatmeal and got up from the table. He put his bowl into the sink, filled it with water, and then returned the milk to the fridge. "I'm headed to work," he said. "You off today?"

"I am now."

"See you tonight, then."

"I'll be here," Topher said. "Thanks for the talk."

As he left the kitchen, Peter turned and said, "Don't thank me, dude. Go write a song."

TOPHER followed Peter's advice and spent the morning in his room. He sat on a rolling desk chair with his guitar on his knee and pages of sheet music on the bed in front of him. He took out the picture of Chris and his friends and set it down next to the sheet music. He strummed his guitar and thought about the black Fender in Stanton's closet. He wondered if getting his hands on that guitar would change everything. Or maybe Peter was right, and a broken heart would be the thing that inspired him. Lord knew he felt rammed and battered. He tried to write a lyric to "Homesick," but his rhyming scheme was off. He felt tired, so he pushed the music aside and took a nap. When he woke up, it was three o'clock in the afternoon.

He went into the kitchen and got a Dr Pepper from the fridge. He returned to his room and grabbed his guitar. He lay back on the bed and began singing his thoughts to the tune of "The Eyes of Texas," which also happened to be the tune of "I've Been Working on the Railroad."

Topher stared up at the ceiling and sang, "I've been working on this damn song, all the fucking day. If by chance you saw me sleeping, please do not turn away. Give me something to grab onto, 'cause I have grown to curse the morn. Oh, show me where to go from here, please, so I won't be forlorn."

Topher felt his phone vibrate in his pocket. His skin began to tingle and his vision sharpened. His senses went into overdrive, like they had that night Bruce Springsteen played "Thunder Road" and Topher kissed Stanton for the first time. He bolted upright and looked at the picture of Chris and his friends. He knew what was coming. He counted it down. In five, four, three, he tasted....

Salt water.

Topher took his phone out and flipped it open. He stared at the blank screen. Then it dawned on him. This was maybe the tenth time it had happened—ten times he had felt the phantom vibration—yet in all those times he had never once considered the obvious.

Topher slowly put his guitar down on the bed. He knew it was just plain stupid, but he couldn't help himself. He raised the dark phone to his ear...

...and said, "Hello?"

At first he heard only silence, then,

Hello, Topher.

He jumped off the bed and threw the phone down. He looked around the room to make sure he wasn't being Punk'd. "I'm cracking up," he said out loud. Topher stared back down at the open phone, still silent and dark. He reached for it and put it back to his ear. He waited for a moment and then tried again.

"Hello?"

Don't throw the phone down, please.

"Who is this?"

Who do you think?

"Chris?"

Silence.

"Have I lost all my marbles?"

No, just the opposite. You've finally found them.

"But how is this possible?"

Think of the phone as a metaphor.

"What kind of metaphor?"

I've been trying to get in touch with you for weeks, but you never pick up your damn phone.

Topher laughed. "You mean I could have talked to you the first day he walked into the shop?"

I have always been here, Topher.

"Holy Jesus Fucking Christ!"

Calm down. Really, there's no need to freak out.

"No need to freak out? Do you even realize what you're saying?"

It's going to take a while for things to sink in, so in the meantime, here's what you need to keep telling yourself: there is only one of us. Got it?

"There is only one of us."

Good. Say it again.

"There is only one of us."

Now breathe, and talk to me. Why do you think we're having this conversation?

"I don't know."

That's because you haven't thought about it yet.

"Okay. I suppose it's because I fucked things up, and now Stanton is pissed that you keep getting in the way. I feel lost. I don't have any experience with this kind of thing, so I don't know what to say to him."

You didn't fuck things up. And I'm sorry I got in the way. I'm on your side, Topher. There is only one of us, remember?

"Yeah, okay. I'll try to keep an open mind."

Good. Because there are some things I need your help with.

"What kind of things?"

Why do you think I keep getting in the way?

"I don't know."

Yes, you do. Take a stab at it.

Topher thought it over for a minute. "Because he hasn't let go. Of you, I mean. For some reason, Stanton hasn't been able to let go."

You're right. I know that's probably hard for you to hear, but I'm not your competition.

"Because there is only one of us?"

See? You're getting the hang of this.

Topher paused. "Will you help me?"

That's why I'm here. I want what you want. For Stanton to let go and move on.

"What can I do?"

Who else might have played a role in this? Who else could have been involved? Think, Topher. What did Ben say to you?

"When?"

The morning Stanton did the piece about Dime Box on the radio. When you talked to Ben on the phone. What did he say?

"He said something about an empty chair at Thanksgiving. Your father has never really forgiven himself for—" Topher stopped. "Your father. That's it, isn't it? Something happened between Stanton and your father, something that's prevented him from letting go all these years."

Yes. All roads lead to Stanton and my father.

"But that's all I know."

Then ask him for more.

"Stanton? He doesn't want to talk about it."

Stanton doesn't want to talk about anything, but you can change that. He used to be fearless, and he can be that way again. With your help, I mean. Do you understand what I'm getting at?

"Yeah. I think so."

Good. Now, what about the music?

"What about it?"

Why are you hesitating?

"I'm not—" Topher stopped himself again and collapsed inward. "Sorry. I don't know if I want it to happen if Stanton's not there. The music career, I mean. I hate this feeling. Being without him."

What about the songs?

"The ones locked in my head?"

Yes.

"You think I can figure that out too? You think I can find the key?"

I know you can find the key. It's all there, Topher. Just put the pieces together.

"Is it the black Fender?"

No, although that's one groovy piece of equipment. I loved that guitar.

"Where'd you get it, anyway? I didn't even know Fender made acoustics."

It was a custom job. One of a kind. But Fender does make acoustics.

"Is heartbreak the key?"

No, but that will make anyone's songs better. Think about what Stanton told you.

"When?"

His warning about using a single word to express an idea.

"Are you saying I've trapped myself somehow?"

Yes. Sometimes you can't find the answer because you're phrasing the question wrong.

Topher paused and thought it over. "It must be the word 'locked'? There is no key because there is no lock. Am I right?"

Yes, you're right. Now keep going. Listen to what you're hearing in your head. How did you describe it to Stanton?

"Fragments, half tones, splintered lyrics. But I still don't get it."

You're not describing something that is locked. You're describing something that is....

Topher finally filled in the blank. "Incomplete."

Yes. Now we're getting somewhere.

"I only have half the songs. But that means—"

The other half is somewhere else.

"Where?

Start guessing.

"In someone else's head?"

That's a good guess. Now, whose?

"Stanton?"

No, too obvious. You know this. You felt it. I felt it too, but I was too stubborn.

Topher tapped his foot on the floor as he considered the possibilities. Then it hit him. "Marvin."

Yes.

"Homesick. I wanted to write a song about home, and he came up with homesick. I can write songs with him?"

You can write great songs with him.

"And I know I can figure out a way to fix things between Stanton and your father. Somehow I can find a way, but how do I get him to see me again? He thinks this whole thing between you and me isn't real. It is real, isn't it?"

You think you need proof that—

"I don't think it, I know it. Even if I can get him to talk to me, if I bring this up without proof, he will just shoot me down again."

You think you need proof that you and I are somehow connected. Actually, I'd like to see the proof that we're not. Stanton doesn't care about reincarnation, or which dates line up, or who sounds like whom. He's not looking for that kind of proof.

"Then what kind of proof is he looking for?"

You tell me.

Topher paused. "It seems he's afraid. Like you said, I mean."

Of what?

"That it's not real. He wants proof that love is real."

Good. And what is the only proof we have that love is real?

Topher didn't need any more prompting. "Music."

Yes. You can reach Stanton by singing him a song so beautiful that it will make his heart beat again. All he wants to know is that love can last, that it's not just a fleeting moment fueled by hormones. We're going to give him that. You and me, together.

"What song should I sing?"

You'll find it. Trust me, and trust yourself. You may not remember any of the details of my life, but we share a melody, Topher. I was one movement and now you're another. Everything that I was and ever hoped to be, I stored it all in the music.

"So I can remember?"

There are different kinds of memory. Go looking for a song, and I promise you'll find the right one.

"Because there is only one of us."

Yes. The student has become the master.

Topher laughed. "You're funny. Why now? Why couldn't I remember anything before?"

Could you have handled this six weeks ago?

"Probably not. I don't think I'm handling it too great right now, if you ask me."

Let's talk about the picture. Look at it. What do you see?

Topher picked up the photograph and said, "Four men. You guys look happy."

Four, Topher. Not one, four. Can't you see they're a part of this too?

"I didn't want to involve them."

Why not? That's the whole point.

"Of what?"

Life. They are here to get involved. This is not a spectator sport, so don't keep them sitting on the sidelines any longer.

"I guess I should at least tell them what's going on."

I think that would be a good idea.

Silence.

"This has been interesting, to say the least."

It has. Now, go find a song.

"Okay. Can I talk to you again?"

You can talk to me whenever you want. I told you, I have always been here.

"Groovy."

They both laughed.

By the way, I like what you've done with our name. Topher. We didn't have that back in my day. I'm jealous. Anyway, don't give up on Stanton, okay?

"Okay. I'll hang in there. Good-bye, Chris. And thanks."

Topher hung up the phone and sat on his bed. He opened his laptop and began searching for a song. As Chris had promised, it didn't take long. He practiced for more than an hour, then heard Peter and the twins laughing in the living room. Topher didn't see the point of dragging this out any longer. He picked up the photograph and got off the bed. When he walked into the living room, they stopped talking and greeted him.

"This is crazy, yo," Robin said. "I'm sorry we've been dicks to you. It's not your fault Stanton broke it off. Stop being sad. Come in and sit down."

"Can we go into the kitchen?" Topher said. "We need to have a meeting."

Peter jumped up and led the way. "Come on, guys," he said. "It seems we got shit to talk about."

They all hurried into the kitchen, gathered around the table, and waited for Topher to begin.

"I think I can say with absolute certainty that this will be the strangest conversation we've ever had." Topher sat the photograph in the middle of the table.

"What's this?" Maurice asked.

Topher pointed to Chris. "This guy is Chris Mead. He was Stanton's boyfriend back in the early eighties. He died of AIDS six days before I was born."

"So?" Peter said.

"I also have his voice."

"His voice?" Maurice asked.

"Yeah. According to Stanton, our singing voices are identical."

"Not to mention your first names," Robin said. He picked up the picture and examined it closer. "Who are the other dudes?"

"Those are his three best friends. Robert, Michael, and Paul."

No one said anything for several moments, but Topher could see the wheels were already spinning.

Peter took the photo from Robert and stared at it. "They look happy."

"That's what I said. All four of them died over an eighteen-month period."

"Died?" Peter asked. "All of them?"

"Yeah."

"Let me guess," Maurice said as he grabbed the picture from Peter. "The same eighteen-month period that we were born?"

Topher nodded and waited. This wasn't going at all like he expected. He thought there would be noisy demands for explanations and protests over the absurdity of the proposition, but his three best friends seemed to be absorbing the information with a peculiar detachment.

"Are we supposed to draw our own conclusions?" Peter asked.

"I'm just telling you what I know," Topher said, "which isn't a whole lot. Stanton doesn't want to talk about it. Marvin's boyfriend, Tyrese, told me about them when Stanton and Marvin were fighting outside on the sidewalk. He helped me sneak this picture out."

"Marvin is Stanton's best friend, right?" Peter asked.

"Yeah," Robin said. "He's the short Jewish guy Stanton brought to our SXSW gig. He's mentioned him a couple of times on the phone."

"We had brunch with them on Sunday," Topher added.

"Brunch?" Maurice asked. "Since when did you start having brunch?"

"Chill," Peter said. "Don't be hating on his new lifestyle."

Topher laughed and slapped Peter upside the head.

"Which one is Michael?" Maurice asked. Topher leaned to the right and pointed him out. Maurice looked at his brother and said, "We're better-looking."

Maurice handed the photograph to Robin, who asked, "Which one is Robert?"

"Okay," Peter said, "you might as well tell me which one is Paul too."

Topher stood up and leaned over the table. He tried to orient himself since he was looking at the photo upside down. "That's Robert and that's Paul," he said as he pointed them out.

"We are not better-looking than him," Robin said. He turned the picture toward his brother. "Did you see this guy?"

"I saw him."

"Paul looks kind of gay," Peter said.

Topher rolled his eyes. "Dude, they were all gay."

"Ooohhh," said Peter and the twins.

"Sorry," Peter continued, "I think we just assumed they were straight and this Chris guy went gay for Stanton. Like you did."

"They died of AIDS," Topher said.

"Oh, right. I guess that would explain why they croaked one after the other."

Maurice snatched the photo from Robin and asked, "Were Robert and Michael boyfriends?"

"I have no idea," Topher said.

"So Stanton is the connection between them and us?" Peter asked.

Topher thought about it. "Yeah, I suppose he is."

"How long have you known about this?" Robin asked.

"Stanton brought it up when he was here in March. That's why I was upset that night, coming home from Travis and Ben's place. But I didn't find out about the other three guys until last weekend."

Maurice set the picture back down on the table, "Why were you upset?"

"It felt like Stanton was using me, to pretend that he was back with Chris. Because of my voice."

Maurice shook his head. "That doesn't sound like Stanton at all."

"I figured that out," Topher said.

"You've known about this for six weeks?" Peter asked.

"Stanton told me it wasn't true, that I should forget about it. What happened in New York was half about this and half about our own problems. He thinks people are going to laugh at him because of the age difference."

"He's right," Maurice said. Robin slapped him on the arm. "What did I say? Do you think some people aren't going to laugh at him?"

"That's beside the point," Robin said. "Use your brain, brother."

"Why are you telling us this now?" Peter asked.

Topher took a deep breath. "I guess you could say I wised up. I was sitting in my room trying to write a song, and even though I didn't get very far with the song, I feel like I worked some things out. One of those things was you three. I don't need to protect you from anything, because chances are, you'll be the ones doing the protecting. I don't want to go through this alone, and I don't have to. That's the whole point of us being friends. We don't have to face shit alone."

No one spoke, and Topher heard their next-door neighbor yell something in Spanish. Robin got up from the table and crossed to the fridge. "Shiner anyone?"

"Me," Topher said.

"Please," Peter seconded.

Maurice stood up from the table. "I'm not stoned enough for this." He exited the kitchen and returned a minute later, exhaling. He set the bong in the middle of the table, and Peter took a hit. Robin returned to the table with four opened bottles of beer. He took a hit as well and then passed it to Topher, who cashed the bowl.

Robin sat down and said, "Let's not pretend this isn't the coolest thing that's ever happened to us."

Peter sighed with relief. "Thank God you said that. I was thinking the same thing."

"Me too," Maurice said. "Are we on some kind of mission from God, maybe?"

"Please," Topher insisted, "let's dial it back a notch, can we? I think it's pretty groovy myself, but—"

"When did you start saying 'groovy'?" Peter said.

"After I saw it in the painting over the fireplace at the W Hotel. Then Stanton told me it was his catchphrase, and now I can't stop saying it."

"What about Stanton?" Robin asked. "You guys broke up. What's going to happen now?"

"I don't know," Topher said. "We've got so much working against us. I don't know how to overcome it all."

"I think I do."

Topher froze and looked at his friends, who stared back at him. None of them had said that. Topher slowly turned around and could hardly believe his eyes. Stanton was on the other side of the screen door.

"Can I come in?" he asked.

The boys jumped to their feet, and Topher ran to the door. He opened it and Stanton stepped inside, dragging a piece of luggage behind him.

Topher hoped that Stanton's sudden arrival signaled a much needed turn of events. "What are you doing here?" he asked.

"I had to see you," Stanton said. "And you live in Austin, so here I am."

"How did you get my address?"

"I called the shop yesterday and talked to Travis."

"You could have called."

"No, I couldn't." Stanton paused and turned to Peter and the twins. "Hi, guys. Have you made your ten thousand back yet?"

"Yesterday," Robin said.

Peter corralled the twins toward the kitchen door. "Let's give them the room. But we're not done with you, Mr. Porter."

They left and Topher gestured toward the table. "Sit down."

Stanton took a seat and nodded at the bottles of beer and the bong. "I interrupted something."

"Just a business meeting."

"Are you stoned?"

"A little," Topher said as he took a seat next to Stanton. "Is that okay?"

"Sure, as long as you offer me some."

"Maurice!" Topher yelled. He waited a moment, and then Maurice poked his head through the door. "Can you reload this, please?"

Like a stealth Navy SEAL, Maurice grabbed the bong off the table and disappeared, only to return moments later. He placed the recharged water pipe in front of Stanton, along with a lighter, then vanished before they knew what had happened.

Stanton took a hit and said, "Thank you."

Topher cleared some space and sat down on top of the table, like he had on the picnic bench that night at Cheer Up Charlie's. "How long have you been single?" Topher asked.

"Awhile," Stanton said.

"Have you loved anyone since he died?"

"I didn't come here to talk about him."

"I know that. But I poured my heart out to you when I said I've never been in love, and you just let me believe you were more experienced than me."

"I have been in love, so I am more experienced than you."

"Okay, but by how much?"

"Ty was exaggerating. I've had other boyfriends."

"How long did they last?"

"A year maybe. Sometimes two."

"Did you love any of them?"

"You mean the way I loved Chris?"

"Yeah."

"No. Never like that."

Topher grinned and reached behind him for a bottle of beer. He took a swig and then kissed Stanton, letting the beer slowly stream into his mouth.

Stanton swallowed. "That was hot. I spoke with my boss, by the way. She has no problems with me dating you. She even thought a piece on Dime Box from my perspective as your boyfriend would be a fresh angle. She agrees with me that music is always personal, so why pretend it's not?"

"As my boyfriend?"

Stanton smiled. "I thought you might zero in on that part. I admit it's not going to be comfortable for me at first. To be honest, I had every intention of never seeing you again."

"I got the message. What changed your mind?"

"I was having lunch with Marvin yesterday, and I told him what happened on the steps of the Met, and how I shut down after that, and how I didn't think I could deal with dating you. He stood up and walked out on me—literally, he got up and waltzed right out of the restaurant. I didn't understand what in the hell I had done, so I called him. His phone went to voice mail for over an hour. When he finally answered, he said I needed to have my head examined. 'A beautiful young man wants you,' he said, 'and all you can come up with are petty excuses about what people will say in the comments section. Jealous, anonymous bitches who would kill for the chance to date a twenty-something pop star.' That's what he said. He called me a coward and told me I wasn't worthy of someone like Topher Manning."

"So you listened to him?"

"I always listen to Marvin. So, now it's my turn to come after you."

Topher thought that was just about the sweetest thing he'd ever heard. Still, he asked, "What about the distance?"

"Marvin said even if I only got to spend one day a year with you, it would still be worth it."

"Marvin is my new best friend. Though I think we can do better than one day a year. This means I can call you my boyfriend, right? You weren't playing with me, were you?"

"I wasn't playing with you."

"And you're going to come visit and hang out with us?"

"If they don't mind hanging out with an old man."

"They'll get used to it. Can you get Marvin to come to Austin too?"

Stanton looked at him, puzzled. "Why?"

Topher slid down off the table and sat on Stanton's lap, straddling the chair. He put his arms around Stanton's neck and kissed him. "We tried things your way, and frankly that didn't get us very far," Topher said. "So now it's your turn to trust me. I want to get to know Marvin, and I just took time off work to visit you. Do you think you could get him to come back to Austin and maybe go camping with us or something?"

"Camping? Me and Marvin?"

"Trust me, remember?"

"Okay, I trust you. Yes, he'll come if I ask him. Nicely."

"Good."

"Did you talk to Travis and Ben again?"

"What do you mean?"

"You have this thing you do."

"What thing?"

"You go from uncertain boy to confident man overnight."

"That's my thing?"

"It's one of them."

"What's another one?"

"You like to crawl on furniture."

"I do, don't I?"

Stanton lowered his head and said, "I'm sorry about last weekend."

"It's okay. I forgive you. Something tells me I'm going to need the goodwill here in a second."

"What did you do?"

"Relax. Breathe. Everything doesn't need to be a reason to raise your blood pressure." Topher reached around and grabbed the photograph off the table. He handed it to Stanton.

"Where'd you get this?"

"Ty gave it to me."

"That's why you had Marvin's book?"

"Yeah, but I did read it. Learned a lot too."

"Ty had no right to—"

Topher shut him up with a kiss. He slid his tongue between Stanton's lips. He tasted marijuana and Shiner, a combination he thought had to be unique to Austin. Then he pulled back and said, "He had every right. Stop being afraid all the time. I bet you weren't always like that."

"What did Ty tell you?"

"Their names and that you and Marvin were like a family with them. He told me they died one after the other, and he thought maybe you've never recovered from that."

"It was twenty-five years ago. Of course I've recovered."

"I told them." .

It took a few moments for that to register on Stanton's face. "You told your friends?"

Topher nodded. "That's what we were talking about when you showed up."

"How did you even start that conversation?"

"I showed them the picture."

"And how did they react?"

"They think it's cool."

"Really? So we're going to proceed as if you are the—"

"It's not important that anyone use the R word. What's important is admitting that we're all connected—you, me, Marvin, and those three guys in the living room. I don't know how, and frankly, I don't see as it really matters much. But you can't sit here holding me like this and tell me you don't feel it too."

Stanton teared up a little. "I feel it. But it's ridiculous for someone my age to believe such a thing is possible."

"Then get over that part. Don't you see we think of you as a gift?"

Stanton didn't answer, but instead, pulled Topher close and kissed him.

When they were finished making out, Topher asked, "Are you ready to meet the band?"

"I guess. It's all weird now, though."

"Stop your fretting. I'll take care of everything."

Topher got up and led Stanton into the living room. He introduced everyone, and the five of them sat down together.

"Congratulations are in order," Stanton said.

"We owe it all to you," Robin said.

"Nonsense. The cream always rises to the top. I just stirred the pot a little."

Topher knew none of them had a clue how to proceed, given all the information that had been downloaded in the span of about an hour. He got up and went into the kitchen, picked the bong up off the table, and returned to the living room. He set it down in front of Stanton with the lighter. "Ty told me that sometimes when you smoke a little weed, you tell the story of the night you and Marvin first had dinner with Chris and his friends."

Stanton looked at them with suspicion, but then he picked the bong up and took a hit. He passed it to Maurice and said, "Are you telling me you want to hear that story?"

"Yeah," Peter said. "Where did y'all meet?"

"Fire Island."

"What's that?" Maurice asked as he lit the bowl.

"It's a vacation spot in New York, off Long Island. One section of it is almost exclusively gay men."

"Is that where the picture was taken?" Robin asked.

"Yes. They had a house out there the summer we met them."

"So what happened at this dinner?"

"Well," Stanton began, "before the dinner there was the bottle of wine. I had told Chris that Marvin said the wine at the Blue Whale was crap. So he had this very large drag queen bring a bottle of the greatest wine on the planet over to the Pines during the Invasion."

"Do you not get stoned very often?" Maurice asked. "Because I don't think I understood two words of what you just said."

Stanton giggled. "Sorry. Let's just say Hutch did a really nice thing for Marvin, and the dinner started with a bottle of wine."

"Who's Hutch?" Topher asked.

"Chris. Everyone called him Hutch."

"Did they call you Starsky?"

"Sometimes. We played the Greatest Game during dinner, then Hutch got out his guitar and sang, and we ended the night dancing at the Pavilion."

"You mean the black Fender?" Topher asked.

"Yes," Stanton said. "You were right. The guitar belonged to him."

"What's the Greatest Game?" Robin asked.

"It was just a stupid thing they made up. Like Penny Can on *Cougar Town*. They played it all the time. This was before things like Trivial Pursuit. Everyone got to pick a category, and then we would all name what we thought was the greatest in that category. You can do it with movies or books or TV shows, but that night we played with music."

"Give us some examples of the categories," Robin said.

"Hutch's was greatest Springsteen song, and Paul's was greatest show tune, and Marvin's was greatest Carly Simon song."

"Let the River Run," the twins said.

"Unfortunately, that wasn't an option in 1981. My answer was 'Boys in the Trees'."

"Can we talk business?" Peter asked.

"Please," Stanton said. "I can only spend so much time on Memory Lane."

"Okay," Peter continued. "It's so weird that you said that, because we scheduled the concert in Dime Box for Memorial Day. Everyone there is totally stoked. The guy who directed our video, Kai, he's going to do the film stuff and all the projections. We'll be on the baseball field over by the school. My dad is building a stage and working on getting extra bleachers. But people can lay out blankets and bring food if they want to."

Stanton turned to Topher. "Is there a new song on the horizon?"

Topher grinned. "There will be."

Peter got out his laptop and asked to go over all the sales numbers with Stanton. Topher put up with all that for about an hour, but then he took Stanton by the hand and announced they would return later. Once inside Topher's bedroom, Stanton looked around at the bare walls.

"So this is where the magic happens, eh?"

"It is now," Topher said. "Lie down on the bed. I want to sing you a song."

"Really? How cool." Stanton sprawled out and put his hands behind his head.

Topher sat down next to him, with his legs crossed and his guitar on his lap. He strummed a few chords and leaned into the first note. Then he sang:

"Che gelida manina,

se la lasci riscaldar.

Cercar che giova?

Al buio non si trova."

Topher opened himself up to the lift and caressed each word.

"Ma per fortuna

é una notte di luna,

e qui la luna

l'abbiamo vicina."

Topher continued singing. He saw tears drop from Stanton's eyes and run down his face, but he half expected that. He relished the high notes that naturally fit his voice, and allowed the crescendo to build, but not overwhelm. As he finished the last note like a whisper, Topher leaned forward and gave Stanton a kiss on the lips. "What did you think, Starsky?"

"Where did you learn that?"

"I listened to the Pavarotti version on YouTube. I can pick things up pretty quick."

"But what possessed you to—?"

"Big voices. You said we both like big voices, and I figured, what's bigger than opera? When I typed that in, though, all I got was a lot of *Phantom of the Opera*, which wasn't really what I intended. I remember my mom listened to some Pavarotti, so I typed his name in, and this is one of the things that popped up."

"He sang that to me once."

Topher grinned. "Yeah, I figured. There are different kinds of memory. And different kinds of proof. This is my kind, Stanton. Does that make sense?"

Stanton nodded and Topher leaned his guitar against the chair. He lay down on top of Stanton and kissed him again. Topher tried to wipe the tears away with his hand, but that only made Stanton laugh. So Topher put his lips next to Stanton's ear and whispered, "He's just homesick sometimes, that's all."

WE TAKE CARE
OF OUR OWN

ON VALENTINE'S Day, Michael insisted on treating everyone to dinner at David's Potbelly, an upscale restaurant near his apartment, as well as tickets to see *La Cage aux Folles*. Michael ordered a bottle of expensive champagne, and they lifted their glasses in a toast.

"To 1984," Robert said. "May it be better than the book."

After the toast, Michael brought up the summer house on Fire Island. "I have a lead on a new place that looks unbelievable. Literally on the water."

"I can't this summer," Chris said.

"What do you mean?" Michael asked.

Robert frowned. "Look, Hutch—"

"Don't call me that. Please, I don't want to be an asshole, but would everyone start calling me by my name? We're not in college anymore. I'm trying to convince people at work to take me seriously."

Paul looked confused. "What does that have to do with what we call you?"

"Carl says it's about perception. I have to take myself seriously before anyone else will."

"So now you're taking life lessons from your brother?" Paul asked.

"You have always called me Chris, so what difference does it make to you? All I'm asking is that everyone else do the same."

"Fine," Michael said. "What do you mean, *Chris*, that you can't this summer?"

"I won't have time. Weekends are when we W&D our biggest customers. We'll spend some of August in the Hamptons with my family, but otherwise I'll be working." Chris looked at his watch and said, "Excuse me, I have to make a phone call." He got up from the table and walked away toward the side hallway.

Michael turned to Stanton. "What's happened to him? W&D?"

"It means wine and dine."

"I know what it means."

"This can't be the first time you've noticed the change," Stanton said. "Robert, you're not blind."

Robert nodded. "I thought he was adjusting. I had no idea he would actually turn into his brother." He covered his nose and sneezed.

"Bless you," everyone said.

Robert apologized. "I haven't been able to shake this cold."

"After the show tonight," Stanton said, "let's go back to our place. Maybe if we all ask him nicely, he'll get out his guitar and sing something."

"We'll try," Robert said.

"Maybe I should talk to him," Marvin said. "We've always had a strong connection when it comes to music."

"If you can get him to listen to you, have at it. But in case you haven't noticed, he keeps coming up with excuses to cancel our Saturday morning breakfasts."

Later that night, after the show, they went back to Chris and Stanton's apartment on St. Marks Place and convinced Chris to pull out his black Fender. The six of them sat around the cramped living room. As usual, Chris asked for requests.

"The Eyes of Texas," Robert said.

"Not again," Stanton protested. After hearing Chris talk about Austin, Robert had become obsessed with Texas.

"What's wrong?" Robert asked. "I'm telling you, we're going to visit next year. All of us. I'm so sick of Manhattan."

"Me too," Chris said as he strummed his guitar.

Paul sighed. "Me three. I hate to say it, but the party's over."

Chris began to sing.

"The Eyes of Texas are upon you,

All the live long day."

Robert and Michael joined him.

"The Eyes of Texas are upon you,

You cannot get away."

Then Paul.

"Do not think you can escape them

At night or early in the morn—"

And finally Stanton and Marvin.

"The Eyes of Texas are upon you

'Till Gabriel blows his horn."

A round of applause filled the room. Then Marvin sat up and said, "Why don't you sing 'Home'. It's your favorite song from *The Wiz,* and I'd like to see what you do with it."

"I don't know if I remember all the words."

"Paul and I will help you out."

"Okay," Chris said. "I'll try."

He had no choice but to take the show-stopping finale and strip it down to something almost conversational. He called these his "Johnny Cash" versions. Stanton had never really listened to the song, and it struck him that Chris didn't realize what he was getting into either, because the song was about finding your way back to a place where things made sense. Stanton realized Marvin had picked it for that reason. At first it seemed to work, but then Chris stopped himself halfway through and said, "I don't want to do this."

"Keep going," Marvin said.

"No. It's not going to change anything."

Stanton reached out and said, "You can quit your job with Carl. And go back to music. It's not too late."

"Right," Chris said. "Because I want to go back to being a loser." He stood up and returned the guitar to its case. "Some of us have to work in the morning, so I'm going to bed. Happy Valentine's Day, everyone. Stanton, are you coming with me?"

"I'll be there in a minute."

Chris disappeared and Stanton showed their friends out. Then he went into the bedroom.

Chris was lying facedown, naked. "Fuck me," he said.

Stanton undressed and sat down next to him. "Roll over."

"No. Fuck me like this. I want you to take your cock and fuck my ass until I can't think anymore."

Stanton pulled a bottle of lube from the nightstand and dabbed some onto his cock. He positioned himself on top of Chris and spread his ass cheeks. He speared his tongue into the hole and heard a groan.

Then Chris lifted to his hands and knees and placed the head of Stanton's dick against his asshole. "Fuck me into tomorrow. You know how I like it, don't you?"

"Yes, I know."

With as much force as he could muster, Stanton slammed all nine inches of his cock in at once. Chris convulsed and buried his face into a pillow. Stanton pulled out and slammed it in again, only harder this time. He held onto Chris's hips and went straight to fifth gear, relentlessly fucking as hard as he could.

Stanton closed his eyes and concentrated. He could only last a few minutes at this pace. Although Chris loved sex talk, Stanton thought it was stupid and hardly said a word. He only talked when he was about to come, which Chris used as his signal to rear up and stroke his dick to completion. Stanton kept fucking until he shot a load deep into Chris's ass. Immediately after, Chris pulled away and curled up by himself under the covers.

SIX weeks later, Robert collapsed in his office, and an AIDS diagnosis followed. Michael, Paul, and Marvin gave him round-the-clock care, but Chris's role was reduced to the occasional visitor because they lived across town. Stanton always wondered if Chris blamed him for that.

Robert died in June of that year. On the day of his funeral, Stanton stood in front of the mirror and stared at his reflection. He never liked wearing a suit. Every man needed one for weddings and funerals, his mother had told him five years ago, when she bought the one he was wearing. He hadn't spoken to his parents in the ten months since he received their letters. He never wrote back and never called, not even at Christmas.

He felt like an orphan.

Stanton buttoned the top button of his shirt and tugged on the Windsor knot of his tie.

Chris walked into the bedroom. "I think I'm going to be sick."

"There's some Pepto in the medicine cabinet." Chris retreated and Stanton put on his jacket. He wasn't really sure how they were supposed to get through this day. He went into the living room and looked out the window. People swarmed St. Marks Place, going about their business as if it was any other Saturday. "We need to get going," Stanton called. "The service starts in thirty minutes."

Chris came out of the bathroom. "Okay, I'm ready."

"What about your guitar?"

He looked confused, but then went into the bedroom and returned with the cased instrument in tow. Neither one of them had eaten a proper meal or gotten a good night's sleep in over a week. Between their jobs and Robert's illness, they barely had time to say hello to each other.

Stanton knew funerals and memorial services had fast become the new dinner parties, but this would be their first. They took a cab uptown to one of the big churches on the Upper East Side. Stanton never understood the distinctions between the different protestant denominations. In his mind, they were only defined by the fact that they weren't Catholic.

The service was solemn and respectful and bore no resemblance to the way Robert lived his life. By now Stanton had gotten used to being around the Upper East Side crowd, even though he clearly did not fit in. The five of them sat in the second row behind Robert's parents. After several readings and a brief sermon, the pastor nodded to Michael. Chris pulled out his guitar and walked to the front with Michael, Paul, and Marvin.

"This was one of Robert's favorite songs," Michael said. "And one of mine too. It seems appropriate today." Then the four of them sang an acoustic version of "While My Guitar Gently Weeps." Robert's mother began to sob, and Stanton found it difficult to maintain his composure as well.

After the service, they returned downtown and gathered at Michael's apartment, where Paul and Marvin now lived as well. Stanton could feel Robert's absence in every square foot. Paul and Marvin went into the kitchen to prepare some food, while Michael disappeared into his bedroom and closed the door. Stanton and Chris took a seat in the living room and sat quietly for several minutes. Then Stanton asked, "Do you think Michael's okay?"

Chris shrugged and stared at his hands. "I doubt very much he's okay."

"I'm going to go check on him."

"Don't."

"Why not?"

"Because he doesn't want to hear from you right now. You still have your boyfriend. There's no way you can know how he feels."

"You'd be surprised."

"What is that supposed to mean?"

"Let's not do this now, okay?"

"Do what?"

"Don't pretend with me. We live together, remember?"

Chris fell silent and Stanton stood up. "I'm going to check on him. I don't care what you say." He went down the hallway to Michael's bedroom and knocked on the door.

"Who is it?" he heard from inside.

"Stanton."

"Oh. Hold on." Stanton heard a rustling and then the door opened. Michael said, "Come in and close the door."

Stanton did as instructed. "Why are you in here by yourself?"

"Get comfortable."

Michael fluffed up several pillows and piled them against the headboard, then lay back on the bed. Stanton took off his jacket and shoes and settled in next to him.

"I can't deal with all four of you at once," Michael said. "Paul and Marvin are smothering me."

"They only want to help."

"I know that. How are things with Chris?"

"We don't discuss it."

"You know he's good at it, don't you?"

"What are you talking about?"

"Real estate. He told me he's really good at it. You of all people understand how charming he can be, and that makes him a good salesman."

"He's never told me that. Can't you see the difference, though?"

"Of course. We all see it. You know what Nietzsche said."

"God is dead?"

"No. Well, he did say that, but I was talking about the other quote."

"What other quote?"

"Without music, life would be a mistake."

"I would like to tattoo that to his forehead."

"Go easy on him. These are growing pains you're having. That's it. You have to push past them."

"Did you ever think of kicking Robert out?"

"Think about it? I did it several times. But I always ended up begging him to come back, so I stopped."

"Just like 'My Man'."

"Yes."

"What will you do now?"

"I don't think I'll need to worry about that."

"Michael, you don't mean…."

"I'm not going to kill myself. But I can feel it. I'm next. I'm tired all the time. I can't sleep. I've lost weight."

"That doesn't mean you have AIDS. The last few weeks would have made anyone tired."

"I have nightmares now too. Well, they start out as nightmares, at least. I'm sitting on the beach with Robert, out on the island. We're lying down on our big yellow and orange towel, and then we fall asleep. When I wake up, the tide has come in and washed Robert away. I panic and dive into the water, looking for him, but he's gone. I can feel my feet being pulled out by the undercurrent. The next thing I know, I'm drowning. My lungs are filling up with water, but just as I'm about to black out, everything changes and I'm standing on a dirt road somewhere. The sky is big and blue, Stanton, like nothing I've ever seen before. And Robert is standing there, in front of me. He looks like he did when I first met him. Young and beautiful and so alive. I say to him, 'We were on the beach and you disappeared. Where did you go?' And do you know what he says to me?"

"What?"

"Texas."

Stanton smiled and said, "Of course."

"He always talked about it like it was Xanadu."

"Even though he'd never been there."

"That was part of the appeal, I think. He told me that if we could just go somewhere new and start over, we'd get it right the second time."

"What happens in the dream, after Texas?"

"Nothing. That's when I wake up, usually in a pool of sweat."

Stanton bit down on his lip. "I took a class in dream psychology at NYU. The prof said it's just a way to blow off steam in your head."

"Maybe."

"He loved you. You know that, right?"

Michael nodded. "Yes. If I had known it was going to end like this, I wouldn't have been such a two-faced jerk. I thought we'd both grow up eventually. I thought we had time."

"I can't wrap my brain around it. Chris said you wouldn't want to talk to me, because I still have my boyfriend."

"He doesn't get it. You and me, we're alike. I recognized that the first night you and Marvin had dinner with us. Hutch and Robert, they need... needed.... Jesus, what verb tense do you use when one person is dead and the other person is alive?"

"They need attention."

"Yes. They need to feel like the world's listening to them, like they're participating somehow."

"I don't need any of that."

"Me neither."

The two men were silent for several minutes, and then Michael said, "I don't think it's going to get better."

"It has to."

"Not before it gets worse. I want you to promise me something."

"What?"

"If you survive this, I want you to promise me that you'll tell our story. That's the only way anyone will ever remember us."

"Don't do this to me."

"Say it."

"What makes you think I'm going to survive?"

"I said 'if'. Now promise me."

"No. Robert is gone. None of us are equipped for this, least of all me."

"Take it back. Say you'll do it."

"No."

"Say it!"

"Okay, okay. If I survive, I will find a way to tell your story. Are you happy? Every time I hear Bruce Springsteen, I will think of you and Robert and Paul and Hutch. But if I know anything about God, I know there's no way he would take all four of you at once. That just seems excessive and cruel."

Michael laughed. "I like you. You have this naïve shock when the world doesn't work the way you expected it to."

"I still can't believe everyone doesn't get free healthcare."

"See what I mean? You and Marvin, you've been good for us."

"I'm glad you think so. I've had my doubts. Not about Marvin, but sometimes I wonder if Chris would have been better off with someone else, someone who could have helped him with his music more."

"There was no magic wand to wave around and make him a great songwriter."

"I know that. I should have found a way to convince him to keep singing."

"You could have been Paul Simon himself and Chris wouldn't have listened."

Suddenly, Stanton heard music coming from the living room.

"Is that Chaka Khan?" Michael asked.

"Oh my God," Stanton said. "It's 'Ain't Nobody'. I love that song."

"Oh, Stanton. Your taste is improving."

They jumped off the bed and flung open the door. They ran to the living room and found Paul, Chris, and Marvin dancing with their hands in the air.

"Join us!" Paul yelled over the booming music.

Stanton looked at his boyfriend and started dancing. He saw tears in Chris's eyes and reached out for him. Stanton pulled him into an embrace and whispered into his ear, "I love you."

Chris nodded in reply and kept dancing.

ROBERT had two dying requests. One, that Michael receive everything he owned; and two, that his friends spread his ashes on the beach at Fire Island. So the day after the funeral, Michael, Chris, Paul, Marvin, and Stanton picked up Robert's ashes at the crematorium.

They didn't rent a house that summer, so they only had time for a day trip. Since it was a Sunday, the train was barely half full. The five men, dressed in Columbia blue, said virtually nothing on the way out. After they crossed Long Island Sound and exited the ferry, they went to the Blue Whale, where they all shared a shot with the bartenders in Robert's memory. Then they began the walk away from the harbor and toward the beach. When they reached the ocean, they stood in a straight line and faced the water. Marvin took the urn out of its box and opened it. He sprinkled some of the ashes onto the sand in front of him and said, "I'll miss you, big brother."

He handed the urn to Stanton, who said, "Robert, this really sucks. I feel like I was just getting to know you. Anyway, I hope you find what you're looking for. Wherever that takes you."

Stanton sprinkled some ashes onto the sand and handed the urn to Paul, who said, "Oh, babe, how are we supposed to do this without you? It's simply not going to be possible. But don't worry, I'll take care of him."

Paul sprinkled some ashes and handed the urn to Chris. "I don't know what to say. You were my best friend. I'll never forget you."

He sprinkled some ashes on the sand and handed the urn to Michael, who turned it over and emptied what remained. Then he said, "Ain't nobody loved us better than you, my beautiful man. I'll see you in Texas."

THAT evening, Stanton made spaghetti and meatballs.

Chris pushed the food around on his plate and occasionally took a sip of wine. "Sorry," he said. "I don't seem to have much of an appetite."

"Me neither," Stanton replied.

"Do you want to break up with me?"

Stanton shook his head. "Have I given you that impression?"

"You don't seem happy."

"And what about you? That's a little pot/kettle, don't you think?"

"I'm trying."

"Christ. If we're both trying so hard, then why are we so miserable?"

"I don't know."

"Michael said it's growing pains. We need to wait it out and things will get better."

"Play the long game."

"Yeah. I guess."

"You're upset."

"Of course I'm upset. The thing I don't understand is why you aren't. Your best friend died, and I haven't seen more than moist eyes from you."

"I'm afraid if I start crying, I'll never stop."

"That sounds like a line from some bad B movie."

"This feels like a bad B movie."

Stanton heard a dog bark outside their door, the one that belonged to the old woman who lived in the apartment next to them. Then he asked Chris, "Will you promise me something?"

"What?"

"That you will get out your guitar and play for me. Music can fix everything that's wrong with us, Hutch."

"Don't call me that."

"Why not? That's the man I fell in love with. Why do we have to erase him?"

"Everyone needs to grow up sometime. I'm not Peter Pan, and we're not the Lost Boys."

"What does that have to do with what I call you in our apartment?"

"I'd just rather you not, that's all."

"Then promise me you'll play more."

"I'm not going to make a promise I can't keep."

"Why wouldn't you be able to keep a promise like that? Help me understand."

"Because it brings the dream back up, and that's too painful right now. This is who I am without a music career. I'm incomplete. Unfinished. Getting out my guitar doesn't make that better. It only makes it worse."

Stanton didn't know what to say, except, "Oh."

"Does that help you understand?"

"I'm sorry."

"That's why I asked if you wanted to break up with me. I know I'm not the same man you fell in love with. I'm never going to be that man again. I'm never going to write a hit song or do anything extraordinary."

"None of that matters to me."

"Then what does matter to you?"

"Making this work."

"Above all else?"

"Yes."

Chris paused for a long moment, and Stanton could see the weariness in his eyes. "Okay," he said. "Let's make it work, then. But I'm done for today. I'm going to get some sleep."

Chris left the kitchen, and Stanton put the leftovers into the fridge. He cleaned up the dishes, and afterward, he stood in the doorway and listened to

Chris's breathing. Then he closed the door and went back into the living room. He thought about watching some television, but was too tired to hunt for the remote. So instead, he listened to the sounds coming from the street and pretended it was music.

The phone rang and Stanton lunged across the room to answer it before a second ring woke Chris up.

"Hello."

Stanton? This is Norma.

"Hi, Norma. How are you doing?"

I'm fine. Colin misses his favorite uncles.

"Sorry about that. Robert's funeral was yesterday."

I know. That's why I'm calling. How is he holding up?

"I can't tell. Everyone copes with these things differently. It just seems like he's not coping at all."

It's going to take time.

"Michael told me today he thinks he's next."

Oh, my.

"That was pretty much my reaction. More and more men we know are dying every day. Not all of us are going to survive this."

Are you and Chris sick?

"No, not yet. But every cough, every spot on my skin—nothing goes unnoticed."

I'm sure they'll find a cure soon.

Stanton laughed. "Sometimes you're more naïve than I am."

It comes with being common. How are you doing?

"I don't know. I like my job. I'm even kind of good at it. The rest of the time I just feel like we're drowning. Everyone is acting so strong and steadfast, and it feels like complete bullshit to me. Robert would have wanted a party, with sex and drugs and Michael Fierman spinning until ten in the morning. But all he got was some constipated service on the Upper East Side."

I wish there was something I could say.

"There isn't. I know that. You've been a really good friend, Norma, but Chris should never have taken that job with Carl."

Are you still in love with him?

"Yes. Of course. I want this to work more than anything else going in my life right now, but AIDS and real estate are killing my buzz."

You're funny, Stanton. I've heard that a sense of humor helps during times like these.

"I've heard that too. Unfortunately, no one's laughing."

Can you and Chris come for dinner next weekend? It's been over a month since you've seen Colin.

"Yes, I'll make sure of it. Thanks for calling."

Good night.

Stanton stared out the window and caught his reflection in the glass. He looked tired and worn. He went to the stereo and thumbed through the albums. He thought about listening to some Carly Simon, but he couldn't decide which one. He kept thumbing until a record caught his eye. Hank Williams? It must have been Robert's. He had recently started to listen to country and western music, and he traded LPs back and forth with Chris all the time. Stanton figured half the records in the pile probably belonged to Robert. He removed the vinyl from the sleeve and placed it on the turntable. He lowered the needle and went back to the sofa.

That night, alone in their apartment on St. Marks Place, Stanton sat back, closed his eyes, and listened to the sad strains of "I'm So Lonesome I Could Cry."

SOULS OF THE DEPARTED

TOPHER could barely concentrate at work. It was a Thursday, twelve days after Stanton had appeared on his back porch and acknowledged their boyfriend status.

After he showed up out of the blue that way, Stanton returned to New York the next afternoon. Topher wished that night had been spent in his bedroom, having sex and listening to music. But after he finished singing "Che Gelida Manina," Robin and Maurice knocked on his bedroom door and asked if they could hear it too. Once his bandmates got Stanton into the kitchen, they were there until four in the morning, talking about music.

As Topher finished changing the tires on a Toyota Tundra, Stanton's arrival back in Austin was just a few hours away. On this trip, though, he would be staying for almost two weeks, through the Memorial Day concert. Being separated from Stanton was just about the worst form of torture Topher had ever experienced. He never felt anything like it—the pit in his stomach, the inability to sleep and focus, not to mention the shit-eating grin that seemed to be permanently plastered on his face.

His phone rang, and he smiled when he flipped it open and saw Stanton's name. "You at the airport?"

Yeah. I'll be there in about four hours.

"You have the three items?"

I have them.

"Sorry, I don't mean to hound you. It's just that Quentin and Jake are all excited about it. Call me when you hit the runway and I'll pick you up outside of baggage claim."

Okay. I can't wait to see you.

"I'm counting down the minutes myself," Topher said, and then he ended the call.

"Everything on track?" It was Travis, who had walked over into his bay.

"Yeah, he's getting on the plane now."

"He got the items?"

"Yeah, I asked him."

"Good. I'll see you tonight, then. Should be fun."

LATER that evening, when Topher pulled up to the airport terminal, he saw Stanton on the sidewalk, his nose in his phone and his luggage beside him. Topher parked and got out of his truck. He walked up to Stanton and kissed him. "Welcome back to Texas. I'll get your stuff. You get in the truck."

Topher opened the passenger door and Stanton got in. He tossed the luggage into the bed of his pickup and crossed around to the driver's side. After he got in, he leaned over and kissed Stanton again. "I sure am happy to see you. I'm going through withdrawal. No one ever told me that once you start having sex, you want it all the time."

"You look hotter than ever, by the way."

"Really? Peter and I have been working out. Is it starting to show?"

"Yes, it is."

"I want you to be proud of me."

Stanton kissed him and said, "I want you to fuck me."

"You want to do it in a bathroom?"

"Like at a gas station, you mean?"

"Yeah, I saw it in some of the porn scenes I watched. Gay guys have a lot of sex in bathrooms. Did you know there's a whole movie about nothing but one truck stop and all the guys who have sex there? I bet we could find one that locks. It'd be hot, don't you think?"

Stanton laughed. "Yes, it would be hot."

Topher drove out of the airport and then pulled over when he saw a 7-Eleven on the right. He got out of the truck and said, "Follow me." He led Stanton inside, and they headed toward the men's room.

"It's empty," Topher said. He looked at the doorknob. No lock. Then he looked at the handicapped stall. That would work. He pulled Stanton into the wide stall and locked the door behind him.

Stanton eyed him nervously. "Do you have a—?"

Topher put his fingers over Stanton's lips and pulled a condom out of his pocket. Then he whispered, "Unlike you, I was a Boy Scout."

"And what would they say about you now?"

"I know. Homophobic assholes." Topher pushed Stanton against the wall and kissed him. The two men fumbled with belts and zippers, jeans got pushed to their ankles, and then Stanton squatted down to suck Topher's cock. When he was sufficiently hard, Topher pulled Stanton up and turned him around. He tore open the condom package and slid it onto his dick. "I don't have any lube," he said.

Stanton looked over his shoulder. "Then spit will have to do. You've already made me your bottom."

Topher laughed hard when he heard that. "Your ass is mine, whenever I want it, yo."

"Yo?"

"Sorry, we watch way too much *Breaking Bad* at our house. We've seen that episode with the fly about twenty times." Topher spread the cheeks of Stanton's ass and tried to maneuver his cock inside. He pushed him down and said, "You're too tall. You need to bend over a little." Stanton did as he was told and lowered his butt so Topher could reach it. Topher let several drops of spit fall from his mouth to his dick. He spit on his fingers too, and greased the rim of Stanton's asshole, which made him moan. Topher pushed his cock past the tight entry point and they fell together against the wall.

"Thank you," Stanton said.

"You needed that, didn't you?"

"Yes, I needed that."

Topher started to fuck him, gently at first, but then the two men froze when they heard the bathroom door open. Topher slapped his hand over Stanton's mouth and they stood motionless. He heard someone take a piss and then wash his hands. Topher stayed hard the entire time. Finally, the door opened and closed again. He waited a few moments in the stillness before he took his hand off Stanton's mouth.

"Fuck me."

Topher slammed his cock into Stanton's ass, and it didn't take long before he felt himself coming. After all, it had been twelve days. Stanton grabbed his dick and stroked himself while Topher reached his climax, but neither of them made a sound.

"Did you come?" Topher asked as he pulled out and removed the condom. He dropped it into the toilet.

Stanton didn't answer, but instead moved to the side so that Topher could see the wall. It was dripping with come.

"Jesus, have you been jacking off at all?"

"Nope. I've been saving it up for you."

Topher grabbed some toilet paper and wiped the come off the wall, then threw it into the bowl and flushed. He pulled up his pants, zipped his fly, and said, "I can't believe we're going to have almost two weeks together. Are you ready for tonight?"

"I don't know. Are you?"

"Yeah. I'm going to nail it, just watch me."

"I have no doubt."

"Did you make it hard?"

Stanton grinned. "It felt pretty hard to me."

"I mean the test, princess. Did you make it difficult?"

"I think so. Marvin helped."

"The boys are really excited about meeting him tomorrow. Marvin, I mean."

"Where are we going camping?"

"Pedernales Falls. It's a state park." Topher paused and thought about his next question. It was something he'd been thinking about for a while. "Can we talk about getting rid of the condoms?"

"Not yet."

"But—"

"Do we really need to have this conversation in a 7-Eleven bathroom stall?"

Topher laughed. "No, sorry. But we are going to have it."

"Fine. Are you ready?"

"Yeah."

"Lead the way, then."

They exited the stall and washed their hands together, grinning at each other in the mirror. Topher bought a bag of chips and a Dr Pepper on the way out. He thought it was only right after their impromptu round of public sex.

THE two men barely had time to drop Stanton's luggage off at the house and say a quick hello to the boys before they headed to Travis and Ben's for dinner. Quentin answered the door again. "Hey, guys. Come in."

Ben stood inside with his other brothers. "Oh, man," Ben said immediately. "I'm so glad we got to see you again. I'm sorry about last time."

"Forget about it," Stanton said. "Who are the new additions?"

"I'm Jason, the other brother."

Stanton shook his hand.

"And I'm Jake, the other boyfriend."

Stanton shook his hand as well and asked about Travis.

"He's in the kitchen," Cade said.

"Did you bring them?" Quentin asked.

"Yes," Stanton said.

Quentin smiled. "Thank you so much for doing this. Both of you."

They filed into the dining room and took seats around the table. Travis came in from the kitchen and looked around. "We doing this before supper?" he asked.

"Yeah," Ben said. "That okay?"

"Sure. It's not going nowhere." Travis pulled up a chair and sat down next to Ben.

"One second," Quentin said, "we're almost ready." He huddled together with Jake around a camcorder. Jake flipped a switch and stood behind Stanton. He pointed the camera at Topher from across the table. "Okay, we're all set. Go ahead."

Stanton reached into his pocket and pulled out three rings. Topher watched as Stanton placed each one in front of him. He stared at them for a moment and then picked up the first one. It was a class ring from Columbia. Familiar, but it felt like a trick. The second one made Topher laugh. It was a toy ring, the kind that came out of those big gumball machines at the Laundromat. Topher picked it up and held it in the palm of his hand. It would be just like Topher to give Stanton a toy ring, and he was pretty sure Chris Mead had the same kind of playful streak in him. Topher picked up the third ring. It had a heart with a crown on top, and two hands around it. Topher turned it in his fingers and tried it on. It didn't fit. Way too big. He put it down and picked up the Columbia ring again. He tried it on and it fit perfectly. He took it off and laid it back on the table.

He could feel everyone watching him. The whole thing felt off, but he couldn't put his finger on it. He picked up the heart ring again, and then the one that looked like a toy. When he tried the toy ring on, it fit as well. The heart ring was the only one that didn't fit. Topher hesitated. He looked over at Stanton's hands and that's when it dawned on him. Of course. He took off the toy ring and picked up the one with the crowned heart and hands.

"This is it," he said. "But it wasn't his." Everyone looked at Topher, who looked at Stanton and handed the ring back to him. "It was yours. He gave it to you."

Stanton nodded. "He's right."

"Whoa," Travis said.

"Was the Columbia ring even his?" Topher asked.

"No. It was Robert's."

"Can I have it?"

"I was going to give it to Robin."

"Why would you do that?" Quentin asked.

"Quentin," Topher said, "if you're interested in turning this little class project of yours into a real documentary, we should talk after dinner."

"What about the toy ring?" Jason asked.

"I bought that at the deli next to my apartment," Stanton said. "It's the kind of thing Chris would have done."

"How do you feel?" Quentin asked Topher. Jake still had the camera pointed at him.

"I'm not sure. I had a one-in-three chance of getting it right. Those don't feel like very convincing odds to me. But I was pretty certain of the answer."

Quentin signaled for Jake to move around to the other side of the table. Then he asked, "Stanton, what's going through your mind right now?"

"I'm not surprised he got it right. I'm getting used to it, as long as it doesn't upset him. And he's convinced me it doesn't."

"Do you believe in reincarnation now?" Quentin asked Stanton.

"I don't know. I used to believe that God was a cruel bastard. He took everything away from me once, and now... I don't know what to believe anymore. I don't want to limit my experience by naming it with a single word."

"When did he give it to you?" Topher asked. "The ring, I mean." Quentin motioned for Jake to reposition himself so he could get both Topher and Stanton in the shot as they talked.

Stanton shook his head and laughed. "He gave it to me the day we met."

"He gave you a ring on the same day he met you?"

"That takes balls," Ben said.

"It's an Irish tradition. How you wear it tells people if you're available or spoken for. If it's pointing out, away from your heart, you're available; if it's pointing in, you're taken. When he first gave it to me, I wore it with the point facing out."

"When did you turn it around?"

Stanton laughed again and said, "Two days later. After the Springsteen concert. We were coming back into the city on the New Jersey Transit, and he had fallen asleep with his head resting on my shoulder."

"You *are* a hopeless romantic," Topher said, "but why do I get the feeling there's something about that story you're leaving out?"

"I'll tell you about that part later, but think 7-Eleven."

"What is that supposed to mean?" Jake asked.

"Never mind," Topher said. He couldn't help but notice Stanton had put the heart ring on his finger with the tip facing in, and that made Topher pretty damned happy.

Travis grabbed Cade and they disappeared into the kitchen. They returned a few moments later with several platters of barbeque and side fixings. As they began to eat, Quentin pulled Stanton and Topher into an extended discussion about past life regressions and recommended a few books they might want to read. At one point, Jason and Jake butted in because they wanted to talk to Stanton about being a music critic. Topher watched and smiled as Stanton interacted effortlessly with the teenagers. He challenged their assumptions about pop culture and argued that not only would Phillip Phillips win *American Idol*, but he *should* win it.

"Do we really need another white guy with a guitar?" Jake asked.

"Excuse me," Topher said. "I'm sitting right here."

Stanton laughed but then answered Jake's question. "We do if he's the singer who captured the attention of a nation."

"The tween nation, maybe," Jason sneered.

"Who do you think put Elvis on the map? Or the Beatles? Or Frank Sinatra? Or Justin Timberlake? Or Bieber? The tween nation is the most powerful star-making force in this country. Who do you think is buying 'Beaches on the Moon'?"

"Okay, okay," Jake said. "I can tell you're one of those people who has an answer for everything."

Stanton turned to Topher. "Tell them how wrong they are."

Topher nodded to Jason and Jake and said, "You're wrong."

After dinner, Cade excused himself to watch TV and left an empty seat next to Topher. Quentin moved into the chair and asked, "What did you mean by that documentary comment?"

Topher said to Stanton, "Do you want to tell them?"

"I suppose. But I'm just going to give them the facts. Everyone can draw their own conclusions. And some of this is going to be new to you too."

"What do you mean?" Topher asked. "There's more?"

"Yes, there's more. Jake, you might want to turn your camera back on." Stanton paused as Jake reached for his camcorder and started shooting again. Stanton took a drink of water and began his story.

"First, there's the part that Topher already knows. Chris Mead had three friends. They also died in the eighties, all within about a year and a half of each other. Their names were Robert, Michael, and Paul. That's the same year and a half that the other three members of Dime Box were born. As I'm sure you know, their names are Robin, Maurice, and Peter. There seems to be a remarkable similarity between the four men from the past and the four men in the present. Or it could be a series of coincidences. Whatever it is, it appears to extend beyond Topher and myself."

"No fucking way," Ben said.

"There's more. This is the part Topher doesn't know about. Ben, you said you thought maybe you and Travis were in love before this, as two different people. Well, it may be another coincidence, but I think I might know who those two other people were. Topher, if there's a connection here, it goes beyond me and your bandmates. It includes Travis too, and Ben. I went to high school with a guy named Brendan Baxter. He's the one who used to live in your garage apartment, Ben, when he was going to law school."

"Law school?" Ben said.

"Yes, he wanted to be a lawyer, just like you. The four of us, we were friends. Me, Chris, Brendan, and Trent Days."

Travis sat up. "Trent Days?"

"Do you know who that is?" Stanton asked.

Travis chuckled. "I'd hope to hell I do."

"Then you might want to brace yourself."

Topher sat back and listened as Stanton told them the story of Brendan and Trent. When Stanton finished two hours later, Topher stared at Travis in silent disbelief. Travis looked at Ben and said, "Things sure make a whole hell of a lot more sense now."

Ben kissed him and said, "They sure do. Quentin, I think you should get in touch with PBS."

Stanton smiled. "I know someone you can talk to."

THE next day, Topher and the twins packed up their trucks with tents and camping equipment. It was a Friday, and they had all taken off work for the weekend. Peter and Stanton left around noon to pick Marvin up at the airport. Stanton told Topher Marvin was excited but a little nervous too.

Topher knew he didn't need to be. When they returned from the airport, Marvin and Peter were already joking with each other. And when Topher introduced Marvin to Robin and Maurice, the twins engulfed him in a bear hug. The boys took Marvin inside to show him the house, and Topher turned to Stanton and asked, "How'd it go?"

"Just as I expected. I sat in the backseat and barely said a word. It felt like old times."

"Were Marvin and Paul close?"

Stanton chuckled, "Close? They were like sisters."

"Sisters? What does that—? Never mind, we need to hit the road. If we don't get past Oak Hill by three, we'll be sitting in traffic all afternoon."

On the drive out to Pedernales, Stanton rode with Topher, the twins rode together, and Marvin rode with Peter in his car. They had camped at all the state parks in the area and liked most of them, but Pedernales had the biggest sites. It was also just a short drive to Enchanted Rock, which had better hiking trails. Topher explained all this to Stanton, who rolled down his window and asked, "What's enchanted about it?"

"It talks."

"Talks?"

"Well, not really. It's made of granite. It heats up during the day, and when it cools off at night, it makes cracking and moaning sounds, so the Indians thought it was enchanted by a spirit."

When they arrived at the park, Topher, Peter, and the twins began to set up the three large tents. Robin put Stanton and Marvin in charge of unpacking the rest of the equipment. The sleeping arrangements fell along the same lines as the driving ones. Topher would normally have been fine roughing it in sleeping bags on the ground, but to accommodate Stanton, he bought a queen-size air mattress and brought bed linens and pillows too. They packed a grill, a propane gas cooking range, and three coolers of food and drink. Topher got a kick out of watching Stanton and Marvin, since neither one of them had ever been camping before, but after the first few hours, they adapted nicely and settled into the nothingness of camp life. Even better, they were so far out in the middle of nowhere that Stanton lost all reception on his phone. That made Topher smile, because sometimes he thought his only competition for Stanton's affections were his goddamned Twitter followers.

After supper, as the sun began to set, Peter and Marvin decided to go for a walk. Stanton produced some battery-powered speakers and plugged his iPhone into the jack. Then he said to Maurice and Robin, "A little bird told me that your favorite band is Linkin Park."

"No question," Maurice said.

"*Hybrid Theory* was one of the seminal CDs of our youth," Robin added.

"Well, you know I spent a couple of weeks with them, doing a piece for NPR about the new album. It doesn't come out until next month, but Chester and Mike gave me permission to play it for you. If you're interested, of course."

Maurice turned to his brother and squealed, "He just called them Chester and Mike!"

Topher couldn't believe how nice it was that Stanton would do that for his friends.

"I think we're interested," Robin said. He put his arm around Maurice's neck and pulled him into a headlock. "Can you believe this?" he asked his brother. "An advance copy!"

Maurice kept his arms around Robin and said, "Hit the play button, please."

They listened to all the songs without saying a word. They smiled, nodded, and tapped each other on the hand at certain moments. As the last track played, the twins sat quietly in awe, their arms folded on the picnic table, their chins resting on their arms. When the track ended abruptly, they all raised their heads in surprise.

"Wow," Maurice said. "I was so into that last song, and then it just stops."

Robin turned to Stanton and said, "Cool, eh? Like the end of *The Sopranos*. What did you think?"

"You tell me first," Stanton said.

"Well, their sound is way more polished than the early stuff. I miss that garage feel *Hybrid Theory* had."

Maurice nodded. "Me too, but Chester has never sounded better."

"I agree," Stanton said.

"The ballad in the middle," Topher said, "'Castle of Glass'? That was amazing. The whole second half is more like a soundscape than a collection of songs."

Stanton smiled at him. "That's exactly what I said to Chester."

Robin turned to his brother. "What did you think?"

Maurice shrugged. "I'm not a critic, I'm a fan. I loved it, and I can tell I'm only going to love it more the more I listen to it."

"Yeah," Robin agreed. "We need to hear it again. Is that cool?"

"Let's get a fire going first," Topher said. The twins grumbled a little, but then got up and pulled some logs from the bed of their truck. They built a campfire, and shortly after that, Peter and Marvin returned.

"Dude," Maurice said to Peter, "you missed it. Stan played Linkin Park's new album for us. An advance copy."

"No way," said Peter. "Can I hear too?"

Topher leaned over to Stanton and whispered, "Do you mind if he calls you Stan?"

"As a rule, I hate Stan. But Maurice can call me whatever he wants."

"Really?"

Stanton nodded. "He was always my favorite." Stanton played the album a second time so Peter could hear it, and after that, *Living Things* became the soundtrack of their weekend.

After a few hours around the campfire, Topher and Stanton excused themselves and headed toward the showers. They shared a stall and soaped each other clean.

When they returned to their tent, they threw off their towels and lay naked on the air mattress. They turned onto their sides and faced each other.

Topher kissed Stanton and said, "You know they think you hung the moon, don't you?"

"It's all part of my evil plan."

Stanton rolled over onto his stomach and Topher crawled on top of him, kissing his back. "What do you think of your first camping experience?"

"I like it."

Topher felt his cock growing hard. His confidence in the sack had grown significantly since their first weekend in New York. Travis had told Topher about rimming, but he hadn't gone there yet. He kissed the flying horse on Stanton's shoulder and worked his way down. As his lips came to rest in the small hollow above Stanton's ass, he said, "You should get a tattoo right here."

"A tramp stamp?"

"Is that what they call it?"

"Yes, that's what they call it. Thanks, but I think I'm a one tattoo kind of guy."

Topher slipped down further until his tongue came into contact with Stanton's asshole.

Stanton jumped and cried, "What are you doing?"

"Be quiet, old man."

Topher spread Stanton's legs and put his tongue back onto his asshole. When he pushed, Stanton groaned from a place Topher had never heard him groan before. He moved his tongue up and down along the crack. Each time he pushed in, he got the same response, only better. Topher smiled when he realized he had found yet another way to turn Stanton on. He nestled in between Stanton's legs and spent the next ten minutes eating ass and enjoying it, then he slipped on a condom and fucked Stanton senseless. As they intertwined their limbs and were about to fall asleep, they could hear Peter and Marvin cackling from inside their tent.

"Would you two shut up!" they heard Robin yell, but that only made Marvin and Peter laugh louder.

"What's going on over there?" Topher asked.

"I told you," Stanton said. "Sisters."

THE next morning after breakfast, Robin and Maurice announced they were heading to Enchanted Rock for a hike.

"I'm in," Peter said.

"Hiking?" Marvin asked, clearly reluctant. "I don't mind a short walk, but I'm too old for anything more. I'm going to stay here and read."

"I want to go," Stanton said.

Topher saw the opportunity he'd been waiting for. "I'm going to stay here too," he said.

Stanton and Topher's three friends piled into Peter's car and headed out of the park. Marvin went to his tent and got a book, then settled into one of the camping chairs.

"What are you reading?" Topher asked.

"*Rock and Roll Always Forgets: A Quarter Century of Music Criticism.*"

"Who wrote that?"

"Your boyfriend's nemesis."

"Stanton has a nemesis?"

Marvin chuckled. "I exaggerate, of course. Chuck Eddy. They started at the *Village Voice* around the same time. Chuck got one of the first national interviews with the Beastie Boys back in the eighties. Stanton really wanted that one. Someone told me Chuck lives in Austin now, so you'll probably be meeting him one of these days."

"I hope he likes our music."

Topher went to his truck and retrieved his guitar from the small cab behind the passenger seat. He sat down on the picnic table and opened the case. He took out his guitar, a pick, two pencils, and several pages of handwritten sheet music. Then he started to work on his new song.

As Topher had hoped, Marvin soon asked him, "What's that?"

"The new piece I told you about. I'm calling it 'Homesick'."

"Let me hear it."

"I can't seem to get the chord progression right."

Marvin got up from his chair, put his book down, and walked over to the picnic table. He began looking over the sheets of music. "Why are you using a major scale?"

"I write everything in a major scale."

"Well, there's your first problem. This is a song about longing. If you changed it to a minor scale, that would shift the tone and give you access to the kind of chord progression you're looking for."

"How do I do that?"

Marvin sat down and picked up one of the pencils. "Do you mind?"

"Not at all," Topher said, grinning inside.

Marvin began to erase and scribble, erase and scribble, on one of the sheets of music. "Here," Marvin said. He turned the piece of paper around so Topher could read it. "Try that."

Topher started to play. Marvin had transformed the melody, adding a gentle melancholy that had been absent before.

"See what I mean?" Marvin said.

"Man, that sounds so much better. But why don't we move that last note an octave higher? My voice sounds better up there."

"Good idea." Marvin erased and scribbled again.

Topher played it a second time and said, "That's it."

Marvin continued to study the pages. "Why did you use this elementary ABAB rhyming pattern in the lyrics?"

"I don't know. Aren't most pop songs either ABAB or AABB?"

Marvin looked at him over his reading glasses. "Most of the bad ones, maybe. Let's try nesting some of your rhymes, so that they're more unexpected." Marvin started to scribble again. "And we should hold off any rhyme to the word *homesick* until the very end. Otherwise, the piece will resolve too early."

"We should rhyme it with guitar pick."

"Well, I don't know about that, but—" Marvin stopped himself and squirmed with excitement. "But that could be the central narrative metaphor. The character in the song collects guitar picks as he travels around the country."

"No," Topher said.

"You don't like that idea?"

"I love it, but what if he leaves them behind instead. In bars and hotel rooms and honky-tonks. Like bread crumbs. He leaves them as a way to find his way home."

"Fucking brilliant."

Topher picked up one of the sheets and handed it to Marvin. "What do you think of the chorus?"

Marvin looked it over and said, "You should cut it."

"Cut the chorus? Are you joking?"

"I never joke about music. Some of the greatest songs don't have a chorus."

"Name one."

"Thunder Road."

"That has a chorus. When he sings the title."

"That's a verse. A chorus, by its very definition, must be repeated throughout the song. Springsteen never repeats that section. Getting rid of the chorus will make it less cookie-cutter pop."

"We'll have to write some new material, then. Otherwise it will be too short."

"'Yesterday' is two minutes and three seconds long. Wouldn't you agree that's one of the greatest songs ever?"

"Yes, but another verse wouldn't kill us. Or a bridge, at least."

"That's a better idea. A bridge will work."

Topher put his guitar down and picked up the other pencil. He sat down on Marvin's left, and they began writing the bridge. They played off each other's ideas and worked together like a well-oiled machine.

"Have you ever written a song before?" Topher asked.

"Me? I tried when I was younger, but it was a disaster. I could never finish anything. It was like… I don't know."

"Like you only had half the song?"

Marvin turned his head and looked at Topher. "How did you know that?"

Topher shrugged in response. "Why didn't you ever try writing a song with Hutch?"

"He never asked. He didn't even have a band, let alone write songs with other people. Besides, I'm a critic, not a songwriter."

"Could have fooled me. You're getting credit on this. You know that, don't you?"

"Don't be ridiculous. I'm just helping out."

"Don't you be ridiculous. We're writing this song together. If you can't see that, then you're not as smart as Stanton says."

"Are you serious?"

Topher winked. "I never joke about music either."

Marvin fell silent and put his pencil down.

Topher waited a moment before he picked the pencil up and handed it back to him. "Please. I only have half the songs too."

Marvin looked away for a moment and cleared his throat. Then he turned back and glanced down at Topher's arm. Something must have caught his eye, because he reached out and touched a part of Topher's tattoo. "What's that?" Marvin asked.

"What do you mean? It's a tattoo sleeve."

"No, I mean that part right there. Those numbers."

"It says 4:33," Topher said. "It's a Bible verse. Acts of the Apostles, chapter 4, verse 33. It's my mom's favorite." Topher quoted the King James version: "'And with great power gave the apostles witness of the resurrection of the Lord Jesus: and great grace was upon them all.' My mom isn't really a religious person, but she likes that part of the Jesus story. She raised me to believe that love could conquer anything. Even death. So when I was putting together the design for the tattoo, I added those numbers to remind me of that. Why? Do they mean something to you?"

"There's a piece by a man named John Cage called '4'33'". It's four minutes and thirty-three seconds of a musician not playing his instrument. I used to argue with Hutch about it."

"You mean it's four minutes and thirty-three seconds of silence?"

"More or less."

"And people actually play it?"

"Yes."

Topher smiled and shook his head. "Damn. Makes you wish we'd thought of that, don't it?"

Marvin chuckled. "Yes. That's what makes him John Cage."

Topher patted Marvin on the shoulder. "You okay? Stanton's kind of gotten used to this. The coincidences, I mean. But it's still pretty new to you."

"I'm okay. It's one thing to believe in something theoretically, but that tattoo is the kind of detail that borders on...."

"Science fiction?"

"Yes."

"Welcome to my world."

Marvin paused. Then he picked up the pencil and said, "Okay. Shall we write a song?"

Topher grinned and stood up. "You want a beer?"

"Yes, please. Do you have any potato chips?"

"We got four different kinds."

"Great. We'll need those too."

The two men worked for the rest of the day. When the others returned late in the afternoon, Topher announced he and Marvin had written Dime Box's next song. As he played it for them, the people in the campsites around them stopped what they were doing and listened too. When Topher finished, it seemed as if the whole park broke out into applause.

"Dude," Maurice said, "that's the best thing you've ever done. You wrote that with Marvin?"

"Yep. Now I know how Lennon and McCartney felt."

"Please," Marvin said, "let's not get ahead of ourselves. We haven't heard from our resident pop expert yet."

They all turned to Stanton, who said, "It's perfect. The opposite of pedestrian. The trail of guitar picks broke my heart, and the minor key—"

"That was Marvin's idea," Topher said. "He's going to arrange the harmonies too, and we're hiring a chamber orchestra for the studio version and the concert."

"Of course you are," Stanton said. "Nice work, there, buddy. Who'd'a thunk?"

Peter put his arm around Marvin and said, "It's going to be a huge hit."

THAT night, they grilled a massive dinner feast with steak, vegetables, potatoes, and garlic bread. They sat down at the picnic table, with Stanton and the twins on one side, and Topher, Marvin, and Peter on the other.

Maurice slathered his potatoes with butter and asked Marvin, "How long have you worked at the *New York Times*?"

"Fifteen years. We'll see if it can survive fifteen more."

Robin frowned and admitted, "I've never read a newspaper."

"Never?" Marvin asked.

"Nope. I read everything online. You're into classical music, right?"

Marvin smiled at Stanton across the table and said, "Yes, you could say that."

"That's cool. Like Mozart and shit?"

"Yes, I have a soft spot for Mozart."

"We watched that movie a couple of months ago," Peter said. "*Amadeus*?"

Marvin nodded to Peter on his left. "I've seen it several times."

"I didn't get what all the fuss was about," Robin said. "I mean, he wrote some nice music, but it's not like he's the be all to end all."

"I would argue just the opposite," Marvin said. "He never revised, he composed his first symphony when he was eight years old, and the music itself was a gift from God. Name one contemporary musician who can match his output, his complete grasp of musicality, and the sheer inspiration with which he was so obviously blessed."

Robin thought it over for a moment. Then he said, "Prince."

"Prince?"

"Yes," Robin said. "He writes everything, he produces everything, arranges everything. Did you know he played twenty-seven different instruments on *For You*? Twenty-seven!"

"His grasp of musicality isn't just theoretical," Maurice added. "It's practical."

"His output so far has been staggering," Robin continued. "I heard he has five hundred unreleased songs in some vault in his house. Not to mention what he's done for other artists. From what I can tell from that movie, old Wolfgang was the Axl Rose of his day."

"What a douchebag," Peter mumbled.

"And no offense," Maurice said, "but one person's sheer inspiration is another person's noise."

Marvin put his fork down. "Are you saying Mozart's music was noise?"

Peter patted Marvin on the shoulder and said, "Now, calm down there."

"You have to understand something," Maurice said. "When we talk about music, the gloves come off. Since you're a music critic, I think we assumed you could hold your own, but if you need us to back off when you're losing an argument, you just say so and we'll try to accommodate you."

Stanton laughed, almost uncontrollably. "My, how the tables have turned. It's like they've been planning their revenge for thirty years."

On the other side of Marvin, Topher heard Peter whisper, "I don't think Maurice was suggesting that Mozart's music is noise."

"I wasn't," Maurice said. "I was trying to foreground subjectivity, which is something Stanton's been teaching us about."

Stanton raised his right hand over Robin's head, and Maurice tapped it in a high-five gesture.

Marvin glared at Stanton. "So I have you to thank for this. I should have known."

Maurice chuckled and asked Marvin, "What's up with the way you couch someone's musical talent in religious terms like that? Gift from God? You can't turn your analysis into some nebulous, spiritual mumbo-jumbo. I mean, anyone who says 'God is on my side' can win an argument. Shit, we learned that from Dylan."

"Whoa," Stanton said. "Okay, you know I love you, buddy, but that was stunning. I wish I had thought of it myself. In fact, why didn't I think of it myself?"

Marvin looked at Maurice and asked, "Where did you go to school?"

"UT."

"Did you all go there together?"

"Nope," Peter said. "Maurice was the only one smart enough to get in. So we all moved to Austin with him when we graduated from high school—to keep the band together, of course."

"Except for me," Topher said. "I had to finish my senior year before I moved."

Marvin smiled and paused for a moment. "Okay, I admit, it was a very nice rhetorical move on your part, Maurice. I may not enjoy being put in my place by a boy half my age, but—"

Stanton pulled out his phone and swiped upward to expose the camera. He pointed it at Marvin and said, "Hold on. Can you say that again so I can tweet it later? The part about you being put in your place."

"Stop it," Marvin said, but Topher could tell he enjoyed the teasing.

Maurice leaned over and whispered something into his brother's ear. Robin looked across the table at Peter, who reached behind Marvin and tapped Topher on the shoulder.

"What's going on?" Marvin asked.

"They want to play that game," Topher said. "The one Stanton told us about. The one you played when you first met them."

"The Greatest Game?" Marvin asked.

Topher nodded.

"I say we roll with it," Stanton said. "They were asking me questions about Robert, Michael, and Paul all day. If they want to play, let's play."

"I never said I had any objection." Marvin turned to Peter, Robin, and Maurice and asked, "Do you know the rules?"

"Music categories only," Peter said.

"No repeats," the twins said.

Topher raised his foot and pressed it against Stanton's crotch under the table. "Ultimate final category rule."

"Wait," Marvin said. "There's something missing."

Stanton slapped his hand on the table. "He's right! We forgot the weed. This game is way more fun stoned. But we shouldn't in public. We don't want to get arrested."

Maurice stood up, saying, "You don't have to smoke to get stoned." He walked over to one of the coolers and pulled out a freezer bag with brownies inside. He returned to the table and set the bag down in the middle. "They'll take a while to kick in, but no one will ever know."

"I haven't finished my steak yet," Marvin said.

"We have this saying in Austin," Topher said. "Dessert first."

"Where did you learn how to make pot brownies?" Marvin asked.

"Our mom," Robin said.

Everyone grabbed a chocolate square and the game began.

"Okay, then," Marvin said. "Who wants to go first?"

"I will," Stanton said. "Greatest song by a boy band."

"Oh," Topher said, "that's an easy one. 'Tearin' Up My Heart'. It put 'N Sync on the map, and really, it never got better than that." Topher imitated Justin Timberlake's signature head bob. "Let's do it, boys."

Topher and his friends jumped up and moved into a clearing next to the picnic table.

"What's going on?" Marvin asked.

"We performed this for a school assembly back when we were fourteen," Peter explained.

"I was only thirteen," Topher said. They broke out into "Tearin' Up My Heart," complete with the original dance routine from the video. Stanton and Marvin stood up and rocked along with them.

When they finished and sat back down at the table, Stanton leaned over and gave Topher a kiss. "That was so hot."

Robin shook his head and laughed. "Can we keep going? I know this sounds random, but I love 'The Call'."

Maurice started to crack up. "My brother, the Backstreet Boy. He wanted to do 'I Want It That Way' for the assembly."

"Shut up. That's a great song."

"Then why didn't you pick it?"

"Have you heard the Thunderpuss remix of 'The Call'?" Stanton asked.

"I don't think so."

"If you love that song, the remix will change your life. Forever. Trust me."

Marvin leaned forward and said to Robin, "In case you haven't noticed, Stanton loves hyperbole."

Topher elbowed Marvin. "Oh, we've noticed. You know what he said about one of my songs? 'Worst thing I've ever heard in my life.'"

"Can I go next?" Peter asked.

Marvin turned and said, "There is no asking to go next in the Greatest Game. It is strictly first come, first serve."

"Then how about Boyzone's cover of 'You Needed Me'?" Peter said. "My mom listened to Anne Murray in the house growing up, and I've always thought their version was just about the sweetest thing."

"You would," Robin said. "I've never even heard it."

"I Want It That Way," Maurice said.

Robin turned to him. "See? That's why I didn't pick it. 'Cause I knew you would."

"We now have two for the Backstreet Boys," Stanton said. He looked at Marvin for his answer.

"I'm forced to go old school."

"New Kids on the Block?" Stanton asked.

"Yes. What's the one they shot in black and white?"

"'You Got It'. But you probably remember it as 'The Right Stuff'." Stanton sang, "Oh oh oh oh oh."

"That's it. Before Jordan Knight's hair got bigger than the Empire State Building. The New Kids were the blueprint for everything y'all have mentioned."

Peter and the twins laughed and banged on the table.

"Marvin," Maurice said. "I don't know if we can handle it if you start saying 'y'all'."

"Why not?" Marvin said. "I like it. It's a perfectly good second-person plural pronoun. Wow, that's a lot of Ps."

"The brownies are kicking in," Maurice said.

Stanton wrapped up the category. "Although I'm disappointed no one said 'MMMBop', I'm going with, 'I Want to Hold Your Hand'."

"What?" Robin said.

Maurice pushed his brother back so he could ask Stanton, "Did you just reclassify the greatest rock-and-roll band of your generation as a boy band?"

"Of our generation?" Marvin said. "Are they not the greatest rock-and-roll band of *all* generations?"

"Frankly, no," Maurice said. "I think Springsteen is greater. Maybe when you first started listening to him in the prehistoric seventies, it didn't seem like you could ever compare him to the Beatles. But now look at his body of work."

Stanton nodded. "It's hard to argue with him."

Marvin looked at Maurice. "You do realize that Springsteen is my generation, and I was ten when the Beatles broke up?"

"I'm just saying," Maurice said, "that people my age don't have the same reverent attitude toward the Beatles. I think it's brilliant that Stanton rebranded them as a boy band, because that's exactly what they were in the beginning."

Marvin looked back at Stanton. "You've really got them blowing smoke up your ass, don't you?"

"I had nothing to do with it," Stanton insisted, but then he and Maurice high-fived over Robin's head again.

Maurice took a swig of beer and said, "We're good, Marvin. You know I only talk trash with my friends, right?"

Marvin smiled and said, "I consider it an honor and a privilege to be hashing out our musical differences."

"Good. Me too. I'll go next, then. Greatest Michael Jackson song. No, wait, wait, wait. Greatest song by any Jackson, group or individual."

"No!" Robin yelled. "That's impossible."

"Calm down," Peter said. "'Rhythm Nation'. See how easy that was?"

"Billie Jean," Topher said.

"ABC," Marvin followed.

"Man in the Mirror," Stanton said. Topher and his friends stopped and looked at him. "What's the matter?"

Topher grinned. "We just closed one of our shows with a cover of that."

Under the table, Stanton pressed his foot against Topher's crotch and said, "You guys have good taste."

"I'm going with 'Control'," Robin said.

"Then I'm going to say 'Beat It'," Maurice said. "There's nothing more iconic than that red leather jacket."

"Uh," Topher said. "The white glove?"

"Oh, right. Almost, then. Marvin, you want to go next?"

Marvin looked at the faces around the table and said, "Let's see if you're old enough to pull this off. Greatest Elvis song."

"Old enough?" Robin scoffed. "I'll show you old enough. 'Hound Dog'."

"Suspicious Minds," Peter said.

Maurice closed his eyes and scrunched up his face. "All Shook Up."

Topher reached down and rubbed Stanton's foot, then he said to him, "Go ahead."

"No. You go first."

Everyone looked at Topher. "I'm going to say 'Return to Sender', because that's the Elvis song my dad used to sing when he was drinking a beer after he mowed the lawn. But I can guess what Stanton is going to say."

"You want to answer for me?"

Topher stood up, leaned over the table, and kissed him. "I bet it's 'Can't Help Falling in Love'?"

"He's right."

"How did you know that?" Peter asked.

"Because," Stanton said as Topher sat back down, "I'm way more predictable than you realize."

"I'll finish with 'Heartbreak Hotel'," Marvin said, and then he nodded to Robin.

"I'm going to bring things home here to Texas," Robin said. "Greatest country and western song. Ever."

"Oh, I'm in trouble," Stanton said. "This is not my strong suit."

Marvin shook his head. "Just think about all those LeAnn Rimes remixes you've heard at the Pavilion."

"What's that one I liked from about five years ago?"

"'Suddenly'. And it was more like ten."

"Suddenly," Stanton yelled.

"I Hope You Dance," Marvin said.

Robin reached across the table and tousled Marvin's hair. "Now just how in the hell does a classical music critic know who Lee Ann Womack is?"

"Be careful," Stanton said. "When it comes to music, Marvin is the second-smartest person I've ever known."

"Who was the first?" Peter asked.

"Yeah," Topher said. "I would like to know the answer to that myself."

Marvin popped the last bit of brownie into his mouth. "Who do you think?"

"Hutch?" Topher asked.

Stanton and Marvin both laughed. "In his dreams, maybe," Marvin said. "No, when it came to music, Robert schooled us all."

Stanton nodded. "We used to go out to Queens on Sundays to have lunch with Marvin's parents. We would get high before the train ride back, and Robert would lead these amazing discussions about music."

"I called them the Stoned Subway Seminars," Marvin said. "I thought I was such hot shit when I first met him, spouting off the way I did. But he taught me everything I know about listening to music."

"He taught us all everything we know," Stanton said.

Topher kicked Robin under the table and said, "See? I told you."

"Can we continue with the game, please?" Maurice said. "I'm going with 'I Fall to Pieces'."

"Do you remember the big drag queen that first summer on the island?" Marvin asked Stanton.

"Patzi Klein. Only she spelled it with a *z*, like Liza. And Klein, like Calvin Klein."

"Ty was right," Topher said. "You two do talk about it like it's some Greek myth."

"Sorry," Stanton said. "I bet I know what you're going to say, though. For greatest country and western song."

Topher laughed. "How would you know?"

"Because you've already picked a song your father used to sing. You told me his three favorites were Bruce Springsteen, Otis Redding, and Buck Owens. So you're going to choose a Buck Owens song. And what other Buck Owens song would you choose, other than—"

Robin raised his hands and said, "I've Got a Tiger by the Tail."

"No fair!" Topher said. "But you're right. Dammit."

Robin shook his head and leaned toward Stanton. "I will never understand his obsession with Buck Owens."

Stanton nodded. "It's that red, white, and blue guitar."

"Excuse me? I'm sitting right here."

Robin and Stanton laughed, and Topher liked the way that made him feel. Then Peter said, "I'm going with 'I Walk the Line'."

"I promise not to tell a story about what Johnny Cash means to me," Stanton said.

"Now," Topher objected, "I didn't mean to shut you up or anything."

Stanton flashed him a grin, and Topher could tell his brownie was kicking in too. "It's just that Chris used to take these big songs and strip them down," Stanton said. "He called them his Johnny Cash versions."

"We call that unplugged," Maurice said. He nudged Robin. "What's the last word on C and W, brother?"

"I'm So Lonesome I Could Cry."

Maurice sighed and said, "That is my all-time favorite Hank Williams song."

"I know it is. Our dad was a worthless piece of shit, but he had great taste in country music."

"It's my favorite Hank Williams song too," Stanton said.

Topher rubbed his chin in jest and said, "I guess you're not as predictable as we thought."

"Peter," Robin said, "it's your turn."

Peter glanced around the table. "Help me out here, boys. We need something truly awesome." There was a long pause as Topher, Robin, Maurice, and Peter considered their options.

Then Maurice clapped his hands together and said, "I got it." He stood up, leaned over the table, and whispered something into Peter's ear.

"Oh, that's good," Peter said. "Okay, greatest *American Idol* performance of all time."

Stanton lowered his head and said, "Best. Category. Ever. Are we limited to what was performed on the show in competition?"

Peter tapped Topher on the shoulder, and Topher nodded. "Yes," Peter said.

"Fantasia's version of 'Summertime'," Maurice said. "No one can argue with that."

"Mad World," Topher followed.

"See?" Maurice said. "That's why I thought you were gay. Your obsession with Adam Lambert."

"I am not obsessed with Adam Lambert. It's the voice, stupid."

"Those are the two most obvious," Stanton said. "After that, it's between David Cook's cover of 'Always Be My Baby' and Kelly Clarkson's 'Stuff Like That There'. I have to go with David Cook, since he's my favorite Idol of all time."

"Elliott Yamin," Marvin said.

"Which one?" Maurice asked.

"A Song for You."

Maurice shook his head. "That's a slip on your good taste meter, my friend."

"Hemorrhage," Robin said.

Stanton grunted beside him. "I hate Chris Daughtry."

Maurice laughed. "No high-five for you, bro."

"Where's Carrie Underwood?" Peter asked.

Maurice bounced up and down and said, "That Heart song!"

"Alone," Stanton said.

"Yes," Peter confirmed. "That's my answer." He leaned forward and looked across Marvin at Topher. "The pimp slot is yours."

Topher looked around the table. It was a sight. Then he said, "Greatest song ever. That's ultimate final category, right?"

Marvin nodded. "You are correct, young man."

"Well," Maurice said, "I'm not going to steal my brother's answer, because he didn't steal mine. So the second-greatest song is 'Smells Like Teen Spirit'." Topher and his friends bowed their heads for a moment of silence. "If there is any band we feel a reverence for, it's Nirvana."

After an appropriate pause, Marvin said, "I'm sticking with 'Redemption Song'. It speaks to me now more than ever."

"The original Bob Marley?" Peter asked.

"Of course."

Stanton smiled at Topher. "Mine is still 'Bridge Over Troubled Water'."

"Shadow of the Day," Robin said.

"Greatest Linkin Park song ever," Topher added.

"I don't know about that," Stanton said. "'In The End' is widely considered to be their best."

"I don't care," Robin said. "Have you seen the clip of Chester singing 'Shadow of the Day' in Madrid? That is going to be you someday, Topher."

"I know it's overexposed," Peter said, "but Leonard Cohen's 'Hallelujah' is still considered one of the greatest, isn't it?"

"Yes," Stanton said.

"Completely overexposed," Robin added. Then he turned to Topher for the final answer of the night.

Topher considered his choice carefully, then he said, "The thing I noticed playing this game, is that it's never really about the greatest anything, is it? It's always about what's your favorite."

"Hear, hear," Stanton said quietly.

Topher warmed inside that his boyfriend agreed with him. "Sometimes, it's even about your favorite at this moment. Honestly, off the top of my head, the greatest song ever is the Killers' 'Human'. But someone slipped a song onto my iPod a few days ago, and at first I thought, 'What is this crap?' Then I listened to it a couple of times, and I have to say, I changed my mind.

Stanton, if that's how you feel about me, then I'm the luckiest man in all of Texas."

"What is it?" Robin asked.

"Only Yesterday," Topher said. "By the Carpenters."

"Stanton," Robin said. "The Carpenters? Seriously?"

Stanton nodded to Marvin. "Some things never change."

MARVIN flew back to New York after the camping trip, but he made plans with the band to return with Tyrese for the Memorial Day concert in Dime Box, where they would debut "Homesick." Marvin wanted to do all the musical arrangements, which meant he e-mailed them the new material in bits and pieces over the days leading up to the concert. Marvin also contacted the resident string quartet at UT and enlisted them to play the orchestral part for both the concert and studio version. Peter's dad used his staff to build the stage and set up the extra bleachers around the baseball field. Mr. Moses was so proud of his son, and the speed at which the band had paid off their loan, that he insisted the lumberyard sponsor the event and foot the entire bill. Mr. Moses also worked with Kai, now the band's official filmographer, and together they set up giant screens for multimedia projections and live close-ups. Kai also assured them he would edit the footage and post it on YouTube within twenty-four hours.

News of the free concert spread throughout Central Texas, thanks to a promotional platform Stanton designed. Stanton spent the week with Topher and the band in rehearsals, helping them fine-tune their playlist, even though the members insisted on keeping their signature closing cover a secret. In addition to the instrumental arrangements, Marvin also e-mailed pieces of the vocal harmonies for "Homesick" on a daily basis. They were the most difficult the boys had ever attempted and required hours of extra rehearsal. Once again, they were averaging four hours of sleep a night, but none of them dared complain. Peter even posted a sign in their garage that read, "No stinking divas!" Stanton suggested they invite other bands to play during the day, as a way to make the trip worthwhile for fans and to generate goodwill within the Austin music scene. Topher remembered him saying something about a rising tide lifts all boats. Stanton used his connection with the critic at the *Austin Chronicle* (the one who loaned him the car that broke down and caused Stanton and Topher to meet) to help contact other bands and arrange the lineup.

When the day of the concert arrived, Topher and Stanton drove to Dime Box late in the morning and had lunch with Topher's mom and sister. Topher knew his mom was a little wary of Stanton's age, especially since Topher had only recently come out to her. Stanton, however, demonstrated he could muster considerable charm when required. At one point, Topher noticed Stanton and his mom talking alone in the kitchen, while he and Trisha caught up in the living room. After that, his mom seemed to be okay with everything and treated Stanton like one of the family. As they left the house, Topher nudged Stanton, asking, "What did you say to her?"

"I told her she had nothing to worry about, because if anyone's heart was going to get broken, it would be mine. I told her once you had set your mind on this, I couldn't sway you otherwise, as hard as I tried. And I did try. She understands your tenacity. I asked her to empathize with me."

"Your heart is not going to get broken."

The first band started playing around four o'clock. The crowd began to swell soon after, and by seven, Mr. Moses estimated about two thousand people had arrived. The town turned into a parking lot. By seven thirty, the organizers sent someone to tell the still arriving cars they would have to turn around, because the concert had reached capacity.

Topher hung out with Stanton in a makeshift green room they'd set up in the school. Topher enjoyed getting to know the other musicians. They were in separate conversations when Topher saw Peter rush up to Stanton. Peter whispered something into Stanton's ear, and then Stanton looked over at Topher. Topher pulled himself away from his chat with a local bass player and walked over to them. "What's going on?" he asked.

"Marvin and Ty are here," Stanton said. "We have a surprise for you."

"A surprise? What kind of surprise?"

"Follow me."

They went into the school hallway, where Marvin, Tyrese, and the rest of the band were waiting for them. At first Topher didn't understand what was going on, but then he saw Marvin holding a guitar case. "Is that the black Fender?" he asked.

"Yes," Stanton said. "It's yours now."

Topher shook his head and fought back tears. "Did you have to do this to me now?" he said, half serious and half joking. "I can't sing if I'm all blubbery." Marvin handed him the case. Topher set it on the floor and opened it up.

"I had it restrung," Marvin said. "I've been playing it all week to break in the new strings."

Topher picked up the guitar and held it in both hands. The strap was a deep red with "HUTCH" branded in white letters. He lifted it over his head and took out one of his "Austin" picks. He played the opening bars of "Homesick." Then he stopped and said to Stanton, "Thank you."

His voice cracked a little.

"You're welcome. It's a beautiful instrument, and it shouldn't be sitting in the back of my closet. He would have wanted you to have it. I'm certain of that. It belongs to you now."

Robin yelled, "Group hug!" Everyone gathered around Topher and threw their arms around him.

When Dime Box took the stage around eight o'clock, the crowd welcomed them with a thunderous ovation. They opened, as always, with "Beaches on the Moon." They played for more than an hour, until it was time for the debut of "Homesick." As the string quartet came onto the stage and took their places, Topher flipped the black Fender onto his back and stepped up to the microphone.

"We want to thank everyone for coming out and making this pretty much the most amazing day of our lives. We want to thank Peter's dad, Mr. Moses, for making it possible, and Kai Jackson for filming it. Kai, you've really become a part of our family, in case we haven't told you that yet. We want to publicly thank Stanton Porter for talking about us on *Morning Edition* and starting this whole rollercoaster ride. And finally, we want to introduce the newest member of Dime Box, my writing partner, Marvin Goldstein." Marvin, who was standing off stage, stepped up and waved to the crowd. "Marvin and I wrote this song together when the band went camping last weekend at Pedernales. I hope y'all like it."

Topher waited and the crowd settled down. Then he sang the opening line, intentionally written in the highest part of his register. The violin joined him, followed by Peter's deep bass voice, accompanied by the cello. The twins were up next, and the melody crescendoed, their voices doing battle with the strings, building to a fevered pitch, and then breaking. Not a sound could be heard for a full measure. Then Maurice gently tapped his drumsticks and the song switched gears. Topher told a story about a young musician, moving from city to city, wanting desperately to make his way home. He looked over at Stanton and hoped he wasn't too unnerved by what he saw.

One voice, one song, one guitar.

Christopher.

When they finished up "Homesick," the fans roared their approval and began stomping their feet for more. After a full five minutes, the throng quieted down long enough to allow Topher to speak. "Okay, one more. As a lot of you know, we always close our sets with a cover. This one is dedicated to four men we've never met, but who somehow managed to reach across the years and connect with us in a way we sure as hell never expected. Their names were Hutch, Robert, Michael, and Paul."

The five projection screens around the stage went black. Then, one by one, the screens lit up with pictures of the four men: dressed in Columbia caps and gowns at their graduation, clowning around in front of Madison Square Garden, sitting at a sidewalk cafe, hanging over the edge of a bridge in Central Park, and of course, on the beach at Fire Island, with their arms wrapped around each other's shoulders. Peter picked up his microphone and moved it next to Topher's. Maurice came out from behind the drum set, and he and Robin joined them.

"You ready, boys?" Topher asked.

The other three nodded and Topher began. He strummed the opening bars of Simon & Garfunkel's "The 59th Street Bridge Song," more commonly known as "Feelin' Groovy."

HOURS later, Topher drove back to Austin with Stanton. Maybe it was because he felt invincible, or maybe it was because it still seemed like time wasn't on his side, but for some reason, Topher picked that moment to ask Stanton about Joseph Mead.

"I don't want to talk about him," Stanton said.

"Why not?"

"Because this was one of the most incredible days of my life, and I would like it to remain that way. Joseph Mead is nothing but a buzzkill."

"Ben told me about the empty chair at Thanksgiving. He told me Chris and his father weren't even speaking to each other when he died, and that Mr. Mead has never forgiven himself. What was there to forgive?"

"You're not going to let this go, are you?"

"Highly unlikely. That's the Topher tenacity, remember? It had something to do with you, didn't it?"

"Maybe."

"Please, tell me."

"Topher, I'm fine. Really. I'm embracing this—us—as a good thing. Why do you want to drag Joseph Mead into it?"

"Because I don't want anything left unresolved. For your sake, not for ours. I don't want you to spend any more of your life being angry at somebody, and I know you still are. I can tell by the way that vein in your neck pops out when you talk about him."

"Pull over, then."

"Why?"

"Because it's a long story, and I don't want to tell it to you while you're driving. Find a place to park. You must know these roads like the back of your hand, even at night."

"Okay," Topher said. He drove a short ways and took a turn down FM 1624. They found a deserted nook off the road, and Topher parked his Ranger underneath a large oak tree. They got out, and Topher pulled down the tailgate of his truck. The two men sat and Stanton began.

"It started the day I got home from visiting my family. I hadn't seen them in two years because of the way they reacted when I wrote them my coming out letter. I had just flown back to New York from Ohio, and I remember it was raining really hard. I took the shuttle bus from LaGuardia and had arrived soaking wet at our apartment on St. Marks Place, the one I shared with Chris...."

DARKNESS ON THE EDGE OF TOWN

STANTON stepped into the tiny foyer of their apartment and dropped his bag onto the floor with a thud. He went back out into the hallway, took off his wet jacket, and shook it dry. The cold September rain that greeted him at the airport sent chills down his neck. He returned to the foyer and placed the jacket over one of the hooks in the wall. He closed the door and locked it behind him. Stanton walked into the living room and glanced toward the kitchen, then the bedroom. The door was closed. That struck him as odd, since they never closed the bedroom door. He walked across the living room and put his ear to the wood. He didn't hear anything, so he reached down and turned the knob. He pushed the door open and stuck his head in. When he saw what was waiting for him on the bed, he opened the door the rest of the way. Chris was lying asleep, naked, his arms wrapped around the torso of another man. Stanton didn't know what to do, so he went into the living room and sat down on the sofa. A few moments later, he heard the bedsprings squeak and a pair of bare feet hit the floor.

"Stanton?" Chris called.

"Get him out of here."

"Fuck." A mad commotion from the bedroom followed, and a few minutes later, Chris and the unknown man walked through their living room to the front door. Chris let the man out and replaced the deadbolt behind him. He walked back into the living room and sat down in the chair opposite Stanton, wearing nothing but a pair of gym shorts.

"In our bed?" Stanton said. "I know we've been having problems, but you couldn't go to his place? You had to throw it in my face like that?"

"I'm sorry. He lives uptown. It just happened."

"What do you mean, it just happened?"

"I was coming home from the office, and we caught each other's eye on the train. I thought you weren't supposed to be back until four."

"It's four thirty."

"Oh. We must have fallen asleep."

"What's wrong with you? Were you trying to get caught?"

Chris didn't answer right away, but then he said, "Maybe."

"I feel like I'm going to be sick. What were you doing in the office on a Sunday?"

"I told you, we're working on a big deal with Trump."

"You never told me that."

"Yes, I—"

"Did you use a condom?"

"Yes."

"Is this because I went to visit my family without you?"

"No. I don't know. Maybe. Jesus Christ, why couldn't you stand up to them? I stood up to my family when they wouldn't invite you to Thanksgiving. You caved. How do you think that made me feel?"

Stanton's mouth fell open in disbelief. "We talked about this. You told me to go."

"What else was I supposed to say? I didn't want you to pick me because I told you to."

"Pick you? What kind of passive-aggressive bullshit is that?"

Chris put his head down. "I'm sorry. It won't happen again."

"You're damn right it won't happen again." Stanton stood up and began walking toward the door.

"Where are you going?"

"To stay with Marvin. Good thing I'm already packed."

"This isn't all my fault, you know."

Stanton stopped and turned back. "What is that supposed to mean?"

Chris got up and faced him. "You want to blame me for this. You think I don't know that? You want to believe this is happening because I gave up on my music and took a soulless job with my brother. You want to believe I've changed, because then you can pretend it was all my fault. Well, here's a newsflash for you—it wasn't all my fault. There have always been two of us in this relationship."

"I'm not the one who cheated."

"There is more than one way to cheat."

"Oh, really? Please, explain that to me."

"When you stop fucking your boyfriend, that's cheating."

Stanton couldn't believe what he was hearing. "I can't take this."

"Of course you can't. God forbid you listen to anything that contradicts the Little Miss Perfect image you have of yourself."

"Stop it. You know I don't see myself that way. What in the fuck is the matter with you?"

"When was the last time we had sex? Do you even remember?"

Stanton didn't reply.

"Neither do I," Chris said. "That's cheating too."

"We're in a monogamous relationship. We made a promise to each other, and I kept that promise."

"No, you didn't. You think you did, but you're wrong. You won't even touch me anymore. How is that keeping your promise? You're supposed to love me. What happened to that?" Chris walked across the room and reached out, but Stanton immediately recoiled from the gesture. "Do you see what I mean?" Chris said.

"You think I want you to touch me now? After you've been with someone else?"

Chris laughed and shook his head. "You finally have a good excuse, don't you? You've been pulling away for months, and we both know why. You think I'm next and you don't want to catch it."

"It's a virus. If one of us has it, we both have it. Most likely."

"See? You're still holding onto that sliver of hope, that maybe you can get out of this alive. If you stop having sex with me, then maybe it's not too late."

"That's ridiculous."

"Is it? Why do you even care who fucks me if you're not? You're only marking time anyway, waiting for an opportunity to bail. Well, here it is. We both know you don't have the balls to leave on your own, so instead you've been making our lives miserable in hopes that I'll do it for you. Isn't that what you want? Okay, then, I'll do it. Get the hell out of here. Go. I've given you the perfect setup to make your escape. Blame it all on me if that helps you sleep at night."

Stanton teemed with anger. "What did you expect? I fell in love with a man named Hutch. Do you remember him? Because I haven't seen or heard from that guy in ages. I did not fall in love with your brother."

"So I'm right. You do blame me. Why does it matter what I call myself, or if I'm a musician, or sell real estate, or dig ditches. I'm still the same person inside."

"No, you're not. I don't care what you do. If you want to dig ditches, go right ahead, but you're not the same person. Music made you extraordinary, and I'm not talking about talent or fame. I'm talking about the thing that used to light you up, the thing that connected us. You're a shell without it."

A piercing silence filled the room. For some reason, Stanton thought of John Cage. The rain lashed against the window and someone's car alarm went off on the street. Hutch's breathing increased, and Stanton heard a dripping sound coming from the hallway. A pool of water was probably gathering on the floor beneath his jacket.

Stanton heard music in the silence.

Chris looked down at the floor, defeated. "I'm losing it, Starsky. All my friends are dead."

"Don't you dare play that card now. They were my friends too."

"I'm sorry. It's just… I'm so tired of pretending that everything is going to be fine, because nothing will ever be fine again. But mostly, I'm tired of pretending that you still love me. It's as if you've already moved on, like you have one foot here and one foot in the future, without me. You act like you're in two places at once, but it feels like you're not anywhere at all."

"That is so unfair."

"Is it? Can you say it to me? Can you tell me you love me? Because I can still say it to you. I love you. I miss you."

"You've got a funny way of showing it."

"This is the first honest conversation we've had in over a year. Can't you feel that?"

Stanton felt nothing. "It's also the last," he said. "This is it. I'm done with you."

"You can't mean that."

"I do."

"Over one stupid roll in the hay?"

"I don't want a boyfriend who cheats on me. Period. You've tortured me enough for one lifetime."

"Don't do this. Not now."

"Then when? How long am I supposed to stick around? When are you going to pull yourself together? You just told me to go."

"I didn't mean it."

"Too bad. I mean it. This is over. I'll be at Marvin's. I'll call you in a few days and we can work out the details."

"Please, don't—"

But before Chris had a chance to finish, Stanton turned around and walked out the door.

AFTER Michael died, a lawyer showed up one day and informed Paul and Marvin the Christopher Street apartment now belonged to them. At the funeral, Michael's grandmother had thanked them for taking care of her grandson until the very end. Now that Paul was gone too, Marvin lived there by himself.

A soaking wet Stanton arrived about twenty minutes after leaving St. Marks Place. His shoulders ached from carrying his bag across town to Christopher Street.

Marvin opened the door and his face crumbled. "What happened?" he asked.

"It's over."

Marvin closed his eyes for a moment before he said, "Come in. Put your bag in your old room and change into some dry clothes. I'll be in the kitchen."

Stanton didn't want to go into the room he used to share with Chris, so he set his bag down in the hallway instead. He opened it and pulled out a fresh pair of pants, a sweatshirt, and some socks. He went into one of the bathrooms and undressed, dried himself with a towel, and hung his wet clothes on the shower rod. He dressed and went back into the kitchen. Marvin was making a pot of coffee.

Stanton opened the fridge and pulled out a bottle of beer. "You want one?" he asked Marvin.

"No. I'm good."

Stanton twisted off the top and threw it into the sink.

Marvin took the bottle cap and tossed it into the trash. "What happened?"

Stanton shook his head. "He was in bed with someone else when I got back from Ohio."

"In *your* bed?"

"Yes. I walked in on them sleeping. They were taking a nap and lost track of time. You should have seen the picture they made together. I wanted to puke."

"Oy vey. How long has this been going on?"

Stanton shrugged. "I didn't even think to ask him that. There was something about one roll in the hay, so I assume it was the only time. Do you think he's been doing this for a while?"

"It wouldn't surprise me. You two haven't exactly been in sync lately."

"It doesn't matter anymore. Can I stay here for a while?"

"You'll move in permanently if I have anything to say about it. I can't stand it here by myself. I cry every time I pass their rooms. But we can't give up on him."

"You can't, maybe. I'm done."

"Don't say that."

"All my instincts about him were wrong. Remember when I first met him? When I told you I thought he was the one? What an idiot I was. Men are such shits."

"You're upset."

"How am I supposed to trust myself again? I thought I had everything figured out. Jesus, was I wrong."

"You're putting the cart before the horse. Now is not the time to second guess yourself. Now is the time to eat ice cream, listen to *Torch,* and watch *The Way We Were.* That's what Paul used to tell me, at least. You can deal with your trust issues later."

Stanton sat down at the table. He took a swig of his beer and then started to peel the label off the bottle, a nervous habit he'd picked up standing around Uncle Charlie's, before he met Chris. "How did we get here?" he asked Marvin. "Everything was going so perfectly. Now we're back to just you and me. No offense."

Marvin sat down next to him. "None taken. I don't know what happened. I keep thinking one of these days I'll walk in here, and Paul will be practicing his up tempo audition number, or Michael will be making breakfast for Robert."

"Nothing will ever be right again."

"You don't know that."

"Yes, I do." Stanton pushed the half-empty bottle of beer away and stood up. "I'm going to lie down. Do you mind if I take Michael and Robert's bed? I don't want to face our old room, even if it's all Paul's stuff now."

"Help yourself. Just don't sleep in my bed." Stanton started to exit the kitchen, but then Marvin stopped him by saying, "There's a test now, you know? We both need to get one."

"A test? To tell if you have AIDS?"

"To tell if you have the virus."

"What's the difference? It's not like there's even a treatment. If you have it, you die. Period."

"I thought it would put your mind to rest, if it came back negative."

"Fat chance of that happening."

"Do you think that Chris—?"

"Let's talk about this later, please? I can only process so much catastrophe in one day."

"Sorry. I didn't mean to…. Get some rest. You look exhausted."

A WEEK later, Stanton called his old number and got their machine. He had to listen to Chris's chipper outgoing message:

Hi. You've reached the home of Chris Mead and Stanton Porter. It's 1985, so we figure you know what to do after the beep.

Stanton left a brief and curt message. Three days went by, and Chris did not return his call, so he tried again. When that message also went unanswered, he tried a third time. "Look," he said into his phone at work, "It's been almost two weeks. I don't like having to do this either, but can you fucking return my call so we can get it over with?"

When Stanton still did not get a return phone call, he decided to drop by their apartment during the day, when he knew Chris would be at work. Since they lived a few blocks from the *Village Voice* offices, he could quickly stop by at lunch. When he let himself in, the smell of rotting food hit him in the face.

"Chris?" he called.

No answer. He went into the kitchen and saw dirty dishes piled in the sink. He opened the fridge and found a Styrofoam container with fuzzy stuff growing on the contents. He tapped his foot onto the trash can lever and threw the container away. He walked through the apartment toward the bedroom, but stopped himself when he saw the blinking red light of the answering machine. He counted the blinks. Seven messages. He pressed the play button and heard his first message to Chris, then his second, then Norma's voice:

Stanton, this is Norma. Christopher is in the hospital. He passed out at a construction site this morning while he and Carl were doing an inspection. He's at Mount Sinai. The doctors say it's pneumonia. Call me at home.

Stanton closed his eyes, and an icy feeling trickled down his body. He listened to the date stamp. Four days ago. He picked up the phone and dialed Marvin's number at work.

Marvin Goldstein.

"Chris is in the hospital."

Marvin paused for a split second, and then asked, *Which one?*

"Mount Sinai."

I'll meet you there.

"Where is it?"

Hold on.

Stanton heard a snapping sound as Marvin flipped through the pages of a phone book.

Ninety-Eighth and Madison. Take the four, five, or six train uptown to Ninety-Sixth Street. But don't take an express, because it won't stop there.

"Okay, I'll meet you on the street at the top of the stairs."

Stanton rushed out of the apartment and locked the door behind him. He ran the one block to the Astor Place subway station. He fumbled for a token and made his way through the turnstile. A train arrived a few minutes later, and he checked to make sure it was a local before boarding. When Stanton reached Ninety-Sixth Street, he exited the station and waited for Marvin on the corner. He looked around him, and with a mighty weight, the reality of the situation settled onto his shoulders. The outcome was inevitable. Chris was going to die. All of their problems seemed petty and insignificant in the face of that one simple fact. Stanton was about to lose the only man he had ever loved, and there was nothing he could do to stop it.

Marvin finally appeared at the top of the stairs. They found the hospital entrance and asked the receptionist what room Chris was in. She informed them he was on the fifth floor, but that it was a private room and restricted to immediate family only. Stanton ignored her and got on the elevator. Marvin followed him.

"She's calling up there now," Marvin said. "We're not going to get very far."

"I don't care."

"You don't have any claim. You broke up with him."

"I doubt his father knows that." Stanton watched the light above the door go from two to three.

"Did you read the paper this morning?" Marvin asked.

"No, I've been writing on deadline. Why?"

"Rock Hudson died yesterday."

"Great. That's exactly what I needed to hear right now."

When the elevator door opened, they stepped out and a security guard greeted them. The goon politely told Stanton and Marvin they would have to leave. Stanton glanced down the hallway and saw Chris's father watching them. Then Joseph Mead walked away.

"Come here!" Stanton yelled. "I know you saw me, you son of a bitch!"

Joseph Mead turned as Stanton lurched forward, but the guard caught him and held him back. Mr. Mead walked down the hallway toward the elevator and said, "I'll handle this."

The security guard released Stanton and stepped away.

"Let me see him," Stanton said.

Joseph Mead shook his head. "Go home. There's nothing you can do for him. He's getting the best medical attention money can buy."

"Let me see him."

"Why would I do that? You don't deserve to be here. You're the problem, boy. My son and his friends were fine until you showed up. Haven't you noticed that, Stanford? All this death? It started when you came along. You did this to them. You're like a poison."

"Oh my God," Marvin said. "You can't seriously believe that."

Mr. Mead ignored him. "Get out. Both of you."

Stanton did not move. "If you don't let me see him, he will never forgive you. Are you going to let him die like this? Without me?"

"I have no intention of letting him die. Now that I'm in charge, Chris is going to recover, and once he's feeling better, we'll be taking him home. Where he belongs."

"He's not going to get better," Stanton said. "Even you can't make that happen."

"He will get better. No son of mine is going to die of AIDS. I'll fly him to Paris if I have to."

"Haven't you read the paper? That didn't work for Rock Hudson, and it won't work for Chris."

"This conversation is over. You have no legal right to see him, and I have every legal right to stop you."

Stanton choked as he held back his tears. "What happened to you? Really, I want to know. What made you so fucking angry that you can't see past your hatred of me? You have the power to let me see him. Just nod your head. All I want is the chance to say good-bye. Please don't take that away from me. Five minutes, that's all I'm asking for, and then I will leave you—and him—alone. I promise. Five minutes, Mr. Mead. I'm begging you."

Joseph Mead looked at him hard, and for a moment, Stanton thought he might break. But he didn't. "No," he said. "You've caused enough trouble. I won't let you infect him for one more minute."

"Mr. Mead," Marvin said, "you're about to do something you will regret for the rest of your life."

Joseph Mead looked back and forth at each of them and said, "I doubt that very much." Then he turned and walked away.

"My name is Stanton, you monster!"

"Don't let them near my son's door," Mr. Mead shouted to the security guard as he waved a cheerful good-bye. The guard stepped in front of Stanton and Marvin and nodded toward the elevator.

"Okay," Marvin said. "We're leaving. Come on, let's get out of here." Marvin pushed the elevator button and the doors opened immediately. He grabbed Stanton by the arm and pulled him in.

"Norma," Stanton said as the doors closed. "I've got to call Norma. She can get me in."

"Let's find a payphone downstairs."

"I don't remember the number. It's in Chris's address book, next to the phone in our apartment."

"Is it listed?"

"Of course not. The Meads are never listed."

They took the subway back to the East Village and the apartment Stanton once shared with Chris. He went to the phone table and grabbed the address book. He leafed through the pages and found the number. He dialed and waited.

Norma answered on the second ring.

Hello?

"Norma, it's Stanton."

Stanton, why haven't you returned my call? I left you a message four days ago.

"I know, I just got it. Chris and I had a fight, and I've been staying with my friend Marvin." He didn't want to tell her that he and Chris had actually broken up. "We just came from the hospital. Joseph wouldn't let me see him."

Why didn't you call me first? I could have run interference for you.

"Can you get me in?"

Not anymore. I could have worked around him, but now that he knows you're trying, you'll never get past the desk.

"There's nothing Carl can do?"

He would never cross his father like that.

"Can you get Chris to call me?"

Joseph had the phone removed from his room.

"Jesus Christ. Has he asked about me?"

No. He's hasn't spoken to anyone.

"Can you at least tell him I was there—that I tried to see him?"

Yes, of course. I'll tell him.

"Maybe he can talk his father into changing his mind."

He's weak, Stanton. He's too sick to get into a fight over this. He's struggling just to breathe.

Stanton thought about Chris in a hospital bed, hooked up to a respirator. "What am I supposed to do? I can't let him die thinking I don't love him."

A pause.

I can tell him.

"That's not good enough."

It will have to be. I can try to talk to Joseph, but—

"Don't bother. After what I said to him, there's no way he'll let me anywhere near that place."

What did you say to him?

"I called him a son of a bitch and a monster."

Oh. Well, I hope you don't think this is inappropriate, but it's about time somebody told him off. I would have paid good money to see that.

Stanton laughed. "It wasn't as satisfying as I imagined."

It never is.

"Will you call me with updates?"

Of course. And I'll see what I can do, but I don't want to get your hopes up.

"He thinks I did this to Chris."

Joseph said that?

"Yes."

Good Lord, Stanton. I don't know what's wrong with him.

"Tell Chris I'm sorry for everything. Tell him he was right, that it was my fault too. Tell him I see that now."

I'll tell him.

"Can I ask one more favor?"

Yes. Anything.

"Can you play 'Thunder Road' for him?"

What's that?

"It's a song by Bruce Springsteen. It's the first track on *Born to Run*. It means a lot to us. He'll understand."

I'll find it and play it for him. I promise.

"Thank you."

I'll call you tomorrow. Will you be at this number?

"Yes. I'll be here." Stanton hung up the phone and looked at Marvin. "That's it," he said. "There's nothing she can do."

NORMA kept her promise and called almost every day, but her reports were never good. Chris's condition deteriorated rapidly over the month of October. Norma relayed to Chris everything Stanton had told her. She even bought a portable boom box and played "Thunder Road" for him. Norma told Stanton Chris had been too weak to react, except for the tears that welled in his eyes. One night, she said on the phone,

You wouldn't want to see him this way.

But Norma was wrong. Stanton would have given anything to see him one last time and say good-bye. He wanted to hold Chris in his arms and undo all the hurt he had caused. He promised himself he would never love someone to death again. Chris had been right.

There was more than one way to cheat.

CHRIS MEAD died on Halloween, one of his favorite holidays. He loved the costumes and the drunken crowds on Christopher Street. Norma called

Stanton at work in the afternoon to give him the news. She had been warning him for days that it was coming. She asked if she could stop by his apartment. There was something she needed to give him, she said.

Norma arrived that evening with Colin in her arms. The boy reached out and cried, "Stannon." Stanton took him from Norma and led them into the living room. He sat down on the sofa and held Colin close. He kissed his head and inhaled the aroma of baby shampoo. There was something about the child that comforted him, as if Colin had inherited a small piece of his uncle.

"Chris here?" the boy asked.

"No," Stanton replied. "Chris isn't here." Colin took the news in stride and settled into the sofa, resting his head against Stanton's arm.

"How are you holding up?" Norma asked.

"I don't know. I'm keeping the apartment for one more month. Then I think I'm going to leave New York for a while. The *Philadelphia Inquirer* offered me a job as their new music critic."

"Really?"

"It's a good offer. I need a break from this place, but I'm sure I'll be back. Marvin won't let me leave forever." Stanton reached over and tickled Colin, who burst into laughter. Then he said to Norma, "Thank you for keeping me in the loop."

"I wish there was more I could have done."

"Was he peaceful in the end?"

Norma shook her head. "He wouldn't look at his father after I told him what Joseph said to you."

"I never meant to get between them."

"It wasn't your fault. Don't take Joseph Mead's shortcomings onto yourself."

"I have plenty of my own," Stanton said. "I don't need his too."

Norma reached into her purse and pulled out a folded piece of paper. "A few days before he died, when everyone else was out of the room, he asked me to find him a piece of paper and a pen. He wrote this down and told me to give it to you." She rose from the chair, crossed to the sofa, and sat down next to her son.

Stanton reached out and took the note from her. It had his name written on the front. He unfolded it and read the four words, written in Chris's unmistakable handwriting.

Play the long game.

WHAT LOVE CAN DO

TOPHER sat on the tailgate of his pickup truck. He tried to absorb Stanton's story and the meaning of Hutch's final note. Then he asked, "Do you think he planned all this?"

Stanton pulled back and looked at him. "Let's not go overboard here."

"I'm sorry he cheated on you."

"That's not the intended takeaway from—"

"I would never cheat on you. You know that, don't you?"

"I believe you believe that."

"So that's why you changed your mind at the W Hotel, the night we saw Springsteen? The title of the last album I pulled, remember? Something about being in two places at once if you're not anywhere at all. He actually said that to you?"

"Yes."

Topher paused. "You knew all along, didn't you? *Play the long game.* There's no way you could have thought any of this was a coincidence."

"I told you. I didn't know what to believe. I still don't."

Topher shook his head and said, "Damn."

"You can see now why a reconciliation with Joseph Mead isn't possible."

"I don't buy that."

"All these years later, and I still can't forgive him."

Topher thought about his own father and said, "That's because you think forgiveness lets him off the hook, but that's not what it's about."

"I've heard that crap before. Don't do it for him, do it for me. It never worked."

Topher jumped off the tailgate and wedged himself between Stanton's legs. "Are you telling me you couldn't even sit down and give him a chance to say he's sorry? Not even if I asked you to?" Topher grinned and watched as Stanton's facial expression changed from determined resentment to inevitable resignation.

"You're not going to let this go, either, are you?"

"Once again, it's highly doubtful. Just give me permission to talk to Ben and Travis about it. They know him, and from what I've heard, he's changed. Please?"

Stanton kissed him. "You know I can't say no to you."

"So?"

"Yes, you have my permission to talk to Ben and Travis. Although I don't know why you bothered asking. You would have done it anyway, with or without permission."

Topher laughed and wrapped his arms around Stanton's neck. "I'm glad you've figured out how this relationship is going to work."

THE week after Memorial Day, Dime Box rented time at a local studio to record "Homesick" and began shooting additional scenes for the music video. They alternated their evenings back and forth: one night in the studio, one night on the video set. Kai's concept combined footage from the concert in Dime Box with a narrative starring Robin and Maurice. Robin took the role of the man who leaves guitar picks behind him as he tours around the country. In each of the scenes, Maurice is standing in the background watching, like a ghost of the man from his past, or maybe an alternate reality.

Although *Glee* passed on using "Beaches on the Moon," Stanton succeeded in placing it on *So You Think You Can Dance*. Travis Wall choreographed a large group piece to the song, and although Topher didn't know who Travis Wall was, Stanton assured him he was a big deal. "Travis is the successor to Mia Michaels," Stanton explained, even though Topher didn't know who that was either.

In mid-June, Dime Box released "Homesick" to iTunes and Amazon. With Stanton and Marvin's help, they launched the music video premiere on Vevo. Five million views in the first twenty-four hours. Thirty million views in the first week. The *New York Times* ran a feature story on how one of its music critics had come to cowrite a pop song. As a result, Topher became a sensation among classical music and opera enthusiasts. At Marvin's suggestion, he recorded his version of "Che Gelida Manina" and released it as a free bonus track with "Homesick."

One day, Stanton got a call from someone he knew at *Saturday Night Live*, putting out feelers for a fall spot. That pretty much made it official, and the boys quit their day jobs. Topher and Marvin talked about writing more songs together, and a plan for the future unfolded. They would spend the rest of the summer putting together a new set list and then begin touring in September. Stanton would go on the road with the band, doing a series of stories for NPR and writing a book about his experience. He told Topher the book would also include the story of Hutch, Robert, Michael, and Paul.

Everyone agreed to the concept of dual residency in both Austin and New York. Topher didn't see any reason to choose between them. He and his friends would find a larger house with a room for Marvin and Ty (plus a larger bedroom for Topher and Stanton, with its own bathroom). As for the living arrangements in New York, one night Marvin presented the boys with his solution.

The announcement came two weeks before July 4, when they were gathered in the room of three thousand records at the W Hotel. Stanton, Marvin, and Ty were in Austin for some local promotion. After a toast, Marvin handed Maurice a manila envelope.

"What's this?" Maurice asked.

"Open it," Marvin said.

Maurice opened the envelope and pulled out a stack of papers. He began reading, but then stopped and looked up at Marvin. "I may not understand this correctly, but did you just give me an apartment in New York?"

Marvin smiled. "I did."

Robin looked as if his jaw had dropped to the floor.

"It never belonged to me," Marvin said. "Not really. Ty and I found a new place nearby, so we'll still be neighbors. We've wanted to move for a while now, but I couldn't let just anyone live there. It's got three bedrooms, so there's enough space for all of you. I think you'll feel right at home."

Topher knew Maurice and Robin had learned to cover up their emotions long ago, given their nightmarish parents, but this gift broke them both.

Maurice put his arms around his brother and wept. They actually owned a home that no one would ever be able to take away from them.

Topher leaned over to Stanton and whispered into his ear, "Do you have any idea what that means to them?"

"I think so."

Peter went over to Marvin and hugged him. "Dude, you're killing us here. 'Too much of a good thing'—"

"Is wonderful," Ty said.

"Mae West," Stanton said. "Right?"

Ty nodded and replied, "Very good."

"We've been talking," Peter said. Everyone stopped their blubbering and paid attention to him. "Me, Topher, and the twins. We want to visit this Fire Island you've told us about, where that picture was taken. Will you three take us back there?"

"Funny you should bring that up," Marvin said. "When Stanton met Topher back in March, I had a hunch something like this might happen. So I called my real estate guy and asked about a house on the island for the week of July 4." Marvin turned to Stanton. "The house behind the Pantry was available, so I put down a deposit."

"You mean the one on Lone Hill Walk?"

Marvin nodded.

Stanton shook his head, asking, "You knew back in March?"

"No, but I wanted to be prepared just in case. You know I always have a plan."

"This was the same house they were living in?" Topher asked. "The summer you met them, I mean."

"Yes."

Topher looked at his bandmates. "Well, boys, I guess we're going to New York next week. We need to check out Maurice's new digs."

"*Our* new digs," Maurice said, correcting him. "Marvin may have put my name on the papers, but it belongs to all of us."

"There's one more thing," Marvin said. "In the envelope."

Maurice put his hand inside and pulled out an antique gold lighter. "What's this?"

"It belonged to Michael. It was his grandfather's."

"And you want me to have it?"

"Yes," Marvin said. "He once told me that all he ever wanted out of life was Robert, his friends, and a good buzz."

THE next morning, Topher put Stanton, Marvin, and Tyrese on a plane back to New York. Topher and his friends would join them in a few days. That evening, he stopped by the Walsh house to talk to Travis and Ben. When he got there, they sat down at the dining room table, Quentin included.

"Travis told me what this is all about," Ben said. "I asked Quentin to be here because he's the closest to Joseph."

Quentin nodded. "I'm the only one who has his cell phone number."

"How did you manage that?" Topher asked.

"I'm naturally adorable and people just flock to me."

"Now you're sounding like a Walsh," Ben said. "I'm going to call Colin and put him on speaker. He can give us some background." Ben set his phone on the table and then swiped the screen. He tapped it a few times and it started to ring.

A moment later, Topher heard the voice of Colin Mead, the little boy from Stanton's story, the one who called him "Stannon" and sat on the sofa when Norma brought over the note from Hutch.

"Hey, Colin," Ben said.

Hello, Walsh. Who's all there?

"Travis and Quentin. And Topher, the guy I told you about. Topher Manning."

"Hi, Colin," Topher said. "It's nice to meet you."

The pleasure is all mine. I saw Jason's tweet about your new song. I'm a huge fan.

"Thank you. Did you know that's your uncle's guitar I'm playing on stage? The black Fender?"

I did not know that, but it's a nice segue into Operation Heal the Big Wound, isn't it?

"Colin—," Ben said.

Please, Walsh, I am thrilled at the prospect of my grandfather putting that damn empty chair away at Thanksgiving. It's not a Seder, and from what I understand, my uncle was no Elijah. Here's what you need to know. My grandfather used to be a real prick. Everyone acknowledges that, even him. But when his wife died ten years ago, he changed, completely. I've asked about Chris, but he simply shakes his head. Quentin is the only person he's ever talked to about it. Everything I know comes from my mother. Topher, did Stanton tell you about the scene at the hospital?

"Yeah, he told me."

I think the old man would give anything for the chance to apologize.

"Then we need to get them to sit down together," Topher said.

If Stanton is on board, then that part should be easy. But Ben and I talked about this earlier, and we both agree. Quentin should be the one to ask Joseph.

"I'll do it," Quentin said. "I know all about Chris, and Colin is right. Joe wants to apologize to Stanton. I don't know what kind of asshole he used to be, but he's not that guy anymore. Besides, it's not the reconciliation between Stanton and Joe that's important here." He looked at Topher.

"We're not going to tell him, are we?" Topher asked.

"No," Ben said. "We're not going there."

I agree. It's far too unorthodox an idea to present to my grandfather. By even hinting at the R word, you run the risk of undermining what you're trying to accomplish. We need to keep the focus on Stanton and Joseph.

"Thank God," Topher said. "The way Quentin was looking at me, I thought he was going to pull out the Ouija board."

Quentin glowered at Topher. "If you think Joe's not going to notice, then you haven't been paying attention."

"Oh, I've been paying attention, trust me. Do you know he called Stanton poison?"

"I told you," Quentin said, "he's not that guy anymore."

"He'd better not be. For his sake."

I love all the testosterone in the room, really. But back away from the steroids, boys. When are we doing this?

"I'm coming to New York in a few days," Topher said into the phone. "We're going out to Fire Island for the Fourth, but we'll be in the city beforehand checking out our new apartment. Maybe we could have lunch or something? You and Joseph and me and Stanton."

Brilliant idea. If need be, we can run interference and diffuse any tension between them. Quentin, call the old man tomorrow and then text me. I'll drop by his office after work.

"Got it."

"Colin," Topher said, "how is it that you don't have your own grandfather's cell phone number?"

Don't get me started.

"Are we finished here?" Ben asked. Everyone nodded.

"Thanks, Colin," Topher said.

You're welcome. Any friend of the Walsh brothers is a friend of mine.

Cade walked into the dining room and asked, "Who's on the phone?"

"Colin," Ben said.

Cade lit up and yelled, "Dude, tell your boyfriend I'm happy to kick his ass in fantasy baseball anytime."

Topher could hear Colin laughing.

He told me you were beating both him and Travis. Good work, Cade.

"At least I'm in second," Travis said. "Tell David he really needs to play his roster better."

Another laugh.

I'll tell him. Good night everyone.

As Topher was leaving that night, Quentin followed him out to the street. "Do you mind if I give you some advice?" Quentin said.

"Do I have a choice?"

"Not really. Tell Joe about your father. And yes, Travis told me the story. Don't be mad at him. I stick my nose where it doesn't belong. It's what I do. Just tell Colin and Stanton to get lost for a few minutes when you go to lunch. It's important that Joe hear your story. Trust me on this."

"Okay," Topher said, "I'll see what I can do." Then he got into his truck and drove away.

WHEN they arrived in New York on the last Friday in June, the members of Dime Box went directly to their new home on Christopher Street. Stanton, Marvin, and Tyrese were waiting for them when they arrived. Marvin and Tyrese had moved out the week before, so when they walked in, it was completely empty.

The boys ran through the apartment. They checked out each bedroom and discussed who would take which one. Stanton, Marvin, and Tyrese stood back and watched.

Topher walked up to his boyfriend and gave him a kiss. "See? I was right. You are now officially the coolest person I've ever met."

"I didn't do this," Stanton reminded him.

"Thank you, Marvin," Topher said. "There's no way we'll ever be able to repay you."

Marvin leaned toward Stanton and said, "He still doesn't get it, does he?"

They spent the weekend shopping for furniture and sightseeing around Manhattan. On Monday, Stanton and Topher had their lunch date with Joseph and Colin Mead. About a half hour before, Stanton panicked and wanted to bail, but Topher talked him out of it. They met uptown at a restaurant Stanton picked out. When they arrived and Stanton saw Mr. Mead sitting at a faraway table, he grabbed Topher by the arm and said, "I can't do this."

"Yes, you can. You're not a kid anymore. All you have to do is listen."

Topher led Stanton to the table, and the Meads stood up to greet them. Topher couldn't help but notice that Colin looked an awful lot like Hutch. He turned to Stanton and could tell he saw it too. "Are you Colin?" Topher asked.

"Yes. It's nice to meet you in person, Topher."

Topher shook his hand and said, "Thanks, you too."

"This is my grandfather, Joseph Mead."

Topher turned to Mr. Mead and offered his hand. "Topher Manning. Nice to meet you, sir."

"Thank you, young man. Would you say your name again?"

"Topher Manning."

"Right," Joseph said. "Topher. That's short for Christopher, isn't it?"

"That's correct. Colin, I don't think you've ever met Stanton Porter as an adult."

Colin offered his hand and Stanton paused for a moment. Then he reached out and shook it. "Sorry. It's just... you look so much like him." Stanton turned to Joseph Mead and said, "Surely you see it."

"Of course I see it," Mr. Mead said. "Stanton, I have a lot to apologize for, but will you begin by letting me say hello?" He reached his hand out across the table.

At first, Topher thought Stanton might turn and run, but then Stanton shook his hand. "Hello, Joseph."

The four of them sat down. They made small talk about Topher's music career until the waiter came and took their order. When they finished, Mr. Mead seemed to understand the ball was in his court.

"I'm sorry, Stanton," he said. "I understand what I took away from you that day, and I know it's something I will never be able to give back. Your friend Marvin was right. I have regretted it for the rest of my life."

Stanton looked down at his plate and fidgeted with the fork. "I accept your apology, but I'll always remember that I never got the chance to say good-bye to him."

"That's fair," Mr. Mead said. "I never got to say good-bye to him either. He stopped talking to me once Norma told him what I had done."

"Whose fault was that?"

Topher reached out and took Stanton's hand.

"Topher," Mr. Mead said, "Colin tells me you're friends with Travis. He's a colorful young man, isn't he?"

"Yes, sir, he is. We work at the—Sorry, I mean, worked. I just quit my day job. We worked at the same auto shop."

Mr. Mead nodded. "Did you know he and Ben are bringing their brothers up to our house in the Hamptons for an August holiday? You and your band should join us, and you too, Stanton. Bring Marvin along. I read his column in the *Times* and follow him on Twitter."

"That would be very cool," Topher said. He turned to Stanton. "What do you think?"

Stanton didn't reply.

Then Mr. Mead said, "I'm trying to make amends, Stanton. I don't know what else I can do."

"I know. My own father has come a long way in twenty-five years. I don't know why I doubt that's possible for you. If Topher wants to go, then we'll be there."

"Will you teach us how to sail?" Topher asked Colin.

"I would be delighted to teach you how to sail."

Topher took a drink of his water, and then he turned to Stanton and Colin. "Would you two give me and Mr. Mead a chance to talk privately?"

Stanton looked surprised. "You're not going to—?"

"No. Trust me, please."

After a pause, Stanton looked at Colin and said, "Come on, let's get a drink at the bar. You can tell me about your mother. Did you know she and I used to be friends? I was your favorite uncle, once upon a time."

They got up and walked away. Topher wanted to put Joseph Mead at ease, so he immediately said, "Quentin suggested we talk for a few minutes."

Mr. Mead's expression changed from caution to joy. "Ah, I see. Well, when Quentin suggests something, I strongly advise listening to him. He's like a little Zen master, that one."

"He said I should tell you about my father."

"Your father? Is he alive?"

"No. He died about ten years ago, of a heart attack. He was still pretty young."

"I'm sorry to hear that."

"I don't ever talk about it, but—"

"How old were you? When he died, I mean."

"Seventeen."

"What happened?"

Topher took another drink of water. "I came home from school one day and there was this confirmation letter for the SAT test. You know, the one people use to get into college? Only problem was, I didn't register for the SAT test, because I had no intention of going to college. So that could only mean one thing—my dad had registered for me. This had been going on since I was thirteen, him pushing me toward UT. It started right after I picked up my first guitar. I knew that I wanted to play music, to write and sing songs, but he didn't want to hear any of it. All he cared about was my education.

"Well, I was so mad I stormed out of the house. I drove around the back roads for two hours, just as pissed as all hell. It was like he wasn't even listening to me. I had told him again and again that I didn't want to go to college, but there it was, me registered for the SAT test, against my will. When I finally went home, they were eating dinner—my mom and dad and my sister. My dad and I got into it, screaming at each other, and I was begging him to hit me so I could run away and get the hell out of there. Then I said it—that thing a son says that he can never take back. I told him I hated him and that I wished he wasn't my father. I told him to stay out of my way and to never speak to me again. My mother was crying. My sister left the house. I went into my room and slammed the door. I was shaking, like I was possessed or something. That night, my dad got up to take a piss and dropped dead of a heart attack on the bathroom floor. He died thinking I hated him."

Joseph Mead put his hands in his lap. "He didn't think that."

"How do you know?"

"Because I'm a father, and I've made terrible mistakes. Awful ones. He would never have held that against you. Yes, I'm sure it hurt. He only wanted something more for you, something better than what he had."

"What he had was fine. He was happy. I didn't understand why he couldn't let me be happy too."

"You were just a boy. When I cut Stanton off from my son, I was a grown man. I have no excuse for what I did."

"You were just scared."

"Perhaps, but being afraid isn't a very noble excuse."

A busboy stopped by their table and filled up their water glasses. Then Topher said, "We're in the same boat, you and me."

"It would seem that way. I'm sure that's why Quentin wanted you to tell me this story. My son died with our entire relationship in shambles, and your father died the same way, with you. I've lived a long life, young man. It doesn't get any worse than that."

"You had a problem with your son being a musician, right?"

Mr. Mead nodded. "What worked for Carl never worked for Chris. I was an angry man back then. Angry at things that had nothing to do with my children."

"It seems to me that it doesn't much matter where you start out in life. The only thing that really matters is where you end up. Maybe we can hang out some more, Mr. Mead. When we come visit you in August, I mean. I don't know about you, but I think that would be really groovy."

A wistful look crossed Mr. Mead's face. "So would I. And please, call me Joe."

"Thanks, Joe. You can call me Topher. Or Christopher. Either one's fine."

Joe pulled his phone out of his pocket. "Let me give you the number to my cell phone. I want you to call me anytime, do you hear?"

Topher smiled. "I hear."

LATER that evening, in Stanton's apartment, he and Topher were about to sit down to watch a movie when the buzzer next to the front door sounded.

"What's that?" Topher asked.

"The security guard downstairs in the lobby." Stanton walked over to the intercom and pushed a button. "Hello?"

Mr. Porter, there's a Norma Mead in the lobby to see you. Says she's got some papers or something.

Stanton looked at Topher with a raised eyebrow. Then he pushed the button again and said, "Can you please send her up?"

Sure thing, Mr. Porter.

"That's Colin's mom, right?" Topher asked.

"Yes. And before you ask, I have no idea what this is about, but I am very excited to see her again." A few minutes later there was a knock on the door. Stanton opened it and said, "Norma, look at you."

"Hello, Stanton. Is this a bad time?"

"Not at all. Please, come in."

Norma stepped into the foyer and Stanton closed the door behind her. He held out his arms and gave her a hug. Then Norma said, "I would have called, but Joseph only gave me your address."

"You talked to him?"

"Yes, after you had lunch."

Topher walked across the room and introduced himself. "Hi, I'm Topher, Stanton's boyfriend."

Norma extended her hand and said, "It's so nice to meet you. Joseph had nothing but good things to say about you, young man."

"Joe is awesome."

Norma looked at Stanton, who laughed and said, "Come in, have a seat. Can I get you a drink?"

"No, I can't stay long. We're heading out to the Hamptons this evening, for the holiday." The three of them sat down in the living room, with Stanton and Topher on the sofa and Norma in the chair opposite.

Stanton sat forward and said, "I'm sorry I haven't kept in touch. I ended up moving to Philly after Chris died, like I told you. Anything that reminded me of him, I just couldn't—I'm sorry."

"I understand," Norma said. "I've thought about you many times over the years. When my son met Ben Walsh, I remembered you telling me about your trip to Austin and the couple you stayed with."

"You knew?" Stanton asked.

"We never met Ben's parents, so I didn't know for sure."

"I used to work with Travis," Topher said. "The Walsh boys talk about you a lot, especially Cade. White River, South Dakota. That's what he tells everyone about you, that you're from White River, South Dakota."

Norma laughed and said, "Yes, that's me. When Joseph told me about your lunch and what he was going to do, I asked if I could deliver the papers." She looked at Stanton and added, "Since I already played the messenger once before."

"What papers?" Stanton asked.

"Topher, I don't know what you said to Joseph this afternoon, but whatever it was, it made quite an impression." Norma reached into her purse and produced a legal-size manila envelope. She handed it to Topher.

"What's this?" Topher asked.

"Open it."

Topher chuckled. "You're not giving me an apartment, are you?"

Norma considered the question and then said, "I would say this is substantially better than an apartment."

Topher opened the envelope and pulled out the contents. The papers looked like some kind of legal document or contract. Topher began reading, but then quickly gave up. "This doesn't make any sense to me," he said as he handed the papers to Stanton.

Stanton looked the document over. "Is this—?"

Norma interrupted him. "Joseph has transferred Chris's trust fund into Topher's name."

"Excuse me?" Topher said.

"As you know, Stanton, Chris never touched his trust fund. Joseph never dissolved it, even after he died. So, it's been sitting there all these years, drawing interest. I've begged him to turn it into a scholarship, or give it to an AIDS organization, but he has always shut me down. It's just like that damn empty chair at Thanksgiving, like he's convinced Chris is going to come back and need it someday."

"But why me?" Topher asked.

"I don't know," Norma said. "Joseph Mead has never been the kind of man to explain himself."

"I can't accept it. I just told him a story about my father. I shouldn't get a trust fund for that."

"Then don't take it for you," Stanton said.

"What does that mean?"

"Take it for your band. Instead of renting a bigger house in Austin, now you can buy one."

"But we're making money," Topher said. "A lot of money." Stanton laughed, and Topher knew what was coming. "Okay," Topher said. "I deserve that."

"If you know what I'm going to say, then there's no need for me to say it."

"What was he going to say?" Norma asked.

Topher turned to her and grinned. "He was about to tell me that if I plan to put all my long-term eggs in the music basket, then he has some excellent oceanfront property in Austin for sale, and maybe I might be interested in buying some."

"I was going to say Arizona, but Austin is better. The money you're making today could evaporate tomorrow. You know that as well as I do."

"Yeah," Topher said. "I get it."

"You're not taking anything away from anybody," Norma said. "The fund is sitting there doing nothing. If Chris knew that it was helping someone with his music...." Norma looked at Stanton.

"Are there any strings attached?" he asked.

"No, except that he cannot touch the principal until he turns thirty. Otherwise, there are no strings. Please, Topher, at least think about it. It would mean so much to Joseph if he could help you."

"Okay, I'll think about it. And talk it over with Stanton. If he says it's a good idea, well, then, I tend to listen to him when it comes to shit like this."

Norma smiled at Stanton and said, "I see you found yourself another winner."

LATER that night, as they lay naked in bed, Stanton and Topher found themselves staring at the ceiling.

"It's just one thing after another," Topher said.

"One *good* thing after another. The valleys will come. Don't complain about the peaks."

"Did you see how much money it is?"

"I saw. The Meads don't fool around when it comes to cash."

"Can we talk about something?"

"What?"

"Condoms. How much longer do we have to use them?"

Stanton grumbled. "We should wait at least a year."

"A year? Seriously? That's ridiculous."

"It's irresponsible of me to lull you into some false sense of security."

Topher sat up in bed. "Are you trying to make me angry? You're not lulling me into anything. And what's so damn false about it, I'd like to know?"

"Getting rid of the condoms is the ultimate gesture of trust, and trust should be earned."

"When was your last test?"

"Just before I met you."

"And how long had it been since you had sex with someone else? Before that, I mean."

"About a year."

"I got tested last month, and I haven't had sex with anyone else in over a year, either."

"Okay. So?"

"So. This isn't about the possibility that we could be anything other than negative, is it? This is about you not trusting me. You think I'm going to cheat on you."

"Don't put words in my mouth."

"Well, then, how about I put them in mine? I didn't go through all this just so I could come back and disappoint you."

Stanton didn't reply.

Topher lay back down and said, "Sorry."

"Will you promise me one thing, then?"

"You know I will promise you anything," Topher said.

"If the day comes when you want to have sex with someone else, then tell me. Please. I will be able to handle it."

"We will never have that conversation."

"You can't say that and mean it forever."

"I want you to fuck me."

"What? Don't change the subject like that."

"I've wanted to try it for a while now, but I don't want to use a condom, and I don't see why we have to."

"Because it's only been three months. The endorphins haven't even drained from our brains yet. If we make this our practice and then one of us screws up—"

"This is because he cheated on you, isn't it?" Topher jumped out of bed and walked around to the nightstand. He opened the drawer, reached inside, and pulled out a string of condoms. He began tearing them open and pulling them apart, then he reached into the drawer for another string and shredded those as well.

Stanton got up and wrapped his arms around Topher's shoulders. "Stop," he said. "I'm just trying to be responsible."

Topher grabbed Stanton and held on tight. "Stop trying so hard."

"Then promise me."

"I'm not going to cheat on you."

"That's not the promise I asked for."

"Okay, okay. If I ever want to have sex with someone else, I will talk to you about it."

"Nothing behind my back."

"Nothing behind your back. I promise."

"And you will never stop playing the guitar."

"Never." Topher pulled back and looked up at Stanton. "Are you happy now?"

"Yes."

"Then fuck me like I asked. With nothing between us."

Stanton kissed Topher and eased him back onto the bed. Topher lifted his legs and brought the tip of Stanton's cock to meet his ass. "Do you want me to get some lube?" Stanton asked.

"No, Travis says lube is for wusses. Just use some spit."

Stanton slicked up his hand and rubbed it around the head of his dick. He pressed it against Topher's hole and it slipped right in.

"Whoa," Topher said, inhaling rapidly, "it's even bigger than it looks."

Stanton leaned forward and kissed him. Topher grabbed him by the neck and pulled himself onto Stanton's cock in one violent motion. He gritted his teeth and said, "It's like jumping into Barton Springs. Just take the plunge and get it over with."

They were still for a moment. Topher could feel his sphincter muscle involuntarily clasp down on Stanton's cock. "Can you stand up?" Topher asked.

"Like this?" Stanton pulled Topher close to him and backed up off the bed. With Topher's arms around his neck and legs around his waist, Stanton stood up. He could easily support Topher's weight.

"How does it feel?" Stanton asked.

"Like my guts are getting ripped open."

"At least you're honest."

"You're inside me. That's all I care about right now. Can you turn around and sit down on the edge of the bed?"

"You're topping from the bottom. You know that, don't you?"

"Sorry. Can you just do it, please?"

Stanton did as instructed. He sat on the edge of the bed. Topher faced him as Stanton's cock jutted up into his ass. They settled for a moment. Topher pulled Stanton close and said, "Now we shan't never be parted."

"Oh, no. I knew it was a bad idea to let you watch that movie."

"Are you crazy? It was a great idea. I know just how Scudder feels."

"Fine. But no quoting *Maurice* in bed."

Topher wiggled around on Stanton's lap. "It's starting to feel good. My dick is getting hard again."

Stanton lay back, exposing Topher's erection. Together, they stroked and edged Topher's cock. Stanton lifted his hips in a cadence that made Topher shiver. Then Stanton flipped him onto his back and kissed him deeply. Topher felt like his orgasm was rising up from his toes. He wanted to come, but he couldn't yet. He closed his eyes and lost himself in the sensation of having Stanton inside him. "Fuck me," he said. "Fuck me harder." Stanton increased his pace, and Topher's orgasm got closer, up to his knees this time. That was when he figured out the two things were connected. "Harder," Topher repeated. "Fuck me harder."

Stanton increased his pace again. Topher pulled his knees to his ears and allowed Stanton to pound into his ass at the deepest possible angle. He positioned himself over Topher, like he was about to do push-ups, and then slammed his cock into Topher's asshole as hard as he could. Stanton was good at this, and soon Topher could feel his orgasm sitting just behind his balls. He growled, bit down on Stanton's shoulder, and came face-to-face with Pegasus. In a fit of sexual delirium, Topher thought he heard the horse whinny and say, "Fly. Fly!" As Topher reached between them and touched himself, chunks of come blew across his chest and stomach, each spasm stronger than the one before it. He could feel Stanton's cock swell and explode inside him. Stanton kept fucking him, but his rhythm slowed. They came to a stop and collapsed into each other's arms.

"Are you okay?" Stanton asked.

Topher nodded. His head was buried in Stanton's neck. He lifted it to breathe, and then he said, "Yes, I'm okay."

"Most intense orgasm ever?"

"How did you know?"

"You've been fucking me for three months, remember?"

"Me, bottom. You, top."

"Now, that's not fair."

"Okay. We take turns. What's that called?"

"Versatile."

"No, Travis had another name for it. What do they call it in porn, when the guys fuck each other?"

"Flip-flop."

"Right. That's it. Flip-flop."

THE next morning, as they were heading out to Fire Island on the train, Topher told his friends about the trust fund.

"What is going on?" Maurice said. "We've gone from nothing to millionaires practically in a span of three and a half months."

"We didn't start with nothing," Peter said. "We've always had each other. What did Stanton say?"

"That we should use it to buy a house in Austin. That way we'd have a permanent home in both places. What do you think?" They all nodded, and Topher continued. "We should look for a big place with lots of bedrooms and a garage apartment, for guests and kids."

"Kids?" Robin said.

"Yes, kids. Peter, you're going to want to get married someday, and I plan to have kids with Stanton."

Maurice chuckled. "Does he know about this plan?"

"Not yet," Topher said. "When the time's right, I'll bring it up. I see Travis and the way he is with Ben's brothers. Stanton and I would make great parents."

"I can take care of the house," Robin said. "I'll start looking when we get home. A big place with lots of bedrooms."

"And a backyard," Maurice added. "It has to have a backyard. And a porch."

"Anything else?" Robin asked.

"No," Maurice said, "that's all. You'll know it when you see it. I trust you, bro."

Topher wasn't crazy about the mad dash that transpired between the train platform and the shuttle buses to get to the ferry. There were inevitably more passengers than seats, and more luggage than space to carry it. Topher and his friends all agreed they would rather rope a wild steer than wrestle one of those guys for a spot on that bus. But by the time they were on the ferry and headed across Long Island Sound, a calm had settled over Topher.

He didn't know what to expect, but what he found surprised him. When they pulled into the harbor and got off the boat, Topher followed Stanton down the pier. There was only one word to adequately describe what he was feeling:

Underwhelmed.

He didn't hyperventilate like the night of the Springsteen concert, when he had kissed Stanton for the first time. He couldn't even say it felt familiar. They waited on the boardwalk while Ty went into the real estate office to get the keys. Then he and Marvin led them around a corner and away from the harbor. The house was literally one of the first ones they saw.

"This is it," Marvin said as he stepped up to the door and unlocked it. They all went into the house. It was a large single space that included a dining room, an open kitchen, and living room. Across from the entrance was a set of stairs leading to the second floor.

"There are two bedrooms upstairs and two bedrooms downstairs," Marvin said. "And a pool house."

"Like Ryan on *The O.C.*?" Peter asked.

"Yes," Stanton said.

"Travis loves that show," Topher added.

"We have Wi-Fi," Tyrese said. "Which is important, because cell reception is spotty out here at best."

Maurice whispered something into his brother's ear. Then Robin asked, "Which way is the—?"

Topher interrupted him. "Do we have to do that right now?"

"Come on," Robin said. "You can't blame Maurice for being excited."

"What's going on?" Stanton said.

"Can I tell him?" Topher asked Robin.

"Yeah. I wanted it to be a surprise when they saw the cover, but someone's got to take the picture, I guess."

Topher turned to Stanton and Marvin. "We want you to take a picture of us. In the same spot. You know. The one of them on the beach, I mean. We want to use both photographs for our album cover, along with the water tower from Dime Box."

"Damn," Marvin said, tearing up. "I can tell now, I am not going to be able to keep it together this week."

"Remember what I said thirty years ago?" Stanton asked. "Someday we'd invite some cute boys out to lounge around our pool and drink our liquor, and maybe if we got lucky, they'd let us suck their dicks. Well, guess what, buddy? I got lucky. Let's take them down to the beach. Come on."

Marvin shook his head. "After all these years, you are still as disturbing as ever."

The seven men walked the distance from the harbor to the ocean, located on the other side of the island. They descended a set of wooden stairs to the sand. When Topher looked out over the water, it finally struck him. He grabbed Stanton by the arm and said, "This feels right."

"It should. This was his favorite spot on earth."

Topher felt exhilarated. He kicked off his shoes and ran toward the water. He splashed against the waves and dove headfirst into the surf. He smacked his lips and relished the taste of salt water. When he waded back to the shore, Stanton was waiting for him.

"I'm wet!" Topher said.

"Yes, you are."

Topher shook his head and water sprayed everywhere. He kissed Stanton and then bent down. He rummaged around in the sand and asked, "Do you know how to skip stones? Me and Trisha used to do it all the time when we went to Galveston. I used to be able to skip three at once, in a single throw. Do people do that up here?"

Stanton got that wistful look on his face, and Topher grinned, because now he knew what that meant. He must have done something that reminded Stanton of Hutch, and that was okay now.

Marvin started taking photos while Topher and his friends horsed around. After a few minutes, Maurice took the original picture out of his cargo shorts and handed it to Stanton.

"Do you remember where this was taken? Exactly?"

Stanton showed the picture to Marvin, who remembered the location. They had to walk about a quarter of a mile, but they eventually found the spot. Topher, Robin, Maurice, and Peter lined up in precise imitation of the poses in the photograph. Marvin used a real camera, while Stanton and Tyrese started snapping away on their phones. Topher even remembered to blow Stanton a kiss instead of saying cheese.

THAT night after dinner, Stanton took Topher up to the rooftop deck. Topher knew he was almost finished, but he still had one more thing to do. One more thing before Stanton would be able to move on. They lay down on one of the lounge chairs together, with Topher curled up in Stanton's arms. "I have an idea," Topher said.

"I'm not sure I like the sound of that."

"It's a good idea. I promise."

"Okay," Stanton said. "I'm listening."

Topher paused. Then he said, "You can talk to him."

"What does that mean?"

"You can talk to Hutch. Through me."

"Topher, don't be ridiculous. How am I supposed to do that?"

"On the phone."

"What?"

"Hear me out. I know I'm not him, but you said it yourself, I have his voice. I feel connected to him. You know that. And I can speak for him. You saw my face the first time I laid eyes on the black Fender. It's the music, Stanton. That's how I know all this is real. So I'm going to walk away, and in a few minutes, I'm going to call you. And when you pick up the phone, Hutch will be on the other end of the line."

"You mean you're going to channel him?"

"Something like that. It's hard to explain. But I can do this. Trust me. I've done it before."

"You have?"

"Yeah."

"How?"

"That's not important. This is the last piece. The last part of your story that's still unfinished."

Stanton hesitated. "I don't think I can."

"No more arguments. I'm not messing with your head. I promise to take care of you and always be loyal. Let me do this for you. Please."

Stanton waited for a moment, but then he silently nodded his consent.

"I'm going downstairs," Topher said. "Then I'm taking a walk, and then I'm going to call you. Okay?"

"Okay."

Topher got up and left the deck. He headed toward the harbor and found a quiet bench away from the crowds. He sat down and took out his phone, the phone that started it all the moment he first laid eyes on Stanton at Groovy Automotive. He flipped it open and put it to his ear. "You there, Hutch?"

A long pause.

Yes, I'm here.

"You ready to do this?"

I've been ready for twenty-six years.

"Okay. I trust you know what you're doing."

I promise you, Topher. This is going to work. And thank you. For everything.

"You're welcome. There's only one of us, remember?" Topher tapped through his contacts until he found Stanton's number, then he dialed it and put the phone back to his ear.

"Hello?"

Stanton? Is that you?

A pause.

"I don't know if I can do this, Topher."

Another pause.

I'm sorry I said those things. In the apartment that day you left. I was only trying to get you to open up. I shouldn't have pushed that hard.

"Hutch?"

Yes, it's me. I'm also sorry about what my father did. He had no right to cut you off like that. I was too sick to fight with him, but I should have tried.

"It's not your fault. I blamed everything on you. I didn't fight hard enough for your music."

We both know that's not true. There was nothing you could have said that would have changed my mind.

"I'm sorry I wasn't there at the end. We never even got to say good-bye."

That's what we're doing now. Finally. Do you remember that first walk we took on the beach? You told me you liked Air Supply, and I gave you that ring.

"How could I ever forget? You compared Air Supply to *Romeo & Juliet*."

That's right. "I must be gone and live, or stay and die." Turned out to be more prophetic than I intended. I just thought I was being cool, quoting Shakespeare to you.

"It was sweet."

Thank you for burying the hatchet with my father.

"It was the right thing to do. And it's what Topher wanted."

A pause.

You know he's in love with you, right?

"I hope so, because I've been in love with him since the day I met him. I just didn't want to get my hopes up."

Go ahead. Get your hopes up. Anyway, this is it. I need to go. Time to say good-bye.

"Already?"

Yeah. Don't you see, Stanton? We won. We played the long game and we won.

"I guess we did."

And now it's time to move on.

"You're right. I'm ready. Good-bye, Hutch."

Good-bye, Starsky. Take care of Topher, okay? He's going to need you to help him through all this.

"I'll take care of—"

Topher heard Peter yell something at Stanton, and then the line went dead. Topher panicked. He put his phone away and sprinted through the harbor toward the house. As he rounded the corner of the Pantry, he had to dodge a man pulling a red toy wagon full of groceries. He stopped and saw Stanton waiting for him on the boardwalk. Topher ran up and threw himself into Stanton's arms.

"Thank you," Stanton said. "I can't believe you did that for me. I love you so much."

"I love you too."

And then, right there on the boardwalk, in front of God and everybody, Stanton got down on one knee and produced the toy ring from the Dalai Lama test. "I never thought I'd be able to ask another man this question, but Topher Manning, will you marry me?"

"Can we do that?"

"Yes, here in New York, at least."

"Holy shit. Of course I'll marry you." He held out his left hand so Stanton could put the ring onto his finger. "Can we do it out here? On the beach?"

Stanton stood up and said, "We can do it anywhere you want."

"And can we have kids too?"

"Children? Me?"

"Yes. You'd make a great father. And the boys would help raise them, plus Marvin and Ty too. Wait a minute. Why did I run all the way back here? What did Peter say to you before we got cut off?"

Stanton smiled one of the biggest smiles Topher had ever seen. "Follow me," he said.

They went into the house, where everyone was gathered around the big dining room table. Tyrese sat with a laptop opened in front of him.

Stanton turned to Topher and said, "Come look. Your bar, remember? For success? The night we went to see Springsteen, you told me your bar was to see one of your songs in the top ten on iTunes. Well...." Stanton gestured toward the laptop, and Tyrese stood up and stepped away.

Topher sat down and looked at the screen. On the right, under the Top Singles, he saw "Homesick" at number four. Topher turned to his bandmates and yelled, "We did it!"

Tyrese's phone, which was sitting next to the laptop, began to light up with a series of notifications. Tyrese picked up the phone and swiped the screen. "The Twitterverse is blowing up about something," he said as he stepped into the living room and sat down.

"Number four on iTunes!" Robin said.

"Unbelievable," Peter added. "Stanton thinks that once people get tired of 'Call Me Maybe', we might even have a shot at number one."

"It's possible," Stanton said. "I still say it's the wrong season for a song like 'Homesick'. It would be number one if you had released it in the fall or winter, but you can't time everything perfectly. You needed to build on the momentum from 'Beaches on the Moon', and now you've done that. Congratulations. This calls for a celebration."

"A double celebration," Topher said as he held his hand up. "Did you see this, boys? I'm engaged."

"What?" the twins said.

Tyrese got up and walked back over to the table. "Hold on, everybody. You might want to hear this."

"Hear what?" Marvin asked.

"I've traced it back to a blog post from one of the guys out here on the island." Tyrese looked down at his phone and read aloud:

"Hello, loyal readers. We apologize for not keeping up with our posts, but a mystery has been unfolding around us and we simply had to investigate. Here's what we didn't understand—what's up with all the guys in their fifties holding hands with boys in their twenties? So far this season, we've counted forty-one couples with at least twenty-five years between them. Now, we understand that the daddy/boy thing is as old as Adam and Steve, but this is an epidemic! Is it a sign of the coming 2012 apocalypse, or maybe something to do with the hundredth monkey theory? We don't know for sure, but an explanation is being floated, and it starts with the letter R. Stay tuned, gentle readers, because you haven't heard the last of this story. Not by a long shot."

Tyrese continued. "There's more. After this post got passed around, it started trending on Twitter as #TheReturn. San Francisco, Chicago, Miami, everywhere. It's the same story. Guys in their fifties dating boys in their twenties. In record numbers."

Topher grinned and turned to Stanton. "You mean it's not just us?"

BRAD BONEY lives in Austin, Texas, the seventh gayest city in America. He grew up in the Midwest and went to school at NYU. He lived in Washington, DC, and Houston before settling in Austin. He blames his background in the theater for his writing style, which he calls "dialogue and stage directions." His first book was named a Lambda Literary Award finalist. He believes the greatest romantic comedy of all time is *50 First Dates*. His favorite gay film of the last ten years is *Strapped*. And he has never met a boy band he didn't like.

Please visit Brad on the web at http://www.bradboney.com or follow him on Twitter at https://twitter.com/BradBoney.

Also from BRAD BONEY

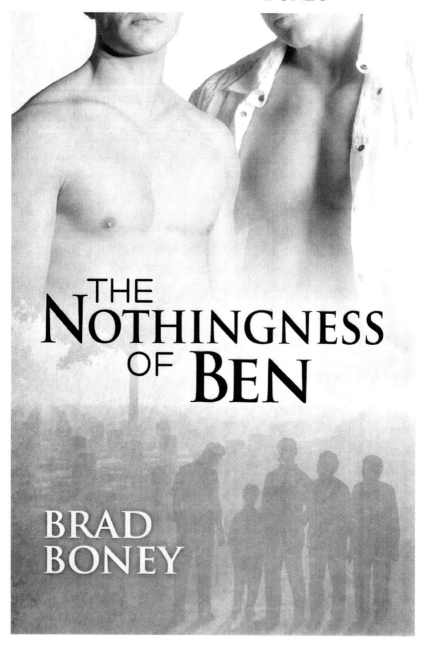

THE
NOTHINGNESS
OF BEN

BRAD
BONEY

http://www.dreamspinnerpress.com

Also from DREAMSPINNER PRESS

Good to Know

D.W. MARCHWELL

http://www.dreamspinnerpress.com

Also from DREAMSPINNER PRESS

THE ONE THAT GOT AWAY

Rhianne Aile ·
Madeleine Urban

http://www.dreamspinnerpress.com

Also from DREAMSPINNER PRESS

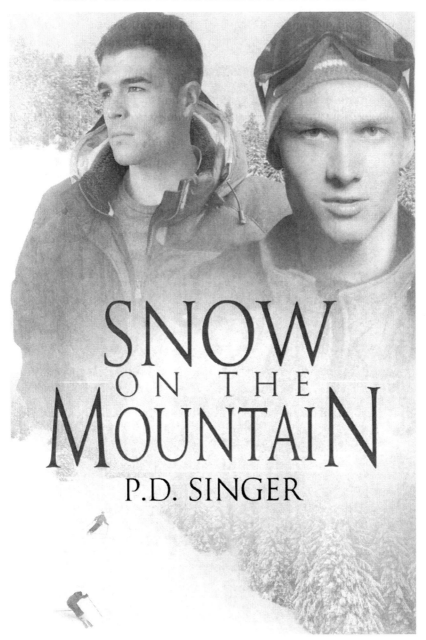

SNOW
ON THE
MOUNTAIN

P.D. SINGER

http://www.dreamspinnerpress.com

For more of the
best M/M romance,
visit

Dreamspinner Press

www.dreamspinnerpress.com

CPSIA information can be obtained at www.ICGtesting.com
Printed in the USA
LVOW05s1202110114

368941LV00004B/695/P